Queen Anne's County Free Library
and 21617
S0-BJL-572

SHADES
of
RED

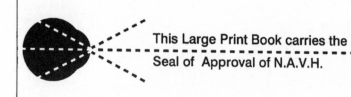

This Large Print Book carries the
Seal of Approval of N.A.V.H.

SHADES
of
RED

Doris Mortman

Thorndike Press • Waterville, Maine

Queen Anne's County Free Library
Centreville, Maryland 21617

Thomson Gale 2895 5/05

Copyright © 2005 by Doris Mortman, Inc.

All rights reserved.

Published in 2005 by arrangement with
St. Martin's Press, LLC.

Thorndike Press® Large Print Americana.

The tree indicium is a trademark of Thorndike Press.

The text of this Large Print edition is unabridged.
Other aspects of the book may vary from the original edition.

Set in 16 pt. Plantin by Ramona Watson.

Printed in the United States on permanent paper.

Library of Congress Cataloging-in-Publication Data

Mortman, Doris.
    Shades of red / by Doris Mortman.
      p. cm.
    ISBN 0-7862-7564-2 (lg. print : hc : alk. paper)
    1. Mothers and daughters — Fiction. 2. Cosmetics
industry — Fiction. 3. Sibling rivalry — Fiction. 4. Serial
murders — Fiction. 5. Sisters — Fiction. 6. Large type
books. I. Title.
PS3563.O8818S53 2005b
 813′.54—dc22   2005002024

For David, Lisa,
Alex, Loren, and Mom,
with love

National Association for Visually Handicapped
------------------------- *serving the partially seeing*

As the Founder/CEO of NAVH, the only national health agency solely devoted to those who, although not totally blind, have an eye disease which could lead to serious visual impairment, I am pleased to recognize Thorndike Press★ as one of the leading publishers in the large print field.

Founded in 1954 in San Francisco to prepare large print textbooks for partially seeing children, NAVH became the pioneer and standard setting agency in the preparation of large type.

Today, those publishers who meet our standards carry the prestigious "Seal of Approval" indicating high quality large print. We are delighted that Thorndike Press is one of the publishers whose titles meet these standards. We are also pleased to recognize the significant contribution Thorndike Press is making in this important and growing field.

Lorraine H. Marchi, L.H.D.
Founder/CEO
NAVH

★ Thorndike Press encompasses the following imprints: Thorndike, Wheeler, Walker and Large Print Press.

Acknowledgments

As a fiction writer I've always had a fascination with heroes. They are, after all, the mainstays of the novel. After 9/11, however, my definition of what was heroic changed, probably forever. The difference between real heroes and those who are created was never as stark. So first and foremost, I'd like to thank those who provided the inspiration for *Shades of Red* — the men and women who serve the public, both in our Armed Forces and in our neighborhoods. I'm humbled by your sacrifice.

On a personal level, I'd like to thank my support system: My editor, Jennifer Enderlin, for her enthusiasm — it's contagious — and her talent — it's prodigious. Matthew Shear and my other friends at St. Martin's for making the process so enjoyable. Peter Lampack for always providing backup. My friends for being fans. And my family for being my family.

Prologue

It's hard to remember a time when I didn't hate her. Despising her feels as natural as breathing, as ordinary as putting one foot in front of the other. Not a single day goes by that I don't think of ways to torment her, yet I don't consider this an obsession. It's simply part of my emotional gestalt: Hating her is who I am.

I used to lie awake at night planning things to do to her. I'd invent exquisite tidbits of torture that would infect her with fear, small, excruciating moments of persecution that would gnaw at her like hungry maggots and make her skin crawl with the terror of anticipating what I'd do next.

How thoroughly delicious those crucifying imaginings have been!

But I've had enough imaginings. They don't satisfy me anymore. It's time to move on, to make my punishing fantasies a reality.

I'm certainly well prepared. Over the years I've amassed a stockpile of ways to make her life miserable and I intend to execute each and every one of them.

And then, I plan to execute her.

Chapter 1

JUNE 2002

Vera Hart's mouth went dry. She was a powerful woman who rarely felt helpless, but just then her knees were weak. An avalanche was threatening to bury her in a ferocious storm of accusations. If she couldn't divert it or stem it or stop it, everything she had taken a lifetime to build would be destroyed.

"Hart Line International is guilty of gross accounting irregularities which must be addressed before the next peer review. If they're not corrected, you run the risk of being investigated by the government, which could result in enormous fines and possible imprisonment. At the very least, with today's climate of consumer rage against corporate corruption, it's likely that you could wind up becoming a scapegoat for the sins of others. At worst, your company will go under."

Vera read the memo for the third time, still in a state of disbelief.

When she came in that morning there was an envelope on her desk stamped FOR YOUR EYES ONLY. It was unsigned, but the details described the author as someone who was more than slightly familiar with the inner workings of Vera's corporation. As she read the comparison of the public financial statements for HLI, the parent company, and the internal financial statements, she realized that she was indeed in serious trouble. As the nameless whistle-blower put it, "your books have been cooked."

It infuriated her that something this potentially catastrophic had caught her so off guard, but to be fair to herself, she didn't conduct regular line-by-line reviews of the company's financials. That's what staff was for. Years before, when she added clothing and accessories to the Hart Line's cosmetics business, she'd put together an outstanding team of business and accounting specialists and gave them control over the numbers. It was a move that was alien to her basic, control-freak nature, but early on she recognized that she simply couldn't do everything and be everywhere.

She was the centerpiece of an enormous conglomerate that manufactured all manner of lifestyle products, from nail polish to sectional sofas. She was also the public face of Hart Line International, marketing herself and her talents every waking minute of every single day. She did the weekly television show, *Vera Hart at Home*, made public appearances, edited the magazine *Hart to Heart*, promoted the various products at stores and malls throughout the country, supervised the addition of new merchandise, and personally tested each and every new idea that came her way. She didn't have time to be a bookkeeper as well.

Aside from the unthinkable prospect of her stock tanking and taking HLI with it, what disturbed Vera was the notion that she could be targeted for investigation. Enron had collapsed. Tyco was in shambles. WorldCom's stock wasn't worth the paper it was written on. And yet she knew the whistle-blower was right: Given the opening, the government would look to make her the poster girl of corporate corruption. The reasons were obvious: She was a woman in a man's world, she had been an actress, not an MBA graduate, before going into business, and she had been extremely successful. It seemed unfair to Vera that once again she was about to be screwed over by a system that judged her on her celebrity rather than her success and by her gender rather than her judgment.

Vera Hart had been a star from the day she made her cinematic debut in *Little Girl Blue* at the age of nine. Until her film career came to an end, her name on a theater marquee had practically guaranteed eight-figure grosses. Her face had graced the cover of every high-circulation magazine in the world. And her image had spawned so many desperate wannabes that at least once a month some well-known psychologist took to the airwaves to urge teenage girls not to disparage themselves if they looked in their mirrors and came up short. Vera Hart, they explained, was simply exceptional.

She was tall and model-slim yet with enough curves to be described as sensuous, her skin was gardenia-white, her nose so perfectly sculpted for her face it was as if the proportions had been mathematically calculated. She had a wide mouth with full, ripe lips that always seemed to be teasing for a kiss and eyes that positively startled. Framed by wing-shaped brows, they were large, clear, aquamarine demilunes that could glisten with emotion one minute, go dead and cold the next. Straight across on the bottom, softly rounded on top, they were neither a true sapphire blue, nor an absolute emerald green, neither the pale, yellowless blue of a Vermont sky in winter, nor the bleached-out green of a backyard pool overdosed with chlorine. They were pure aquamarine gems: rich and precious and mesmerizing.

At fifty-nine she owned a penthouse in New York, an oceanfront mansion in Palm Beach, an estate in East Hampton, and a compound in Westchester that included a television studio that was the envy of the networks. She had been named to the Best Dressed List Hall of Fame fifteen years before and even with the natural effects of aging was still considered one of the most beautiful women in the world. More important, she was one of only two females on the New York Stock Exchange. Her personal wealth was calculated in excess of five hundred million dollars; Hart Line International was a multibillion-dollar-a-year enterprise. She was a force to be reckoned with.

Again, she went over the figures. Then she picked up the phone and instructed her secretary, Tess, to set up a six-thirty meeting that evening with the CFO, the COO, and the heads of the various Hart Line divisions. She didn't care if anyone

15

had social plans or family obligations. There were to be no absentees and no excuses.

"If they're not at the meeting tonight," she said, "they don't have to bother coming to work in the morning."

There were days when Bryan Chalmers hated his job. He was an assistant district attorney for the city of New York, sworn to uphold the laws of the state and to ensure that justice was done. That part of it he loved. What he hated was that after the police and the Crime Scene Unit and the DA's office had gathered the evidence and sorted through the facts and put together a case that would obtain a conviction and take a criminal off the streets, the system kicked in with loopholes like plea bargains and parole and, most laughable of all, time off for good behavior.

Take the case he was working on: A woman was gang-raped under the boardwalk in Coney Island. She was so badly beaten that three months after the assault she was still in a coma and therefore unable to assist the police in making a positive ID on her attackers. DNA had led the police to two of the assailants. They needed help nabbing the other three: an eyewitness who could place them at the scene, a snitch who'd heard one or all of them bragging, another forensic clue, or, as happened here, for one of them to roll over on the others.

Once Bryan explained the hard-time consequences of their night on the town, Ramon Ramirez gladly ratted out his friends. In exchange for that noble exercise in civic cooperation he demanded — and received — immunity from prosecution.

A knock on Bryan's door announced the delivery of a package. It was from Tony Borzone, a detective from the Central Park Precinct. A young woman had been accosted in the park, savagely beaten, and raped.

The victim, a white woman in her mid-thirties, had suffered multiple blows to her face and head. The beating was so savage she was almost unrecognizable. If not for an alert patrolman finding her driver's license in nearby brush, they would have had to rely on dental records.

Her pants were down around her ankles. Her bra had been ripped off so violently it had sliced into her skin. Her T-shirt remained on, but her arms had been twisted in such a way that her right arm coiled around the left side of her neck, her left arm snaked around the other side. Her wrists were lashed together with a shoelace from one of her sneakers; a twig served as a garrote. If she struggled too hard to escape, the shirt would tighten around her neck and make it difficult for her to breathe. One of her socks was stuffed in her mouth as a gag.

A wave of nausea washed over Bryan as he studied the photographs. Whoever did this had stalked this woman, swooped down on her, beaten her just enough to immobilize her, then raped, sodomized, and bludgeoned her to death. When he was done, he painted her face and body with lipstick.

In his note, Borzone promised Bryan a clean collar.

Bryan promised the victim there would be no plea bargains, no loopholes, no deals.

Greta Hart had a headache the size of Ohio. First, Vera's secretary had informed her there was a mandatory meeting at six-thirty in the boardroom. A few minutes later, her date, Bryan Chalmers, called and canceled. He was sweet about it, and she obviously had to work late as well, but Greta couldn't bear to give up a single moment with him, let alone an entire evening.

They had only been seeing each other for a few months, but she hadn't felt this way — ever.

Then her secretary handed her a copy of the program for the Women of the Year Banquet. The cover was Hart-red paper with a satin finish and a richly embossed Hart Line logo. It was simple and elegant, the only flourish a red rope tipped with a feathery tassel that ran down the spine of the booklike program. Greta opened it and leafed through the white pages, each of which featured the bio of a recipient. She was more than a little surprised when she came upon the 2002 Hart Foundation honoree for scientific achievement, Dr. Marta Phelps.

Normally Greta was afforded the opportunity to screen the nominees for the various categories. She wasn't on the Foundation board, so she didn't have a vote per se, but her opinion mattered. If there was someone she felt was completely wrong for the Hart Line's image, or there was a candidate whom she felt was undeserving of recognition by the Foundation, she said so. Since she didn't abuse the privilege and the few times she'd raised objections they'd been borne out, the board heeded her warnings.

There was the time the nominating committee had proposed a young pianist for the award in arts achievement. A Russian émigré, she had made a splash on the classical music scene by winning a major competition. Everyone on the committee was wowed by the woman's musical genius. The fact that she was extremely good-looking didn't hurt; the Hart Line, after all, was a cosmetics company. Greta, who over the years had created a network of informers and had several very private detectives on her payroll, was told that Tatiana Godonov's real talent was in the bedroom. According to Greta's sources, Tatiana had slept with every one of the judges — male and female — and probably would have slept with a Great Dane if it would ensure her victory.

The nomination was hastily withdrawn.

Then there was Bess Whitelaw. She ran a rehab facility for teens. Her track record for turning out recovered addicts who went on to complete high school was beyond remarkable. She seemed like a shoo-in. Until one of Greta's private eyes told her that not only was Bess skimming the money she received through charity events, but also she had a sideline venture with her brother who dealt the very drugs that hooked those kids in the first place.

Her name was also removed from consideration.

Logic dictated that the only reason Greta wouldn't have been given the complete list of this year's candidates was if Vera had specifically told the head of the Foundation not to do so.

Typical, Greta thought.

Much as she liked to believe she was her mother's confidante, Vera kept her own counsel. She told others, Greta included, only what she wanted them to know, when she wanted them to know it. Like when Greta had asked Tess what was on the agenda for that evening's meeting, Tess said she knew nothing other than it was a command performance.

As Greta read Dr. Phelps's bio she tried to swallow the jealousy that quickly soured her throat. Greta was a highly accomplished woman. She was the COO of a major public company, a Harvard graduate with an MBA from Harvard Business School, and a well-respected, much envied doyenne of New York society who, like her mother, had graced the Best Dressed List many times. Yet suddenly she felt like the fourth runner-up in a backwater beauty pageant.

It was the quality of the achievements,

she supposed. This Dr. Phelps was like some super Girl Scout who went around winning merit badges for performing beyond the norm; Greta simply made money.

Also, Marta Phelps was perfectly gorgeous.

In an almost Pavlovian response, Greta grabbed a mirror and studied her reflection. Even to her highly critical eye, she was indisputably attractive. Her pale, snow-white complexion, complemented by lustrous auburn hair that fell softly to her shoulders and aquamarine eyes combined in a palette as delicate as a watercolor. In contrast, her aristocratic nose and high cheekbones were sharp and angular. While that sort of sculptural classicism was deemed enviable by most, Greta felt it made her appear hard, underscoring the soberness of her personality.

Her eyes, those fabulous azure orbs, were a genetic gift from her mother and unquestionably her most arresting feature, yet there too she found a negative. Despite their luminous color and the fact that they were enlivened by a keen intelligence and unceasing curiosity, they were often void of humor. Greta studied and perused and considered; she rarely twinkled or sparkled or gleamed.

And then there was that damnable scar beneath her right eyebrow. No one else noticed it. It was barely visible and easily covered by makeup, but to Greta it stood out like a red badge of imperfection. Despite the oohing and ahhing of the fashion press about her stylishness; despite the accolades from the business community about her managerial cunning; despite what she knew to be true about who and what she was, that damnable scar served as a patent reminder that she was flawed.

Greta shoved the mirror back in its drawer and slammed it shut.

The phone rang. Startled, Greta hesitated before picking it up. Her head was throbbing; the last thing she needed was more bad news. Then again, maybe her date was back on. A romantic late-night supper would be lovely. She popped two Tylenol into her mouth, took a quick gulp of water, and picked up the phone.

"Hi," she said, purring even before she heard his voice.

"What the hell do you think you're doing?"

Greta smiled and leaned back in her chair. She'd been expecting this call.

"Whatever do you mean?" she said in her best Melanie Wilkes voice.

"There is no way I'm giving you a divorce!"

"I take it you got the papers."

"Yes, I got the papers."

"Well, I'm sure you're as devastated as I am that our marriage has actually come undone, but really, Tripp, we've always known that ours was not one of those happily-ever-after unions. Eight years wasn't a bad run and it was fun while it lasted."

"Fuck you!"

From the shrill timbre of his voice she knew his face was hideously florid.

"You wish."

She hung up the phone, but that wouldn't be the end of it. Trevor Runyon III, known as Tripp, was a libertine. Work was not his strong suit, leisure was. As someone lucky enough to have been born into a family with a pedigree, he adhered to the philosophy that lineage translated into entitlement. His idea of a good day was brunch, golf or polo, drinks, a nap, not necessarily alone, drinks, dinner, never alone, drinks, and then to bed, again not necessarily alone. Work was what he did when he wasn't playing.

Greta had married him because he'd been a terrific catch. He was handsome in that fair-haired, blue-eyed, chiseled Wasp way. He looked spectacular in a tuxedo or a navy blue blazer, the two requisite wardrobe pieces for the socially prominent male. He'd graduated from Princeton, thanks to numerous tutors and a generous endowment from the family trust. And while he could never be mistaken for an intellectual, he had a certain savoir faire, was at ease on a dance floor and adept at witty cocktail party repartee. Most important, he was a Runyon.

The Runyons were Mayflower descendants who owned the Seafarer Bank of Boston, a lending institution established in the late 1700s to finance international trade for the Colonies. Skillfully run by Trevor Runyon, Junior, the family continued to maintain its niche position as a venture capital source for the shipping industry with branches in New York, San Francisco, Seattle, and Miami. Lowell Runyon was the executive vice president. Malcolm Basking, husband of Bethany Runyon, was a senior vice president. And Bethany served on the Seafarer board. Tripp was the only Runyon who didn't work for the bank. He worked for HLI.

By divorcing him, Greta was also firing him. She couldn't imagine that he would go quietly, but no matter what he said, did, or thought, he would go. He had been a husband of convenience. He was no longer convenient.

It was a redbrick Tudor-style home on a quiet street in a modest neighborhood in Mercerville, New Jersey. There was an open, square porch off the dining room at the back, two large oak trees in the front whose roots had entered into a territorial battle with the sidewalk, an old-fashioned one-car garage with a door that could only be raised manually, and at the rear of the small yard a willow tree overlooking a pond that in summer became a breeding ground for mosquitoes.

Inside were three bedrooms, one and a half baths, a kitchen with a dinette, a living room, dining room, and small den — each decorated within an inch of its life with Hart Home Line products. Everything from the carpets to the cachepots were inspired by Enid Polatchek's idol, Vera Hart. Several rooms had been reproduced directly from Hart Line catalogues. Others had been cloned from episodes of *Vera Hart at Home*. Enid's greatest regret in life, and she had many, was that her husband, Dolph, wasn't rich enough to allow her to change décor as often as Vera did.

For Enid the joy of cooking was being able to work alongside Vera Hart. Of course, that meant Vera was on television and Enid was in the kitchen, but she didn't quibble about such details.

This afternoon the mission was Arctic Ambrosia, an all-white cake that looked as if it had been constructed of icy glaciers and snow-peaked mountaintops. Enid's eyes darted from the television mounted on a shelf to the mixer on the island countertop. Small beads of sweat dotted her forehead as she concentrated on whipping the egg whites to the proper consistency: not too wet, not too dry.

Vera lifted the whisk out of the bowl. The glob of shiny white meringue stayed on the whisk, sparkling with perfection.

Enid lifted the whisk out of her bowl, examined her egg whites, and smiled. They too seemed perfect.

Step by step she followed Vera's directions, stuffing the meringue into a canvas piping bag fitted with a wide-mouthed tip and squeezing its contents onto the top of a three-layer white cake that had already been frosted with vanilla cream.

"Squeeze a large, lovely dollop of meringue onto the top of your cake. Then swirl the top around, narrowing it as you go. Twist the tip just so," Vera said, flicking her wrist and gazing at her effort with gushing admiration. "It should look like a tiny bell atop a jester's hat."

Squeeze. Swirl. Twist. Make each white cap exactly the same size and height as the one next to it. Watch Vera. Squeeze. Swirl. Twist.

"There!" Vera exclaimed, proudly displaying her finished product. "How gorgeous is that?" she asked her adoring audience. Her face glowed as if she could actually hear millions of viewers clapping their approval.

Enid watched enviously as Vera bent down to perform the final check. With a cathedral hush to accompany her, she eyeballed the high, round cake, carefully verifying that each white cap was precisely the same height as the others. When she was satisfied, she tilted the cake forward so the camera could get the full effect and uttered her signature line: "If it's from Vera Hart's home, it has to be flawless."

She smiled. The credits rolled. The show was over.

Enid examined her Arctic Ambrosia. Two peaks were higher than the others. A third had drooped. A fourth had collapsed altogether. She looked at the cake, looked at the fading image of Vera Hart on her screen, curled her lip down in disgust, and dumped the cake into the garbage.

Tim Polatchek walked into the kitchen just as Enid's Ambrosia met its inglorious end. If he could have sneaked out before she spotted him he would have. He'd forgotten what time it was. Visiting his mother before or after *Vera Hart at Home* was never a good idea. She was either too ecstatic to talk about anything other than how she kept up with the miraculously gifted Goddess of Perfection or too despondent to do anything other than mourn the fact that she wasn't worthy of sharing the same air as the High Hoo-Hah of Hearth and Home.

"Having a bad day, Mother?"

"It wasn't flawless," she said with the same breathless incredulity as someone trying to explain how a gun went off accidentally and killed a philandering husband. "I tried, but as usual, it wasn't perfect."

Tim didn't bother to console her. Words wouldn't soothe her, nor would they alter the script. After the mea culpa came a few tears. Then there would be the diatribe on how if Dolph really cared about what made her happy he would make enough money for her to go to cooking school so she could be in the same kitchen with Vera Hart and not be humiliated by harebrained mistakes such as not being able to get two dozen gooey egg-white balls to stand at attention.

"I brought you some things that might make you feel better," he said, handing her a box of Harty Chestnut hair dye, a red vinyl pouch with makeup from the Hart Line's fall color story, and a peach velour warm-up suit from the Hart Line Leisure Collection, size 12.

Like a daytime game show contestant who'd just won a refrigerator, she jumped up and down, giggled, and clapped her hands with delight. When she grabbed the hair dye box and didn't throw it back at him, Tim breathed a sigh of relief. Enid's latest incarnation, Harty Titian, was an abomination. In her eternal quest for Hart-like beauty Enid tended to go overboard, especially when it came to hair and makeup. She thought if you could put it on and wash it off if it didn't work, it couldn't be a bad thing. She was right, but she was wrong. She wasn't doing anything dangerous or permanently scarring, but more often than not the results were scary.

For the last couple of years she had been on a fruit and vegetable kick when it came to her hair, dying it shades that could only be described as orange, eggplant, carrot, pepper, kumquat, cherry, or cantaloupe. As for her makeup, the palette coordinated a bit too closely with the hair. The concept of subtlety was completely absent from her maquillage.

After she had gone over every item — twice — she kissed her son and patted his cheek lovingly.

"You're such a good boy. Thank you, Timmy."

"It makes me happy to see you happy, Ma." Tim had repeated that sentiment so often over the course of his lifetime he wondered if that was destined to be his epitaph.

For as long as he could remember, pleasing his mother was Tim Polatchek's unattainable goal. As hard as Enid tried to be Vera Hart, Tim tried to be a good son. The task of eliciting a smile or a word of praise from her became more important than any other achievement, a misapplication of effort that resulted in a life steeped in mediocrity. While he did have some successes over his forty-three years, Enid had set the bar so high that unless they were spectacular they felt like failures.

As a boy Tim was smart, but too undisciplined to be an honor student. He had attitude problems with teachers. They thought strictness might be a more effective motivational tool; he had enough of that at home. He was an okay athlete, but not a particularly likable kid, so he was the last one picked for a team, a distinction that didn't inspire a great deal of esprit.

He wasn't cootchy-coo adorable as a child, but as he grew into manhood his aspect enhanced to where he was attractive, though hardly an Adonis. Six feet tall and well built, he had the slender frame of a runner with muscles toned by weights from regular workouts in a gym. His face was wolfish, with a wide forehead, a shock of thick pitch-black hair, and an attenuated jawline rough with stubble. Bushy eyebrows that hooded flat, deep green eyes the color of seaweed added to the sense of a man whose personality was guarded, hidden in a thick emotional swamp at the bottom of which was a bubbling anger rooted in a need for approval.

He'd gone to college, tried his hand at a number of different occupations, but ultimately wound up an accountant, like his father. To Enid that was anathema. She couldn't imagine a more dead-end job. And said so, over and over and over again.

Then Tim landed a position with Hart Line International. Suddenly he was the sun and the moon and the stars. The fact that he was one of many financial managers didn't matter. Her son worked for Vera Hart. If he were President of the United States she couldn't have been more impressed.

"So how's work?" It was her favorite question.

"Fine. Same as usual." It wasn't. He'd heard a few rumors, but he wasn't one of the privileged few. If something was happening he wouldn't know about it until it was a fait accompli or his inside sources filled him in. As of that moment, those sources had been extremely closemouthed.

Enid's nose crinkled with dissatisfaction. She relied on him for the inside scoop on her idol. "Fine" didn't cut it.

"I am going to the Hart Foundation Awards Gala," he said, knowing it would thrill her, annoyed that something so trivial was more important to her than what was really going on in his life. "Someone gave me a ticket."

Enid almost fainted. "Will you take pictures? Can you get me her autograph? Can you get me a ticket?"

"No to all three." He shook his head. He

hated when she sounded so sophomoric. But it upset him more when she got that look of tragic disappointment on her face. "I'll bring you whatever souvenirs I can. Okay?"

She patted his cheek again. "That's a good boy."

Tim nodded dumbly. Sometimes he felt more like her pet than her son, but like any good cocker spaniel he continued to jump through hoops for her favor. The only thing he would never do was roll over and play dead.

He did that once. It didn't turn out too well.

The boardroom at the Hart Line's head office was more feminine than most corporate headquarters. There was no chintz and no frills, but the sensibility was decidedly distaff. Instead of wood paneling, the walls were upholstered in a quiet, café au lait flannel, a shade that complemented the long, highly polished mahogany table and Empire chairs that centered the room. Thick crown moldings were painted a shade lighter than the walls; the sisal carpet was three shades darker. Instead of elaborate draperies, simple canvas shades dyed to match the walls covered the windows that overlooked Fifth Avenue. And instead of recessed spots, an eighteenth-century Russian chandelier with two tiers of cascading crystal illuminated the room.

Vera stood at the head of the table taking attendance with her eyes. Greta was to her left; she was the COO of Hart Line International. Craig Hemminger, the CFO, was seated to her right. Around the table were the presidents of the various divisions — cosmetics, furniture, kitchen and bath, clothing, accessories, floor and wall coverings, and media operations. In front of each of them lay a copy of the whistle-blower's warning. Vera watched their reactions as they read it

"We have a traitor in our midst," she said in a low, rumbling voice. "If that person is in this room, identify yourself. If you do, the worst that will happen is you'll be fired. If you don't, I will hunt you down and feed you to the dogs."

Even Greta was shaken by Vera's seething belligerence.

After a few minutes of fraught, tight silence unbroken by a confession, Vera took her seat.

"When I hired each of you, I did so because I believed that you would bring a high level of skill and commitment to the

Hart Line. At the time, I told you I believed that the concepts of individuality and teamwork were not mutually exclusive. While I would design the overall strategy, your division was yours to run. As long as you produced, you were in charge.

"I kept my part of the bargain. I allowed each of you your fiefdom. In exchange for extremely generous compensation, I asked that you do good work, be honest, and be loyal. For reasons I cannot fathom, all of you betrayed my trust. One of you may have gone so far as to provide the government with information that could be damaging not only to the company as a whole, but to me personally."

Several people sat stunned and silent. Others offered immediate denials. Vera pounded her fist on the table. Her eyes flamed.

"When the government goes looking for a villain, none of you is going to be named. It's my neck that's going to be slipped into the noose. My reputation that's going to be savaged. And my ass that's going to be sitting at the defense table in federal court."

There were some who raised their voices in support. Vera ignored them.

"Since I no longer have confidence in anything any of you tell me, I'm going to bring personnel in from the outside to conduct a thorough oversight."

"That's unnecessary," Greta said, harrumphing to hide the fact that she'd been taken completely off guard. "I can oversee an accounting review."

Vera laughed at her. "You were supposed to be overseeing it in the first place and look where we are."

Greta's headache became a migraine as she tried to hide her humiliation. It didn't make her feel any better to listen to Vera go down the line and shame each of her colleagues. She called Craig Hemminger an incompetent. She called the rest of them thieves. The woman was raging like a tsunami.

"While I was out building this company into an international powerhouse," Vera railed, "you greedy little bastards decided the hundreds of thousands of dollars you make each year wasn't enough. So you started stealing from me behind my back. Well, thanks to you, we're all in danger of being prosecuted and Hart Line International is in danger of going under."

She placed her hands on the table and leaned on them. The veins in her neck were so taut they looked as if they might burst.

"Since none of you seems to remember what I told you the day you joined the Hart Line, let me reiterate company policy: I am Vera Hart. The Hart Line is my life. I care deeply about it and will do whatever I have to do to save it. I don't give a shit about any of you."

Martie Phelps didn't like labels. They defined people and things in black and white terms, and if life had taught Martie anything, it was that nothing was ever black and white or absolute.

She had been labeled a hero and given medals to prove it, but she didn't consider her actions heroic. She had been a soldier in Desert Storm, so she knew firsthand that everyone who wore the uniform was a hero.

She had also been labeled a survivor. She was, but setting aside her own ordeal, her time as a doctor in an urban ER and on the battlefield in Iraq had taught her that no one ever completely survived a trauma.

She'd been hailed as a humanitarian, and while it was true she'd headed up a team at Rockefeller University that had produced a laudable breakthrough in the treatment of metastatic skin cancer, she'd simply been doing her job.

Her latest label was as a Hart Foundation Woman of the Year. As such, she'd been invited to attend their upcoming gala and accept the Award for Outstanding Scientific Achievement.

Martie found that ironic for many reasons, but especially since just that afternoon she'd been informed that the position that had produced that achievement was in jeopardy.

Abner Kaplow, the head of Rockefeller and one of her mentors, had told her that the grant which funded her research was going to be renewed, albeit slightly reduced. Martie would have to cut staff or trim her salary or both, none of which was appealing or practical. She couldn't afford a salary cut, nor could her group function with a depletion of personnel.

As she walked through the wrought-iron gates of Rockefeller University and turned north onto York Avenue, it made her sad to realize that sooner rather than later, she would have to look for another job. And when she did, she thought wryly, those black and white words that people insisted on painting her with — *award winner, hero, survivor, humanitarian* — would not be on her résumé. They were labels, not qualifications.

On her way uptown to her apartment, she considered her options. At that moment they seemed limited to a research grant somewhere else, a return to the ER, or a teaching job at a university — all long shots.

By process of elimination, the Women of the Year Banquet hosted by the Hart Line Foundation had leaped from ironic to fortuitous. Not only did the award come with a check for twenty-five thousand dollars, but also it provided the perfect occasion for networking. There would be hundreds of important people there, loads of press, and, she hoped, a few choice opportunities to explore.

She was nearing her apartment on Eighty-first and East End Avenue when her cell phone rang. Martie didn't recognize the number, but the voice and the desperation in it were all too familiar.

"I know it's late and I should have called sooner. I hate to do this to you, but I can't make dinner tonight."

"Why not?"

"Something's come up."

"Like what?"

"Just . . . something."

"Where are you?"

It took a minute until an address was forthcoming.

40

"I'll be right there," Martie said. Without a moment's hesitation she grabbed a cab and headed downtown.

Delilah Green reminded Martie of the Scarecrow in *The Wizard of Oz*: blond, spindly, and so loose-limbed she looked as if a flick of a finger could upend her; she appeared to have more sinew than skeleton. Her eyes were round, the pale blue of a winter sky, but they were never calm. They darted about constantly, surveying the area, greeting everyone she met with suspicion. The world had not been kind to her, so she didn't trust easily. Nor did she play well with others. She was a loner who skirted the edges, not following the rules, not keeping in step, and not caring what anyone thought of her refusal to be one of them. She held society at arm's length and they held her in contempt.

Delilah hailed from Piney Hollow, a coal-mining village in the hills of West Virginia. Her father died from black lung disease when she was ten. Her mother took in laundry to survive. Delilah went to school, worked two jobs, and helped care for her three brothers and two sisters. When she left home at seventeen, she ran as far and as fast as she could.

She had tried to make something of herself, but between then and now events had conspired to retard her progress and dilute her confidence. As each of her opportunities disappeared, another layer of her emotional strength was excised. Soon Delilah had little left except the primal instinct to survive. And even that was precarious. Along with her other failings, like the Scarecrow, Delilah believed she lacked courage.

Martie knew for a fact that wasn't true, but convincing her friend — and others — of that reality had become a decade-long struggle.

She was sitting on a park bench in Washington Square Park watching the pigeons peck for food and the old men playing chess.

Before she approached her, Martie took a good hard look at Delilah. She was a mess. Her hair was stringy and in need of a wash. Her outfit teetered between hooker and just plain horrible: a short skirt that left little to the imagination, clunky high heels, a denim jacket lined with something that looked like faux squirrel, a low-cut, acid-green sweater that probably had started out fuzzy but now looked like a matted bath rug, and hoop earrings large enough to hold a parakeet.

"I can certainly see why you had to cancel our date," Martie said, taking a place on the bench. "You're much too busy."

Delilah laughed. "Hey! I have birds to feed and people to advise," she said, pointing to the men hovering over the stone checkerboard.

"Noble tasks," Martie said. "But what does any of that have to do with meeting me for dinner?"

Delilah's smile faded. She fidgeted with the edge of her sweater, rolling it around in her fingers like a wad of cookie dough.

"I can't afford dinner," she muttered, her chin down, her voice laden with shame. "I'm out of work."

The last Martie had heard, Delilah was manning a checkout at Gristede's. Before that she'd been waitressing at a coffee shop in Brooklyn. Before that she'd been a bartender in the East Village, a receptionist at a beauty parlor, and for a brief time a truck driver in Wisconsin. Before that, she'd worked the line at a Toyota engine plant in Buffalo, West Virginia.

"What happened?"

"Unfortunately, my career in foodstuffs came to a halt. Just like the rest of my assorted careers."

"When?"

Delilah shuffled her feet and followed an imaginary bird with her eyes.

"When?" Martie asked again.

"A couple of weeks ago."

Probably more like a couple of months. By the looks of her she was flat broke, possibly homeless. Martie couldn't bear to think about what Delilah had been doing for food and shelter.

"Look, come on home with me. You'll get cleaned up and we'll have dinner in."

Delilah's lower lip stuck out the same way Martie's daughter Lili's did when she had done something wrong and Martie was about to discipline her.

"Are you upset with me?" Her voice trembled.

"Why would I be upset with you?"

" 'Cause I can't hold a job. And because I'm such a loser."

"You are not. You've just had a run of bad luck."

"Thirty-something years is more than a *run*, don't you think?"

"Okay, so it's closer to a marathon than a sprint. So what? Are you deliberately getting yourself fired?"

"No."

"Then shake it off!" Martie said, rising from the bench and taking Delilah with her. "Move on to the next."

As they walked out of the park, Martie was tempted to tell Delilah that they were both in the same situation, but that wasn't really true. She had a college diploma, a master's, a medical license, and a notable career history. Delilah had a string of no-end jobs.

"It's tough to shake shit like this off when you don't know where next is," Delilah said, her liquid blue eyes brimming with frustration.

"I know, but you can do it, Delilah. I know you can."

"I'm getting weighed down by the baggage, Martie." Her voice was small. "Know what I mean?"

Martie knew very well what Delilah meant. They shared an uncomfortable history and carried the same baggage.

"It doesn't help to dwell on the past."

"I don't dwell on it. I shut it out as best I can, but it just keeps on coming back," Delilah said. "It's kinda like a piece of bread crust that gets stuck in your throat and won't go down."

Martie wanted to tell her to fight harder, that even if the nightmares never completely went away eventually they eased, but over the years Delilah had chosen alcohol and promiscuity as her means of escape, neither of which Martie wanted to encourage.

"If you can't swallow it, you've got to spit it out."

Delilah forced a grin and snapped a salute. "Yes, ma'am!"

Martie laughed as she ran out into the street to flag down a cab, but her smile quickly faded as her own truth surged up from her gut and confronted her. She could tell Delilah to shake it off or spit it out or do whatever, but the ghosts were powerful. They followed Martie too, lurking over her like an ominous gang of thugs. She had appeased the past slightly, but it was insistent, looming in its thick gown of gray, circling, threatening to unleash the force of its secrets. She could try to run from it, to hide from it, to deny it. But the past was always there.

It was just a question of when it would leap out and grab her.

Chapter 2

The Rotunda at the Hotel Pierre was one of Martie's favorite venues. One couldn't help but feel elegant and grand standing in this lavishly decorated room with its tromp l'oeil murals, domed ceiling, and twin marble staircases leading up to the ballrooms. She didn't go there often, but whenever she did, she surrendered instantly to the seductive charm of Old World opulence.

Recently, she brought her six-year-old daughter Lili here for tea. In truth it was a reconnaissance mission. Martie had wanted Lili to see the hotel in advance so that she wouldn't be overwhelmed or frightened when she came this evening. It had been a good idea that turned into a fabulous afternoon. Lili was positively awestruck. She thought she had stepped into a veritable fairyland. The fact that the wait staff was smitten and fawned all over her didn't hurt. They brought her finger sandwiches and freshly baked madeleines and hot cocoa with extra whipped cream.

The only thing that even came close was the Palm Court at the Plaza — mother and daughter had done high tea there as well — but that, as Lili reminded Martie, was Eloise's domain, referring to the children's book character who lived at the landmark hotel. This, Lili declared, sweeping her hand around to take in the entire Rotunda, was going to be hers. Martie thought it was a lovely idea — every little girl should have a make-believe realm of her own — and for the past several weeks had been calling her daughter Lady Lili, the Princess of the Pierre.

Speaking of Lili, Martie wondered what had happened to her. Hugh Phelps, Martie's father, was in charge of his grand-daughter this evening. They had been there only a few minutes when he decided the room was too crowded for someone Lili's size, so the two of them had em-barked on a sortie, of sorts. Martie wasn't worried, she simply felt a little awkward standing by herself. And, to be honest, she was a little nervous. There were several people she didn't want to run into.

As she looked around at the crowd, she chuckled to herself. This was not like the award dinners she usually attended. Those were, as she politely called them, geek gatherings, full of scientific types who cared more about the chemical composition of the fabric in one's dress than the name of its designer. This was a full-blown, full-court social event with New York's elite prominently on display.

Since she'd presumed the haute caliber of the guests, Martie had bought a new gown for the occasion: a long, black silk jersey slip with spaghetti straps and a low, gently curved bodice. She'd have to wear it once a week for ten years to amortize the cost, but it was worth it. If she'd shown up in the only other gown she owned, which she'd purchased some five years before, she would have stood out like a weed in one of Vera Hart's perfectly planted gardens.

With nothing better to do until it was time to enter the ballroom, she checked out the women standing near her. Some sported elegant upswept hairdos, others favored more casual short crops. Martie's chestnut hair hung straight and free to her shoulders. Wrists, ears, and a few necks were ablaze with expensive jewels. She wore delicate gold briolette earrings tipped with pearls and on her wrist a jumble of slim ropes strung with freshwater pearls. Intertwined with the pearls was a slim gold chain that held a dime outlined in gold. It was her good luck charm. She never went anywhere without it.

The one thing she didn't have, but wished she did, was a watch. She needed to know how much longer it would be before everyone moved into the ballroom. Her feet were beginning to hurt. Three-inch-high heels were not part of her lab uniform.

Needing to find a chair so she could take off her shoes and sit for a minute, she headed for the ladies' room. She had just rounded a corner when she found herself face to face with Vera Hart.

Vera seemed as stunned as Martie was, but her recovery was quicker. "Marta, I'm delighted to run into you."

"It's nice to see you too," she said.

"I'm so glad you came. It's going to be a wonderful evening."

"I was honored to be one of the recipients. Thank you."

Vera proffered a throaty laugh. "I'd like to take the credit, but in truth the selections are up to the Hart Foundation board. They're the ones who decided your contributions were meritorious enough to be singled out. My job was simply to agree or disagree. I wholeheartedly agreed."

Martie was touched.

"Your work is stellar, Martie. You should be very proud of yourself."

"I am."

"Good. One should always take pride in one's work."

Vera paused.

Martie couldn't tell whether she was assessing her ensemble, waiting to be told what a fabulous job she'd done with the Hart Line, or deciding what to say next.

"By the way, when you were in Washington did you receive a note from me? And some flowers?"

It had been so long ago, Martie had forgotten about them.

"Yes. I did." They had been delivered to the hospital when Martie returned stateside. "It was very kind of you. I'm sorry I didn't thank you properly."

Vera waved her hand dismissively, forgiving the breach in manners. "I was concerned for your well-being and wanted you to know that."

Martie's knee-jerk reaction was to say that if she'd been really concerned she would have contacted Martie in person. But this was neither the time nor the place for that, so she simply acknowledged Vera's thoughtfulness with a nod.

"Well, it's been lovely chatting, but if

you'll excuse me, I have to check on some last-minute details."

With that, Vera was off.

Martie felt as if she'd just had an encounter with the Ghost of Christmas Past.

Hugh and Lili were wandering through the Pierre when Hugh sidelined one of the catering managers. He explained that they were there for the Hart Foundation dinner, his daughter was one of the recipients, and he thought it might be nice for his granddaughter to see the room without all the people. Happy to oblige, the man led the two of them to the Grand Ballroom. When he opened the doors, Lili's eyes boggled and she giggled with delight. Everything was red.

Sumptuous ruby red brocade tablecloths created an opulent field. Red Hart Foundation programs rested atop gold-rimmed plates. Votive candles wrapped with rose petals flickered politely. Low, lush floral arrangements of red and black roses mixed with dried burgundy hydrangea and dark purple grapes, which spilled onto the table, served as centerpieces. Rising above them and highlighted by red-gelled spots were ivy-covered wires molded into large, leafy hearts. The room looked like a Valentine.

As Lili looked around, she clapped her hands, thoroughly enchanted.

"Does the Queen of Hearts live here?" she asked, imagining herself an Alice in Wonderland.

"Sort of."

Hugh turned and there was the Queen of Hearts herself.

Vera looked spectacular. She was wearing a low-cut gown of champagne chiffon that seemed to float as she walked toward them. Her hair was pulled back in a soft chignon that rested at the nape of her neck and provided a dark frame for the perfection that was her face. Her makeup was simple yet exquisite, her only accessories large, pear-shaped diamond drop earrings, a lacy diamond cuff, and a ring with a diamond large enough to qualify as a planet.

"Do you like it?" Vera said to Lili, transfixed by the little girl in the pink party dress.

"It's so fun." Lili turned to Vera and gifted her with a huge grin.

Her mouth was exactly like Martie's, Vera noted. Wide and full and simply made for grinning.

"I'm glad you think so." Vera bent down and touched the child's cheek gingerly. She hadn't done that in a very long time.

Lili stuck out her hand. "I'm Lili

53

Abrams and I'm pleased to meet you."

Vera shook the little girl's hand and smiled. "I'm Vera Hart and I'm pleased to meet you."

Lili heard Vera's name and a flash of recognition passed across her face. Vera waited expectantly.

"You're the lady who's giving my mommy a reward."

"Award," Hugh corrected, keeping his eyes on Vera.

A sharp inhalation of breath revealed that it never dawned on Vera that someone wouldn't know who the world-famous Vera Hart was, especially this child.

"Award," Lili repeated dutifully.

Hugh caressed the back of her head in a gesture of approval. His gaze still rested on Vera.

"She's very smart, your mother."

Hugh wondered if Vera said that for Lili's benefit or his.

"She's the best!" Lili glowed with such unadulterated pride and love it appeared to stun Vera, almost to disturb her.

"Well, Hugh, you're as handsome as ever," she said, moving to his side and bussing him on both cheeks.

Lili found that curious. "How do you know my grandpa?"

"I met him a long time ago. Before he was your grandfather."

"Did you like him a long time ago?"

"Yes," Vera said. "As a matter of fact, I did."

Lili looked up at Hugh with adoring eyes, then at Vera. "In my 'pinion, he's really special."

"Gee, that's my 'pinion too."

Lili giggled.

"You have very good taste in men, Miss Abrams."

"My gramma used to say that too."

"Is your gramma here tonight?"

Lili shook her head. Her lower lip curled downward. "Gramma's in heaven."

Vera looked at Hugh, whose mouth had grown tight.

"She died two years ago. Breast cancer."

"I'm sorry," Vera said. It was impossible not to notice that Hugh was still feeling the loss.

The moment was awkward but short-lived, thanks to the appearance of a tall man with thinning brown hair and a dyspeptic look on his face. At first Hugh thought it was another catering manager needing approval for a last-minute detail, but the manner in which he approached Vera seemed possessive.

"I don't mean to intrude," he said, although his impatience made it clear that was exactly what he'd intended. "They're about to open the ballroom."

Vera nodded. Traditionally, she made a quiet entrance from the side, after all the guests were seated and the award recipients had taken their places on the dais.

"Craig, this is . . ."

She hesitated only because she wanted to get his rank right. Hugh interpreted the gap as her uncertainty about whether or not she wanted their past relationship revealed.

"Lieutenant General Hugh Phelps, retired." He offered his hand, which the other man shook. "And this is my granddaughter, Lili."

"I'm pleased to meet you," Lili said, once again displaying her manners.

Hemminger didn't shake her hand as much as he brushed her fingers.

"Hugh, this is Craig Hemminger. He's the CFO of Hart Line International." She smiled. Hugh recognized it as one of her professional smiles. "Now, if you'll excuse me."

Hugh gave a slight, courtier's bow. "Certainly. It was nice seeing you again, Vera. Good luck this evening. I hope everything goes well."

"I hope so too." She didn't know whether he was referring to the gala or something else, but she wasn't about to ask, especially in front of Hemminger. Instead, she bade Lili a good evening. "Maybe I'll see you later."

"Where will you be sitting?"

Vera pointed to the dais. "Up there."

Lili looked at her grandfather. "Is that where Mommy's going to be?"

Hugh nodded and turned to Vera, a sly twinkle in his eyes. Ever since he'd heard about Martie's award he'd been suspicious of Vera's motives. It had been years, but people didn't change much. Vera had engineered this. He wondered why.

"I'll wave to you," Lili said.

Much to Hugh's surprise, Vera promised to "wave back."

As Craig and Vera walked away, Craig said, "Who are they?"

"None of your business," Vera replied.

Martie had just returned to the Rotunda when someone touched her arm. She hoped it was Hugh.

"Martie?"

She hadn't heard that voice in years, but it still had the power to make her heart flutter.

"Bryan," she said, offering him her hand and a quick smile. "This is a surprise."

That was an understatement. Of all the potential run-ins she had anticipated, he was not one of them.

There were a few lines around the corner of his mouth now. The mischievous glint that had characterized his earthy brown eyes was gone. His hair was longer than the flyboy buzz cut he used to sport, but he was still one of the handsomest men she'd ever met. Athletic-looking even in the elegant tuxedo he was wearing tonight, Bryan had a commanding presence, always had. It was a dignity of bearing that reminded her of her father. There was also a duality to him that was highly charismatic. Most of the time he appeared poised and fully at ease with his surroundings, no matter what they were. Yet he exuded a powerful, restless aura that felt like an energy field. He seemed to be perpetually idling, ready in case something happened that required a rapid response. Martie found that sexy.

"It's a surprise for me too. A very pleasant one, I might add."

His eyes fixed on hers, holding her in place as if they were stun guns. He'd always been direct and intense.

"Likewise. How've you been?" She could have kicked herself. She hadn't seen Bryan Chalmers in eons. *How've you been* sounded so lame.

"I've been good. How about you?"

She nodded her head, praying something brilliant was rattling around in there and would find its way to her mouth.

"Good," she said.

A slow smile started to cross Bryan's lips, but he stifled it. He could see how uncomfortable she was.

"Are you here with anyone?"

"I'm one of the honorees," she said shyly.

His brown eyes widened. "Really. I'm impressed."

Martie laughed. "Me too. Scientific achievement. It sounds rather lofty, don't you think?"

"I think it sounds terrific."

She flushed. Bryan couldn't remember her doing that before; it wasn't that Martie lacked modesty, but whenever she set out to do something she worked hard to accomplish the task and took pride in its completion. Her attitude was: If you weren't going to do your best to make sure you did the job right, you shouldn't attempt it. The worst failure was not a lack

59

of success, but a lack of effort.

"So what exactly did you achieve?"

"The short version is that we found a way to manipulate certain genes so that someone with melanoma would be more sensitive to chemo and therefore have a greater chance of being cured."

Bryan whistled. "That's way better than terrific." He furrowed his brow and studied her. All that beauty combined with all those smarts. "Is there anything you don't do well?"

She wanted to say relationships, but he knew that already.

"I have a list, and believe me, it's long."

"Somehow, I doubt that." His voice grew soft, almost intimate.

"And you?" Martie quickly changed the subject. "What have you been up to?"

"I'm still catching bad guys, but instead of doing it for the army or the FBI, I'm in the DA's office."

She smiled. "With you on the job, I'm surprised there are any bad guys left."

"You put one away and three more crawl out of the woodwork."

A bell rang. Heads turned as hotel staffers invited the guests to enter the ballroom.

"I'd better go." As awkward as this reunion was, Martie was reluctant to break it off.

Bryan was also. "Would you like me to escort you to the dais?"

"That would be nice, but I have to help my guests find their table."

As if Lieutenant General Hugh Phelps, combat veteran of Vietnam, Desert Storm, and Bosnia, couldn't find his way to a table. What was it about Bryan that was making her sound like such a complete idiot?

He looked disappointed. She almost changed her mind and asked him to escort her upstairs, but then he said, "It was great seeing you again."

He took her hand and squeezed it affectionately. As he pulled his hand away, his fingers felt something familiar. He looked down and spotted the dime. He swallowed hard before looking up at her. She appeared as unnerved as he felt.

He reached into his pocket, pulled out a handful of change, and rummaged around until he found the mate to Martie's good luck piece: another dime outlined in gold.

Martie looked in his hand. She could barely breathe. She wanted to talk to him, to ask him why he still had their dime, but she couldn't. Not now.

"I have to go."

"Of course you do."

He dropped the dime back into his pocket and watched as she walked away from him, again.

From the landing at the top of the stairs outside the ballroom, Vera observed the conversation between Martie and Bryan. She couldn't hear what they were saying, of course, but it was interesting to watch the emotions that played across their faces as they conversed and to read their body language. Whatever scenario she might have conjured in her mind, the look on Bryan's face when Martie left spoke volumes. Theirs was a love story that hadn't had a happy ending.

Vera knew all about stories like that.

Martie was uncomfortable. Black tie galas were not her milieu. Her daughter, on the other hand, appeared quite at ease in this very grown-up world. Then again, Lili was a very sophisticated six-year-old who'd already experienced a great deal of upheaval in her young life. Lili's father had died when she was two; Gramma Connie had died when she was four. When Martie relocated to New York she'd had to make new friends and adjust to new surroundings, but she'd done it all with a smile on her face and an older-than-her-years acquiescence to change.

"I feel particularly privileged to be introducing Dr. Phelps," Abner Kaplow said.

The speeches had been going on for some time. Martie had only been half listening. Hearing her name, she snapped to attention.

Abner was a stocky, bespectacled oncologist with a halo of silver hair and a sense of humor that seemed remarkable considering that he'd spent most of his life trying to find a cure for pediatric cancers.

"Aside from my obvious respect for her scientific acumen, her background astounds me."

His head turned and his green eyes peered at Martie through round rimless glasses. His smile carried a silent apology. Over the years, they'd developed a highly collegial relationship. He knew how private Martie was and how much she disliked certain aspects of her life being discussed in a public arena. He also knew that under certain circumstances, she understood it was expected.

"She sailed through the University of Virginia in three years and graduated NYU's combined med school/honors program at the top of her class. Then she did something most of us might never have thought of doing. She joined the army."

Spontaneous applause greeted that revelation. Martie looked at her father. His face remained implacable, but his eyes glistened with amusement. It surprised people to learn of those who could have pursued careers in the civilian sector yet volunteered to serve in the military, especially women, but they didn't know what a close, welcoming clan the uniformed community could be.

"After eleven weeks of basic training at the Army Medical Department Officers Basic Course at Fort Sam Houston in Texas, she was commissioned a first lieutenant. Then came seven weeks in the Army Flight Surgeon Primary Course in Fort Rucker, Alabama, where, among other things, she learned to fly a helicopter.

"And in case she hadn't achieved enough distinction, Dr. Phelps decided to try for the esteemed Expert Field Medical Badge. Her final exam was marching twelve miles in under three hours carrying a thirty-five-pound backpack." His eyes widened and he sighed as if he had tried marching alongside her, but couldn't keep up. "There were sixty people in her group when the course began. Eight graduated. Martie was the only woman."

Again, the audience expressed its respect.

"Her internship in emergency medicine at Walter Reed Army Medical Center was cut short in August of 1990 when she was sent to the Gulf. During Desert Storm, Lieutenant Phelps was a flight surgeon in the 229th Attack Helicopter Battalion of 101st Airborne Division. She was on a search and rescue mission when her Black Hawk helicopter was shot down. Six of the eight crew members were killed."

Even now those deaths devastated Martie. She could still see their bodies lying in the desert, still recall the last words she had spoken to each of them before their Black Hawk went down.

"Within minutes of the crash, she was captured by the Iraqis and for nine days was subjected to harsh interrogations in an effort to pressure her into betraying her country, which she steadfastly refused to do." Abner smiled as the audience rose to give Martie a standing ovation.

This was why she didn't like her service record to be discussed. She was proud of her time in the military, but she had been one of twenty-two POWs and she wasn't the only woman. All of them had been mistreated in one way or another. She didn't like being singled out for doing what she'd been trained to do: stay alive long enough for her comrades to free her. She acknowledged the applause, but remained in her seat. Her cheeks felt warm.

When the room was quiet again, Abner went on to explain Martie's work in the field of skin cancer.

"And so, I'm delighted to call up my colleague and my friend, Dr. Marta Phelps."

Martie winked at Lili, rose from her seat, and headed toward the podium.

He glared at her from the back of the room, aiming his hatred at her heart. She didn't even fidget in her chair. It was as if she were wearing Kevlar. Instead of writhing from the heat of his animus, she was making light conversation with one of her tablemates. What really galled was he knew he could have been standing next to her and she probably wouldn't have noticed him.

Wanting to hide his ire, he buried his face in the program and studied the page devoted to her achievements. She might come off like a hero to others, but to him,

Martie Phelps was a curse. Thanks to her, his dreams had been crushed, his life ruined. Thanks to her, he had spent years in ignominy, toiling away like a serf in jobs well beneath his talents just to rebuild his reputation. And now, just when things were going well, just when he was on the brink of having everything he ever wanted, she reappeared.

He gulped his drink and signaled to the waiter to bring him another. His head was throbbing, but over the years he'd found that alcohol in large quantities numbed what ailed him.

What rankled was that this predicament had occurred because he had slipped up. He had believed she was permanently ensconced in Washington, so he had let down his guard and had not maintained proper vigilance. He supposed it served him right. While he was napping, she had come to New York, invading *his* space, polluting *his* universe.

The waiter brought his drink and he downed it quickly, unsuccessfully trying to sedate his agitation.

Each time the audience applauded, he grew more depressed, more unsettled.

She could ruin everything for him.

Or, he thought, bilious, self-righteous

67

anger rising in his throat, he could ruin everything for her.

Greta had passed furious a couple of hours ago and was quickly approaching apoplectic. She had missed the cocktail hour and probably most of the dinner. Gone was her dramatic entrance. Gone was the hobnobbing with business connections and dishing with her cronies. Gone were her photo opportunities. Gone was her face to face with the eminent Dr. Marta Phelps.

And, she cautioned, if she wasn't careful running up these stairs, gone would be her five-hundred-dollar Jimmy Choo shoes.

Greta stopped, took a deep breath, and tried to calm down, but she couldn't. Vera had done this deliberately. She had barged into Greta's office just as Greta was about to leave and demanded that she prepare pertinent files for each of the subdivisions likely to come under government scrutiny. Greta protested. Vera insisted. Greta repeated what she had told Vera privately after that emergency meeting/public flogging the previous evening: Whatever precautions they took and whatever adjustments they made should be kept very close to the vest.

"The whistle-blower didn't give his

name because it's someone inside HLI, probably the same someone who's giving the government information in exchange for immunity. Don't give him any more ammunition than he already has."

Vera accepted the logic behind her argument, yet she ordered Greta to prepare the files anyway.

An hour and a half later, elbow deep in profit/loss statements, it dawned on Greta that this was a ruse. Vera didn't want Greta at the Foundation gala and this was her way of keeping Greta busy.

As she approached the entrance to the Grand Ballroom, Abner Kaplow had just begun his introduction. Greta stood in the doorway and listened. However intimidating Dr. Phelps's accomplishments had seemed when she first read them in the program, amplified by a microphone and underlined by spontaneous, enthusiastic applause, her record became positively daunting.

Quietly, not wanting to draw attention to her tardiness, Greta slipped inside and made her way onto one of the low balconies that rimmed the ballroom. Aside from providing a better view of the dais and the front tables, it allowed her the privacy to have whatever reactions she was going to have without feeling the need to censor herself.

It proved to be an excellent choice, because minutes later, when the audience gave Martie a standing ovation, Greta flinched. She wasn't envious of Martie's time as a prisoner of war — she wouldn't have wished that on anyone — only that her survival seemed to prove that no matter how horrific the challenge, Martie Phelps could rise to the occasion and triumph. Greta was tough, but not in the same way. She never would put herself in those situations in the first place, and while she knew that didn't make her a coward or a bad person, neither would she ever be a hero.

She was about to sneak onto the floor and join her table when everyone sat down. A few seconds later, Martie arose and started to walk toward Vera.

Whenever Greta had visualized this evening, and she had many times over the past several days, she imagined that Vera handing Martie the Foundation award would be an unpleasant moment. It was, but it paled next to the sight of a tall, distinguished-looking, silver-haired man in the front row gazing up at the stage and beaming with pride.

It was déjà vu all over again.

* * *

Bryan's Blackberry vibrated. Discreetly, he slid it out of his pocket and read his e-mail. It was from Borzone: *The vic didn't die from the beating. ME says mercuric chloride poisoning.*

Bryan was confounded. He'd read the initial autopsy report. This woman's injuries were horrific. A sadist who got off on watching his victims suffer beat her with his fists as well as something hard, like a rock. There seemed to be little question about cause of death.

Then again, the Central Park jogger had survived a similar attack.

Mercuric chloride struck Bryan as an extremely odd choice. It was hardly your everyday poison. An under-the-sink cleaning agent was far more typical. The other question was how he got this woman to ingest the compound. Did he force it down her throat at the scene or had he been with her somewhere else and slipped it into her drink like a Mickey?

Either way, a woman was dead, and somewhere out there a sick bastard was on the loose.

Martie had waited for this moment all evening.

What would she say? What would she do?

The run-in outside the ladies' room didn't count. They'd both been unprepared.

But Vera had planned for this. So had Martie. In the weeks leading up to this event she had run through a variety of possibilities and tried to come up with an appropriate response to each one, but now that it was actually here, her insides were churning.

How could they not be? Vera Hart was Martie's mother.

"I realize this award doesn't carry the same weight as your Bronze Star, your Purple Heart, or your Distinguished Service Medal, but on behalf of women everywhere, I thank you. Please accept this with our gratitude for a job well done."

Vera handed Martie an envelope and a red velvet box opened to display a small eighteen-karat gold heart suspended from a short, wide, red satin ribbon.

As Martie accepted the gifts and the bejeweled hand, she looked deep into Vera Hart's eyes, hoping to find some maternal warmth, some sign that this was the first step in a greatly desired reunion between mother and daughter.

Instead, Vera remained distant, formal, and completely impersonal.

"Thank you," Martie said politely, kicking herself for expecting and wanting more.

As she returned to her seat, she was disappointed, but, she told herself, her spirit wasn't crushed. Her life wasn't ruined. She and Vera had a brief encounter, she accepted an award, and in a few minutes she would take her child and her father, go home, and put the notion of a reconciliation with her mother back in storage.

Then Vera did something Martie never would have expected: She waved at a little girl in a pink party dress.

Chapter 3

Lili fell asleep the minute her head touched her pillow. Hugh and Martie were exhausted, but neither was ready to even attempt sleep. Instead, Hugh doffed his jacket and tie, Martie did a quick change into a T-shirt and sweatpants, and they debriefed in her living room with a pot of hot tea and a plate of doughnuts.

"First, I had this bizarre run-in with her outside the ladies' room," Martie said, curling up on the couch. "One minute the two of us are exchanging awkward pleasantries. The next minute she's oozing concern over my war injuries. Two minutes after that, she's gone."

She made it sound as if Vera were deranged.

Hugh smiled. Their conversation was a bit peculiar.

"Then there was our encounter on the dais. She smiled, congratulated me, and presented me with a check. The whole thing was so: Hi, 'bye."

Martie's aquamarine eyes narrowed as she tried to define her feelings.

"It was like looking into the face of a stranger, only stranger."

Her face reflected a mix of disappointment and resignation.

"I suppose I expected something more. Something extra. Something that said there was a connection between us."

She shrugged, as if she should have known better.

"But Vera repeated the same moves with me that she used with the other award recipients. There was nothing special. I was nothing special."

Hugh's heart ached. Martie was thirty-five, yet at that moment she sounded no older than Lili.

"I disagree," he said gently. "I think she handpicked you for that award."

"Maybe, but I don't see why. We hardly know each other."

Martie was eight when her parents separated. Originally, the terms of the divorce took into consideration the two parties' peripatetic schedules and the enormous distances the children would have to travel. Hugh was posted in Europe and would visit Greta whenever he could. Martie was to visit Vera in California for

75

three weeks over the summer.

Martie visited California twice; both times the length of the trip and the re-adjustment from home to home took such a tremendous toll that Hugh petitioned the court to require Vera to come to Martie, which she did, twice. Once she had the Hart Line up and running — and Hugh had married Connie Vaughn — she claimed that as much as she wanted to maintain contact with her daughter, as a single parent without adequate support, financial pressures made it impossible for her to get away.

Over the years, Martie and Vera had ex-changed occasional letters and perfunctory gifts, but there had been no further visits. Once Martie went to college, all contact ceased. Until this evening, Martie hadn't seen her mother in person since she was twelve years old. Any information she had about Vera — or Vera had about her — came from newspaper or television reports.

"Contrary to what you thought," Hugh said, "Vera has kept close tabs on you."

"Do you think she knew about Lili?"

Hugh revisited the meeting between grandmother and granddaughter.

"No."

"Then would you please explain what

was going on between them?"

Hugh laughed. "It's simple. The Queen of Hearts answered the wave of the Princess of the Pierre."

"Excuse me?"

Hugh told her how they had run into Vera in the ballroom.

"She was utterly charmed by our Lili," he said with unvarnished pride. "And Lili was utterly charmed by her."

Martie was skeptical.

"Was she charmed by you too?" Like her, this was the first time Hugh had seen Vera in years.

Hugh laughed. "Mildly, perhaps, but not utterly."

That seemed impossible to Martie, who was still her father's biggest fan, but since she hadn't been there, she couldn't debate.

"She does look fabulous."

Hugh agreed, but added, "Looking fabulous was never difficult for her. Putting herself second was."

"Which brings us back to this evening," Martie said. "Let's say you're right and she engineered my appearance. What was the point? I just can't figure it out."

"Then don't bother. Cash the check and forget it."

Easier said than done, Martie thought.

★ ★ ★

Greta remained at the hotel long after everyone else was gone. As the cleaning crew came in, she moved out from the shadows toward the front of the low balcony and stared out onto the floor of the ballroom. In her mind, she replayed the image of Vera waving at that child in the front row.

Greta had been completely thrown by the uncharacteristic gesture. When she located the recipient of the wave, she almost fell over; the power of the moment was that strong. A little girl with a heart-shaped face, chestnut brown hair, and aquamarine eyes was waving at Vera with one hand and holding on to Hugh with the other.

Suddenly Greta was eleven years old. She wasn't at the Pierre, she was in the foyer of the house on Roxbury Drive. She was standing by Vera's side, but her mother wasn't paying attention to her. Her father had started for the door with Martie, who was eight, in tow. Greta panicked. She didn't know what to do.

If she changed her mind and moved toward Hugh, her mother would be hurt. If she didn't say something or make a move, her father would leave without her.

Greta could still remember how she felt standing in that hallway: frightened, unsure, angry with Martie for not having to make a decision, and thoroughly conflicted about the one she had made. She wanted desperately to stay with one parent, yet she wanted just as badly to go with the other.

Greta recalled how inside her head she screamed at Hugh to offer her an alternative. She begged Vera to say something that made it essential for her to stay. But they were too busy hurting each other to see what they were doing to Greta.

Hugh took Martie's hand and walked out.

Vera slammed the door and ran to her bedroom in tears.

Greta was left alone in the hall.

Just as she was now.

Despite the lateness of the hour, Hugh left Martie's apartment and walked home so he could clear his head.

There were certain days in everyone's life that stood out: historic moments that were so significant in their impact that ultimately, they changed that life.

Hugh had a handful of those days: March 16, 1962, at Fort Bragg when Vera Hart came to entertain the troops and their love affair began. October 25, 1963, when Greta was born, and August 28, 1966, when Martie was born. August 20, 1969, in Vietnam's Queson Valley when more than sixty American troops were killed during a fierce drive to reach the wreckage of a U.S. command helicopter. February 25, 1991, when Martie was captured by the Iraqis. March 22, 2000, the day he lost Connie. And May 12, 1973, when his younger daughter posed a question that ultimately ended his marriage: "Why doesn't Mommy love me?"

The substance of her question was jarring enough, but the when and where of its asking made it even more striking. They had paused on the corner of Foothill Road and Carmelita Avenue, halfway through their regular Sunday morning walk around Beverly Hills. Normally they talked about school, TV shows, her friends, why Hugh was a Yankee fan living in Dodgerland, and other equally innocuous topics. For her to blurt out something like that in the middle of what was usually a casual, before-breakfast hike was disturbing.

"Of course she loves you, sweetheart." Pat assurances were hideously insufficient, but until he knew the root of her anguish they were all he had to offer.

Martie wasn't buying. She shook her head. Her lips were pursed as if she were holding back tears, but her eyes were dry and certain.

"You're her baby. How could you think such a thing?"

She shrugged, raising her shoulders slowly, looking up at him with apologetic eyes. "I just do."

Martie was seven at the time. Vera had been Hollywood's darling for more than twenty years. For eleven of those years, Hugh had been Vera's husband, so he knew how difficult life could be when one was part of a movie star's retinue. As much as you loved them, it was hard to compete with the thrill of an adoring audience or to make up for the devastation of fan indifference. It was also difficult understanding that with a superstar self-absorption was not only a given, but a necessity.

"Sometimes your mother just gets caught up in what she's doing."

Martie listened as Hugh ticked off a list of what was expected of a public persona and nodded politely, but he could tell she didn't find "busy" a reasonable explanation for what she was feeling.

Hugh tried again. "It's hard being a big star."

Even harder when that star was waning, he thought.

"It's hard being a soldier, but I know *you* love me."

Hugh reached down, caught Martie up in his arms, and hugged her. "You bet I do!"

Her small arms wrapped around his broad shoulders. Her face nestled in the crook of his neck.

"I'm going to miss you," she said, clinging to him.

"Me too you." He hugged her again and set her down. "I'm only going to be gone for a couple of weeks, punkin."

A tear fell onto her cheek. Tenderly, he kissed it away.

Hugh was a major in the United States Army, which meant he was off on assignment a great deal of the time. His frequent absences were hard on all of them, but short of resigning his commission there was nothing much he could do.

"I'll be back before you know it."

"Okay." Her lower lip quivered, but she was trying very hard to be brave.

Staying home with one's mother shouldn't require bravery, he thought.

"Does Greta feel the same way? About Mom, I mean."

Martie shrugged. The sisters weren't particularly close.

"We're different."

They were, but Martie wasn't presenting an analysis of their contrasting personalities. In her little-girl way, she was pointing out how each related to their parents. Greta idolized Vera to the point of worship and spent her life bending over backward in an effort to please. Martie also coveted her mother's love and approval, but Hugh seemed more accessible and more responsive.

"What makes you think Mommy doesn't love you?" he asked. "Did she do or say something?"

What Vera had done was become distracted and edgy. She missed Martie's school play, which was odd, since she had rehearsed with Martie until she could recite her lines in her sleep. She had the nanny take Greta to her ballet lessons, an activity she usually adored. And she snapped at the girls when they came into her dressing room to play makeup, which was *really* odd, because makeup was Vera's favorite game.

Greta said Vera's change of mood had something to do with her movies and nothing to do with them. Since Greta always seemed to know everything about everything, Martie took her sister's word for it.

Then she overhead Vera talking to someone about being a mother. Martie didn't hear the whole conversation. All she picked up was, "The older one was planned, the younger one was an accident." And, "No one ever told me that in show business having two children would be a major liability."

Martie had no idea what a liability was, but she knew people avoided accidents. When she fed that information into her young brain, the words she didn't understand became jumbled with the concepts she did, and out came, "She said I shouldn't have happened."

Vera was too wound up to sleep. The gala had been a smashing success; aside from the staggering amount of money they had raised, the public relations the Hart Line accrued from an evening like that was priceless, especially now. But it was the personal moments she was relishing. She had reacquainted with her younger daughter, sort of, and she'd finally met her granddaughter.

Vera smiled just thinking about Lili.

What a positively enchanting child she was.

Not unlike Martie when she was Lili's age, Vera thought wistfully.

Publicly, when asked about her career and the course of her life, Vera claimed she had no regrets.

"You do what you have to do and deal with the consequences later," she said. "If you do something for the right reasons, no matter how it turns out there's always an upside."

The example she cited was that while she had missed out on a normal childhood, she'd been rewarded with a star on Hollywood's Walk of Fame and a legion of life-long fans.

The example she kept to herself was that while agents and studio executives insisted children were a liability to her ingénue image — she had two fabulous daughters. And therein lay the source of her one real regret: the sacrifice of her family on the altar of her career.

It was never easy being a working mother. Whether you were a movie star or a waitress in a diner, the conflict was constant and the pressure was unbearable, but if a mother was working there were reasons for doing so.

Many women worked because they had talents they wished to contribute to society and because, like men, they found that success in one's chosen arena provided a sense of fulfillment that nothing else did.

Most women worked because their families needed the money.

Vera qualified in both categories. She was talented and adored what she did, but also she'd been the primary support of her family since she was nine years old: first her parents, then her husband and children.

The United States Army was known for many things, but lavish salaries was not one of them. Whatever Hugh made paled in comparison to what Vera brought to the household. And since the household was predicated on her financial contribution, the Phelpses' lifestyle would radically change if that contribution were eliminated. Unfortunately, the only one who couldn't own up to that reality was Hugh.

Hugh. Vera recalled the jolt of emotion she'd experienced when she ran into him earlier this evening. He was still the handsomest, most exciting man she'd ever known — and that included most of her costars and all of her lovers. He still owned a piece of her heart, but back in the day,

Hugh Phelps had been a tough guy to live with. She didn't know if he'd mellowed any with the years — or with Connie — but when they were a couple he'd been so heavily steeped in old-fashioned conventions, he'd been oblivious to her struggle to maintain a balance.

He was married to a woman whose earning capacity dwarfed his, yet he continued to trumpet the male/female division of labor that set the male on the upper tier as the breadwinner and decision maker of the family, and the female on the lower tier as the one who bore the children and kept the home fires burning. He and Vera shared incomes, passion, and children, but not responsibilities.

When they'd first married and her career was still in full flower, Vera didn't rebel against the disparity in their roles because the stereotype felt oddly comfortable. Her childhood was so abnormal that having a Donna Reed adulthood made her feel secure and cherished and deliciously average, as if for once in her life she fit. She had a house, a husband, two children — everything but a dog.

Then her career began a precipitous slide. She couldn't talk to Hugh about her fears because he was away. Even if he'd been home he probably wouldn't have been particularly helpful. He didn't understand the industry and he couldn't understand why Vera was so stressed out. She was a major talent. Why couldn't she just hire another agent or take on different roles? She was a loving mother. Why was she always complaining about having to juggle her emotional need to be there for the girls and her professional obligations? He did both; why couldn't she?

She didn't think he realized he was doing it, but when he said things like that he trivialized her career and, by extension, her. What he was really saying was that he dealt with important issues like war and peace; she made moving pictures.

She couldn't confide in her mother because Ilona refused to listen to talk of retirement; her income depended on Vera's career. So too did Vera's agent, her manager, and her publicist. As for her children, they were . . . children. They were supposed to be shielded from life's larger problems.

So, like other mothers torn between career and family and inhibited by the fear of damaging their husbands' egos, Vera was left to deal with her life crisis alone. Without a core of advisors looking out for her and not themselves, without the full support of her husband, and overwhelmed by the possibility of everything she'd worked for being taken away, she messed up. Her husband walked out. He took her younger daughter with him. And despite all her efforts and her sacrifices, her career died anyway.

Now Vera Hart was rich and powerful. Since she had enough money and enough influence to be certain that neither could be completely taken away from her, she decided it was time to rid herself of her one regret. She was going to get back what she'd lost.

She knew she couldn't simply call Martie and say, "I want to be part of your life." The consequences from the errors she'd made years before had snowballed to where it was going to be difficult to dig herself out. She'd have to earn Martie's affection and she'd have to do it without launching a heavy-handed campaign or issuing demands.

She devised her plan months ago, subtly ensuring that Martie would be considered for the Hart Foundation Award. When the committee put Martie's name before her, she enthusiastically approved her nomination. Everything was in place. The gala was the first step. She planned to take Martie's emotional temperature toward her, present the award and move on to step number two.

But now the Hart Line was in trouble. Once again, Vera was going to have to juggle the demands of career and family. The difference was that this time she was determined to wind up with both.

Martie's first encounter with Captain Bryan Chalmers was on the driving range of the Silver Wings Golf Course at Fort Rucker. After two weeks of intense classroom study she desperately needed what she called a blue-green break: blue skies, green grass and trees. The quickest nature fix available was the golf course, so that's where she headed.

Having grown up around army bases, which often had their own golf courses, golf was not a foreign subject for Martie, although she would never have been so bold as to declare herself proficient in the sport. That kind of braggadocio always proved dangerous. It dared the golf gods to visit hideous curses like the chili dip or the dreaded shank on one's game.

She borrowed a couple of clubs from the pro shop, found a slot at the far end of the range, and started hitting balls. She wasn't swinging particularly well, but she didn't care. She was outdoors. It was a gorgeous day. The air was sweet and she had the entire afternoon to herself. Life was good.

After hitting half a bucket of balls — few of them straight — she became disgusted and decided it was time to focus. Little by little, something that resembled a golf swing returned. But it was hot out and her T-shirt was beginning to stick to her body. Since she was the only woman on the range, she felt self-conscious about a clingy wet T-shirt, so she pulled it out of her shorts and let it hang loose. She also removed her hat, welcoming the feel of the sun on her face.

It didn't take long before her eyes began to water from the glare. She reached into her rucksack, found a handkerchief, and dabbed at her eyes.

"It's not that bad," a male voice said. "You're just coming too far inside."

"Excuse me?" Martie turned around to find an extremely handsome man in khaki shorts, an olive green T-shirt, a tan Silver Wings baseball cap, and gold-rimmed aviator glasses.

"That's why you're going to the right. You're bringing the club too far inside."

He took his own club and imitated her swing.

"Most beginners do that, but it's easily corrected." He showed her how. "Try it."

Martie wasn't a beginner, she wasn't crying, and if this was a pickup line, she wasn't buying.

When she didn't jump to do as he suggested, he stepped behind her.

"Here, I'll show you."

Before she could stop him he wrapped his arms around her and covered her hands with his. As he swung the club up and through, her T-shirt moved up and down. His head was so near hers she could feel the brim of his hat against her hair. His body was closer than that.

Shaken by his proximity and annoyed at the cheesy come-on, she quickly pulled away. She also tucked her T-shirt back in her shorts.

His expression fell midway between a leer and frank admiration.

"See?" he said. "It's easy." Again, he illustrated the correct movement of the club, as if to emphasize that his up-close-and-personal swing demonstration had indeed been a lesson.

"You mean like this?" She took the driver, teed up a ball, and slammed it dead straight over the two-hundred-yard marker.

She turned around to her erstwhile tutor with a what-do-you-say-to-that! expression on her face.

"Whoa!" His eyes were wide and his hands flew up in a gesture of surrender. "Hey, look, I saw you flailing away. You started to cry. I was trying to help. Obviously, you don't need any."

"If I need help, I ask for it," she said, returning her attention to the driver. "But thanks anyway."

The starter yelled, "You're on the tee," and in a flash, he was gone.

Two days later, they met again. This time they were in flight suits, not shorts, standing in front of a Black Hawk helicopter, not a driving range, he was the instructor, she was the student, but this time it was for real. Captain Bryan Chalmers was standing before ten flight surgeon candidates, charged with the task of teaching them how to fly rotary-wing aircraft.

He didn't single Martie out or make a comment when he called her name, so at first she thought he didn't recognize her. As the class began, she wondered whether he had recognized her and was deliberately ignoring her.

He introduced himself and then introduced the Hawk.

"The UH-60 is the Army's frontline utility helicopter. It's used for air assault, air cavalry, and medical evacuation. It's designed to carry eleven combat-loaded troops or four litters, plus medical personnel. If you make it through your seven weeks here, that would be you."

Clothing aside, he looked completely different. It was the setting and his seriousness of purpose, she supposed. There was a no-kidding tone in his voice and an all-business cast to his approach as he pointed out the salient features of the Hawk, taking particular notice of areas directly related to medical evacuation. Without any personal aggrandizement, he mentioned his experiences with both the Black Hawk and the Apache in combat situations as a way of emphasizing the importance of rotary-wing aircraft in the army's arsenal.

Someone next to her whispered that Captain Chalmers had been involved in the military action in Panama. Martie found it interesting that a guy who'd seemed so macho at the golf course was so modest and measured in the field.

She respected that. And, if she was honest, found it very sexy.

"The Hawk flies at a speed of one hundred and fifty knots and has a vertical rate of climb of one hundred eighty-five feet per minute. It also has built-in resistance to small arms fire and most medium-caliber high-explosive projectiles."

"Good to know," one of the men said.

"What's better is to know how to handle one of these babies so you can jockey out of the line of fire," Chalmers said. "Teaching you how to do that is my job. Paying close attention and learning everything you can about the Hawk is your job."

He invited them to climb into the cabin and move around, get the feel of it. When they were finished, he told them when and where they would meet the next day for their first hands-on session and then asked if any of them had any questions. No one did.

Bryan scanned their faces. When his eyes fell on Martie, he stopped. His gaze was so heated she felt the skin on her neck prickle.

"Fine, but if you need help," he said, his eyes firmly fixed on hers, "just ask for it."

Several weeks later she did. It was during her first training flight. He took the Hawk up. She was just getting used to the ear-splitting noise of the blades cutting through the air when he handed the controls over to her.

"What are you doing?" she asked.

"You came to Rucker to fly, so fly." He leaned back and folded his arms across his chest as if he were watching a football game.

His attitude was infuriating, but it had been ever since she had shown him up at the golf course. When she asked a question, he answered it respectfully but perfunctorily. She aced all her written tests, yet he appeared unimpressed. He chatted with others in the class, but most of the time treated her as if she were a vapor.

"I'm not sure I'm ready," she said. He was deliberately intimidating her, she was certain of it.

"Well, you'd better be, Lieutenant, or we're going to hit the ground, hard."

Angry at his arrogance and the nerve of his challenge, she put her feet on the pedals, grabbed the collective, which controlled the pitch of the rotary blades, and tried to remember everything she had learned. After a few jerky moments, she stabilized the copter by working the pedals, which controlled the tail rotor.

"Change the angle of attack," he commanded.

She used the cyclic to adjust the swashplates, increasing the craft's lift and altering its flight angle.

"Left."

She adjusted the pitch of the tail rotor. The Hawk changed direction.

He shouted more orders at her. She executed each of them with precision.

"Fun, isn't it?" he said, grinning.

"It's the best!" she enthused, realizing that for the past several minutes she had been flying solo.

"Now land."

"What?"

"Take it down."

"I don't know how."

"Hmmm. Then you'll just have to ask for help."

She glared at him, knowing she had no choice but to give him his victory.

"Okay, okay. Help."

His lips curled into a satisfied smile. "With pleasure."

He guided her to the ground. The landing was rocky, but not bad for a first-timer.

"Nicely done," he said. "I have one more thing I'd like you to do."

Her eyes were aglow with the thrill of what she'd just accomplished.

"Name it!"

"Meet me at the Officers' Club tonight for a drink."

Bryan's face overwhelmed Martie's dreams. She turned over onto her side, hoping to change the picture in her head, but Bryan wouldn't budge. Even in her somniferous state, Martie smiled.

"Persistence is my middle name," he used to say.

He was persistent back then, but she couldn't help being resistant. It wasn't that she didn't love him; she did. He wanted to make their relationship permanent at a time when she wasn't certain there was such a thing as permanence.

She was still recovering from the effects of her captivity. Her physical wounds were healing, but the residual effects from her nine-day ordeal lingered. Post-traumatic stress disorder, they called it. She sought professional help as well as the counsel of former POWs. She welcomed the loving support of those closest to her and the encouragement of her fellow soldiers. But PTSD was an open-ended, obstinate condition that seemed to sheath her spirit in Teflon. No matter what anyone said or how much proof they presented to show her that she was safe, it didn't stick. She remained in a simmering state of agitation, certain that a serious and lethal threat lay just around the corner.

Her breath came in short quick puffs. Her heart beat faster. She could feel herself sinking into a familiar whirlpool. She turned onto her back, closed her eyes, placed her hands on her chest, and resorted to yoga breathing to calm her system and invite sleep.

In. Out. Slowly. Rhythmically.
In. Out. Slowly. Rhythmically.
In. Out.

A loud jangling pierced the soft fog of sleep. Martie's eyes popped open. She blinked and tried to focus. Her head swiveled from side to side as she searched for the source of the noise. When she realized it was the phone, she grabbed it and placed the receiver next to her ear. A glance at the clock told her it was six-thirty in the morning.

"It's me," Delilah said.

Martie sat up, still half asleep.

"What's wrong?" Calls from Delilah usually signaled disaster. "Are you all right?"

"I'm fine. I just called to tell you I'm going to do like you said."

Martie struggled to remember what that

might be. After Martie had brought Delilah home from the park, they'd talked for hours about a lot of things, mainly taking charge of one's life.

"You were right about my anger getting in my way."

Delilah's PTSD manifested itself in spurts of rage. Someone, particularly a man, would insult her or raise his voice in a threatening manner, and inside she panicked. Verbal assaults were simply preludes to physical assaults. She yelled back or struck back, usually salting her language in a way that bystanders, and her employers, found unacceptable. It was usually after such a public outburst that she was fired.

"I'm going over to the shelter this morning."

Martie wiped the sleep from her eyes and willed herself to concentrate. If Delilah called at this hour of the morning, she'd been up all night.

"They have a head-shrinker who comes in to counsel the women there. I'm going to speak to her."

That opened Martie's eyes.

"Seeing a therapist is a good decision, Delilah. It helped me. It'll help you."

"I hope so. I'm tired of being nowhere."

"We talked about this," Martie reminded

her. "We decided you can either stay stuck at nowhere or get headed somewhere. Your choice."

"I know. And I've decided to head out."

"Good girl! The first step's always the hardest."

"Actually, the shrink's the second step. The first one is I got me a job."

"Wow. You are just full of surprises," Martie said. "Where?"

"When I called the shelter to ask about that doctor, I asked if they had anything for me to do. I was thinking of sweeping up or working in the kitchen, that kind of thing. The lady in charge said she needed help in the office and asked if I had any experience. I told her I took a couple of courses and stuff and that I worked a bit here and there, but I was up front. I told her I never stayed at one gig long enough to get really good at it. She said that was okay. She'd give me a try."

"That's great!" Martie said, trying to buoy the hope she heard in Delilah's voice. "Just do the best you can and don't be afraid to ask for help."

"I'm not real good at that either," Delilah said. She paused. "And speaking of help, thanks. For the clothes and the food and . . . all that."

The "all that" was money Martie had given her to get a room and some essentials.

"It's my pleasure. You know that."

"Yeah, but . . . still."

It pained Martie to feel Delilah's embarrassment. Need often demanded that pride step aside, but it never moved easily.

"I loved seeing Lili," Delilah said, hurriedly shifting the conversation onto a more appealing subject. "She's terrific."

Martie chuckled. Her daughter was a wonderful child. Somehow she sensed Delilah's enormous thirst for affection and gave it to her in buckets. When they were together it was like watching two children at play.

"She loved seeing you too. You're her favorite big-girl friend, you know."

"That's nice."

Delilah paused. Martie could almost see her smiling. Lili had that effect on people.

"Hey!" Delilah said, suddenly remembering something. "I saw you on TV last night. You got some kind of award."

"I did, yes."

Another pause.

"I'm real proud to know you, Martie. You're an amazing woman."

"Thanks." Martie wasn't comfortable

with adulation and quickly moved on. "Call me later. I want to know how your first day went, okay?"

"Scout's honor."

After she hung up, knowing sleep was no longer an option, Martie slid out of bed and retrieved the *New York Times* from outside her front door. She made herself a cup of coffee and climbed back into bed.

When she opened to the front page, her breath caught in her throat. Above a none-too-flattering picture of her mother was the headline: HART LINE INTERNATIONAL ACCUSED OF MASSIVE ACCOUNTING FRAUD.

According to the article, the federal government had initiated an investigation into HLI's accounting practices seeking evidence of securities fraud, insider trading, and filing false financial certifications. The most serious charge against Vera was that she directed the inflation of company profits to the tune of nearly a billion dollars. Immediately following that accusation was the insinuation that Vera misused company funds for her personal enrichment. Among other things, the reporter pointed out that HLI paid Vera Hart $1.5 million a year in rental fees for use of her various properties.

A spokesperson defended the practice by saying, "Vera Hart's residences are used for segments of *Vera Hart at Home*. Ms. Hart's fans want to see how she lives, not how a set designer decorates a sound stage."

An anonymous source scoffed, claiming that "Vera Hart uses HLI as her personal piggybank. If she wants something, she gets her financial gurus to figure out a way for HLI stockholders to buy it for her."

There were further implications of widespread fraud and others who could be indicted, but it was obvious that Vera Hart was the primary target.

Stunned, Martie dropped the paper onto her lap and put her coffee cup down on her night table. As she did, her gaze landed on the envelope Vera had handed her the evening before. She'd never even looked inside. She picked it up, carefully tore it open, and lifted out the check. As she did, another piece of paper fell out — a handwritten note from Vera asking to see her.

Chapter 4

"This place is a dump!"

"It's a diner, and don't be such a snob."

Vera spread her napkin on her lap and smiled at the waiter who put her food down in front of her and poured her coffee.

When she arrived home last evening there was a message on her answering machine from Tripp Runyon insisting on a private meeting, ASAP. She agreed to meet him at the Empire Diner on Twenty-second and Tenth Avenue. The last thing she wanted was to be alone with him. Or to be seen with him — hence the out-of-the-way location.

Vera had never liked Tripp, but she could understand Greta's initial attraction. He was handsome in that neatly groomed, Ralph Lauren way, and he came packaged with all the appropriate credentials. Vera had always found his looks and his affect a bit effete. She preferred broad-shouldered men who wore their masculinity as comfortably as they wore their five-o'clock stubble and as boldly as they wore their boots. Tripp's various sporting activities kept him in decent shape, but his sinew was on a narrow frame and his clothes were always too freshly pressed, his shoes too highly polished. Even after eighteen holes of golf in hundred-degree weather, his slacks held a crease. In Vera's mind, at least, that made him less appealing than, say, a man who didn't mind getting his hands dirty, a man like Hugh Phelps.

"We need to talk," Tripp said, stretching his upper body across the table so that he was only inches from her. Up close, his navy blue eyes appeared tired and bloodshot. He drank too much and it showed.

"You really should try the French toast," she said, ignoring his obvious agitation. "It's positively exquisite."

"She's divorcing me."

Vera took her time pouring maple syrup on her toast. When she was satisfied that she'd dispensed enough to sweeten the bread without drenching it, she graced him with her attention.

"I know, dear, and I'm sorry," she said. "I didn't realize you'd be so heartbroken."

His jaw clenched in frustration. "It's not

about losing Greta, it's —"

"About money," Vera said, completing his sentence. She chewed a piece of toast and moaned with pleasure, further infuriating her companion.

Tripp didn't bother to argue; she was right. Instead, he went straight to the reason for this morning's tête-à-tête.

"I'm not going to sign those papers until I get assurances from you that my funds won't be cut off."

Vera put down her fork, raised her napkin to her lips, and dabbed at them with the raised-pinky delicacy of a Victorian grande dame.

"Since we both need to be on the same page for this discussion to have any value, let me refresh your memory on the terms of our arrangement. When you married my daughter, I gave you a job at Hart. You proved to be not only a flagrant incompetent, but a disaster waiting to happen. Instead of firing you and causing both your family and mine a lot of unnecessary embarrassment, I kept you on the books as a vice president in charge of something innocuous, provided an office in one of our branches, and made sure you received regular paychecks. The only condition was that you were *never* to cross the portal of my offices again."

"And I didn't."

He was practically whining. That made Vera ill. She loathed wimps and bellyachers.

"True, but now my daughter has decided to end her in-name-only marriage, which means that I can end our in-name-only employment arrangement."

"And what am I supposed to do for money?"

Vera shrugged. "I paid you to not work for me. Since I'm sure your business skills would be just as catastrophic to the Seafarer Bank, I suggest you negotiate a don't-work contract with your family. Let *them* pay you to stay home."

"I always said you were a bitch. Like mother, like daughter."

Vera wasn't at all fazed by his insult.

"You've received your last check from me, Tripp. Now be a good boy, sign the divorce papers, and go on your merry way."

"Not until you pony up a healthy settlement package."

Vera opened her Hermès bag and pulled out a thick envelope. She opened it and placed some photographs on the table in front of him, lining them up one after the other after the other. As each snapshot hit the table, Tripp's perpetual tan faded, shade by shade. His eyes filled with out-rage, then fear, then panic. She could almost see his heart pounding in his chest.

"Are you out of your mind?" he said, shoveling them into a pile and turning them over so no one would see.

Vera sipped her coffee.

"What the fuck are these and why are you showing them to me?"

"I believe they're photographs."

"Of a man doing some very nasty things to a very young boy." His expression was one of wild-eyed hysteria.

"Uh-huh."

It took a minute for her intent to register.

"That's not me," he insisted, shaking his head. "That is not me!"

"No?"

"You know damn well it isn't."

Vera took the pictures from him, slid them back into their envelope, and put them back in her bag.

"What either of us knows doesn't matter. It's what the world sees that counts."

"I'll deny it!" he sputtered. "And I'll sue you for defamation of character."

"Then it'll be your word against mine. Guess who the world will believe?"

She slid off the banquette, collected her

belongings, and headed down the narrow aisle toward the door. As she passed the register, she pointed to Tripp and said to the man sitting behind the counter, "He'll take the check. He always does."

Greta was too absorbed in running an Internet search on Martie to hear him come in. When the door to her office closed, she was so startled she jumped and spun around to confront her intruder. Her heart pounded when she saw who it was.

"I waited," Bryan said, sounding like a rejected suitor. "It was when they started clearing away the coffee cups that I figured out you were a no-show."

As he approached her desk, Greta minimized the image on her computer screen.

"Very funny," she said, trying to recover.

He slid into the seat facing her desk, his smile ebbing. She looked paler than usual.

"I called your apartment. When I didn't get an answer, I worried. Are you all right?"

He'd seen the newspapers that morning and assumed Greta had spent most of the night tied to her desk.

She disarmed his concerns with a wave of a hand. "I'm fine. I got tied up here. By the time I left, I had such a mind-numbing

110

headache I went home, turned off my phone, and climbed into bed." She reinforced her lie with as contrite a smile as she could muster. "Forgive me. I didn't mean to stand you up. It was simply unavoidable."

"Been there, done that," Bryan said, sympathizing with the rigorous demands of her job.

He didn't know the half of it, Greta thought.

"While I understand the reason for your absence, I did miss you," he said.

"I'm glad." She wondered how understanding he'd be if she told him she'd been only a few feet away from his table having a temper tantrum on the balcony.

"Was the evening a hideous bore?"

She wanted him to say yes.

"Actually, the award-winners were quite impressive."

The knot in Greta's stomach twisted. "Anyone in particular?"

"They were all incredible. Funnily enough, I knew one of them in the service, Dr. Marta Phelps."

Greta didn't find that funny. "What a coincidence," she said, forcing a fascinated smile onto her lips.

"Quite. And by the way, in case you were

wondering, your mother was spectacular."

"Quel surprise." Greta didn't have the energy to suppress her sarcasm. She was exhausted from a sleepless night of comparing herself to Vera Hart, then to Dr. Marta Phelps, and then, during a moment of total insanity, to a pink-clad mini-Martie. "That's why being her daughter is such a struggle. She's perfect and the rest of the world, including me, isn't."

"Perfection is highly overrated."

Greta appeared doubtful. "According to whom?"

"My mother, for one. She never believed in perfection." He laughed, tickled by memories of youthful indiscretions that had tested his mother's patience. "She thought my brother, my sister, and I were terrific, warts and all."

"Lucky you. So to what do I owe the pleasure of this visit?" she asked, changing the subject.

"Other than wanting to know why you bailed on me, I have a meeting with your mom."

Greta arched a suspicious eyebrow.

"Last night, just as I was leaving, she asked me to come by the office today. She said she had an offer she hoped I wouldn't refuse."

"I have a few of those myself," Greta said, leering at him suggestively.

Bryan smiled, but declined her invitation with his silence. Instead, he asked, "Any idea what this is about?"

Greta shrugged. "I take it you've seen the headlines."

"I have."

"I'm sure it has something to do with that."

"How crazed is everyone?" He thought Greta was astoundingly calm considering that she was HLI's COO. If indictments were handed down, she would probably be in receipt of one.

"Vera hasn't been in the office all day, so I don't know about her mental state. As for the rest of us, we're gearing up for a very rough ride."

Bryan wondered if Greta realized just how rough it could get. He'd witnessed several federal witch hunts during his tenure at the FBI.

"Good idea," he said. "Government investigations tend to get nasty."

"It's the press I'm worried about. Enron and Tyco aren't companies with names the public relates to. The Hart Line is not only the name of the corporation; it's the name on each of our products. Damage one and

113

the other is damaged as well."

He hadn't thought about that, but she had a point. Other companies might be able to weather a public lashing. For a company that relied on name recognition, a slanderous stain would be devastating.

Greta's intercom buzzed. It was her secretary. The call was brief. When Greta put down the phone, her jaw was tight.

"Her Highness is in residence and has requested a moment with me. I was told to ask you to wait."

"No problem," Bryan said. But it was clear by the look on Greta's face that there was a problem.

"Close the door."

Greta obeyed the command, but in a small act of defiance remained where she was instead of taking a seat as she was expected to do. She folded her arms across her chest, protecting against the onslaught.

"I understand you're divorcing Tripp." The words were casual. The tone was not.

Greta said nothing. Obviously Tripp had said plenty already.

"Why would you do something like that?"

"Because I can't stand him."

"What difference does that make?"

Greta was so offended by Vera's selfishness her teeth itched. The only reason she'd stayed married to that jerk all these years was because Vera insisted the relationship was valuable to the Hart Line.

"I am thirty-nine years old. Your company is a whopping success. It's enough."

"You should have spoken to me first."

"Why? I don't need *your* permission to dissolve *my* marriage."

"You do when *your* divorce affects *my* business."

Tripp must have threatened Vera. "Please don't tell me that Mr. Penny Loafer managed to intimidate you," Greta said, amazed and amused.

"Hardly. I simply don't appreciate being taken by surprise."

Actually, Vera hadn't been surprised, but Greta didn't have to know that. After Tripp called, Vera called Greta's attorney, a very pragmatic gentleman who recognized that it was to his advantage to give Vera a heads-up on a potentially troublesome situation. As for the photographs, she'd acquired them years before. Vera had always known that sooner or later Tripp Runyon would try to shake her down. It was his nature to be avaricious. It was her habit to be prepared.

"And I don't appreciate being told what

to do with my life," Greta said. "Whether you like it or not, that farce of a marriage is over."

Vera shook her head. Her expression bordered on pity at Greta's foolishness.

"You didn't think this through, Greta. We're about to become the target of a federal investigation. The last thing we need is the Runyons lined up against us."

Greta threw her head back and laughed. "That's rich! Since when do the Runyons give a damn about Tripp? The only thing they care about is the same thing you care about, and that's the bottom line. So rest easy. They're not going to line up against us. They can't afford to."

Greta wasn't wrong. Over the years, the Seafarer Bank had become HLI's primary source of capital. If the Hart Line was tainted by accusations of fraudulent accounting practices, so were they.

"I just don't trust the depth of their commitment to HLI," Vera said, more to herself than to Greta.

"You never trust anyone's commitment, Mother."

Greta was still smarting over a decision Vera had made nearly a year before when Greta had asked to be named Vera's successor. Vera had denied the request, reminding Greta in no uncertain terms who was in charge. She also made it clear that the only way she was going to leave her office was feet first. Just then Greta would have been happy to oblige.

"Commitment is all about self-interest," Vera said, refusing to be baited into an old argument. "How committed someone is depends on what the project or the relationship is and how much they want to get out of it."

"Sort of like a marriage."

Every now and then, Greta tweaked Vera about the one glaring failure in Vera's perfectly orchestrated life. Greta hated Hugh for walking out and leaving her behind, but his exit gave her something to hold over Vera's head, and for that she was grateful.

"I never got anything out of my marriage, but as long as it didn't interfere with the rest of my life I stayed in it. When it started to get in the way, I got rid of Tripp so I could move on to bigger and better things. You understand that, don't you, Mother?"

"You're being snide, Greta. It's unattractive."

"Maybe so, but it's honest." She started for the door. "It would be nice if you could be happy for me," she said, turning back to face Vera. "I've got someone really terrific in my life, someone who makes me feel positively blissful. Tripp was a business deal. This guy is the real deal."

Greta waited, hoping for a word of encouragement or approval or congratulations.

"When you get back to your office," Vera said, "tell Mr. Chalmers I'll see him now."

"The government is alleging fraud, conspiracy to inflate company earnings, and insider trading," Vera said the minute Bryan's butt hit the chair. "I want you to represent us."

Bryan whistled. "You don't waste any time, do you?"

"I don't have any time to waste. I haven't been formally accused of anything, but if you read between the lines, they've already ordered an orange jumpsuit with my name on it."

With all the corporate stink in the air, it didn't surprise Bryan that another company was about to come under fire. HLI was an enormous conglomerate. Its stock was sold on the New York Stock Exchange. And its owner was ubiquitous. America drank Hart Line coffee in Hart Line mugs, slept on Hart Line sheets under Hart Line blankets on Hart Line beds in rooms with Hart Line carpets and Hart Line drapes. They cooked with Hart Line pots, wore clothes, shoes, and makeup from Hart Line collections, learned to cook, garden, and do repairs via Hart Line magazines and Hart Line television shows. Millions of people believed Vera Hart could do no wrong.

The Justice Department felt otherwise.

"Well?" Vera didn't bother to hide her impatience.

"With all due respect, Ms. Hart, you have a stable of lawyers, each of whom is extremely competent."

"They've been living large for too long. It's made them soft." She pursed her lips and peered at him, taking his measure. "I've been following your career, Bryan. You're bright and capable and extremely ambitious. I like that. I also like the fact that you've refused to suck up like so many other ladder-climbers I've met over the years."

Bryan accepted that as a compliment, but he wasn't prepared to give her an answer just yet and said so. "I need to think it through."

This would be an extremely high-profile case with all the attendant publicity of a circus. It would also be difficult to defend. Legal issues notwithstanding, public sentiment was running high against big business. In the collective consciousness of the nation, the words, *corporate* and *corruption* had suddenly become one and the same. In that climate finding a jury or a judge that would hear a defense argument without prejudice would be difficult at best.

Another consideration was that he'd put a lot of years in at the DA's office building a reputation and creating a foundation for a possible foray into the political arena. Leaving would mean giving up a number of appealing options for a position with a lot of risk and no guarantee of reward.

As if intuiting his thoughts, Vera said, "What's there to think about? You and Aaron Liebman" — the New York district attorney — "can't stand each other. You're biding your time until the political climate becomes ripe for you to run for office. He's biding his time waiting for you to overreach or commit some bureaucratic blunder so he can toss you out without being accused of petty jealousy. This could be the stepping-stone you've been waiting for, Bryan."

That might be true, but Bryan wouldn't

know that until after he'd burned his bridges at the DA's office.

"In case you could use some financial incentive, I'm prepared to pay you three times what you're making now. And to offer you a substantial signing bonus."

Bryan was flattered. A powerful woman was trying to woo him by throwing influence and wealth at his feet. Bryan had neither of those things. Being human, he wouldn't mind a little of each, but his ambitions had never been about acquiring wealth.

"I need twenty-four hours."

"And I need a lawyer who believes that fighting for a just cause is a good fight."

Her tone was sharp. She wasn't used to people refusing her.

"I didn't say your cause wasn't —"

"Look," Vera said, interrupting him. "The only reason I'm at the top of the government's list is because I'm a woman. If they think my books are cooked, fine. Let them prove it. But they should be fair about it. They've already acquired warehouses full of evidence on the executives of companies that have bankrupted their employees and their stockholders, yet not one of those male CEOs has been indicted. They're going about their lives as if nothing's changed, while my face is plastered all over the front pages like wanted posters. Why is that, do you think?"

Bryan's lips curled in an admiring smile. She had done her homework and knew just which buttons to push. More than once, Bryan had spoken out against the glass ceilings that prevented women from moving up professional ladders.

"Tomorrow, I'm having a meeting at my estate in Westchester. I have to be there in the morning to tape some upcoming cooking segments for my television show. If you have the time, I'd like you attend."

"I think I can manage it," he said.

"Good. I'll send a car for you." Vera was obviously pleased. "If by the end of the day you're still not convinced my company is worth saving, I'll know I'm in trouble."

"Because?"

"Because I've spent my life convincing people to believe what I believe and to do things the way I think things should be done. If I can't do that any longer, I should retire."

The room was dusky, but illumination didn't suit his current mood. He sat in his favorite chair and sipped his brandy slowly, allowing the sting of the alcohol to anesthetize his tongue and its sedative power to salve his anger. On the table next to him was a photograph he usually kept hidden, one of him and Vera Hart back when they were lovers.

They were on a beach in Anguilla, harbored beneath a cavelike turquoise-and-white striped umbrella. He remembered asking the cabana boy who roamed the sands providing towels and drinks to take their picture. She had draped an arm around him, put her cheek next to his, and boldly slid her other hand between his knees. It had been all he could do to control his reaction to the electricity generated by her touch.

She had looked at him adoringly then. She had whispered things to him in the night that he'd probably heard from other women, but coming from her those words had sounded different, felt different, and had elicited a very different response. She had taken him on a sensuous journey to a place from which he'd never wanted to return and then left him alone and helpless.

Her looks, her words, and her passion had been a sham. She hadn't loved him. She had used him to satisfy both her business and her sexual needs. He'd suspected as much at the time, but he'd been so smitten, so in her thrall that he'd willingly enslaved himself to her.

When it ended he was devastated, more than he'd imagined possible. She was hardly his first dalliance — he'd never been an allegiant husband — but his other affairs had never lasted very long and had never tested his emotional mettle. This liaison changed his life because he made the fatal mistake of falling in love. They were together six months; he thought it was the prelude to forever. He was prepared to leave his family and start over with her. She never discouraged him. After he had made his move and severed his ties, she rebuffed him.

He was a man of great pride, yet she stripped him of that. When she summoned him, he raced to her side like a dog on a leash. When she asked for something, he fulfilled her request without hesitation or question. It was later, when their romance was over, that he realized the full extent of his imprudence.

She had made a fool of him, playing him as expertly as Paganini on the violin. When she was done, his heart was broken and he was left with no other choice but to explain his behavior to his wife and hope that she understood. She didn't.

Fortunately, other than during that aberrant time of obsessive infatuation, he was a patient man. He was also a clever man with a bent for revenge.

He put the picture back on the table and reached for a stack of newspapers. He read about the Hart Line's troubles on the front page of the *New York Times*. He devoured every incriminating word against her in the *Wall Street Journal* and the *Washington Post* and the *Chicago Sun-Times*. Tabloid headlines like HART NOT SMART and cartoons like the one that showed a man representing the SEC sticking a fork in Vera's side with the saying, *"She's Done!"* tickled him.

His lips flattened against his teeth in a venal smile of satisfaction. This had been years in the planning, but finally the game was on: The collapse of Hart Line International had begun.

Chapter 5

When the doorman buzzed up to say her visitor was downstairs, Martie experienced a moment of sheer panic. It took every ounce of courage she had not to hide in the closet. If not for Lili rushing to open the door, she might have.

"Hi!" Lili said, thoroughly delighted to see the Queen of Hearts again.

"Hi." Vera tried to imitate Lili's enthusiasm, but it was difficult. Vera wasn't comfortable exhibiting uninhibited gusto. She did gift the child with a smile and a small red shopping bag with the Hart Line logo on the front and oodles of red and pink tissue paper peeking out from within. "I thought you might like this."

Lili looked at her mother before accepting. Martie nodded. Lili grinned and gleefully took the bag. While she dived into the fun task of unwrapping, Martie led Vera inside. Vera panned the space with the affect of an appraiser, making Martie feel as if she were back in the army enduring the staff sergeant's daily inspection of the barracks. Fortunately, Martie was far more confident in her apartment than she had been about her digs at Fort Sam Houston.

The living room was a generous size boasting ceilings high enough to allow for wooden beams, which had been painted black to match the ebonized floors and the noir-colored drapes. The walls were a soft *crème fraîche,* the area rug a honey-toned sisal. The main furnishings, a Chesterfield sofa and several modernized wing chairs, wore fabrics that were a touch lighter than the walls and encircled a low marble table in an easy, unstructured way. In a corner to the right of the entry were a round table of dark wenge wood and four black leather-upholstered shield-back chairs.

Following through on the black and white theme was a Chinese chest, a dark Jacobean writing table, and several black throw pillows. The only splashes of color were a red silk upholstered ottoman that sat opposite the couch, red lampshades, and a number of blue and white Chinese urns, one of which sat on the dining table and held tall branches of flowering quince. It was eclectic, simple, and, to Vera's practiced eye, in very good taste.

"Your home is lovely," she said as she seated herself on one of the wing chairs. "Charming, yet comfortable."

Martie thanked her for the unsolicited critique, but noticed that even as she settled herself Vera continued to peruse the room, visually examining every accessory.

Why had she said yes to this?

When she read Vera's note inviting her to call so they could get together, an inner voice had cautioned her to throw the note away. A second voice warned that she might regret wasting such an opportunity. She'd called Vera fully expecting her secretary to make an appointment for Martie to visit the office. Instead Tess asked if it would be all right if Ms. Hart stopped by Martie's apartment that evening. Martie was so taken off guard she agreed.

"Mommy!" Lili squealed with delight as she presented her mother with the goodies Vera had brought — Hart Line makeup samples that had been scaled down and packaged in pink to appeal to little girls. "Lipstick and cheek powder and eye shadow! Just like you have."

Martie smiled. It was hard not to. Lili was beyond thrilled.

"Wow," she said as Lili gave her each item to examine. "Movie Queen Body

Sheen? This is very grown-up stuff."

Lili nodded, then took another look at her loot. "Yours are bigger. 'Cause you're bigger."

"Exactly. Now what do you say to . . . Ms. Hart?"

Vera displayed no reaction to Martie's discomfort about defining her in any way other than Ms. Hart.

"Thank you, Ms. Hart," Lili said.

"You're quite welcome, Miss Abrams."

Martie was impressed that Vera had remembered Lili's last name.

"Can I go play makeup?" Lili was so eager to slather her face she could barely stand still.

"Just be careful," Martie warned.

A brief tick of Vera's lips prompted Martie to wonder if Vera had realized Martie's daughter enjoyed the same game that had tickled her when she was Lili's age.

The instant Lili left the room, Vera rose and walked over to a large trestle table by the window that held an assortment of photographs. Martie sensed she'd been dying to do that ever since she walked in.

The photographs varied in size but they were framed in silver, as befitted a banquet of life's special moments. There were pictures of Hugh and Connie with Martie and Lili; Hugh and Connie holding a baby and beaming with that goopy expression reserved for grandparents; a group photo of soldiers in desert camouflage; Martie in full uniform receiving her Distinguished Service Medal from her father; Martie leaving the hospital with Lili alongside a handsome man whom Vera assumed was Lili's father.

"Is this Mr. Abrams?"

"Major Abrams," Martie corrected. "Yes. That's Jack."

Vera picked up the picture and studied it. "He's quite good-looking."

"Was. Jack died when Lili was two."

Vera had assumed Lili's father was no longer in their lives. There were no up-to-date photographs of him on the table and no overt signs of his presence in this room.

"He was in a car accident. A bunch of drugged-up kids were joyriding on the Beltway around Washington. They were going so fast they jumped the divider and slammed into him. Both cars burst into flames. Everyone was killed."

She recited the facts dispassionately, but Vera could see a lingering pain in Martie's eyes. She wondered if it was from missing her late husband or because Lili was forever missing her father.

"I'm terribly sorry," Vera said, wondering if Martie had ever missed her.

"Me too."

"Did you love him very much?"

That struck Martie as an odd question considering their relationship, or lack thereof, and incredibly intrusive.

"Okay, let's stop tap-dancing. What's the real reason for this visit?"

Vera turned and eyed her younger daughter. "Actually, I have three reasons."

"And they are?"

"I wasn't aware that I had a granddaughter. Now that I am I'd like to get to know her."

Martie should have expected that. There was no way Vera Hart was going to have a genetic reproduction of herself running around without being able to influence that child's development. And, since that child didn't rise from the ocean on a seashell, it was easy to anticipate what came next.

"I'd also like to reacquaint myself with her mother."

"Why?"

Vera's lip curled in amused admiration. "Why not?"

She reclaimed her chair, tacitly announcing that if Martie wanted her to leave she would have to demand it. Martie surrendered and took a seat on the couch.

"You might not believe this, but over the years I tried to keep up with what was happening to you. I was able to follow your career, but without an intermediary or any contact between us I had no way of tracking your personal progress. Seeing Lili the other night was a shock. A pleasant one, I assure you, but a surprise nonetheless." Her aquamarine eyes fixed on Martie. "It made me realize how much I had missed."

Martie hated that her first response was cynicism, her second, pique. She hadn't orchestrated this family schism. Vera's absence from Martie's life was strictly voluntary. If Vera had regrets, she had only herself to blame.

"How did Lili handle her father's passing?" When Martie didn't comment about how much she had missed having Vera in her life, Vera simply moved on. "It must have been terribly traumatic for her."

"It was, but she had me and her grandparents and a tight community of friends to help her through."

Vera absorbed the sting of Martie's obvious snipe: Lili had two people she thought of as grandparents, perhaps four, and she was not one of them. Again, she moved on.

"Her warm, outgoing personality more than attests to the loving support she must have received, but most of all she's a credit to you. Even from the little I've been able to observe, you're a wonderful mother, Martie."

Martie wanted to say she learned how to mother from Connie Vaughn, but restrained herself; Connie wouldn't have approved. She also thought about saying it was easy when you had such a wonderful daughter, but that raised questions she didn't want to answer.

"Thank you," seemed the easiest response. "What's the third reason you're here?" She was anxious to bring this excruciating tête-à-tête to an end.

Vera also had reached her emotional limit. "I came to offer you a job."

Martie tilted her head to the side and studied Vera as if trying to verify that what she'd heard had actually come from Vera's mouth.

"The future of cosmetics is in skin care. To that end I've been researching ways to bolster our Hart Line Skin Care Line with truly substantive products. So has my competition. We've all been manufacturing anti-wrinkle, anti-sagging, anti-aging creams based on retinol or alpha hydroxy or collagen or some other stopgap, make-pretty ingredient. We've also been putting out foundations that claim to be more than blotch cover, thanks to the addition of sunscreens. They've sold well but women have caught on to the fact that there's no miracle in any of the miracle creams.

"What women want are products with credible science behind them. They care about their looks and they care about their health. When the latter begins to affect the former, they run to the cosmetics counter seeking help. We haven't been able to give it to them.

"You are a nationally renowned expert on skin cancers. What I'd like is for you to consider combining your scientific knowledge with our manufacturing capabilities to produce a scientifically based, truly effective skin care regimen. It would be good business for us, but it would also give you an opportunity to bring your gifts to a larger audience.

"I know how important your work at Rockefeller is and I understand how difficult it would be for you to leave there, but one can contribute to the public good via commerce, you know."

She rose, went to her bag, and retrieved a large manila envelope, which she handed to Martie.

"I've drawn up a proposal that outlines staffing potential, laboratory availability, a generous compensation package, and benefits. I'd like you to look it over, add or subtract whatever you think would be necessary for your personal and professional satisfaction, and let me know."

Martie was flummoxed. She hadn't expected this.

"I . . . don't know what to say."

Vera smiled. "How about, yes?"

Bryan opened the door to his apartment, walked inside, and tossed his keys into a shallow basket on the entry table. He lived in downtown Manhattan in a spacious loft carved from a former factory. It was a large, open space distinguished by walls of windows, fat columns that helped separate the living room/dining room/kitchen areas, dark Brazilian wood floors, and dramatically high ceilings.

As he always did when he needed to think, he retreated to one of two pale taupe oversized couches that opposed each other in front of a flat-faced fireplace. He flipped the switch that turned on the gas-fueled flame, took off his jacket and shoes, loosened his tie, sprawled out, and closed his eyes.

After his conversation with Vera Hart, he'd gone back to his office to sort things out. Greta had called several times, but he'd avoided speaking to her. This decision was complicated enough. Pitting the lofty, long-term professional goals he had set for himself against a here-and-now job with obvious financial benefits created an honest conflict, as did his relationship with Greta. In good conscience he couldn't take this job without considering where that relationship was headed. At best, office romances were sticky. When they ended, they turned ugly.

And then there was the sudden reappearance of Martie Phelps. They had been together for only a few moments. Their conversation had been banal. But it had been electric, as if someone had taken a lamp that had been dark for years and changed the bulb.

When he viewed his feelings for Greta in the glare of that light, he knew that he cared for her. He enjoyed being with her. But he didn't love her, at least not the way he'd once loved Martie.

Then again, he reminded himself, their affair ended years ago. It was unfair to weigh the depth of his feelings for someone now against what he'd felt then. He and Martie were young. Their romance was hot. There was a war.

Still. It hadn't taken much to reignite some of that heat.

The night before, as he stared at Martie on the dais, he'd tried to convince himself that it was natural to relive memories when one had a chance meeting with a former love. It was natural to admire an absolutely gorgeous woman who could wear a sexy gown or army fatigues and be equally desirable in both. It was also natural to wonder why after ten years she still had that dime. And he still had his.

He was a pilot. She was a doctor. They met at Fort Rucker in Alabama, the home of army aviation. He was a flight instructor. She was taking the seven-week Army Flight Surgeon Primary Course, which included learning to fly helicopters used in search-and-rescue missions. Since the military was pretty much a no-makeup, anti-fashion zone, when a woman was nerve-paralyzing gorgeous it was noticed because it was achieved without the usual enhancements. Martie Phelps in a flight suit caused as many raised eyebrows, wolf whistles, and fantasies as the cover of the *Sports Illustrated* swimsuit issue, and like all the other men at Rucker, Bryan wanted to get in her pants.

He thought she might have been attracted to him as well, but she made it abundantly clear that who got into whose pants and what happened after would have to wait until she got her wings. When it came to flying, she was all business.

At first Bryan tried to ignore her, teaching her class the same as he would any other class: He didn't make anything easier for those he thought might have been in over their heads or harder for those with an overdose of arrogance. The problem was that Martie excelled. She was incredibly smart and surprisingly adept. Also, he'd heard that she was the only woman in her group to complete the grueling requirements for the Expert Field Medical Badge, which meant she was gutsy and tenacious. He had no choice but to pay attention to her.

Her class consisted solely of flight surgeon candidates, so it wasn't as if her fellow students were clucks. They were all highly motivated and highly intelligent.

Some had even flown fixed-wing aircraft before, but not everyone took to helicopters or flight the same way. Some couldn't contain their fear. Some didn't see the thrill in piloting a loud, lumbering machine with no doors, and rotors that smacked at the air and made a hideous noise. Others simply preferred plying their medical skills on terra firma. Martie took to it as if she'd been airborne since birth.

Her only complaint — which of course she didn't vocalize within earshot of him or any other superior — was that the newest aviation equipment, the Apaches, were combat craft and only men were allowed to fly them. She was restricted to Black Hawks, the utility helicopters that flew behind Apaches during attack missions. If an Apache was shot down, the Black Hawks, which had assault capabilities, were close enough to rescue the two pilots before they could be captured. While normally Martie objected to restrictions based on gender, this was the army. She'd known when she signed up that there were strict rules about women in combat.

Bryan, who sensed her annoyance, reminded her she was at Rucker to become a flight surgeon, not a fighter pilot.

"In war everyone has a specific job to do

139

and they're expected to discharge their duties efficiently and effectively. Your job is to make sure that the men who fly those babies, men like me, are physically fit to do so. And if they go down, it's your job to rescue them and take care of their injuries so they can get back up. If you don't think that's important, you don't belong in the army."

It was as if he'd taken a bucket of ice water and thrown it at her. Later that day Martie went to his office and thanked him for the wake-up.

They became lovers shortly after.

For two such serious souls involved in such serious business, it seemed almost ludicrous to say that they fell in love at first sight, but that was pretty much the way it happened. Of course, military life being what it was, they no sooner found each other than they found themselves separated. Their affair became a long-distance one until August 1990, when both their units were shipped to Saudi Arabia in advance of Desert Storm. Even though they were stationed in different quadrants, they managed to see each other during their off times.

In early January 1991, on one of those stolen weekends, Bryan and Martie tried to block out the rest of the world and just be together, but it was difficult. The day before, Congress had voted to allow U.S. troops to be used in offensive operations.

"It's anytime now," Bryan said. "Once it starts, it's going to be tough keeping in touch."

Martie grimaced. Impossible was more like it. "I'm going to go crazy not knowing where you are and whether or not you're safe."

"I know, which is why I'm giving you this." He handed her a small pouch, inside of which was the gold-rimmed coin. "As long as you have a dime on you, I'm only a phone call away." He showed her that he too had a dime. "That goes for me as well."

And then, being an oldies-but-goodies fan, he did his groove thing and burst into "Ain't No Mountain High Enough."

They laughed a lot that night and made love a lot that night, but when they parted in the morning and returned to base, love became secondary to military prepared-ness. They were two of half a million troops stationed in the region anticipating the outbreak of war.

During those final days of preparation, anything that made a soldier feel safe or connected to someone he or she loved or brought good luck was important. Some carried photographs from home; others relied on traditional favorites like a shamrock or a rabbit's foot or a lucky penny or a religious token. For Bryan and Martie, it was those dimes. He secured his underneath the inner sole of a boot; his AH-64 was better armed than her helicopter, so the chances of him being shot down and searched were smaller. She had to be more creative. Black Hawks flew lower, which made them easier targets for SAMs, antiaircraft artillery, and RPGs, rocket-propelled grenades. She created a small pocket in each of her bras to house the dime. Even when the worst happened, she was able to claim modesty and get her captors to return her bra to her.

After the war was over and they were reunited, they both claimed it was the luck inherent in those dimes that had saved their lives.

If asked, Bryan would say he kept the memento for that reason, that it had been designed as a good luck charm and no one was so superstition-free as to be able to throw out a good luck charm without fearing the consequences. In his heart he knew he held on to it because it reminded him of Martie and what they had meant to each other.

He reached into his pocket and found the dime with his fingers, touching it as one would a talisman. Those months he'd spent with Martie were the most passionate of his life.

Lying on the couch looking up at the ceiling, he remembered how alive he'd felt, how vital and productive, as if loving her had sharpened his instincts and heightened his responses. He'd been a better pilot, a better soldier, and a far better man when they'd been together. Since they'd been apart he'd used his passions to enable his work rather than to enrich his life. He might not have been happy, but he believed he was content.

Then he ran into Martie. Seeing her, experiencing that familiar frisson of emotion he felt whenever he was around her, made him realize what he'd been missing.

These past ten years he'd been sleepwalking through life, not wrestling with it or relishing it or embracing it. He'd find a project and immerse himself in it. The project would end and he'd move on to the next. Outside of those job-directed enterprises, his life lacked emotional substance.

He dated. He had sex. He even had relationships, such as the current one with Greta. He tried to be committed and loyal and caring. He tried to tell himself this was the one, he was falling in love, this affair was different. It never was.

He blamed himself for the breakups. He'd trotted out that worn expression, "It's not about you, it's about me," so often he truly believed it. But now, remembering what it had been like with Martie, he realized that it was about him. It was also about "her." When he and Martie had been together, Bryan had a visceral need to be near her; he only felt calm and at home when he was. He functioned in the real world, but thinking about Martie was more exciting than being with anyone else or doing anything else, including flying. She was his heart.

When they parted it was a long while before he dipped his toe back into the dating pool. Each time he ventured further into the deep, he'd been disappointed. The women had been beautiful and smart and eager to please, but somehow he and the she-du-jour didn't mesh as a twosome. If he hadn't had Grace and Cal Chalmers as role models he wouldn't have understood it, but he knew that couples weren't crafted by matching tangibles. Couples were about intangibles like compatibility and fit and chemistry. Some couples were about destiny. Bryan had believed Martie was his soul mate, that each had been placed on earth to complete the other. He still believed that.

He fixed on the mesmerizing curtain of fire before him, a profound emptiness weighing on his chest.

How easily the heat of a romance could be doused by the cold splash of impatience, he thought.

Lieutenant General Phelps had been at the Pierre with a little girl who was the spitting image of Martie. That had hurt Bryan more than he'd been willing to admit. That little girl's existence meant that Martie had fallen in love with someone else, that she had committed to him and had a child with him and a life with him. None of which she'd been able to do with Bryan, or so she'd said at the time.

At his table were a couple of members of the Hart Foundation. As discreetly as he could, he questioned one of the women about the award recipients, inquiring about their lives and their families. When she pointed out Martie's father and daughter, he wondered where Dr. Phelps's husband was. All she knew was that Dr. Phelps had requested two tickets. That meant the husband was either away on very important business, or Martie was separated, divorced, or widowed.

He thought about taking a chance and calling her, but then he reviewed their conversation. She hadn't been what one would call encouraging. She had rejected his offer to escort her to a table, for goodness' sake. Somehow he didn't think she would welcome an out-of-the-blue phone call.

When his phone rang, he jumped off the couch. For an instant he fantasized that Martie had picked up on his vibe and decided to make the first move. When caller ID showed a number he didn't recognize, he decided to let his machine take a message. Unless it was a life-or-death emergency, he'd deal with it in the morning.

The minute he heard the voice, he picked up the phone. It was from Tony Borzone and it was a matter of life and death.

Vera walked into her apartment and switched on the lights.

She was so preoccupied with thoughts of Martie and Lili and the hope that Martie

146

would accept her offer that she almost didn't notice the package sitting on her hall table. Her eye caught it only because it was out of place. Vera didn't like anything to be off line or out of place. It jarred her sense of order.

It was wrapped in standard brown packaging paper and tied with ordinary string. There was a shipping label with her name and address on it, but no postmark and no return address.

She stared at it curiously. She assumed Bonita, her housekeeper, had left it there for her; usually Bonita left deliveries in the kitchen.

She carried it into the kitchen, set it down on the marble island that centered the room, and found a scissors. She snipped the string and carefully undid the paper. It was a shoebox from Manolo Blahnik, of all places. Gingerly, she lifted off the top. Inside was a grenade.

And a note: *If you don't make things right, it's all going to blow up in your face.*

Chapter 6

Vera's Westchester estate sat on fifty-five acres up in bucolic Bedford, New York. With two houses, a barn, a clapboard cottage, and five other structures on the property, it was more like a self-contained village than a residence. The barn, the cottage, and the two houses, one a double Colonial that had been built circa 1760 and carefully restored, the other a quasi-Tudor, were used as decorative models, each promoting a different line within the burgeoning Hart Home Line Collection. The Colonial was traditional in feel, the Tudor more contemporary, and the cottage shoes-off, feet-up casual. The barn housed the television studio. There were two enormous greenhouses, one dedicated to orchids, the other to flats of annuals, as well as a vegetable garden that could probably feed a Third World country. There was a private lake that was so clean it looked like a pool, a black-bottomed pool so natural it looked like a lake, a wildflower meadow, and a twenty-vehicle garage that sheltered everything from a golf cart to a John Deere tractor.

Bryan hailed from a humble background, so the opulence of the place astounded him. That was not to say he was a hick. Since his arrival in New York and his name began appearing in the *New York Times* for his prosecutorial skills and on page six of the *New York Post* for his social acquaintances, Bryan had gained entrée into an elevated level of society. He'd been a guest in the homes of people of influence and wealth before — Greta's apartment was hardly a shack — but he'd never seen anything on the scale of Vera's Valhalla.

The size of the property, the staff it took to maintain it, the beauty of the grounds, and the caliber of the equipment, particularly in the kitchens, was perfection, which of course was Vera Hart's trademark. She drove him around in her customized golf cart like a tour guide, but the excitement and pride in her voice as she described the purpose of every structure, its history, and why each looked a particular way reminded him of a kindergartner showing off her arts and crafts projects. She told him about buying the barn in Virginia and having it taken apart, transported, and rebuilt. She waxed poetic about the Colonial, which had been on this land since its construction, and the lakeside cottage, which was where she preferred to stay when she was here alone; she found it peaceful and spiritually restorative. The one spot on the estate where he would have liked to linger was the bunker. Vera described it briefly as they drove by, but her exclusion of it from her tour told him it was something she wanted to remain secure. He respected that.

Over a Hart-Smart luncheon of stir-fried scallops with julienned carrots, leeks, and orange peel, Vera expressed her pleasure at his decision to join HLI. Bryan also detected a sense of relief, which indicated she appreciated the enormity of what she was facing. When she mentioned she wanted to discuss another matter out of earshot of others, he thought it pertained to her suspicions about one of her board members being a possible Judas. Instead, she confided in him about her mysterious package.

"Did you save everything so a forensic team can have at it?" he asked.

She had.

"Did anything unusual precede the receipt of this package?"

It had. Over the past several weeks Vera had received a number of disturbing e-mails. She brought a laptop over to the table and inserted a CD.

The screen was dark. There was a faint ticking sound. As it got louder, a picture came into focus, slowly, as if the camera lens had been buried deep inside something gelatinous but opaque.

The ticking became thumping, beating faster and growing louder, until Bryan felt as if a bass drum had been amplified a thousand times.

On the screen, a large, gray, shapeless form pulsated. When the camera pulled farther away and the black and white image changed to color, Bryan realized it was a heart beating inside an open chest cavity.

The ticking became deafening.

The heart beat faster.

There was an explosion.

The heart stopped.

The screen went blood red.

And running over the bleeding color was the line: HART ATTACKS BRING DEATH. YOURS IS COMING.

"Any ideas about who might have sent this?"

"A disgruntled investor, a rejected suitor, a deranged critic, a dissatisfied customer: take your pick. I've heard from them all before."

"Have you ever received anything with

this heightened element of threat before?"

She shrugged, but not offhandedly. "There are a lot of crazies out there. Narrowing it down to one would be almost impossible."

Bryan didn't disagree, but said, "There are several steps I need you to take immediately."

He was concerned that as she became more involved in the defense of HLI, she might become distracted and overlook something that could lead to the capture of whoever was behind the threats. Bryan knew that all threats had to be taken seriously.

"I'd like you to compile a list of recently fired employees, any correspondence from unhappy customers that had begun to turn nasty, and any other e-mails that sounded odd or potentially menacing. That includes any with a vague sexual innuendo to them as well.

"You are a beauty queen, Vera, and have been for some time. It's not inconceivable that these are from a secret admirer."

Bryan could see from her expression that over the years she'd had many admirers, most of whom had been far more flattering than this particular fan.

"Stalkers who form deranged crushes on

celebrities are not unusual, as I'm sure you're aware. They're intimacy seekers who weave fantasies around the objects of their affections. When that object ignores them, or rejects them, they often issue threats."

Vera acknowledged familiarity with menacing messages. "I've been harassed before and probably will be again. It goes with the territory."

"Maybe so, but how many of the other threats had that level of hostility and this kind of follow-up?"

She shook her head. They both knew that was why she'd raised the issue with him.

"While the majority of those who make threats don't proceed to subsequent violence, you still have to be vigilant, Vera, because *all* of those who turn violent have issued prior warnings."

Vera sipped her lime-spiced club soda.

Bryan noticed she did that a lot. While she was figuring something out or absorbing a bit of unpleasant news or planning a response to a challenge, she lowered her eyes, keeping her emotions hidden. That was probably how she earned her reputation as a sphinx.

"There was something else," she confided. "I don't know if the two are related, but this morning a Lieutenant Borzone from the NYPD called to inform me that a young woman who'd been found in Central Park the other day had died from a poisoned Hart Line lipstick." On this, she made no attempt to hide either her distress or her astonishment.

Bryan didn't tell her that he'd received the same phone call from Tony the night before. Nor did he confess that it was probably Tony's information that had influenced him to accept Vera's offer, but it had. Perhaps it was simply a serendipitous juxtaposition of circumstances, but somehow the fact that the Central Park rape victim had died from a lethal concentration of mercuric chloride which police labs traced to a lipstick from Hart Line Cosmetics, the head of which had just offered him the job of a lifetime, felt like a sign.

"I'm not afraid of those who are out to destroy my company," Vera said with a sangfroid that inspired awe. "This investigation has a decidedly personal tinge to it, but at the end of the day it's about business. No matter how intrusive or upsetting it becomes, there are ways to solve these problems." She smiled at him. "A good defense is one of those ways." The smile faded. "Readiness, as you military types would say, is another."

"Readiness for what?" Bryan asked.

"Let's just say that if this is a personal vendetta, whoever is out to ruin me would be wise to guard against the boomerang effect."

She allowed the scent of vengeance to linger in the air as again she lowered her eyes and sipped her club soda slowly. When her gaze returned to Bryan her expression had become one of frank concern.

"I know you think I should be, and you're probably right, but honestly I'm not afraid of garden-variety lunatics or cyber-stalkers taking their frustrations out with nasty letters and threatening packages.

"What I do worry about, however, is the horrific possibility that some sociopath might think he can get to me by murdering others."

Bryan worried about that as well, but the other, more frightening scenario was that the killing of that woman was meant as a prelude to killing Vera.

He started to say something, but Vera had looked away. He didn't need to see her eyes to know how she felt. She was afraid.

★ ★ ★

Vera had selected the kitchen in the rear of the television studio as the site of her meeting. Its plain wooden trestle table, Windsor chairs, and spartan décor captured the bare-bones tone she wished to convey. There were no refreshments other than bottled water and coffee and no amenities. Since she didn't want notes to leave the premises, there were no yellow pads or pencils either. This was a meeting of Vera's war council, not a kaffeeklatch.

People filed in slowly, nervously seeking their names on the place cards; considering the circumstances, no one wanted to sit near Vera. It felt too dangerous. They were also curious about the gentleman standing by her side. Since neither he nor Vera was smiling, his presence didn't feel like a good thing.

When Greta entered the room and saw Bryan, she was surprised and disappointed, excited and depressed, all at the same time.

As she approached, Vera's expression warned her not to greet Bryan in a personal way. Their relationship had no place in this meeting. Greta obediently took her assigned seat, but not before flashing Bryan a brilliant smile.

He smiled in return, but not as warmly as she would have liked. As she settled in, she tried to put a leash on her paranoia.

When everyone was assembled, Vera positioned herself at the head of the table. Bryan was at her left, Greta on her right. Craig Hemminger sat opposite Vera at the other end of the table. The various division heads filled in the remaining seats.

"This is Bryan Chalmers," Vera said, eschewing any greeting or preamble. "I've retained him to defend the Hart Line against the government's accusations. In case you've been living in a gulag and are unfamiliar with Mr. Chalmers, he was until this morning the rising star in the district attorney's office. Before he was a prosecutor he was an FBI agent, and before that a decorated army pilot. I feel privileged that he has decided to bring his prodigious talents to HLI."

Around the table polite smiles acknowledged the stellar quality of Bryan's résumé, but no one really cared about him. They wanted to know what was about to happen to them.

With the preliminaries out of the way, Vera focused her attention squarely on Craig Hemminger.

"You are the CFO of Hart Line International, which is being investigated for accounting fraud among other sins. I personally am going to be charged with several jailable offenses, all of which are the result of your criminally ineffectual oversight. Give me one good reason why I shouldn't throw your sorry ass out of here!"

"I'll give you two," he said without a second's hesitation. "Greta Hart and Vera Hart."

His defiance stunned everyone. Craig Hemminger was the archetypical Milquetoast, the ultimate accountant whose nimble ability with figures stood in sharp contrast to his plodding, reticent nature. While no one expected such an in-your-face response, he was known to be obsessive about preparation. It made sense that he might have anticipated a public flaying and had rehearsed his defense.

"Greta is my immediate superior. You are hers. I may have the title chief financial officer, but in reality I'm a functionary. My orders were to show a profit, to keep our stockholders happy, and to provide enough goodies and income to keep the two of you happy. I did that by diverting profits to dummy companies, which purchased homes, art, cars, and other luxuries. I leveraged company losses with bogus capital expenditures for the purpose of maintaining an impressive bottom line and, therefore, the price of HLI stock. To be sure, maintaining these figures required some creative accounting, but I repeat, these were not my policies. If you're disturbed by the consequences of your fiscal gluttony, you have no one to blame but yourself."

Vera's face flushed ruby red. "You and key members of your staff are discharged as of this minute. A press release announcing the firings has already gone out. You can watch it on the six o'clock news."

Bryan winced. That was a major tactical error. Vera believed a preemptive purge would place the guilt firmly on Hemminger's shoulders. While that strategy might succeed in assuaging the public's anger at her, it gave those discharged employees a reason to barter information for reduced jail sentences. Also, Bryan guessed the government's plan was to direct the first assault of their case against the CFO and his deputies. Once they proved the CFO's guilt, they would go after Vera. She just accelerated the process.

"There's a car waiting to drive you back to the city," she continued, oblivious to her new attorney's concerns, "but don't bother to return to your office. The door is locked, your records have been confiscated, and your personal items have been packed up and sent to your home."

Hemminger stood and tugged at the lapels of his jacket, straightening it as if it were a bulletproof vest. His injured expression said that even if it were, it wouldn't help. He'd already been mortally wounded.

"Fine," he said, refusing to vacate his space at the alternate head of the table just yet. "I'll go, but mark my words: There will be consequences. You and your devilish spawn have made an adversary of a friend. And you will both live to regret it."

He walked out of the room without a sideways glance, but the heat of his umbrage caused everyone at the table to sweat.

Everyone save Greta and Vera Hart. They remained remarkably cool.

Hemminger saw her just as he was about to climb into the Town Car.

What the hell is a kid doing here?

Playing croquet with one of Vera's minions on the lawn of the Colonial was the same little girl he'd seen at the Foundation gala.

Hemminger scratched his head, trying to conjure a reason for a child to be on the grounds of Vera Hart's Valhalla.

Maybe she was related to that Chalmers guy. No. Hemminger had read about him. He was single, no children, currently the paramour of Greta Hart.

Hemminger studied the girl more carefully, scratching his memory.

She'd been with some military guy. Phelps. That was his name, Lieutenant General Phelps.

A smile graced his lips. She looked exactly like Vera.

His smile grew broader. One of the award recipients also bore a strong resemblance to Madame Hart. Her name was Phelps.

Hemminger almost slapped his forehead in an I-should-have-known type flourish. He had a Ph.D. in all things Vera. How could he not have remembered? Lieutenant General Phelps was Vera's ex-husband. Dr. Marta Phelps was the forgotten daughter, the one who'd had the good fortune to be raised by someone other than Lucifer's Queen.

The little girl was Marta Phelps's child. And Vera Hart's grandchild.

Interesting, he thought as he closed the door of the car.

He wondered if the child's existence had been a surprise. And if so, how Vera had dealt with the double whammy that she was no longer an ingénue and that something had occurred in her world that she hadn't decreed or designed.

Aside from her compulsive fetish to remain forever young, Vera didn't like surprises. A surprise meant she wasn't in control, and if she wasn't in control, chaos was possible. Vera feared chaos the way others feared the ocean or heights or cramped spaces. To overcome that fear Vera strove for perfection. In business she attained it. When it came to male-female relationships, friendship, and parenting, however, she was an outright flop. That vaunted, venerable virago was single, friendless, and as a mother could lay claim only to that harridan Greta as representative of the fruit of her womb.

He laughed. The other daughter, Marta, was rather spectacular, but her father had reared her. Again he laughed.

It must make her crazy that Hugh Phelps, the guy she made out to be a deadbeat dad in their divorce trial, comes off looking like the Parent of the Year next to her.

His laughter faded and his mood grew dark when he thought about how his role as a father had been brutally truncated. He had a son and a daughter he hadn't seen in years. When he and their mother divorced he had been denied all but the most minimal of visitation rights. And why was that? Because he had been stupid enough to have an affair with Vera Hart. Because he had been so swollen with passion for her and so blinded by the gift of her affection, he had forsaken everything and everyone.

When his wife found out about his dalliance and threatened to take him to court, Vera convinced him to give Olivia what she wanted — her freedom, custody of the children, and most of his money. Vera's argument was that if Olivia took him to court, the media would skewer all of them, and that would be terrible for his kids. The unspoken lure was that when he was free, they would be together. After he surrendered his money and his children to Olivia, Vera dumped him. He was alone, deeply in dept, and completely beholden to the architect of his demise.

He'd suppressed his hatred for her because he had to; without his job, his disgrace would have been total, he'd have had nothing. But now that he was no longer tethered to the Hart Line, he was free to do as he wished.

And what he wished was to give vent to that hatred.

Once the directors had gone, Vera invited Greta and Bryan to adjourn to the lakeside cottage for tea. "I have someone I want you to meet," she said.

"Who?" Greta shared her mother's antipathy for surprises.

"A new hire."

"Who?" Greta said again.

"Stop that. You sound like an owl," Vera said as she strode up the shallow brick steps and opened the door to the cottage.

Bryan's eyes had to adjust to the light as he followed Vera from the sun-drenched outdoors through a dim foyer and a short hallway into a fabulous pavilion that felt completely open to the sky and the lake. The room was large and square, set up like a studio apartment — kitchen, living room, and dining area all in one. The ceilings were high and gabled, punctuated by fanlights. Below them were three walls of bare, side-by-side sash windows that acted as frames for the lush, natural landscape. That bright, airy gazebo feeling carried through to the pale, salmon-toned sofas and sand-colored walls. A Persian carpet and honeyed wood wheel-back chairs

164

around a pedestal table provided richness. A brick-faced fireplace and a dado of vertical siding provided texture.

But it was the presence of Martie Phelps that provided both of Vera's guests with a heart-stopping jolt.

"Bryan, this is Dr. Marta Phelps. You might remember her from the dinner the other night. She was the recipient of the scientific achievement award."

It was rare for a high-level prosecutor to display any feeling, let alone raw emotion, but Bryan was clearly thunderstruck. It took a minute for him to regain his composure, but in that splash of time Vera — and Greta — were treated to a startling array of intense sentiment. After the initial surprise, his face registered a joy that would have been difficult to disguise. What was interesting to Vera was that Bryan made no attempt to camouflage his pleasure in seeing Martie, nor she in seeing him.

Greta couldn't conceal her feelings either. Her expression morphed from shock to outrage to jealousy to outrage to heartbreak to outrage, seemingly at the speed of light. At first it was simply the sight of Martie in Vera's cottage that stunned. Then it was the realization that Bryan and Martie didn't simply *know* each other from

165

their time in the army, but they had been intimate and perhaps had never really gotten over each other.

"Actually," Bryan said to Vera, back in charge, "Dr. Phelps and I served in the military together."

"Really?" Vera exclaimed with Oscar-winning amazement at the coincidence.

Two maids entered, one with a large tea service, the other with a plate of sliced fruit and the almond crescent cookies Vera had baked for that morning's show. After they departed, Vera encouraged everyone to take a seat and relax. By subtly pointing here and there, she placed everyone where she wanted.

Bryan sat at the corner of the larger sofa. Martie settled into the corner of the smaller loveseat that L'd with the sofa. Vera positioned herself next to Bryan. Greta was left with the choice of sitting next to her mother or her sister. It was like choosing between death by poison or by drowning. Vexed, she plunked down next to Vera.

"Were you in the same unit?" Vera asked as she poured the tea, leaving it to either one to respond.

Martie found her voice first. "Bryan was my flight instructor at Fort Rucker."

"Aha," Vera said as if that were news to her. "And what did he teach you to fly?"

"Black Hawk helicopters." Martie couldn't suppress the smile that crawled onto her lips.

Bryan nodded his head as he too allowed a smile to appear.

"Is there a joke in there somewhere?" Greta's voice was as tight as spandex. "If so, I'm afraid I don't get it."

Bryan had almost forgotten Greta was in the room. Guiltily he turned and faced her.

"Martie wanted to fly Apache attack helicopters, but they're combat vehicles and as such restricted to men. She didn't think it was fair and said so. The army disagreed."

"What a pity," Greta said, her mouth pinched, the veins in her neck taut.

Bryan was confused at Greta's level of hostility. It didn't seem to fit the situation.

"Would you please explain what *she's* doing here?" Greta demanded of Vera.

"I would think that would be obvious," Martie said, her voice void of any intimidation. "I've been hired to head up the skin care division."

Martie, who'd been quietly observing the dynamics between Greta and Bryan and Vera, decided she'd had enough. She was not about to allow people to discuss her as if she weren't right there in the room. Also, three things were obvious: Vera was playing head games with Greta, and possibly with her; Greta had known nothing about Martie being brought into the Hart Line circle; Bryan and Greta weren't strangers. All of which compelled Martie to wonder the same thing as Greta: What was she doing here?

Aloud, she said, "And in case you're interested, I'm more than qualified for the position."

Greta wasn't interested. She bounded off the sofa and stalked the perimeter of the room, keeping her heated gaze focused on her mother.

"We're being investigated by the government! Our stock is plummeting! You could be indicted for fraud! And you're searching for a new wrinkle cream? Have you lost it altogether?"

"Hardly." Vera's posture remained unruffled, but an edge had crept into her voice. "And for the record, I'm not searching for a wrinkle cream. We already have that. What I want is for the Hart Line to put out honest-to-goodness age-defying products, rather than momentary feel-good, fat-based panaceas. Not only does

Dr. Phelps have the experience to develop such a line, but her name and prestige adds a certain gravitas and credibility. Don't you think?"

Greta's fists were tight balls. "What I think is that you've decided to play Mother Teresa and your first act of charitable beneficence is to give this lab geek a cushy job. And stop referring to her as Dr. Phelps as if she's some kind of Nobel Prize winner."

Bryan was aghast. And even more confused. "What the hell is going on here?"

"Oh, I thought you knew," Vera said with breathless astonishment. "Greta and Martie are sisters. Unfortunately, as you can see, they can't stand each other."

"What kind of malicious game are you playing?" Greta's alabaster skin was mottled with angry red blotches.

"I don't play games," Vera said in a blasé tone. "I have neither the time nor the inclination."

Greta remained anchored to one spot as if her feet had been nailed to the floor. Vera busied herself tidying up after her tea. She had no tolerance for messiness. Or for having her motives challenged.

"You don't expect me to believe that this

sudden reconciliation with your long-lost daughter is truly about business, do you?"

Vera placed the last teacup on the tray and began to collect the napkins.

"You ambushed me!"

"I simply invited you to meet the newest member of the HLI team."

"Nothing you do is simple," Greta countered heatedly. "This is about you making certain that my relationship with Bryan stalls, isn't it?"

"Why would I want to do that?"

"Because if I don't have anyone in my life, I can do your bidding twenty-four/ seven. That's why! You don't want a daughter, you want a lapdog who sits when you say sit and heels when you say heel."

Vera looked at Greta, pulling away slightly as if her last outburst proved her unstable. "If this is any example of filial loyalty, a lapdog might be preferable."

"Charming! Why don't we have that touching maternal sentiment embroidered on a sampler for the Hart Line Heartless collection?"

Vera bypassed the snipe. "You're a very bright woman, Greta, and your contributions to HLI have been legion, but at the end of the day this is my company. Whatever I decide is what's done, whether you like it or not."

"Gee. Call me crazy. As COO I thought I was part of the decision-making process."

"You are, but there are certain matters on which you've proven yourself to be far too emotional. Your sister is one of them."

"I haven't had a sister in more than twenty years. And frankly, I've never felt as if I were missing anything."

"Which is precisely why I didn't ask for your input."

"Oh, please! You thought it would be amusing to shove her in my face."

Vera clucked her tongue in dismay. "Really, Greta, you're so overwhelmed by sibling rivalry you can't see the big picture. Martie is extremely accomplished in a closely related field. She could make an enormous contribution to the success of one of our lines. Why shouldn't I take advantage of her being in New York and being available?"

"Because you can't trust her."

"Why not?"

"Because she probably hates you for abandoning her as a tot."

"That's possible, but she accepted the Foundation award when she could have refused," Vera said. "And she agreed to work for me when she could have refused."

"That doesn't mean she doesn't hate you," Greta warned.

"Are you speaking from personal experience?" Vera asked.

Greta walked out of the cottage without answering.

"I thought Connie was your mom," Bryan said after he and Martie had walked outside, acceding to Vera's request to leave her and Greta to have a private moment alone.

"She was, in every way that mattered."

"Why didn't you ever say anything about Vera?"

"It wasn't relevant."

Bryan's jaw clenched. Obviously he thought it was.

Martie knew Bryan wanted an explanation, but she chose not to give him one. It was complicated and painful and, now that their romance was history, unimportant. If Greta felt differently, she could fill him in.

"I'm curious about two things," Bryan said in an example of extreme understatement. "I gather that you and Vera have been estranged for eons. Since you don't want to discuss that estrangement, I'm getting that it wasn't your choice and it didn't sit real well with you." He watched her face for signs of confirmation or denial, but her expression remained blank. "So why sign on to work with her?"

"This is a vertical move, the hours suit me, and it pays well."

"Okay," he said, "but since it also appears that you and Greta are oil and water, why put yourself in the position of having to see her day in and day out?"

"Because one of the conditions of my employment was that I don't have to see her. I am essentially autonomous. I don't report to anyone except Vera."

Bryan nodded.

He seemed to be hovering between anger and befuddlement. Martie guessed that behind those brooding brown eyes a dozen balls were bouncing in front of him, each of which represented an alternate reality: what was true, what he had believed to be true, who should have said what to whom, what his reaction might have been then, what it should be now. He didn't know what to catch, what to pass.

"Aside from formulating a skin care line, I've been asked to look into another problem at HLI," Martie said, hoping to offer him something to think about other than the uncomfortable fact that his current girlfriend and his former girlfriend were sisters. "Valentine Red."

His meditation came to an abrupt halt. Bryan's eyebrows dove downward into a hawkish vee and his lips pursed. Martie knew that look. He wasn't happy that Vera had discussed a police matter with her.

"Vera told me you're the only other person who knows about that. She also told me it's to stay that way."

His eyebrows resumed their normal position, but his mouth remained tight.

"She wants me to tour the manufacturing plants to figure out how that lot was poisoned and if any other lots were compromised. If she knows the how and the where, she believes the who will follow."

"Hopefully," Bryan said, blatant skepticism coloring his words. "Do you have a proper cover? Any protection? If someone's poisoning lipsticks they're on a mission, which means they're not going to give you a pass to snoop around."

"As the new head chemist, it's not unreasonable for me to visit the facilities and get to know the crews."

"True. But you shouldn't go alone."

"Bryan. I can take care of myself."

He held up his hands. "I didn't mean to make it sound like you need a bodyguard."

His lips curled in an apologetic half smile. "But it's not a totally misguided idea." Again, his forehead furrowed as another disturbing notion surfaced. "Does anyone else on staff know that you're Vera's daughter?"

Martie shook her head and swallowed her conditioned response to that question: *The world doesn't know that Vera Hart has another daughter.*

"No. And Vera has assured me it will stay that way."

"How about Greta?"

Martie laughed, but it didn't resonate with any humor. "Greta didn't readily acknowledge our sorority when we were kids. I doubt if she's anxious to do so now."

Before he could delve deeper, a little girl with gardenia-white skin and chestnut hair came skipping toward them.

"Mommy! I played crocus," she exclaimed. "Just like in the book."

Martie scooped Lili up into her arms and the two of them brushed noses.

"Cro*quet*," she said, correcting her daughter.

Lili giggled and dutifully repeated the word. "Cro*quet*."

"Brilliant!" Martie kissed Lili and set her down. "I'd like you to meet someone," she said. "This is Bryan Chalmers. He and

Mommy used to fly planes together. Bryan, this is my daughter, Lili."

Lili's mouth blossomed into the same entrancing, full-toothed smile he'd always adored on Martie. It was a grin as wide as open arms and just as inviting.

In spite of efforts to quell the memory, Bryan recalled the first time he handed over the controls of a helicopter to Martie. Her whoop of sheer delight affected him like a large gulp of a carbonated beverage: It made him fizz inside.

Her daughter's grin had the same effect.

"Hi, Lili," he said, smiling as he knelt down so they were eye level and extended his hand. "It's a pleasure to meet you."

Lili shook his hand politely, but she had no interest in wasting time on social patter. She was bursting with questions.

"Was Mommy a good flyer?"

"One of the best."

"Was she ever scared?"

"Probably. Everyone's scared at one time or another, don't you think?"

She considered that. "I guess."

He leaned closer. "She just hid it better than others."

Lili giggled. She liked that. "Were you ever scared?"

"You bet."

"What did you do?"

"I had a good luck charm. I counted on that to see me through."

It spilled out of his mouth before he could stop himself. A quick glance at Martie told him she knew he wasn't playing Lili. He was simply telling the truth.

"My mommy has a good luck charm too. She wears it all the time."

Bryan had noticed the chain around Martie's neck. It was the same chain she'd worn on her wrist the other night, so he assumed the dime was at the end of it, but it was tucked inside her blouse.

"How about you? Do you have a good luck charm?" he asked Lili.

"Uh-uh. I don't need one. Mommy says I make my own luck."

"Well, I'd say you're off to a terrific start. Look how lucky you are to have her as your mommy."

Lili grinned at Martie. The love that passed between them was so rich it perfumed the air. Bryan was pleased for Martie yet jealous that he didn't have that kind of tight-knit personal connection in his life.

"When you were a pilot did you know my grandpa, Hugh Phelps?"

"I did."

Lili smiled. Her love for him was evident. "A lot of people are afraid of him because he's a general with a lot of stars. Were you?"

"Actually, I was." *But not because of his rank.*

Bryan and Hugh had gotten along very well in the beginning. They didn't have a great deal of contact with each other due to the war, but he liked the general and for a time he believed the general liked him. It was when Bryan refused to accept Martie's decision not to marry him that things turned ugly.

It took Bryan years to understand that Hugh's reactions were those of a father blinded by the need to protect his child, but even now a part of him resented Hugh's interference. It was unrealistic, fairy-tale projection he knew, but on some level Bryan believed that if not for Hugh, Bryan and Martie would have married and lived happily ever after. Instead, Bryan had been transferred to Korea; his orders had Hugh Phelps's fingerprints all over them. Since he had time left on his commitment to the army, he had no basis on which to object.

"Did you fly with Mommy in the desert?" Lili's curiosity was boundless.

178

"No. I was with a different unit." With another child he might have felt compelled to explain that. This child was the daughter of a decorated veteran and the granddaughter of a general. No explanations necessary. "I flew with your mom stateside. In Alabama."

"Fort Rucker."

"That's right."

"Were you in her class?"

"Sort of. I was her teacher."

Lili's aquamarine eyes became full circles. "Would you teach me?"

Martie started to respond, but Bryan beat her to it.

"You're too small for the kinds of planes your mommy flew, but I know a place where pilots your size are very welcome."

"Will you take me?"

"If it's okay with your mom."

"Really?"

"Really," he said, confirming his promise by making an X on his chest.

"Mommy, can I go?"

"We'll see," Martie said, hedging.

Lili's face fell into a frown. Bryan could tell she was an immediate gratification girl, just like her mother. Also, just like her mother, she didn't accept dismissal easily.

"I would really like to do this," Lili said

with surprising grown-up insistence. "And since you introduced me to Mr. Chalmers as your friend, he isn't a stranger, so it's not bad for me to go with him."

Lili reminded Bryan of a lawyer in the midst of a negotiation. There was a point to be nailed down and Lili wasn't leaving the table until it was.

"Okay," Martie said. "We'll figure it out."

Lili's face waxed triumphant. Bryan didn't even bother to smother his smile.

"When? I want to go soon."

"Okay!"

Lili was so excited she jumped up and down and clapped her hands. Bryan clapped his hands too.

"Wow," he said, noticing the blinking red reflectors on her sneakers. "Those are neat."

On the sides of her little white shoes were plastic red hearts that lit up when her feet touched the ground.

"I wore them today because I was going to see the Queen of Hearts."

"Good choice, then," Bryan said.

Their delight in each other made Martie uncomfortable.

When Jack died, Martie vowed not to marry simply to give her daughter a father.

While she understood the need for that second parent, she had been an eyewitness to the disintegration of a marriage. It wasn't pretty, nor was it something she wanted her daughter to experience.

Fortunately, Martie didn't have to add someone to their lives just to fill the hole in their family portrait. She could support them on her own. There were Hugh, Connie, and Jack's parents to provide Lili with family structure. And there were friends to fill in some of the other blanks. As for her social life, she went on dates and tried to make a couple of relationships work, but having a daughter created additional pressure because it was no longer just about Martie and whomever. Nor was it just about Lili and how she got along with whomever. She and Lili were the core; *whomever* was almost secondary. If a relationship wasn't right for Martie it could never be right for Lili, and vice versa.

She knew that to be an absolute truth because Connie was so perfect for Hugh that their union was perfect for her.

Martie had never questioned whether Bryan was right for her. It was the timing that was wrong. A couple of years after Jack died she thought about calling him but smothered the impulse. She didn't know what to say or how he would greet her or if he would even take her call. Then they ran into each other at the gala. She hadn't stopped thinking about him since.

Now, watching her daughter laugh and talk so animatedly with him, seeing how quickly Lili trusted him and how quickly he'd taken to her, she wondered if destiny had thrown them a second chance.

Then Greta exited the cottage and headed toward them, her eyes fixed squarely on Bryan.

Martie watched her approach and recalled that inside she had sensed that Greta and Bryan were more than business associates. Like a soap bubble, Martie's fantasy burst. It didn't matter whether Martie thought Bryan was her Mr. Right; Greta believed he was hers.

Once again, the timing was wrong.

Chapter 7

Martie was seven when Vera's movie career bottomed out. In an attempt to remind the public and the Powers That Be how much they loved her, Vera's publicist scored a five-page spread in the premier issue of a new lifestyles magazine, *Mainstreet*. The pitch: Vera Hart was an icon. It didn't matter how many movies she made, people clamored for news of everything Vera — her clothes, her makeup, how she lived, where she went, what she did. The hook: The one aspect of Vera's life that hadn't been exploited was her role as a mother. *Mainstreet* was promised an exclusive cover of Vera and her daughters.

In the abstract, the shoot had appealed to Vera. The reality of it was something else again. The crew was tracking dirt onto her carpet. The so-called stylist not only had the audacity to rearrange some of Vera's *objets*, but insisted that Vera and her daughters pose in mother-daughter outfits despite Vera's protests that "I don't do adorable." And instead of Hilary Baron, the assistant editor of *Mainstreet*, prostrating herself at Vera's feet, she was stomping around Vera's dressing room in a disrespectful huff.

"Your husband was supposed to be here," she sniffed, clearly annoyed that Major Hugh Phelps was a no-show.

Vera was in the midst of having her makeup applied. Annoyed at the interruption, she eyed the pesky woman with imperious disdain.

"He's out of the country protecting America from the spread of communism," she said, then turned back for another swipe of blush.

Hugh had flown to Thailand the week before, but even if he'd been in Los Angeles he never would have agreed to this. When Vera and Hugh first met, he'd been as starstruck as any other fan, but he wasn't in love with her fame.

"And your daughters? Where are they?"

Vera stared into the mirror and slowly colored her lips a bright red.

"I have no idea," she said as she appraised the effect. "That's what nannies are for."

Antonio Ravello, the reigning king of the beautiful-people photo world was in charge of the shoot. When he'd completed his lighting check and his prop setup, he declared himself ready.

"Tell them I'm starting in five minutes."

His assistant saluted and headed toward the back. He was at the hallway leading to the bedroom wing when he remembered something.

"There's one that looks exactly like Vera Hart. Hilary wants her in front."

The one that looks like Vera Hart goes in front.

Greta seethed as she stomped down the hall to her bedroom.

How dare he, she thought as she stormed into the pink aerie she shared with her sister.

Martie did look exactly like their mother, but that didn't give her the right to be out front!

Greta slammed the door behind her.

Martie was the last person Greta wanted to see just then, but there she was, standing in the middle of the room, her hands plunked on her hips in a pose of obvious pique.

"Where's my dress?"

"How would I know?" Greta was wearing the ivory lace dress the stylist had brought under protest. She thought it made her look like an old-fashioned lampshade.

"You said you'd get it while I was in the shower."

In fifteen minutes everyone was expected to gather in the living room. Martie was showered. Her hair was brushed. She had on her tights and her shoes. Now she needed her dress.

"I'm going to be late." Her voice was growing shrill from nervousness. "Didn't you ask where it is?"

"Actually, I did."

"Well?"

"They didn't send one for you."

Martie's face fell. "Mommy said we were all wearing the same dress. *All* means me too."

Greta shrugged. "Maybe she changed her mind."

"She said the magazine was sending mother-daughter dresses. I'm a daughter."

Greta leaned down, bringing her face inches away from her sister's. "I told you. They didn't send one for you. And since I'm the only *daughter* with a dress, I guess I'm the *only* daughter they want in the picture."

Martie started for the door.

"Where do think you're going?" Greta

asked, as if Martie needed a hall pass to leave the room.

"To ask Mommy why I didn't get a daughter dress."

Greta lunged for Martie. She grabbed her arm and squeezed it.

"Ow!" Martie wrenched her arm out of Greta's grasp. "You're hurting me."

Greta paid no attention to the red welt on her sister's arm.

"If you go in there and start whining and carrying on, the people from the magazine are going to hear you."

"So what? They were supposed to send me a dress." Martie was flushed with indignation, but her voice wobbled with disappointment.

"That Hilary lady is going to have a fit," Greta warned. "Who knows, if she gets angry enough she might postpone the shoot. Or cancel it altogether." Greta shook her head. "Mom would be real upset if that happened."

Martie didn't budge.

"You spoil this for her and she'll tell Daddy you were a brat."

As expected, Martie surrendered. Upsetting Vera was one thing. Disappointing Hugh was another.

"Maybe next time," Greta said, her face

screwed into a mask of sympathy.

She stifled a smile as she closed the bedroom door behind her and headed for the living room. It was time for her close-up.

"Where's the other one?" Hilary Baron barked, seeing only Greta emerge from the bedroom wing.

Greta ignored her, went over to her mother, and whispered in Vera's ear. "Martie said the dress was awful. I told her we didn't like it either and we were wearing it, but she said she wouldn't put it on. I'm sorry, Mom. I tried."

Vera's jaw tightened. This day had gone from bad to hideous to nightmarish and it wasn't even noon.

"Marta isn't well," Vera announced with a gravitas usually reserved for serious illnesses.

"That's a shame, but we're already running late, Miss Hart," Hilary said.

Vera paused. "Well, then," she said, flashing a megawatt smile. "Let's have at it!"

She made certain her best side was to the camera, placed Greta next to her, turned toward Antonio, and struck a pose.

"Perfect!" he declared.

Vera and Greta smiled on cue. Antonio

clicked his shutter. The crew murmured its approval.

And off to the side a little girl stood and watched, big, sad tears dripping down her cheeks.

The headline on the front page of the *New York Post* blared: FROM MAIN STREET TO WALL STREET TO CENTRE STREET. The accompanying photograph was a triptych: on the left was the cover of a now-defunct magazine *Mainstreet*, featuring Vera and a ten-year-old Greta; in the center were Vera and Greta opening the trading session at the New York Stock Exchange when HLI stock went public; and on the right was the federal courthouse on Centre Street in downtown New York City, where many expected Vera, and possibly Greta, to be tried for fraud.

It took Greta a minute or two to recover from the shock of seeing her face splashed all over the newspaper and from the clear insinuation that she too was headed to court. Quickly, she scanned the articles about HLI's investigation in the *New York Times* and the *Wall Street Journal*. They too foresaw her seated at the defense table. Worse, not one reportorial handicapper predicted a victory for her side. The smart

189

money was on the government's case.

The only bright spot in an otherwise dreary beginning was that *Mainstreet* cover. As she studied it, a whiff of remembered triumph fluttered over her lips.

The morning of that photo shoot, Greta rose early and cut up Martie's daughter dress. She stuffed it in a pillowcase and hid it at the bottom of the laundry basket, eliminating Martie from the carefully orchestrated sitting. Later that night, after poor little left-out Martie had cried herself to sleep, Greta slid out of bed, tiptoed into the bathroom, retrieved the pillowcase, and emptied its contents into the garbage pail in the kitchen, carefully mixing the shredded dress in with the remains of that night's dinner.

As she stared at the newspaper now, seeing that red, ugly scar under her eyebrow on the *Mainstreet* cover, she remembered how joyous she'd felt then, knowing that she had achieved a modicum of payback.

Several months before, on one of those Sunday morning hikes in Beverly Hills the girls used to take with Hugh, they decided to try out the roller skates they'd gotten for Christmas. Hugh advised them to skate in the street, close to the curb, rather than on the sidewalk because the sidewalk wasn't level.

They were going along fine, each at her own pace, when Hugh heard a car turning the corner. He shouted for them to get out of the street and up onto the sidewalk. Greta was slowing down and had just put her foot out to step up when Martie, squealing and speeding out of control, zoomed directly in front of her. Martie's skates hit the curb. She started to fall, but Hugh caught her by the arm and steadied her. Greta, unable to get out of the way and too far for Hugh to grab her as well, tripped over one of Martie's feet and fell forward, her face hitting an uneven piece of sidewalk.

Blood gushed from the wound above her eye. She was dizzy and disoriented and felt as if she might throw up. Hugh took out his handkerchief and pressed it against the angry gash to stem the bleeding. He told Martie to run to the nearest house and tell whoever answered the door to call 911. An ambulance came and took Greta to the hospital. Fifteen stitches and three hours of observation later, she went home. Everyone fussed over her, moaned about what a terrible accident it was, and assured Martie it wasn't her fault, but at the end of the day, Greta was left with that scar.

She never went on another hike with Hugh. And she never forgave Martie.

Chapter 8

One of the perks for Hart Line International employees was the rooftop gym. Lavishly equipped, it was banked on two sides by walls of windows, which afforded incredible views of Manhattan. The other two walls were mirrored, providing ample views of one's self.

The first few days on the job Martie had been too bogged down learning the lay of the land and planning her approach to the Valentine problem to take advantage of this most appealing dividend, but today, she'd come to the office determined. The minute the whirlwind calmed, she grabbed her gym bag and raced upstairs.

Exercise had always been a part of her life; one couldn't grow up in a career officer's home without it. By the time she reported to Officer Basic Course, she thought the physical part would almost be easy. Her home workouts had been that strenuous. Of course, *almost* was the key word; no one coasted through Basic.

Martie's training was done at Fort Sam Houston in San Antonio, Texas. As a physician she entered the army as a commissioned officer; her basic training program was shorter and slightly less rigorous than that for a recruit slated for the front lines. The program, conducted under the auspices of AMEDD, the Army Medical Department, was nine weeks long, including a one-week Field Training Exercise (FTX).

Martie excelled in the classroom. She didn't have a problem with the physical training either, but field training presented a different challenge in the person of Drill Sergeant Vincent Wiggers, the most dedicated, patriotic, well-meaning son of a bitch Martie had ever met. He was, as the slogan goes, an Army of One.

Built like a condominium, he had a round choirboy face and a dimpled smile that was positively oxymoronic considering his fearsome heft and his mountain lion roar. Wiggers was a survivor of the East St. Louis ghetto. He joined the army because, as he so delicately put it, "If I'm gonna have to kick the shit out of someone or get the shit kicked out of me every day of my life, the fight's gonna mean something and I'm gonna make damn sure I come out the winner."

The army became his way out and his way in. His uniform, his stripes, the respect he earned from his peers, and the camaraderie they shared gave him a much-needed sense of pride and belonging. The army was his family. No one was going to mess with it.

At Fort Sam his charges were lieutenants as well as health care professionals. Wiggers wasn't intimidated by their degrees or their rank. Their job was to find fallen soldiers in the field, extract them safely, and tend to their wounds. His job was to turn them into officers and to teach them the survival techniques they were going to need when called into battle, which was why he made the week-long FTX his specialty.

The door of the bus to Camp Bullis hadn't even closed when everyone felt the heat generated by Drill Sergeant Vincent Wiggers. He mounted the steps and turned, arms akimbo, his panther-black eyes peering out from beneath his brown felt campaign hat. Like a hunter stalking his quarry, he paraded up and down the aisle, eyeballing each and every soldier, measuring, assessing. His face was so stony it was impossible to imagine him being able to change expressions. It was as if that old saw, "Be careful your face doesn't freeze," had come true in his case.

Martie was seated toward the back, by a window. On his third go-around he stopped and stared at her, taking her apart like a mechanic stripping an engine piece by piece by piece.

"I don't tolerate slackers, stupidity, or weakness." His voice boomed loud enough to carry throughout the bus, yet he seemed to be directing his comments specifically to her. "I don't give a shit who you are, who you were in your former life, or who you think you're going to be when you get out of here. I don't care if you're going to make a career of the army or you're here for the short run. Either you add to the corps or I'm going to make sure you're subtracted before you do anyone any harm." He leaned over the soldier in the seat next to her, his dark face only inches away from hers. "You got that, Lieutenant Phelps?"

"Yes, sir!"

He moved toward the front of the bus and stood over another female soldier.

"If you ask me, women shouldn't be in the army." He glared at the men, daring any of them to snicker or agree with him. "But you know what? No one asked me.

Women are in the army and my orders are to train them same as I do the men."

Again, he marched up the aisle, looking hard at the other female soldiers. Again, he stopped at Martie's row.

"I'm going to tell you a secret, Lieutenant. I don't give a flying fuck what my orders are. I work my women ten times harder than the men."

Martie kept her eyes squarely on his, refusing to give him the satisfaction of even blinking.

"I'm going to train your ass so hard you're going to scream for mercy."

Her gaze remained steady.

"You hear me, Lieutenant?" he demanded.

"Yes, sir!"

"You going to scream for mercy?"

"No, sir!"

Up ahead, her sisters in combat winced. Martie had just thrown down a gauntlet for all of them.

Twenty-five miles north of Fort Sam Houston at Camp Bullis, the soldiers were divided into squads. Martie was appointed lead soldier of hers. She didn't know whether it was a vote of admiration for standing up to Wiggers or a decision to sacrifice her for the good of the unit, but whatever the motivation, she was out on the field with the other leads early the next morning at the start of FTX.

Drill Sergeant Wiggers wasted no time presenting the squad leaders with their first assignment. He brought them to a fifteen-foot concrete wall modeled after a World War II–style bunker. Their mission was to get their team up and over that wall within a specific time frame. All they had to work with was a length of rope and whatever ingenuity they brought to the task.

"By the way," Wiggers said pointing to the wall with a knowing snicker. "Anything below four and a half feet is contaminated."

He asked if anyone had any questions. Everyone did, but only a few verbalized them. Martie wasn't one of them.

She returned to her squad, briefed her mates, and asked for input. There was some debate and a few suggestions, but whatever confidence they might have had quickly paled when they came face to face with the formidable fifteen-foot slab of concrete.

The first thing they had to figure out was how to use the rope. After some mental calisthenics, one limber recruit climbed a nearby tree in the hopes of being able to toss the rope over the top of the wall. He would follow and anchor the rope for the others. The tree was high enough, but too spindly and ultimately too far away to be useful. His squadmates decided to try bending the tree toward the bunker without shaking him down like a coconut. It wasn't easy, but they finally managed to maneuver him close enough so he could scramble to the other side. He was about to throw the rope back over when Martie shouted a reminder not to let the rope touch the lower section of the wall.

"If it's contaminated, we can't use it."

Once the rope was in hand, the team made several attempts to scale the wall. First they tried throwing their gear over the top. That didn't work; backpacks were too heavy and, as Wiggers barked from the sidelines, tossing an M-16 around was not a good idea.

They knotted the rope in the hopes of making it easier to climb, but the knots slipped loose.

They hoisted one very tall guy above the contamination point and he made it over, but that didn't work for the others.

Eventually they tied the gear to the rope, hauled it up, then concentrated on the squad.

Martie kept a constant eye on the clock, exhorting her team to pick up the pace.

Then one of the team touched the contaminated area.

"Casualty," Wiggers yelled.

Everyone including the "casualty" stopped, unsure as to how they should proceed.

"Soldier down," Martie shouted, trying to remind her squad that they were still in the midst of a fictional battle and still on the clock. "Soldier down!"

As she ran toward the young man whose feet had touched the wall, she pointed at the ground, motioning for him to drop down. He crumpled as if he'd been slimed with chemicals.

"He's immobilized," Martie said. "But we don't leave anyone behind, so let's go!"

Wiggers watched as Martie instructed her team to rig up a sling.

"Hurry! We don't have much time!" she said, shouting instructions and encouragement.

Wiggers crossed his arms and checked his watch as the squad hitched the injured man into the sling and maneuvered him and themselves around so they could haul him to the top.

Ultimately everyone made it up and

over, gear and all, but not in the allotted time. They had failed to complete their mission.

After Wiggers ripped each of them apart and told them what losers they were, he said, "Do you know how many deaths would have resulted from your sloppiness?"

He walked up and down the line, glaring, silently condemning them for their potentially lethal carelessness.

"Look to your right," he commanded. "Now look to your left. One or both of those soldiers would have been sent home in a body bag if you did this in the field."

They were appropriately shaken.

"Did you learn anything from this?" he shouted.

Squad leader Phelps responded, "We learned we need to think things through better and we need to move faster, sir!"

"You bet your sweet fucking ass you do!"

Wiggers spun on his heel and started back toward the wall, where the next squad was waiting to try their luck. Suddenly he stopped and faced Martie's squad.

"In a war you have to be prepared to do two things: make a plan and then be prepared to modify that plan. Burn that into your brains because it's the best advice you're ever going to get. Dismissed!"

He was right. That advice had saved Martie's life during Desert Storm. And had ruled her life ever since.

She stretched, did half an hour on the elliptical trainer, fifteen minutes of lunges, and a hundred crunches. She had just begun lifting weights when a familiar voice sliced the silence.

"You're still the buffest babe I know," Bryan said with blatant admiration.

Martie smiled, but inside she cringed. While he looked fit and fabulous in dry shorts and a T-shirt, she was sweaty, her ponytail was disheveled, and her clothes were wet and blotchy. It wasn't exactly a Kodak moment. She and Bryan hadn't seen each other since the day at the cottage, but with the drumbeat of an all-out investigation getting louder by the day, she'd known a get-together was inevitable. She just didn't think their first sighting would be over a dumbbell.

"Thanks." She dabbed at her neck with a towel, trying to figure out what to say next.

"Quite a place, isn't it?"

Judging by that banality, Bryan felt as awkward as she did. There was an unfinished conversation hovering over them, but she was loath to raise it.

"Vera doesn't believe in half measures," she said, panning the top-of-the-line equipment and exquisite surroundings.

"Neither do you," Bryan observed. "That kind of trait must be inherited."

Martie sighed. "I'd rather not go there, if you don't mind." He minded very much, she could see that, but just then that was his problem. "We have more pressing issues to discuss."

He hesitated, then conceded. "True," he said.

His tone indicated a conditional surrender; he'd postpone the matter of her biographical omission for now, but he'd come back to it.

"I logged on to the ViCAP site," he said, referring to the Violent Criminal Apprehension Program, "and searched for deaths involving mercuric chloride."

Bryan had left the FBI years before, but he maintained friendships with a number of agents who helped him out whenever the need arose.

"Anything come up?"

"A couple of cases, but none where the mercuric chloride was traced back to a lipstick."

Martie nodded and tapped her foot while she thought about that. "Here's the problem: It's not only one lipstick that's been contaminated. Lipstick is made in large batches, which means there are dozens, maybe hundreds of other lipsticks laced with this stuff floating around out there. Valentine Red has to come off the market."

She was right, but a move like that would have serious financial consequences.

"That's going to be a tough sell," he said, imagining Greta's and Vera's reaction.

"No tougher than it'll be once the newspapers get hold of the story and start referring to Vera as a killer. They'll go through their morgues and dredge up every hideous story about the cosmetics industry they can. Lash Lure and Koremlu and Valentine Red will be linked in headlines all across the country."

"What are Lash Lure and Koremlu?" Bryan asked.

"Koremlu was a depilatory containing thallium, which is used as a rat poison. Lash Lure was a mascara substitute that contained an aniline dye that caused such severe allergic reactions that in one instance, it resulted in total blindness. In another, a woman died. This was during the 1920s and '30s when there was no regulation. There was a huge public outcry which forced the FDA to impose controls on the beauty industry."

Bryan winced. His primary focus was building HLI's defense. If a death were linked to a Hart Line product, Vera's public image would be permanently tainted. He was good, but no lawyer would be able to overcome that kind of negative publicity.

"When are you going into the field?" he asked. "I would've thought you'd been out already."

"I wanted to, but a team of FDA inspectors swooped down on the Little Rock plant. Vera didn't want to introduce a new chemist until they were gone. We both thought it might raise undue suspicion."

"Do you think they were called in because of Valentine?"

Martie shook her head. "That factory produces primarily hair products. The inspection was prompted by a complaint brought by a customer several months ago."

Bryan's eyebrows arched.

"I know it seems odd, but Vera says the FDA is always slow to respond. They don't have the personnel to do their yearly factory inspections, let alone follow-ups on every complaint that comes in."

"What was the problem?"

Martie could see Bryan was torn. He was hunting for a link so they could affect a quick capture, but he didn't want the FDA to be the ones who found it.

"The customer said that one of the Hart Hair Line shampoos made her scalp itch. She claimed there was an allergen in the product that should have been listed on the label but wasn't."

Bryan nodded. That was logical, but being suspicious by nature, he wanted to know, "Why now? Why was the FDA suddenly so hot on tracking down the cause of an itch?"

"Vera thinks one of her rivals sicced the FDA on her. Evidently that's not uncommon."

"Nice."

"If this was initiated by a rival, my guess is they decided to take advantage of the negative publicity about HLI and gave the FDA a nudge."

Bryan nodded. "I agree. The timing is a little too perfect."

"Anyway, the inspection is expected to conclude today. Barring any unforeseen circumstances, I'll be able to visit one of the targeted factories tomorrow."

Bryan scowled. He didn't like "unforeseen circumstances."

"Where are you going?" he asked.

"The New Jersey facility manufactures lipsticks. I'm scheduled to head out there in the morning. Since the bulk of their production ships within the metropolitan area, it's possible this is the corrupted site. If I'm lucky and do find evidence of contamination, we can shut that plant down and work on finding the psycho who decided to use Hart Line International as his own personal chemistry set."

"What happens if you don't find anything?"

"I go to each and every plant until we locate the source of the poison."

"And until then?" Bryan said.

They both knew the answer to that: Every woman who bought a Valentine lipstick was at risk.

Craig Hemminger was screening his calls. Most he refused to take. This one he did.

"I figured I'd hear from you sooner or later," he said.

"Then you also figured I'd want whatever tapes you claim you have."

"That did cross my mind."

"What do you want for them?"

"Since you don't have a heart or a soul, I

guess I'll have to settle for what's behind door number three."

"Which, I assume, would be money."

"And lots of it."

"Gordon Gekko may be your idol, Craig, but in this particular instance greed is not good. In fact, in this particular instance greed could be a dangerous impulse."

"Is that a threat?"

"No. It's advice."

"I've had enough advice to last a lifetime. Now I want enough money to last for a lifetime. And you're going to give it to me or I'm going to give the tapes to the feds."

"Some lifetimes are shorter than others, Craig. Remember that."

And some people aren't as smart as they think they are, he thought as the phone went dead. Not only had he taped their conversations about HLI financial matters, but Craig had taped this conversation as well.

Finally, he had her where he wanted her.

Enid's hands were filthy. The floor was dusty and the countertop was a mess, but it was all for a good cause. Enid was planting herbs that would be used throughout the summer in special "Hart and Herbs" recipes. She had set up an assembly line of whatever was needed to complete the transplants: terra-cotta pots, small rocks for drainage, bags of potting soil, trowels, a watering can, and nursery flats of basil, chives, thyme, rosemary, and parsley. Everything the discerning cook would need to create delicious dishes from Vera's new *Hart of the Garden Cookbook.*

With one eye trained on the television, Enid gently lifted a small plastic square of chives from a flat. Then she eased the plant out of its container and replanted it alongside several others already set in a wide-mouthed pot layered with rocks and dirt. She patted the soil around the herb's delicate roots and sprinkled it with water: not too much, not too little, just enough to set the roots in place and welcome them to their new home.

Tim Polatchek walked into the kitchen and shook his head in disgust. If only Enid could see herself, he thought.

Vera Hart was broadcasting from one of her enormous greenhouses, bathed in sunlight and surrounded by flora so lush and perfect the blooms looked as if they were constructed by stage designers rather than grown by horticulturists. It was Eden under glass with Vera starring as Eve.

Costumed in trim black pants, a starched white shirt with the sleeves rolled up *comme ça,* a striped bib apron tied around her enviably slim waist, bright red gardening gloves that matched her lipstick, large diamond stud earrings, and a smile that radiated complete self-assurance, she promised her followers that if they did as she said, they would be rewarded with herbs as fragrant and succulent as those in the planters on the table before her.

Enid was in overalls, a grimy T-shirt, and sneakers. Her herbs looked fine. She was a disaster.

Tim didn't understand why she insisted upon trying to be a Vera Hart clone. It was never going to happen. Then again, Enid was never happy with things — or people — as they really were. He was the prime example of that.

"I thought we were having a family dinner."

Enid shushed him.

"I drove down here because you said we were having dinner."

"Quiet. Vera's not finished."

He wanted to torment her about Vera Hart's imminent demise, but it wasn't worth the effort. Soon enough Enid would have to deal with the fall of her idol. He headed for the nearest exit, escaping the kitchen and the harridan who lived there.

When Tim entered the living room, Dolph Polatchek was in his usual place — parked in front of the TV in his beige corduroy recliner from the Hart Home Line Collection. His eyes were glued to the screen and his mouth drooped in a hangdog expression. Tim couldn't remember the last time his father had laughed.

Dolph was a tall, lanky man with large bug eyes and a thinning pate who looked as if the world beat him up every single day. From personal experience Tim knew it wasn't the world that abused Dolph, it was Enid. He often wondered whether Dolph and Enid had ever been in love or if they'd married because it was what people did and they happened to cross paths at a time when each was getting desperate.

He remembered discussing this once with a friend whose parents had divorced when she was young. She said that as much as her parents fought, their passion for each other was evident. There was no passion between Dolph and Enid. Nor was there any intellectual camaraderie or common interests or complementary traits. They lived in the same house, shared a child, an income, and the meager emotional existence that passed for a life.

Tim found them pathetic. Worse, they were without any sense of self-awareness. They actually had the nerve to wonder why he'd never married.

"Hey, Dad," he said, plopping down on the beige/burgundy/forest green striped couch from the Hart Home Line Collection. "What's happening?"

"I saw your name in the newspaper." Dolph handed his son the *New York Times*. It was folded so that the article about Craig Hemminger's dismissal was front and center.

Tim took it and glanced at the paragraph Dolph had highlighted:

Released along with Chief Financial Officer Craig Hemminger was the entire upper tier of the Financial Division: Franklin Flintoff, Robert Crimmins, Paul Halliday and Ron Grossman, all of whom could be charged with criminal fraud. Also fired was Tripp Runyon, Vice President in charge of Distribution; Susan Peckany, Chief Information Officer; and Roger Kirschenbaum, Assistant Controller. It is presumed that all of these company officers, as well as Harvey

Anikstein and Tim Polatchek, lower ech- elon members of the Financial Division, will be brought into federal court to testify in the government probe into improperly inflated profits. Mr. Runyon is the soon- to-be-ex-husband of HLI COO Greta Hart.

"That's why I came out to the house today," Tim said, returning the paper to his father. "I would've been here sooner, but needless to say, a lot's going on."

Dolph nodded dully.

"When it all shakes out, they're going to have to restaff," Tim said. "I'm going to get you a job, Dad. A good job."

Dolph nodded again, clearly unimpressed with Tim's bravado and unconvinced about his ability to follow through.

Dolph had been fired from Arthur Anderson during that company's purge in the wake of the Enron and WorldCom scandals. Tim had been outraged by Dolph's dismissal. The man had been a loyal employee for over twenty years. His work had been top drawer, without so much as a hint of impropriety, yet when Enron fell and the head honchos at Anderson had been criticized for their colossal failures, men like Dolph were tossed. He'd been out of work for months and had no job prospects on the horizon; his association with Anderson had branded him a pariah.

"I can't believe the feds are really going after Vera Hart," Dolph said, ending any further conversation on his possible employment. "It's kind of unseemly."

Dolph was a traditionalist, so the notion of ganging up on a woman didn't sit well with him. Also, there were men out there who had done much worse and should be going to jail, but seemed to be getting a pass. That irritated his sense of fairness.

Tim didn't care about any of that. Man. Woman. Dog. Sheep. Life wasn't fair. That was a given.

"They should go after her," he groused. "She's no different from those other losers. They all have these big ideas that are going to change the world and make them a bundle of money, but either they don't know how to get the job done or are too squeamish to get their hands dirty. So what do they do? They get someone to do it for them. If it works, they're geniuses. If it doesn't, you're the goat. Hart's no different." He shook his head and ground his teeth in disgust. "Has there been anything on the news about it?"

"She was swamped by reporters as she

left the office." Dolph turned to his son. "She says she's innocent."

"Yeah, and I'll bet she's a virgin too."

"If she's guilty, she should own up to what she did," Dolph said, referring to Vera as well as the higher-ups at Anderson who fired him.

"Little chance of that. She'll do what she always does, she'll blame someone else. Who knows, maybe she'll get desperate and point her finger at me. After all, I'm usually the one people blame when things go wrong." His lips pursed, then relaxed and pursed again, like a fish trolling for food.

"They're not going to come after you, son. You're a small cog in a very big machine."

Tim's pale complexion flushed red with indignation. He'd been considered a small cog his whole life and he hated it. Just once he'd like the world to acknowledge his contributions. Just once.

He was about to object to Dolph's characterization of him when Vera Hart appeared on the screen. She was leaving HLI headquarters in the company of an entourage of bodyguards. Dozens of reporters accosted her, swarming around her, shoving microphones at her face, and shouting questions at her.

"Vera, were your books cooked?"

"Three of your former financial officers intend to plead guilty. Do you?"

"Is Hemminger taking the fall for you?"

"Instead of hiring a skin care guru, shouldn't you have hired a lawyer?"

"Did you cheat your stockholders?"

Vera conferred with a preppy-looking man who looked vaguely familiar to Tim, then turned to the cameras.

"You were given a press release on the Hart Line's newest project. As for your other questions I'm sorry, but I have nothing to say at the present time."

Preppy draped an arm around her shoulders and escorted her toward a waiting car. As the door to the limousine opened, the camera caught another familiar face.

Martie was jolted out of a deep sleep by the sharp jangling of the telephone. Her heart pounded as she groped for the receiver and brought it to her ear. Middle-of-the-night calls rarely brought good news.

"Hello."

No one answered.

She opened her eyes and gazed into the darkness.

"Hello."

No response.

She sat up and leaned against the head-board. She was tired and getting angry.

"Who is this?"

Silence.

Her eyes had adjusted to the darkness, so she searched her bedroom, as if the phantom caller had an ally hidden in the shadows.

"You awakened me for a reason. Now spit it out or hang up."

A click was followed by a dial tone.

Whoever it was had stayed on too long for it to be an accidental wrong number. Either it was some freak getting his kicks by making crank calls at three in the morning or she was the intended receiver of this call. Her gut said it was the latter.

She stared at the phone, daring it to ring again.

When it didn't, she dialed *69.

This feature cannot be activated because the number of your last incoming call was outside the cross-calling area.

That could mean it was a cell phone or an unlisted number or a pay phone in another city. No help there.

If this late-night roust was meant to frighten her, it didn't. It aroused her curiosity. It annoyed her. And, considering the threats against Vera, it did raise a red flag, but she wasn't about to alter her schedule or waste her time on senseless security procedures.

Whoever had placed this call had wasted his time. Martie Phelps didn't scare easily.

Chapter 9

The headlines screamed: HLI MONEY CHIEF OUT; HART LINE FLAT LINES; CFO HEMMINGER HART-LESS. One article after another detailed the government's accusations, HLI's denials, and the ouster of Craig Hemminger.

"He's out to ruin us," Greta said, storming into Vera's office waving the *Wall Street Journal*. "That bastard's promising proof of your knowledge of all his wrongdoings."

"He couldn't have any proof," Vera said confidently. "I never told him to play with the figures."

"He claims he has tapes."

"He can claim he has the Ten Commandments. I never directed him to do anything that could even remotely be described as criminal."

Vera's self-assurance grated.

"What if the tapes are doctored?" Greta insisted. "You could have said things that when edited sound incriminating, or things that on the face of it are nothing but could be twisted and interpreted as having criminal intent. You know how venal prosecutors can be."

"Speaking of prosecutors," Vera said, smoothly segueing into something else, "how are things between you and Bryan?"

It had been almost a week since the drama at the cottage. Greta and Bryan had been playing phone tag; she was convinced he was deliberately calling her back when he knew she wasn't available.

"Strained. That's how things are, thanks to you."

"I can't even begin to imagine why you would think I'm responsible for whatever has come between you and your boyfriend."

"Don't play innocent with me. You knew they had a relationship. Did you think it would be fun to throw us all in a room and shake us up and see what happened?"

Vera dismissed her older daughter's insinuations with a la-di-da wave of the hand.

"Don't be so paranoid, darling."

Greta's already attenuated face grew even narrower as she sucked in her cheeks and gritted her teeth. "Does my happiness disturb you that much?"

"Not everything is about you, Greta," Vera said quietly.

Greta looked at her quizzically.

"I hired Martie because I needed her on staff."

"Since when? You never *needed* Martie."

Vera hadn't wanted to share the information about Valentine Red with Greta, but Bryan had insisted. If someone was gunning for Vera, he might have Greta in his sights as well.

"Since I received a phone call from Detective Tony Borzone."

She told Greta about the woman in Central Park and the coroner's conclusion about cause of death. Greta was appropriately astonished.

"Martie's primary function is to detect how many lots might have been compromised, whether it was done at one or several facilities, and, if possible, to stop any other poisoned products from being shipped. We can't let this get out."

"Are the police keeping a lid on the coroner's report?"

"For now." Her expression was grim. "They're not about to alarm the public if the problem is contained."

"Wouldn't it have been more efficient to get a forensic chemist from the NYPD?

With the chemical analysis and detective work being done by the same person at the same time, the problem is solved, the culprit is arrested, and our exposure is limited."

"Perhaps, but we're under a microscope. The press would have sniffed out a cop in an instant. Martie was a recipient of the Hart Foundation science award. It makes sense to hire her and wonderful press because it appears as if we're moving forward despite the government's efforts to drag us down."

"She saves the day again," Greta mumbled.

Vera asked, "What did you say?" but Greta was gone.

She'd heard enough.

Three hours later, Vera was circumnavigating her office with a determined gait. She'd just received word from the FDA that although they hadn't found anything at the Little Rock factory, since Shreveport also produced products for the Hart Hair Line they were going to inspect that plant as well before issuing their final report.

"This is harassment, pure and simple," she said to Martie, Greta, and Bryan, all of whom had been summoned to discuss strategy. "Either a competitor did this because they're about to launch a new product or it's part of some grand conspiracy to take over HLI. Damn whoever's behind this!"

While Vera's anger created a fiery nimbus around her, the atmosphere surrounding Greta and Martie was positively arctic. The sisters, operating under the delusion that the HLI offices were large enough for them to function on separate tracks, had managed to avoid each other for nearly a week. This morning those tracks crossed and neither was happy about it.

Vera paused at her desk just long enough to issue an exasperated sigh.

"If this Valentine matter hits the papers it could ruin us. Of course, that's what someone would want if they were plotting a takeover, isn't it?"

"The FDA inspections have nothing to do with Valentine." Bryan chose his words carefully. He had swept Vera's office for bugs, but the latest fiber-optic devices were so small they were almost invisible. He would have preferred no conversation about Valentine Red, but since that was unlikely he had advised Vera to keep any conversation about it vague. "One is hair, one is lips."

"They appear to be separate incidents, but I'm beginning to think the person behind the FDA intrusion and the Valentine mishap are one and the same."

Vera was obsessed with the notion of someone working in the shadows to wrest control of her company.

"The best way to bring down a behemoth is to attack its soft spot. Our soft spot is consumer confidence, and whoever's behind this harassment knows that. I wouldn't be surprised if he's the same one who blew the whistle on us to the government!"

"And the reason we've had such a rainy spring," Greta injected sarcastically.

"Vera's point is well taken," Bryan said. "If HLI's competitors are behind the inspections, they're going to spill the fact of them to the press. Otherwise, why bother getting the FDA involved in the first place?"

Greta knew she shouldn't take his comments personally, but every word out of Bryan's mouth felt like a betrayal.

"They *bother* because inspections slow up production," she snapped. "They *bother* because the industry is small enough for retailers to get wind of a problem and cut their orders. They *bother* because it's the way the game is played. If you knew anything about the cosmetics business, you would know that."

Bryan's composure wasn't altered by her verbal fusillade. Neither was his opinion.

"That may be true, but what I do know about are conspiracies. These inspections reek of ulterior motives, which means they might well have been step one in a long-range plan. Step two would be to get the feds involved. And step three would be a press leak about Valentine Red."

"You're seeing a bogeyman behind every door and curtain," Greta said, dismissing his theory with a cluck of her tongue. "You're not in the DA's office anymore, Bryan. Stop building a case."

"Even if these incidents are part of a grand scheme," Martie said, jumping into the fray, "we can't rely on a one-size-fits-all solution. We have to approach them as separate issues and prioritize them."

"Another one who's been in the business for an hour and a half and thinks she knows everything. Spare me!"

"You don't have to be in the business for twenty years to know that finding a tainted vat of lipstick takes precedence over everything else," Martie said. "To me it's a no-brainer."

Greta didn't know whether to be impressed or dismayed by Martie's sangfroid, but it appeared as if GI Jane had come to work with her boots on.

"Clearly you have a solution to all our woes." Greta's tone was mocking, her expression one of faux awe. "I'm breathless with anticipation."

"Whether there's one enemy out there or several," Martie said, doing her best to remain respectful and straightforward, "HLI is being attacked on several fronts. Since the best defense is a good offense, we should counter with something that will neutralize their efforts in the short run while we create a strategy to devastate them in the long run."

Vera halted her peregrination, parked herself in a corner, and quietly observed the exchange between her daughters. She was fascinated, as was Bryan.

Greta was aware of their enthrallment. And disturbed by it.

Martie was completely focused on the matter at hand. "We need to get to the press first and use it to our advantage."

"To say what? We didn't do whatever it is you think we did?"

"It's not what we say, it's what we do. The best way to shore up public confidence is for us to appear confident."

Greta folded her arms across her chest in a physical display of doubtfulness.

"News of a revolutionary skin care line will bump stories of minor FDA inspections to the back page of a newspaper every time," Martie said, turning away from Greta so she could address Vera. "I suggest you make an announcement about my joining the company."

"Now I get it," Greta said. "This whole harangue is about heralding your debut."

Martie ignored her. "The announcement does two things: It allows me to go into the factory sooner rather than later and, as you said before, delivers the message that HLI is alive and well and open for business."

Vera said nothing.

Greta, who realized her churlish hostility was working against her, softened her rhetoric slightly.

"The FDA is inspecting our factories and the feds are inspecting our books. At the same time, the NYPD is investigating a murder involving one of our products. This is hardly the time to trumpet the arrival of a skin care savior."

Bryan cringed. If there was a listening device, whoever was at the other end had hit pay dirt. A few minutes before, Martie mentioned a tainted vat of lipstick. Now Greta tied a Hart Line product to a murder. Not good.

"How about if I go to New Jersey without trumpets?" Martie had had a stomachful of Greta's insults. "What if I just go in quietly, introduce myself, and do what has to be done?"

Before Vera could respond, Bryan said, "The less publicity about anything chemical at this particular juncture, the better, but Martie needs to test the kettles as soon as possible. Also, I would recommend an increase in security, both personally and for the factories that appear most vulnerable."

He figured that if there was an invisible listener, mentioning hired guns couldn't hurt.

"We already have a security firm on retainer," Greta said. "Let's not turn these offices into Guantanamo Bay."

Bryan wished she wouldn't be so negative about everything, but he supposed she was still reacting to being blindsided that day at the cottage. And he'd been avoiding her.

"I'm not talking about uniformed guards," he said patiently. "I'm talking about plainclothes bodyguards. The two of

227

you," he said looking from Greta to Vera, "definitely need extra protection. Since Martie is going to be delving into some sensitive areas, she should also be covered."

He deliberately skirted the issue of Martie being a family member. The last thing he wanted to do was give a potential killer another target. Or two: There was Lili to consider. "If you would like, I have the names of some policemen who moonlight as personal bodyguards."

Vera tapped her lips with her finger as she considered her options. "I have someone I can call," she said.

"Is it someone you can trust?" Bryan wanted to know.

"With my life," she said.

General Security was headquartered in one of the glass towers that banked upper Sixth Avenue. Since most of General Security's clients craved anonymity, there was no name on the thick mahogany doors, simply three gold stars. The offices were spare but well designed, with lots of leather and wood and other masculine appointments.

One of the more appealing features was the private after-hours elevator that was made available to clients who didn't wish to mingle with the public or feared that the daytime crowds around Rockefeller Center could provide easy cover to a stalker. To take advantage of this service one had to call in advance and book a reservation on the elevator. Now and then exceptions were made.

Vera Hart was one of those exceptions. She had called late that afternoon.

As the doors opened, the guard who met her in the lobby and escorted her into the elevator stepped aside so she could exit. Hugh Phelps greeted her, then immediately hustled her into the office. The doors automatically locked behind them.

"Well," Vera said, "that's efficient."

Hugh smiled. "And effective. Some of our clients have been known to grow tails. We like to cut them off before they can do anyone any harm."

Vera laughed and followed him through another set of quick-lock doors down a long corridor with plush carpeting and up-holstered walls that Vera guessed were meant to absorb sound. At the end of that hallway was Hugh's office, a spacious corner with magnificent views of the tree-tops of Central Park on one side and the lights of midtown Manhattan on the other.

A large mahogany desk sat catercornered between the walls of glass, accessorized with just the basics: telephone, pens, pads, and a high-back black leather chair; no computer, no photographs. On the short wall that extended from the doorway to the windows there was a large recessed square divided into cubes that housed artifacts Hugh had collected at his various postings. Vera noted one or two that had been in their Roxbury home.

The carpeting was flat and dusky, intricately patterned in tones of wet bark and deep olive that complemented the autumn brown fabric that covered the walls. The lighting was subtle. And the furnishings were thick and hearty, made of soft leather and rich wood, making it look more like a gentleman's study than the office of a war-hardened general. The only sign of Hugh's past employ was a collection of fanciful scabbards and sheathings — some metal, some leather, some cloth — artfully arranged over one of the couches. Directly opposite, on the largest wall, were several large wenge panels, behind which Vera guessed was a television, a bar, and an assortment of technical gizmos.

There were no visible blinds on the windows, which struck Vera as curious.

Hugh, intuiting her question, said, "There are electric shades to block out the sun and bulletproof glass to repel sharp-shooters."

He offered her a seat on one of two umber brown leather divans.

"Can I get you something to drink? Some wine, perhaps?"

"That would be nice."

Hugh approached one of the lower panels and pressed a button that slid open a cabinet door, revealing a small wine re-frigerator. He selected a bottle of Gavignano, then closed that door and opened another, behind which was a fully stocked bar. As he uncorked the wine, Vera studied him.

He looked wonderful in his charcoal gray suit, white shirt, and steel gray tie. His hair, just a shade longer than army-short, was thick silver shot with white. His skin, which used to be on the pale side, was tanner now and slightly creased, probably from all those years he spent outdoors. Age hadn't hurt him. If anything, maturity be-came him, perhaps because along with it came a solidity born of self-assurance. Hugh had always been strong and sure, but now he seemed even more so.

Vera wondered if it was because he had

managed to translate his impressive military success into an equally successful civilian enterprise. General Security was one of the premier names in global security. With offices in Europe and New York, they provided protective services, security consulting and engineering, background screening, and intelligence investigation services. They weren't as large or as famous as Kroll, but they were gaining.

Vera found his ambition sexy. During their first incarnation she was the driven one. She was the one who insisted that nothing was more important than fame and adulation and the material trappings that came with celebrity. Hugh had his own personal goals, but they were about rank, not riches. At the time, Vera didn't put stars and clusters and scrambled eggs in the same category as diamonds and caviar and multiple mansions. She was myopic then, defining success purely in Hollywood terms. It was only after Hollywood dumped her and she had embarked on a new career that she came to recognize that achievement was different than stardom and that excellence resulted from real, sustained effort.

"This is very impressive, Hugh," she said, taking the wine glass from him and tipping it toward him in a quasi-toast.

He bowed his head in acknowledgment. "Thank you. We have a good team here."

He sat down, took a sip of his wine, then put the glass on the wooden cocktail table and faced his former wife.

"What's up?"

"I need you," she said.

He smiled briefly at the obvious double entendre.

"Normally I'd be flattered, but judging by the tone in your voice when you called, your need is professional, correct?"

"My life's been threatened," she said bluntly. "It's been suggested that who-ever's looking to hurt me might try to do that by inflicting harm on Greta. If it be-comes known that Martie and Lili are re-lated to me, they could be at risk as well. The four of us need protection and you're the only one I would trust with that assignment."

Hugh's forehead crinkled and his lips formed a tight line. He was concerned, as she knew he would be.

She opened her Hermès bag and ex-tracted an envelope containing printouts of the threatening e-mails. Then she reached into a canvas tote and placed the shoebox, the grenade, and the accompanying note on the cocktail table. All three items had been bagged in plastic.

Hugh read the notes, put on a pair of latex gloves he pulled from his pocket, and examined the grenade. It contained a reduced charge, which meant it was used as a practice grenade during military training. There was no fuse, which told him the sender meant to terrorize Vera, not to harm her. At least not then.

"What else?"

"Someone has tainted one of our lipsticks with mercuric chloride. It was used in the commission of a brutal crime and was declared the murder weapon by the coroner's office." Vera's expression was pained. "I don't know which factory has the poisoned kettle, how many batches of this lethal lipstick were shipped, and whether or not any other Hart Line product has been compromised."

She knitted her fingers together and stared at her hands while she gathered herself. Hugh waited. When she was ready, she looked at him.

"Unless you've been living in a cave, you must know I'm being hounded by the government."

"I've read the newspapers."

"This investigation is serious," she continued. "I'm not minimizing its impact on our bottom line or my personal reputation, but that pales in comparison to what will happen if it ever gets out that a woman died from a poisoned tube of Valentine Red."

Hugh pursed his lips and bobbed his head as he digested this information. "Have you tested the kettles?"

"I have a highly qualified chemist going in tomorrow," she said. "Dr. Marta Phelps."

He looked surprised. She couldn't decide whether she was disappointed that Martie hadn't told him of her new situation or was delighted to be able to give him the news herself.

"Just as I hired her to head up our skin care line, this happened."

"What a lucky coincidence," Hugh said, tiptoeing along until he knew whether the field Vera had led him into was filled with tulips or land mines.

"I prefer to think of it as a stroke of fate."

Hugh let that go. He sensed that Vera would have liked him to ask her more about her courtship of Martie, but this wasn't the time.

"I take it the police are cooperating."

She nodded. "They don't want to cause a panic, so they're giving us time to find the site and clean it up before anything else happens."

"How many are on the team going in with Martie?"

"She felt she would be less conspicuous if she went in alone."

Hugh shook his head. "Uh-uh. She needs backup."

"I thought so too," she said. "Fortunately, Bryan Chalmers, a former ADA, also works for me now. He served in the military, worked for the FBI, and has generously offered to provide that backup."

Vera observed Hugh's reaction to hearing Bryan's name. She didn't know whether the two men had known each other and, if they had, whether or not they had liked each other. Hugh's empty expression did little to clear things up for her.

"Mr. Chalmers's face is too well known for him to be effective. I have someone else in mind."

"Whatever you say. You're the expert."

In that small back room in one's brain where extraneous thought lived while the front room was concentrating on something else, Hugh found those words amusing. In the eleven years they were married, he didn't think Vera ever uttered the words, "Whatever you say." She certainly never called him an "expert" on anything.

"Has Greta received any outright threats?" he said, returning to the subject at hand.

"None that I know of."

"And Martie?"

"Most people aren't aware that Martie is my daughter." She waited for him to make some snide comment. He didn't.

"It's probably best to keep it that way."

"I agree," she said, piqued.

It bothered Vera that Hugh was *so* businesslike. She respected his diligence, but they used to be quite passionate about each other. It had been years, but still. Didn't he feel any connection? Wasn't he curious about why she came to him and not another security firm?

He reached behind him and took a pad off a shelf that was hidden behind the couch. He retrieved a pen from the inside pocket of his suit jacket.

"I'm going to need the names of anyone you would classify as an enemy."

"All of my competitors," she said with haughty conviction. "They're jealous and would like nothing more than to either ruin me or take over my company and profit from my hard work."

Hugh understood her umbrage, but had no time to salve her ego.

"Enemies, Vera. We're looking for someone with a serious grudge, someone who might want to kill you, not someone who wants to wave P&L statements at twenty paces."

She wanted to tell him that if someone did poach her company it might kill her, but he probably knew that.

"Are you aware of any ex-employees who left Hart Line and went to work for the competition?"

"None that hate me to the extreme," she said.

"Get me the names of those who've been fired in the last five years. We'll run a check here."

Vera said that she would.

"How about budding entrepreneurs who came to you with deals that you turned down? Or money sources that weren't satisfied with their fees? Or licensees who felt they were getting the short end of the stick?"

She sighed and shook her head. "Too many to mention."

Hugh drummed the pad with his pen,

thinking of other avenues to pursue. Then he remembered who his potential client was.

"How about rejected suitors?" he said.

Vera offered a coy smile. "Also too many to mention."

That wasn't true. She had a small, special list of men whom she had spurned. The thought that perhaps one of them might be gunning for her caused her to squirm in her seat. Hugh noticed.

"Not all men go quietly," he said. "I know you've had your share of romances, Vera. Most of them have been chronicled in the media. I need to know which ones ended badly."

"All romances that end, end badly, wouldn't you say?"

When he refused to pick up on that, she swallowed a sip of wine along with the urge to clarify that the numerous relationships that were chronicled in the media were affairs, not romances. She'd only had one of those. And they hadn't detailed the affairs that ended really badly because those had remained private. The only people who knew about them were Vera, the men with whom she was involved, and their wives.

Hugh watched her hide behind her wine glass and debated how hard to press the issue. Knowing Vera, she would dance around that question no matter how many times and in how many different ways he asked it, so he opted to move on. He just hoped her pride wasn't protecting a potential killer.

"There is something else," she said, shifting the focus of their conversation. "Someone has been goading the FDA into inspecting our factories. Is it possible that it's the same person who sent the e-mails and sold me out to the government?"

"Of course it's possible."

Hugh wasn't certain it was likely, however. Blowing the whistle about accounting fraud and tweaking another government department weren't acts of violence. They were actions designed to disrupt the conduct of business, perhaps permanently, but they were not precursors to murder. A shoebox with a grenade and a series of threats, however, had nothing to do with business and everything to do with hate. And there was the matter of the poisoned lipstick. Where did that fit in all of this?

"You don't think it's probable, though, do you?"

Hugh leaned forward, rested his arms on his thighs, and steepled his fingers. Vera sensed he was measuring his words, assessing how much he could tell her without frightening her to death.

"In my opinion, there are several forces at work here and each has to be considered as a separate battle. You have to look at what was done and then think about why someone might have wanted to do that. In other words: What was the cause of the action and what is the intended effect?"

Martie and Bryan said pretty much the same thing, thought Vera.

"Someone poisoned one of your lipsticks. Was that done to ruin your business? Or, given that the name of the lipstick was Valentine, was someone indulging a homicidal fantasy?

"Someone snitched to the government about financial wrongdoings at HLI. Did he do that to ruin your business, take over your business, or simply to extract revenge on you for something personal?

"Someone sent you a series of menacing e-mails. Then you received a more substantial threat in the form of a grenade. There's no mystery here. That person means to do you physical harm. Again, the question is why."

He looked at Vera, his sky blue eyes fixed on hers. "Get rid of your ego and whatever other bullshit you're holding on to and give me a complete list of possible enemies."

She looked away, her lips tight.

"You're in real danger, Vera. Isn't that why you came to me?"

"Yes," she said, her voice small.

"Well then, don't handcuff me. Either give me what I need to protect you or take your business elsewhere."

That threw her, but not for long.

"What about the girls? Are you willing to put them into someone else's hands?"

"You're their mother. Are you willing to accept responsibility for what happens to them or are they on their own?"

That comment was so heavily layered it landed between them with a thud.

"Believe it or not I came to you because of them, not because of me. In spite of what you think, I don't want any harm to come to our daughters. And while I just met Lili, I care very much about her safety." She examined the pleat in her trousers, then addressed Hugh again. "I'll provide you with a list, but I need something from you."

Hugh encouraged her to continue.

"I want you to work with Bryan Chalmers on this."

"Why?"

There was no mistaking the hostile overtones in his response. Vera's question about how Hugh felt about Bryan Chalmers had been answered.

"Because he's smart and well trained and committed to doing the right thing. And because he cares about them. He and Martie were involved years ago, as I'm sure you know. And recently he and Greta had a relationship, which may or may not be ongoing. He has an emotional interest in both, which under these circumstances is a very good thing."

Hugh crinkled his forehead and tilted his head, eyeing her quizzically. "What are you up to, Vera?"

"I don't know what you mean."

"You have nothing to do with Martie for twenty years and suddenly she's given an award, put in charge of one of your divisions, and is given the lead horse on a posse meant to save you and your company from a public lynching.

"You didn't care enough to come see Lili when she was born or when her father died, but now you're lavishing her with attention and grandmotherly concern? What's wrong with this picture!"

"Nothing is wrong with that picture. What's wrong is the judgment in the eyes of the beholder," she shot back. "Did it ever occur to you that I might regret the distance between Martie and me and when her name was nominated for the award I decided to take advantage of the opportunity?

"Did you ever think it might have been nice if Martie or you called to tell me about Lili's birth, or better yet invited me to come meet her?

"As for being there when Martie's husband died, again, did you call to tell me? Did Martie? Did anyone? No. I'm many things, Hugh, but clairvoyant isn't one of them."

"Fair enough." He paused. He knew he should end the conversation here, but he couldn't help himself. "Why now? Why does it matter now?"

"Because now life is finite."

Her answer was so simple and spontaneous Hugh had to believe it was the truth. But what did that mean? Was she ill?

The telephone rang. He rose and went to his desk.

"Hugh Phelps." As he listened to the caller, his face paled. "I'll be right there."

He replaced the phone in its caddy and turned to Vera.

"I have to go. Lili's been rushed to the hospital."

Vera's heart started to pound like a jackhammer inside her chest. "What happened?"

"Valentine Red."

Chapter 10

Not much terrified Martie, but seeing her child lying so small and still in that hospital bed did. Lili's color was chalk. Her body, depleted by vomiting and diarrhea, appeared frail and thin. Above her head, machines monitored her heart rate and blood pressure. Two plastic bags dangled from metal trolleys, their fluids dripping into narrow tubes that converged into a single passageway into Lili's tiny arm.

When Martie arrived, the head of the emergency team, aware that he was dealing with a fellow physician, had explained the protocol in stark medical terms. After Lili had been brought in, the ER team immediately cleansed her stomach with a gastric lavage and gave her fluids to restore those she had lost. Then they hooked her up to an antidotal IV, which introduced a chelating agent into Lili's system in the hopes of removing the mercury from her bloodstream. The quicker the poison was eliminated, the better her chances of avoiding renal failure. He apprised Martie of the various risks as well as whatever options were available in case this procedure proved ineffective.

Martie couldn't process any of it because she wasn't listening as a doctor. She heard what he said through the filter of motherhood and it paralyzed her. It was as if some malevolent force had invaded her body and emptied it of all its vital organs; she felt that helpless. She couldn't breathe. She couldn't think. She couldn't speak. She could barely stand. All she could do was hold on to the bedrails and plead with God not to take her daughter from her.

Martie held Lili's hand and stared at her, trying to will her well. Tears filled her eyes. She felt so responsible for this it was almost unbearable. The minute she heard about that woman in the park she should have checked the contents of the package Vera gave to Lili. She should have taken the lipstick away. How could she have been so negligent? So careless?

She wiped her eyes, put down the rail, and lay her head down on the bed, her hand still clasped around Lili's.

Due to the din created by emergency room traffic, Martie never heard her parents enter the bay where she and Lili were. The

247

first she knew anyone was there was when she felt her father's hand on her back. She looked up, saw him, and wept.

"Tell me what happened," he said as she stood and he sheltered her in his embrace.

Martie wiped her eyes and told him what Soledad, Lili's nanny, had told her.

"Lili had a friend over. After she left, Lili was playing, and suddenly it was as if her little body exploded. She was throwing up and having diarrhea at almost the same time. The poor thing was so frightened she just stood in her room and screamed. Soledad rushed her to the bathroom and helped her as best she could. When Lili finally stopped vomiting, Soledad gave her water and felt her forehead to see if she had the flu. Since her forehead was cold, Soledad assumed it was something else and beyond her control. She called 911 and then called me."

Hugh reached into a pocket, took out a handkerchief, and wiped his daughter's eyes. His arm remained tightly around her. His eyes were glued to Lili.

"What did the doctors say?"

"It's mercuric chloride. She had put on so much of that damn lipstick that she had practically eaten the whole thing."

Behind her, a soft gasp told Martie

someone else was in the room. When she turned and saw Vera, she was shocked. Also surprising was the horrified look on Vera's face. The sight of Lili in that bed, multiplied by the thought that one of her products had put her there, had bleached out every last ounce of color.

"I'm so sorry," she said. "I had no idea."

Martie couldn't bring herself to forgive Vera that easily. She didn't know whether it was because of Lili or because of all the things Martie believed Vera should have felt sorry for over the years, but her inability to respond was visceral. She turned away from Vera and looked at Hugh for an explanation as to Vera's presence.

"Vera came to see me about having General Security provide a protection detail. She was in my office when you called."

"Is she going to be all right?" Vera asked.

Martie's expression remained hard. "I don't know. There might be kidney damage."

Vera heard the unspoken accusation. Having neither a retort nor a salve nor any right to remain in that room, she turned to leave.

Martie made no attempt to stop her.

Lili wasn't assigned a room until nine o'clock. Once she was comfortable and

Martie was settled, Hugh went home, albeit reluctantly.

Soledad had returned to Martie's apartment, packed a few essentials, and brought them back to the hospital. At Martie's request she also bagged everything that had been in the package Vera had given Lili.

At ten o'clock, Bryan arrived. Martie hadn't wanted to involve him in something so personal, but Lili's health took precedence over her desire to maintain an emotional distance. She had called him on his cell, told him what had happened, and asked if he could take everything to the NYPD lab and have it analyzed; she needed to know if this was from the same batch that killed that woman.

"How is she?" Bryan said, closing the door behind him.

Martie rose from the other bed where she had been trying to read. She appeared haggard. "Resting. They're still giving her fluids and an antidote, but they're optimistic that there wasn't any permanent damage."

Bryan approached Lili's bed. His forehead was pleated with concern. He didn't like visiting children in the hospital. He had five nieces and nephews and only once did he have to do that. One of his nephews had suffered a ruptured appendix. Connor was eight years old and Bryan's buddy. Seeing that little guy so sick had been tough. Seeing Lili this way wasn't easy.

Bryan eyed the sleeping child. Even ill, she was adorable.

"Her color looks good," he said. "Almost normal."

Martie nodded and sighed, her breath trembling as it left her mouth. "This afternoon she was beyond pale."

Bryan turned to Martie. "How are you doing?"

Martie shrugged and offered a wan smile. "As well as can be expected."

Just then she noticed that Bryan was wearing a suit and didn't have a briefcase with him.

"Did I interrupt your evening?" she said, guessing that she had. "I'm so sorry. I had no idea, I just called because you were involved with this Valentine thing and I thought —"

"Stop." Bryan raised his hand to silence her. "It's okay. This is more important." He touched the sheet on Lili's bed, almost protectively. "Now tell me what happened."

She repeated what she'd told Hugh earlier that day. When she was finished she handed

Bryan the plastic bag Soledad had brought.

"I've already notified the detective on the Central Park case," Bryan said. "His name is Tony Borzone and aside from being a great cop he's a good friend. He'll have this looked at first thing in the morning."

"Thanks."

Lili stirred. Martie and Bryan looked to see if they'd awakened her. She snuffled a bit, shifted slightly as if trying to find a more comfortable position, then fell back to sleep.

Bryan's brown eyes grew dark and narrow. "We'll get this guy, Martie. If I have to hunt him down personally, I promise you we'll get him."

His jaw was clenched and his voice reverberated with the same fervid determination she'd noticed every other time they had discussed the Valentine murder.

"Don't get me wrong, Bryan, I'm grateful for your resolve and I don't mean to pry, but even before Lili you were in serious vigilante mode. Do you have some connection to this Valentine thing I don't know about?"

He didn't answer, which was answer enough.

"I take it it's something personal."

"Very, but I'd rather not discuss it here." He looked over at Lili.

Martie nodded. Whatever it was, it could wait.

"I gave you whatever was in the goody bag. Could your friend Tony have the other products tested as well? It looks to me as if Lili was so busy playing with the lipstick and the blush that she never opened the other items, but I don't want to take a chance. For all we know, we have more than one poisonous cosmetic on our hands."

"I'll take care of it."

"Mr. Chalmers."

Lili's voice was weak, but trilled with delight.

Bryan walked over and grinned at her. "In person."

"Did you come to see me?"

"I did. How're you feeling?"

She pursed her lips. "Not so good."

"Yeah. That's what Mom said."

"My stomach was sick so they attached my dinner to my arm." With her free hand she pointed to the IV setup. "Not too tasty."

"Saves wear and tear on your teeth," he quipped. Lili rewarded him with a giggle.

"Once your stomach's had a chance to rest you'll be back to all your favorites. They'll probably tell you to take it slowly, though. No Whoppers or triple-scoop banana splits."

"And no more lipstick," she declared. "I'm never *ever* going to wear it again. It's yucky."

Martie looked skeptical.

"Never. Ever. Ever," Lili insisted.

"I'll tell you what," Bryan said. "Wait ten years and then see what you think."

Lili considered that. "Okay," she said. "Ten years. Then maybe."

A nurse came in to take Lili's temperature and other vitals. Bryan used her entrance to announce that it was time for him to go.

"Do you have to?"

"You and your mom need to rest, so yes, I have to."

"Will you come see me tomorrow?"

He glanced over at Martie to see if that was all right. A quick nod said that it was.

"I'll be here the minute they open the gates. How's that?"

"That's great," Lili enthused. "See you then."

Martie offered to show Bryan out while the nurse tended to Lili. In the hall, she hugged him.

"Thank you," she said.

"For what?"

"For making my daughter smile and for being her new best friend."

"She's easy to befriend, Martie. She's a terrific kid."

Martie's eyes welled and she found it hard to speak. Bryan put his hands on her arms and looked deep into those aquamarine pools.

"She's going to be fine," he said with quiet confidence. "And we're going to get the sick bastard who did this."

"I know." Her confidence level sounded shaky.

"Now you go get a good night's sleep. I'll be back in the morning after I finish up with Tony, okay?"

"Okay." Her voice was low and unsteady.

For Bryan it was a déjà vu moment. The last time Martie looked this vulnerable was just after she'd been rescued and brought back to base from Iraq. The memory stabbed him.

Surrendering to an impulse, he wrapped her in his arms and kissed her. Then, before either of them could comment, he left.

Delilah sounded so frantic, Martie ran down to the lobby to meet her. When she got there, Delilah was pacing, her pool blue eyes overflowing with tears.

"Soledad told me what happened to Lili. Please tell me she's going to be okay."

Martie should have expected this. Delilah had been at the apartment visiting Lili before all this happened. There was no way she wouldn't have felt responsible. No matter how remote, Delilah felt responsible for every negative happening short of an earthquake.

"The doctors say she'll be fine."

Delilah sniffled and took a deep breath, trying to get control over her emotions.

"When I left, she was okay." She seemed confused as to how things could be fine one minute and horrendous the next. "She was laughing and joking . . ."

"I know. Soledad said Lili had a great time with you. The stomach pains and the vomiting started later." Martie hoped to reassure Delilah. "What were you two playing?"

Delilah shrugged as if Martie should have known. "Makeup. It's Lili's favorite game." She laughed. "I'm lucky I didn't get arrested. She put so much eye makeup on me and teased my hair up so high I looked like a hooker."

Martie's eyebrows knitted. "How about

lipstick? Did you use the lipstick?"

"Uh-uh. Lili wouldn't share. She said the little tube was hers." Delilah flushed. "She gave me one of yours. I hope Chili wasn't your favorite, 'cause it is gone, honey. I mean totally!"

Martie smiled. She could just imagine what Delilah looked like when Lili got finished painting her.

"I'm not sure it was my best color, so don't worry about it."

"Was it something she ate?"

Before Martie could respond, Delilah answered her own question.

"Couldn't be. We had PB&J. Lili's not allergic to peanuts and as far as I know no one ever threw up from Skippy and Welch's grape jelly."

"It doesn't matter, Delilah. Lili's fine."

As they walked to the door, Martie asked Delilah about her new job.

She flushed. "Actually, I'm doing real well. I'm working the phones and filing. I'm even getting pretty good at the computer, thanks to my boss. She says I'm a quick learner."

Martie smiled. "This is good stuff, Delilah. Keep it up."

"I'm tryin'."

After Delilah left and Martie returned to

Lili's room, she realized that the other makeup hadn't been compromised. If it had been, Delilah's eyes would have been broken out or burned or something. They were fine. It was hard to label it good news, but it appeared that only the lipstick her daughter used had been poisoned.

Greta was waiting at Bryan's apartment when he got home. It was after midnight.

"I was beginning to think you'd been abducted by aliens," she said.

She'd made herself comfortable on his couch, jacket off, feet propped up. Diana Krall was singing in the background and a large brandy snifter sat on the table in front of her. It was half empty.

"Might I ask where you went?"

They were at La Golue in the middle of dinner when Martie called. Bryan had apologized profusely but told her he had an emergency. She refused to be ditched, so she asked for his key.

"There was another incident involving Valentine Red," he said.

Greta hadn't expected that.

"Did someone else die?"

"Fortunately, no, but it was close."

Greta didn't ask him the patient's name, for which he was grateful. On the taxi ride home from the police station he'd decided that despite the consanguine connection, he would respect Lili's privacy.

"Do you have any idea who's doing this?" Greta said. There was an edge to her voice.

"No. I have an early morning meeting with the detective who's handling the Central Park case. He's going to send the evidence from this victim to the lab to see if there's a connection."

Greta rose from the couch and slipped into her shoes. She smoothed down her skirt and fussed with her hair. Her movements were sharp, almost jerky.

"Speaking of labs, where the hell is the great Dr. Phelps?" Her voice rumbled with malicious sarcasm. "I thought she was supposed to go to the plants, ferret out the bad guys, and save the world from extinction."

Bryan detected a nervous tinge, but someone was out to destroy her family's business. Her credibility was on the line. It was hard to fault her for sounding anxious.

"She was supposed to start her inspections tomorrow." Whether she would or not, he didn't know.

Greta was pacing up and down the gallery that ran the length of the loft. Her high heels clickety-clacked against Bryan's hard-wood floors.

"She's not going to find anything, you know. It's simply a colossal waste of time. Anything that's been in the stores recently was produced months ago."

Bryan had raised that point with Martie, but she felt an inspection couldn't hurt. Even if they couldn't pin down precisely when it was done or where, they might be able to pick up a lead from one of the workers. Also, criminals were often careless.

"And what is your detective friend doing other than hanging around the station-house waiting for fresh victims?"

"Really, Greta." Patience had turned to exasperation. "Don't you think he would make an arrest if he could? He has an open homicide on his desk and a near-homicide in the hospital."

"And I have thousands of people who will lose their jobs if the Hart Line tanks. Everybody's got problems."

Bryan couldn't remember ever seeing Greta this tightly wound. His eyes caught sight of the brandy snifter. He wondered if it was the alcohol speaking.

"How about a cappuccino?" He started for the kitchen.

Her cell phone rang. Before answering, she checked the caller ID.

"I'm leaving now," she said to the person on the other end. To Bryan she said, "I have to go."

She retrieved her jacket and her purse and headed for the elevator. As she said good night her expression was hostile and mocking.

"Do let me know if either member of your crackerjack team comes up with anything."

"Sure thing." He gladly watched the doors close behind her.

He brought her brandy glass into the kitchen and thought about all that had happened this evening. For him, it had started and ended the same way: being with Greta and feeling uncomfortable.

He met her for dinner and almost immediately she initiated a discussion about the state of their relationship; he'd expected that to be on the agenda when he accepted her invitation. She wanted him to explain his sudden distance. He parried, using his new position as an excuse for his obvious distraction. Not only was he representing HLI in the government investigation, but also he'd become part of the crisis management team.

"Are you sorry you accepted Vera's offer?" Greta had wanted to know.

"No. Despite the long hours and the pressure, it's an incredible opportunity," he said.

That was the truth, but not all of it. While professionally this presented challenges few lawyers would turn down, personally it presented nothing but complications. If he was still in the DA's office he would simply break off his relationship with Greta as gallantly as he could, mourn the loss, and move on.

"Are you pulling away because we're now colleagues as well as lovers?"

"Our circumstances have changed," he admitted.

Greta continued to press. He continued to dodge. Then Martie interrupted them.

When he came home after being with Martie and Lili and found Greta ensconced on his couch, his reluctance to continue their dinnertime discussion became overwhelming. He didn't want to hurt Greta, but he didn't want to lie to her either. They were never going to be more than a passing affair because, bottom line, he didn't love her. And he'd known that for some time.

He shut out the lights and went to his

bedroom. As he always did when one of his relationships ended, he wondered whether subconsciously he'd used the memory of Martie as an excuse for his refusal to commit to someone else. It wasn't an unreasonable conjecture. He was sure many men clung to the notion of "the one who got away" as the reason they never made that long march down the nuptial aisle. How convenient to sigh and allude to a former love who might have been his greatest love. No one wanted to be labeled second best and no one wanted to compete with a phantom.

He emptied his pockets and went to put his change in a dish he kept on his dresser for that purpose. Its usual spot was on the left. Tonight it was more in the middle. He moved it back to its customary place and filled it with his coins. His eyes lingered on the gold-rimmed dime, but only for a moment. He hung up his suit and dumped his laundry into the basket in his closet.

He might have used the specter of Martie to justify his lack of commitment in the past, but not this time. He didn't want anything permanent with Greta and he didn't need to pull a phantom out of the hat to justify his lack of feeling.

Seeing Martie had simply reminded him what being in love felt like.

Still, despite the kiss tonight and the flood of memories that had deluged him since he ran into her again, Bryan hadn't completely shaken his irritation about Martie lying to him. If she lied to him about who her mother was, what other untruth had she told him?

That she loved him?

Bryan washed up and got ready for bed. A quick glance in the mirror told him he could use a good night's sleep.

Bryan's bedroom, like the main loft space, was relatively spartan, or, as his designer preferred, "elegantly utilitarian." After sharing a bedroom with his brother, plus his years in the service, followed by several financially lean years at the Bureau, Bryan had grown accustomed to living with the bare basics. He didn't crave luxury, nor was he comfortable with excess. Simple and functional was who he was and how he lived.

His bed was queen-sized and built into a sleek wooden unit containing an upholstered headboard and deep shelves for books and magazines. Two protruding shelves served as end tables. There was a reading lamp and a telephone on one, a clock radio on the other. Across the room, anchored by a flat sisal area rug, were two easy chairs and a low table he'd brought back from Korea. The floors were wood and stained a dark brown. The drapes were cocoa and plain. There was no television.

Bryan climbed into bed and set his alarm. He turned on the light and noticed that the portable phone was out of its cradle. He put it back in its place and reached down to grab a magazine so he could decompress, but they weren't lined up the way they should have been. Instead of being neatly stacked on the front of the shelf, they were shoved toward the back. One or two were off kilter. He looked inside another cubby, the one where he kept his books. Usually they were arranged in descending order, the one he was currently reading on top, those he intended to get to underneath. The top two were out of order.

His coin dish had been in the wrong place.

When he'd opened his top drawer to put his credit cards and wallet away, the leather box that held his cufflinks was on the other side of the box that held his watch.

The phone was off its cradle.

He got out of bed, walked to the far wall, and observed the scene. It took a minute before he spotted it. On the floor by the entrance was a leather frame he'd recently retrieved from a storage box and placed on his nightstand.

The photograph was of Martie and him posed in front of his Apache. They were in desert cams and floppy hats, holding on to each other and grinning at the camera. He'd just painted a goofy heart on the side of the fuselage with BC LOVES MP inside. Lots of pilots embellished their planes with slogans or love notes or warnings for the enemy. Bryan's copilot, Arnie Gravenas, had painted SA-DAMN-YA HUSSEIN on his side of the AH-64A. Different strokes.

He bent down and picked up the frame. It was empty. It didn't take a genius to figure out what had happened. Greta must have divined that Martie was involved in Bryan's emergency. Encouraged by her brandy, she must have worked herself up into a Martie-rage, snooped around, found the picture, and ripped it from its frame.

That was fine with Bryan. He'd miss the photograph, but it had served a purpose. Now they both knew it was over.

Martie was sweating, but the air was cool. Her body felt heavy, yet she felt no pain. She tried to move, but something hard was pressing against her chest. Unsure as to where she was and what had happened, she lay still and attempted to get her bearings.

The world around her was eerily silent. There was none of the usual sounds of war. No shooting or yelling. No screaming tracers or loud, thumping rotor blades.

The sky above her was thick with gray smoke and wet soot from the burning oil fields in Kuwait. The ground beneath her was soft and warm.

Her right eye was closed for some unknown reason. Using only her left, she looked to see what was holding her down. A large hunk of metal that she recognized as coming from her Black Hawk was splayed across her. It was part of the fuselage. She turned her head to the side. Whatever remained of her helicopter lay on the sand like a dead animal, steaming and smelling and broken to bits. She didn't see any of her crew, but for that she was grateful. If they were alive they were hiding or had escaped and would return with reinforcements. If they weren't alive, she wouldn't be able to bear the sight of their bodies.

She turned her head to the other side. Not too far away was a yellow flame. Her heart thumped inside her chest. The fuel lines might have been cut. Severed electrical wires might start to spit sparks. There could be an explosion at any moment.

Quickly, she tried to extricate herself by pushing the wreckage off her, but when she pressed her right hand against the metal a sharp pain ripped through her. Her instinct was to scream, but she stifled it for fear of alerting the enemy to her position. Her hand was broken — even a layperson would have known that — but that yellow flame didn't know or care about her broken bones or her pain.

Desperate now, she tried to dig her heels into the sand and push herself out from under the fuselage. That's when she learned that her right foot was also broken. The shock from the crash must have numbed all her nerve endings.

Think! Don't panic. Think!

Whatever numbness she'd been blessed with after the initial impact was gone, but pain or no pain, she had to get out from under that wreckage before it exploded. Frantically shoveling sand with her left hand and left leg, she wriggled about like a crab, sliding her body sideways into the depression she was creating. Fortunately the sand was soft and moved easily. She chewed her bottom lip rather than scream from the pain she was inflicting on herself, sucked it up, and persevered.

Scoop the sand. Slide it away. Shimmy sideways.

Repeat that action, she commanded, finding comfort in the pretense that she wasn't alone, that someone was issuing orders and she was following them.

Scoop. Slide. Shimmy.

In her head, her drill sergeant was shouting at her: "If you want to avoid disaster, you have to move faster."

Scoop. Slide. Shimmy.

Finally, after what seemed like an interminable amount of time, she wriggled out from under the fuselage. Now she had to figure out how she was going to get away from the smoldering, spitting Black Hawk.

She turned onto her left side and began to "swim," using a sidestroke in the sand just as she would have done had she been in water. Her right side was immobilized, which helped minimize the pain, but it was slow going. She pushed with her left leg and pulled with her left arm, keeping her eyes trained on the horizon.

Little by little she inched away from the copter and away from the flame. Then everything went dark. Even the small amount of light that had bullied its way through the oil soot and the smoke had been somehow overwhelmed. She thought it might be a cargo plane that had blocked the sun or a fresh billowing of thick, viscous smog.

She turned her head skyward, but instead of dirty air she found herself surrounded by dark boots worn by tall men with mustaches brandishing AK-47s. Their red berets identified them as members of the Iraqi Republican Guard.

There were six of them hovering over her, staring at her as if she were a scorpion. One reached down, grabbed her right arm, and jerked her to her feet. She sliced the night with her screams. Stunned, the soldier dropped her arm and recoiled. Martie struggled to steady herself, which wasn't easy to do on one leg in the sand. She swallowed as much pain as she could so she could stand at attention.

Two of the other guards came at her. They snatched her pistol from its holster and removed her survival vest. The younger of the two stuffed her radio in his pocket like a trophy. The other one stripped off her flak jacket and helmet. Her chestnut hair fell to her shoulders. Judging by the look of shock on their faces, they hadn't known their prisoner was a woman.

There was an outburst of agitated Arabic as they huddled to reassess the situation.

While they talked, Martie panned the landscape hoping to spot signs of an imminent rescue. To her left lay the bulk of the wreckage, charred metal chunks of what had been a powerful machine. It was still smoking, but she spied no sparks, no threat of an explosion.

Confused, she looked beyond the copter toward the horizon where earlier she thought she'd seen flames. The sky was black.

To her right was detritus from the accident, bits of the engine, boxes of medical equipment, stretchers. More disturbing, she could see dark lumps peeking out of the sand or out from under a large hunk of metal. Those lumps were the bodies of her crew.

She stared at the undulating landscape, studying the sandy graveyard and wondering who lay where. Her vision blurred and for the moment she thought one of the lumps moved. She blinked. She could have sworn one mound of sand had shifted, but her head was woozy.

She looked again, harder this time, concentrating as best she could, but there was no movement.

She felt faint, but her dizziness was born of immense sadness and rising fear. Stillness meant she was the only survivor of the crash. There was no one to back her up. No one to radio the base with her location. No one to tell Command that she was alive.

At their base in Saudi Arabia she and her colleagues often talked about the what-ifs of war. Most, including Martie, had assumed they would be killed rather than captured. Air force or navy pilots ejected from high-flying jets and parachuted to the ground; most of them were captured. Army helicopters flew so low crews didn't even wear parachutes. And they didn't worry about being captured. If the copter crashed, the likelihood was they'd be killed. She was living their biggest fear: surviving the fall.

Martie thought about what she'd heard about the abuse and torture visited on the Kuwaitis and shivered. She recalled the pictures of American pilots who'd been captured early on, beaten until they agreed to make videos denouncing the war.

She and Bryan had actually practiced blinking out Morse Code messages.

The leader of the Iraqi squad barked at his comrades and pointed at Martie. One of them pushed her forward. She fell. He screamed at her. She pointed to her right foot and arm, gesturing to indicate that they were broken. A couple of the soldiers nodded sympathetically. One extended his hand to help her up. She took it and again, balanced on one leg.

She visualized herself hopping through the desert with AK-47s pointed at her back and, in a bizarre, out-of-body, out-of-her-head moment of hysteria, a giggle bubbled up inside of her. A voice in her brain was singing: Tip-toe through the desert, through the desert will you follow me?

Quickly, she stifled her inner gremlin. There was nothing funny about the look in the eyes of the man they called Tariq.

He shouted at her. His words were Arabic, guttural utterances awash with venom. She was wearing the uniform of his enemy and he hated her. So did his friends. They were snarling at her and slapping each other on the back, congratulating themselves on bagging an American.

Martie remained expressionless. She was a POW and there were rules of behavior for them and for her.

"What's your name?" Tariq demanded in English.

"Lieutenant Marta Phelps."

She thought about pointing to the flight surgeon's badge on her jumpsuit. According to the Geneva Convention, medical personnel were not supposed to be made prisoners of war. If they were not caring for their soldiers who were also prisoners, they were supposed to be returned to their side.

Three things stopped her. One, she remembered her commander telling her unit that the Iraqis didn't like doctors. During the Iran/Iraq war, Iranian doctors tortured Iraqi soldiers. Two, she didn't want to be treated differently from other officers. And three, she suspected Tariq was a guy who didn't like rules, or those *who pointed them out to him.*

But Tariq was more observant than she gave him credit for being. Two of his men had carried over a stretcher. He ordered them to throw it away. Instead, he pushed her to the ground, gripped her by the hair, and began to drag her through the desert.

Before she blacked out from the pain, she heard him say, "Welcome to Iraq, Doctor Phelps."

"Dr. Phelps."

The nurse touched Martie's arm, not wanting to frighten her.

Martie's eyes shot open. She stared up at the young black woman, disoriented.

"You're in New York Hospital." Martie looked blank. "With your daughter. You must have been having a nightmare."

Martie bolted upright and looked over at Lili, who was sleeping peacefully.

"Don't worry. She's sedated. She didn't hear you."

Martie gathered from the nurse's inflection that everyone else on the floor did.

"I'm sorry," she muttered, not knowing what else to say.

"It's all right. What if I give you something to help you sleep?"

Martie rubbed her eyes and tried to jump-start her brain.

"I have an important appointment in the morning," she said.

"I won't give you a knockout pill. Just something to relax you so you can get some sleep and wake up feeling rested." She noted Martie's damp clothes and sweaty brow. Also, her body was trembling. "I think you could use it, Dr. Phelps."

Martie agreed, but as she swallowed the small white tablets the nurse gave her she knew that even if she slept, she wouldn't wake up feeling rested.

Martie hadn't felt rested in ten years.

Vera was exhausted and depressed. Instead of returning home after she left the hospital, she went to her office. She planned out a month's worth of television shows covering everything from growing orchids to making a quilt from dime store bandannas. Then she read over a dozen new product proposals for her housewares line, and signed whatever correspondence Tess had left on her desk. Also, she compiled a list of possibly disgruntled ex-employees. Work was a balm.

Throughout, the image of Lili lying in that hospital bed haunted her. Too, the utter disgust in Martie's eyes when she spied Vera in the room.

She knew it wasn't her fault that Lili was there, but she also knew she wasn't completely faultless. She didn't know what she had done to inspire someone to turn Valentine Red into a chemical weapon, but whoever it was hated her enough to randomly poison innocent people with something that would specifically lay the blame for that atrocity at her feet. The fact that one of those innocents was her granddaughter seemed like a macabre bit of poetic justice.

It wasn't often that Vera cried, but alone at her desk that evening that's what she did.

When Greta got home, Tripp was waiting for her. He'd made himself comfortable watching television on the couch in her den. Within easy reach were a double scotch and a plate of caviar. Greta was the only woman Tripp knew who never had orange juice in her refrigerator, but always had a fresh tin of beluga.

"To what do I owe the pleasure?" he said, stuffing his mouth with black fish roe.

"I had a bad day." She threw down her purse and took off her jacket.

"So you call me? I don't get it. Last time I looked, you sneaked behind my back and divorced me. Did I miss something?"

"No. This is a house call."

Tripp laughed. "Ah, I get it now. The lady needs to get laid." He laughed again. "I guess you're the one who's missing something." He made a lewd gesture and licked his lips.

Greta glared at him and unzipped her dress. "Just fuck me and get out."

He rose from the couch, took his drink with him, and walked over to where she was standing. He put the glass to her lips and encouraged her to drink. Then he slid the dress off her shoulders, letting it pool at her feet. "I thought you had another fish on your hook."

She reached down, unzipped his fly, and reached inside his pants. "He was too small. I threw him back."

Tripp finished his scotch and tossed the glass onto a nearby chair. He unhooked her bra and indulged himself by ravishing her breasts.

She leaned back, giving him free rein, and continued to stroke him until he was hard.

"I thought you didn't want anything to do with me anymore," he said, gliding his hands down her body, reaching into her panties and returning the favor.

"I don't, but you're all that was available on such short notice."

And he was good. Tripp wasn't the brightest bulb on the tree, but he knew his way around a woman's body. Greta wouldn't admit it, but there were times she simply thought about him and got hot.

"You want it, you're going to have to come get it," he taunted, moving away from her, knowing that she was past the point of being able to stop.

She stood there for a moment, furious that Tripp would throw her need in her face, but she didn't stay mad for long. She'd already been rejected once this evening.

She walked over to Tripp, undid his belt, lowered his pants, snaked her arms around his neck, and lifted herself onto him. She wrapped her legs around his waist and dared him to resist.

"Do it," she said.

His fingers teased her.

"Do it."

She was practically begging. That turned him on.

He held her away from him and flicked his tongue across her nipples, delighting in their quick response. Then he teased her again. Her body was writhing against him, pleading with him.

"What if I say no?"

"You wouldn't dare."

Again, he licked her. "I'm the one in control, babe, or hadn't you noticed?"

She released her arms from his neck and her legs from his waist and, before he knew what was happening, pushed him down onto the floor and climbed on top of him. She took him in her hand, guided him to where she needed him most, and rode him until she was satisfied.

When she was finished, she climbed off him, and stood over him like a conquering warrior.

"I'm the one in control," she said. "And don't you ever forget it."

She picked his clothes up off the floor and threw them at him.

"Now get out."

It was well after midnight when Vera got home. She headed straight for her bedroom, stripping off her clothes as she went. When she opened the door to her massive walk-in closet and clicked on the light, her heart leaped to her throat.

Hanging in front of the mirror on the

back wall was a large paper target with her face pasted on top of a man-sized black body. Her mouth was smeared with a nasty sprawl of lipstick. In the middle of the chest where her heart would be were several bullet holes. Sloppily drawn red splotches tracked a bloody trail down from the bull's-eye, each bloodstain drawn with a different lipstick, the various shades notated in a scrawl made by a fat black Sharpie.

Vera recognized the colors as coming from her current New York Night line. But instead of *Copa, Colony, Stork Club, Café Carlyle, Le Club,* each shade of red had been renamed to better fit her tormenter's theme of death: *Hate. Passion. Rage. Vengeance.* And *Massacre.*

Chapter 11

The Hart Line plant in Carteret, New Jersey, was in a large industrial park just off the turnpike. It was a massive structure, wide rather than tall, and built around a courtyard. It reminded Martie of the Pentagon.

Inside it looked more like the starship *Enterprise*. Long hallways padded in white and dove gray vinyl connected one sector to another with fenestration that reinforced the feeling of being in a vehicle capable of intergalactic travel. The outer walls were striped with thin rectangular windows that only let in slivers of light. The windows on the inner walls were larger, squarer, and spaced farther apart, each one framing a view of the spectacular garden that monopolized the courtyard.

As Martie was led from the administrative wing, which was in the eastern quadrant, to the lipstick production quadrant in the north, she couldn't help but admire the lushly floral landscape. The colors were so riotous it looked like Matisse at the height of his Fauvism.

"It's gorgeous," she remarked to Stella, her pale blond, reed-thin guide.

The young woman, who was garbed in the white lab coat that appeared to be a Hart Line must, had been very impressed with Martie's credentials. Eager to please, she readily explained the theory behind the garden.

"Ms. Hart believes that beauty inspires beauty. The garden inspires us. Our work inspires the garden," she said, sounding a bit like a robot. "The flowers are changed to coincide with the current color story."

Martie had done some quick research on the beauty industry and knew that a "color story" was the way a cosmetics company packaged a season's collection. Tuscan Summers. Napa Valley Wine. Tropical Splendor. Whatever name the marketing division believed would entice customers to their counters. Gazing at the luxuriant sea of reds and oranges, Martie guessed that something like Mexican Sunset or California Mornings was the latest tag.

Stella corrected her. "Those have been done. This season we're 'On the Beach in Tahiti.'"

She said it as if it were highly original,

rather than the same idea wrapped in a new sarong.

When they reached the door to the production area, Stella pressed the photo ID tag she wore on a white string against the front of an electronic identification box. A red light went on. She pressed her thumb against the box. When finally it beeped its approval, she pushed a button that prompted a display asking for a number. She responded "One" verbally, touched "1" to confirm, and asked Martie to press her visitor's tag against the same ID panel.

Security was taken seriously around here.

A door slid open, admitting them to a large room that housed a series of enormous kettles that looked like overgrown pressure cookers. Stella informed Martie that each kettle held thirty to fifty gallons of product. In case Martie thought that didn't sound like a lot for a company like the Hart Line, Stella reminded her that a lipstick only weighed about 3.6 grams.

Mentally, Martie crossed off the kettles as the source of the poisonous batch. Someone would have to have wheeled a small dumpster of mercuric chloride in here to compromise such large containers.

Beyond the kettle room was a spacious,

well-lit laboratory, a work zone that felt far more familiar to Martie. A dozen men and women in the ubiquitous white lab coats were hunched over tables performing various tests. The equipment didn't look any different than that which Martie employed in her Rockefeller University lab: glass beakers, Bunsen burners, racks filled with test tubes. The difference was that this lab was a beehive of activity. People seemed to be constantly coming and going, some carrying small cups of colors and paper swatches, others swiping finished lipsticks on the backs of their hands and holding them up to the light.

Stella told Martie that all color labs faced north.

"That's the best light for matching color. Direct sun is way too yellow."

At one table Martie noticed a woman grinding what looked like coffee in a pestle.

"This factory also produces eye shadow," Stella explained. "Helen is searching for the perfect cinnamon for our Fireside Fall campaign. When she's satisfied that she's matched the swatch sent over from the head office, she'll give it to a technician, who'll press it into a pan. That goes to the head colorist here, and if she approves, it goes on to New York for Ms. Hart's okay."

"Does everything go to Ms. Hart?"

Stella reacted as if Martie had questioned the color of the sky.

"There is nothing Ms. Hart doesn't pass on, and thank goodness for that. Her color sense is exceeded only by her ability to keep her finger on the public pulse."

Stella was positively gushing.

"A couple of years ago, all the other cosmetics companies decided to target teeny-boppers. They put out a completely pink palette with the emphasis on lip gloss. Ms. Hart decided that if the competition was going after the very young with gloss or barely-there lipstick, the Hart Line would fill in the blanks and go after the thirties-and-up. Since most post-teenagers don't wear bubblegum pink, or shouldn't, the Hart Line sold them a Rose Garden. Tea Rose remains one of our bestsellers."

"Smart woman, Vera Hart," Martie said.

"Very."

"Is she tough to work for?"

"Tough only begins to describe it."

That was the first time Stella had said anything even vaguely negative about Vera.

"Really? How so?"

Stella realized she had breeched the

Hart Line code of silence and dummied up. Instead of answering Martie, she reverted to Roboguide.

"Lipstick is basically pigment contained in a stick of wax, usually carnauba," she said, piloting Martie through the lab. "That gives the lipstick shape. Oil is added to make the lipstick glide. Frosts make lipsticks hard. Metallic pigments, known as lakes, make lipsticks mushy."

At that moment Martie agreed with Lili: lipstick was yucky.

The two of them treaded softly so as not to disturb anyone. Stella was speaking in a near-whisper. Martie was keeping an eye out for anything that might prove helpful. What made that particularly nerve-racking was she had no idea what she was looking for.

"How long does it take to produce a lipstick?" she asked, hoping to establish a time line.

"The first set of lab samples could be completed in a few weeks. Usually, though, there are corrections and the process has to be repeated. Ms. Hart demands perfection."

Don't I know it, Martie thought.

"How long does that take?" she said.

"Eight weeks is about average for a final approval."

"What about colors that remain in the line season after season?"

"The tried-and-trues? Those formulations can be run off almost automatically." Again, Stella looked as if a mechanical hand were going to reach out from behind a wall and slap her for her insolence. "Of course, even they're carefully checked by Ms. Hart. Her eye is infallible."

"I'm sure," Martie said.

Since Valentine Red was certainly a tried-and-true, it might be left to second-tier chemists. Lead chemists would probably be assigned to the newer colors, the ones without previously established, Vera-approved formulas. Martie made a mental note to find out how many new chemists had been hired in the past year and where they'd worked before.

Stella led her down another hallway into the production room. There, in a space large enough to shelter a small plane, white-robed women with paper shower caps on their heads and latex gloves on their hands guarded the Hart Line Lipstick Line, intently scrutinizing each of the uncapped lipsticks moving past them on a conveyer belt. Other surgically garbed personnel operated complicated-looking machines that processed the liquid lipstick until it was cooled and squeezed into tubes and, finally, capped.

Martie wondered whether the samples Vera had brought Lili were made here as well.

"I love those gift-with-purchase promotions," she said with wide-eyed enthusiasm. "I get to sample a new color or a skin care product. And I get travel sizes of my favorites, to boot."

"They are wonderful."

"Are they produced here as well?"

Stella nodded and led Martie back into the lab. "We have to change the molds on the line, but yes."

That meant the crew was the same no matter what size the end product was. The same person could have poisoned both batches.

When they had completed their tour, Stella introduced Martie to the staff, following what Martie assumed was hierarchical protocol. She was introduced to the head chemist, Ian Bardwill, his assistants, and then their assistants. Each welcomed her graciously, but with the expected reserve; new leaders often meant new personnel. This group also had the additional stress of knowing their company was under investigation.

Martie thanked them for allowing her to interrupt their day and assured them that her primary function was to develop the Hart Line Skin Care Line of the future. The purpose of this visit was to meet all of them and to get the lay of the land.

"We don't produce the Skin Care Line here," one woman said. "Will you be changing that?"

"No. Skin care will still come out of the Suffern plant. As for me, I'll be commuting between there and the lab at the New York headquarters. I will be staffing up, though, so anyone with expertise in skin care, please feel free to apply." She smiled invitingly. "I'm going to need all the help I can get."

Some the faces relaxed. Others remained suspicious.

She thanked everyone again and allowed them to get back to work. She and Stella were about to leave when Martie noticed two people pouring beakers of liquid lipstick into bullet-shaped molds. It looked as if each chemist was filling several dozen tubes.

"What are they doing?" she asked Stella.

"Preparing a batch of samples. Those are colors that have been given final approval."

"Where do those samples go?"

"Probably to the sales force. We often send small lots to the people in the field so they can show their customers what's coming or to use the new colors themselves to test consumer reaction."

"Anyone else?"

"Why do you ask?" Stella had shifted into protective mode. Her tone was crisp, guarded.

"Since I'm going to be creating a new line of products, I'm curious about how the Hart Line goes about test-marketing."

That must have made sense, because Stella responded easily.

"It depends. For skin care or face makeup, we often have focus groups try the product for a period of time so they can rate the effect the product has on their skin."

Martie nodded as if that had answered a burning concern. "And after they've passed those focus groups and go into the market? How do you tease the consumer into purchasing it?"

"During the prelaunch stage we might supply samples as giveaways for things like charity luncheons or golf tournaments."

"I thought goody-bag fillers came from promotional overruns."

"Most of the time they do, but if an event comes up just as we're about to launch a major promotion for a new product, we'll do a tease."

"And otherwise? Do you ever make up samples of in-the-line items?"

"Absolutely. Ms. Hart wants to be sure we're noticed, so if it's big enough we'll do something event-specific. Like putting out a pale shade of pink for a breast cancer outing or a red nail polish for an AIDS function." She looked at Martie as a memory struck. "You were at the Hart Foundation Awards Gala. That's the perfect example. Everyone got a goody bag with a specially packaged gold tube of Valentine Red."

Martie's heart began to pound. Four hundred people had been at the Pierre that night. That meant four hundred possibly poisonous tubes of lipstick were out there waiting to be used. She had one of those bags at home. She had to get that lipstick to Bryan ASAP.

"I've taken up enough of your time, Stella," Martie said, anxious to leave. "I think I'm going to start back to the city now."

"But we haven't visited the southern quadrant yet where the packaging is done."

She sounded so distressed, Martie wondered whether she would be docked pay for not completing the tour.

"Next time."

As Stella reluctantly led Martie back to the east-wing entrance, Martie thought she spotted a familiar face. The setting was so completely incongruous she looked twice, certain she was wrong.

"Who are they?" she asked Stella, nodding toward a squad of men dressed in gray overalls.

"That's the early-day cleaning crew." She checked her watch. "They're finishing up now."

Martie looked confused. "Early-day?"

"Ms. Hart is obsessed with cleanliness, so we have crews come in three times a day." She beamed. "Every year Hart Line factories are cited for being the cleanest in the country."

"Definitely something to be proud of," Martie said, watching the men check out at the front desk.

"Oh, we are," Stella said.

"Well, thank you again," Martie said as she turned to leave.

She was almost out the door when one of the men in the gray overalls winked at her. She could barely stifle the giggle that bubbled at her lips at the sight of her former drill sergeant, Vincent Wiggers.

Wally Crocker, Ian Bardwill's assistant, went to his locker to retrieve his cell phone. Claiming a need for fresh air, he took his break in the garden, where he wouldn't be overheard.

"Do you know a Dr. Marta Phelps?"

"Why?"

"Because she toured the plant today."

"And what did she find?"

"Nothing out of the ordinary."

"Let's keep it that way."

"Absolutely."

He ended the call, pocketed the phone, put it back in his locker, and smiled as he returned to the lab.

Who said bench work didn't pay?

"Good morning, sir." Bryan shouldn't have been surprised to find Hugh Phelps outside Lili's room, but he was taken aback nonetheless.

"Bryan." Hugh gave a quick nod of his head, but didn't extend his hand. "What are you doing here?"

General Phelps had always been abrupt and to the point. That much hadn't changed.

"I came to visit Lili and to speak to Martie."

Hugh couldn't help but notice a large gift box swathed in pink ribbon and a spray of pink flowers.

"About?"

Hugh's manner made Bryan feel like an adolescent picking up his date for the prom. He fought the instinct to stammer and shuffle his feet and instead looked the general in the eye.

"The lipstick that poisoned Lili."

Hugh's silence was an expectant one. Bryan continued.

"Before I joined HLI, I was working a similar case involving Valentine Red."

Since Hugh's expression remained the same, Bryan gathered he already knew about the woman in Central Park.

"Last night Martie gave me the other items in Lili's gift bag for testing."

"Do you have any results?"

"Not yet, but I have a friend on the job who's shepherding it. It'll be done as quickly and discreetly as possible."

Hugh nodded, but said nothing.

"If you don't mind my asking, sir, is Martie here?"

"No, she's not."

"Do you know if she went to New Jersey?"

"Yes, she did."

Bryan clenched his jaw.

"Does that bother you?" Hugh asked.

"Yes, sir, it does. I would have preferred it if she'd taken someone with her."

"Still trying to tell her what to do?"

Bryan bristled. At first, he wasn't going to respond. The man before him was a three-star general and deserved his respect. He was Martie's father, Lili's grandfather. He was also the man Bryan blamed for costing him the love of his life.

"No, sir. I'm still just trying to keep her safe."

"No need. I took care of it."

Phelps was baiting him. Bryan knew it but bit anyway.

"I'm sure you did. Whether she wanted it or not." He'd resented this man's interference before and he resented it now.

A nurse approached. Bryan stopped her. "Would you mind giving these to Ms. Abrams, please?" he asked as he handed her the package he'd been carrying.

"Not at all," she said. "Sure you don't want to give these to her yourself? The doctor will be finished in a minute."

"I'd love to, but I have to go."

"Okay." She shrugged and went into Lili's room.

"I would have given them to Lili if you really had to go," Hugh said.

"No need," Bryan said, taking his leave. "I took care of it."

The elevator doors opened and before Bryan could take two steps into the lobby, he collided with a tall, angular blonde who looked strangely familiar. When they separated, she appeared to recognize him too.

"Captain Chalmers?"

The voice fit the face. It was a smaller voice than one might have expected from a woman of Delilah's height, but it matched the woman she believed she was inside.

Bryan's mouth spread in a surprised smile. "Delilah Green."

"That's me."

She looked older, of course. A gray shadow veiled her light blue eyes and there was a sallow cast to her skin, physical testimony to Delilah's continuous bout with the harder side of life. Still, her mood was upbeat.

"Wow," he said. "How are you?"

His eyes scanned her, but there was no judgment, only curiosity and genuine pleasure at running into her.

"I'm hangin' in. How 'bout yourself?"

"I'm good. Really good. What are you

doing here?" The instant the words left his mouth he noticed a bouquet of daisies in her hand. "Lili?"

"How'd ya guess?"

He laughed. So did she, but in the back of her brain a thought itched. She knew why she was there. His presence raised a number of questions.

"I thought you and Martie were yesterday's news."

A wry chuckle escaped his lips. "We are, but we . . . It's complicated."

"Wasn't it always?"

He thought about that. "No, not always."

The regret in Bryan's eyes tugged at her. "Are you two rekindling?" she asked hopefully.

"We're working for the same company, that's all."

Delilah gave him a yeah-sure nod of the head.

"And I suppose you're here because Lili also works for this company."

Bryan laughed and shook his head. "I met Lili a couple of days ago and was utterly charmed by her."

"Oh, please. Spare me the horse poop! You're here because you and Martie are like grits and gravy," she said. "You two belong together, so no matter how complicated it appears to be, make it work!"

"I can't do it alone, Delilah."

"Maybe not, but you gotta try. Life don't hand out three and four chances at happiness. Most people only get one. Those who are really lucky get two. Catch my drift?"

Bryan smiled. "That's like a ninety-seven-mile-an-hour fastball into the center of the glove: I couldn't miss it if I tried."

Just as Martie's taxi pulled up to the hospital, she saw Bryan climb into another cab. It sped off before she could stop him.

When she got to Lili's room, Lili was sitting up in bed playing with a plump, colorful stuffed airplane. Her dresser looked like a flower shop with a dozen vases standing together in an efflorescent crowd. One large arrangement of red roses in a heart-shaped vase dominated all the others. Martie didn't have to guess who that was from.

On the nightstand next to Lili's bed was a small arrangement of pink flowers in a simple glass vase. Judging by its solo position, Martie guessed it was from someone special.

She was about to assign that offering to

her father, when Lili said, "Mr. Chalmers was here. He brought me this to play with until we can go flying for real and he brought me those." She pointed to the pink blooms. "Aren't they pretty?"

Martie smiled. Her daughter had a major crush on Captain Chalmers.

"They're beautiful, sweetheart." She kissed Lili's forehead. "How're you feeling?"

"Much better. Dr. Sanborn says I can go home."

Martie had spoken to the nurse before coming in to see Lili, so she already knew that.

"GG says he'll help me take home my flowers."

When Lili was a toddler she heard everyone calling Hugh, "General." She thought that was his name, so she began calling him Grandpa General, which wound up being shortened to GG.

"Did Mr. Chalmers come in to see you?" Martie said.

Lili said no and expressed her disappointment. "GG said he had to go."

Martie turned to her father for an explanation.

"He said he had things to do."

Martie narrowed her eyebrows and shot him a look. Hugh remained defiant. Martie surrendered. It was tough staring down a three-star.

"Did you see the flowers the Queen of Hearts sent me?"

"Hard to miss. Was she here today?" Martie asked Hugh.

He shook his head. "Find anything interesting on your sojourn?"

She smiled. "Tell Wiggers gray isn't his best color."

Hugh laughed.

"What's so funny?" Lili wanted to know.

"GG surprised me today."

Lili looked at her grandfather. "Did you send Mommy a present?"

"Sort of," Hugh said. "Now, how about we get you out of here?"

Delilah heard Hugh's voice, turned away from Lili's room, and hotfooted it back to the elevators. The general didn't like her and she didn't like him. In addition to whatever he found distasteful — her appearance, her accent, her lack of education — she was a physical reminder of what had happened to Martie in Iraq. He didn't want her around and had never been shy about letting her know it.

Martie used to try to excuse his boorish behavior by saying he was a father trying to

301

protect his daughter. But Delilah had served in Iraq; she too had been a POW. General Phelps had been her superior officer. He was supposed to care just as much about what had happened to PFC Green as he did about what had happened to Lieutenant Phelps. And he didn't. Delilah never said anything to Martie or anyone else, but that hurt.

Chapter 12

As Vincent Wiggers frequently reminded his troops, "Teamwork only succeeds if you work as a team."

It felt odd to think of herself on the same team as Vera, but she was. It felt strange to be on the same team as Bryan, but she was. It felt good to team up with her father again; the thought of Vera and him working together was surreal. As for Sergeant Wiggers, having him on her side was reassuring. His no-nonsense approach helped any team he was on. The only one Martie was having a hard time sharing bench space with was Greta. She didn't trust her and she didn't like her, but if co-operating with Greta was the means to finding the bastard who put Lili in the hospital and that woman in the morgue, Martie would suck it up and get along.

She had said as much when she proposed that this cobbled-together squad get together to combine information and brainstorm a strategy. Hugh thought it was a wonderful idea and suggested she host the meeting at her apartment.

"You're not going to want to leave Lili," he pointed out.

He also reasoned that her place was less conspicuous than the Hart Line offices and less likely to attract media attention than Vera's apartment.

"Since the press hasn't caught on to the fact that you're Vera's daughter, you're still able to fly under the radar."

"It's nice to know that being inconspicuous can turn into a benefit," she said.

Vera arrived early. To throw the paparazzi off track, she had changed clothes in the office, bypassed the executive exit, came out the front of the building, and fought for a taxi like any other workingwoman in New York. Her disguise was brilliant because it was ordinary: black slacks, a white T-shirt with a cocoa sweater draped over her shoulders, black velvet loafers, sunglasses, her hair pulled back into a ponytail, and a black baseball cap.

When Martie opened the door, the ghost of a lifetime past was standing in her hallway. Instead of Vera Hart/corporate mogul/international personality, there was the Vera Martie used to see around the

Roxbury house: no jewelry, no labels screaming status, no fashion-layout hair or photo-perfect makeup. Just a naturally beautiful woman with an innate sense of style and elegance.

"Thank you for doing this," Vera said as she entered.

Though she and Martie hadn't seen each other since that night in the hospital, she'd called a dozen times for updates on Lili's condition. She'd also sent over dinner so Martie didn't have to cook, as well as assorted pastries and fruit for the meeting.

"Since Lili came home this afternoon, I'm sure it's a hardship. I apologize for the inconvenience."

"It's all right," Martie said, momentarily shaken by the memories that had come through the door with Vera.

"Would you mind if I peeked in and said hello to Lili?"

"Not at all."

It surprised Martie to realize that she didn't mind.

She led Vera down the hall to Lili's bedroom, a happy-go-lucky confection that started with a candy-colored, harlequin-patterned carpet. There was a pink-and-white-upholstered chaise tucked in a corner and a dozen delicate watercolor clown paintings flanking the window bay, six a side. A pale blue tufted headboard looked down on a bed dressed in pink and white linens. A dresser, two end tables, and a hutch overflowed with books and dolls and stuffed animals and Lili's get-well flowers.

Vera's extravaganza occupied center stage on the dresser. Bryan's smaller offering brightened the nightstand, as did the toy airplane.

Lili was sitting up in bed playing Candyland with Soledad.

"Hi!" Vera said, grateful to see the color back in Lili's cheeks.

Lili grinned at her. Vera smiled back.

"Soledad, this is the Queen of Hearts," Lili said excitedly.

"It's nice to meet you, Soledad."

"A pleasure, ma'am."

Martie chuckled to herself. Soledad had looked from one to the other and did a double-take at the unmistakable resemblance.

Lili invited Vera to join their game, which she did, quite gladly it seemed.

Again, Martie was awash with memories, this time of counterpane games she'd played with Vera when she was Lili's age.

The doorbell rang. Reluctantly, Martie

left so she could let in her other guests.

Bryan and Hugh must have met up in the lobby. Judging by the chill emanating from both of them, there had been little or no conversation in the elevator on the way up.

Martie was delighted when two minutes later Vincent Wiggers disembarked. Grateful for the distraction, she left Bryan and Hugh to fend for themselves while she reunited with her former drill sergeant.

Hugh headed immediately for his granddaughter's room.

Bryan, thankful that he wouldn't have to subject himself to another round of Hugh's disapproval, gave himself a tour of Martie's living room, eventually making his way to the table that held all her photographs. It was fueled by morbid curiosity, but he couldn't help it. He needed to see what her life had been like without him.

The pictures of Lili were sweet, even those with her grandfather.

He lingered over a picture of Connie and silently mourned her passing. He'd gotten along a lot better with her than he had with her husband.

He spotted a group photo of Martie's Desert Storm unit and picked it up so he could inspect it more closely. Having visited her base so often in the buildup to the war, he knew most of her crew. As always when he looked at pictures of army buddies, it was difficult to gaze upon the smiling faces of those who didn't make it back. It was also curious to look at those who did and wonder where they were, what they were doing, who they had become.

He returned that picture to its place and turned to those he'd been avoiding, the ones of Martie and her late husband, Jack Abrams. He was nice-looking, Bryan supposed: Martie's height and slim, with a shock of dark brown hair and what looked like hazel eyes. The morning after the gala, Bryan had asked around about Abrams. The Internet informed him of his fatal accident. The word from people who knew him was that he was a dedicated doctor, super bright, straight arrow, nice guy. Bryan had hoped to hear that maybe he cheated at cards or golf or didn't get along with the guys or wasn't a favorite of the nurses. But Jack Abrams had been universally well liked. Bryan didn't expect anything less from Martie, but he felt jealous nonetheless.

And while he knew it was completely unreasonable, he was pained by his lack of presence on Martie's memory table.

Hugh was just outside Lili's room when a familiar laugh filled the hallway, a full-throated chortle he hadn't heard in years. A smile tickled his lips as he heard Lili's higher pitched version of the same laugh join in. Not wanting to disturb them, he quietly peeked in. Vera and Lili were grinning at each other and laughing, thoroughly engaged in whatever they were doing. He knew how charming Lili was, so Vera's fascination with her newly discovered granddaughter didn't surprise him. It was Lili's enthrallment with Vera that intrigued.

He stood against the wall and eavesdropped. At first the conversation amounted to gibberish about girly things like scrunchies versus skinny bands for ponytails and nightgowns versus jammies.

"I prefer nightgowns," Vera said as if she had given considerable thought to the question, "but my younger daughter loved baby doll pajamas."

A picture of Martie running around the Roxbury house in shortie pajamas flashed before Hugh's eyes.

"Me too!" exclaimed Lili, throwing back the blankets to show Vera the truncated bottoms of her pink pajamas.

"How about that!" Vera said, sounding

totally amazed at the coincidence.

After they had exhausted that subject, he heard Vera ask about the toy airplane.

"My new friend Bryan Chalmers gave it to me," Lili explained. "He taught my mommy how to fly. He promised to take me flying, but I got sick so he gave me this until I'm well enough to go in a real plane. Isn't that so nice?"

"So very nice," Vera said in an encouraging tone that set Hugh's teeth on edge.

He was overreacting, but he couldn't help it. He had counted on Bryan Chalmers to care for Martie in her time of need. Bryan had let him down. Instead of backing off gracefully the way Hugh had suggested and giving Martie space, he pressured Martie to marry him, which made things worse. Hugh didn't forget and he rarely forgave.

As if on cue, Bryan rounded the corner into the hall that led to the bedrooms. He thought he'd pay a quick visit to Lili. The look on the general's face made it clear that was not going to happen.

"She's busy," Hugh said, walking toward Bryan. "Besides, we're supposed to be having a meeting."

Bryan swallowed his annoyance, turned around, and reentered the living room.

He'd visit with Lili when her three-star guard dog wasn't around.

A few minutes later Vera joined them, counted heads, and suggested they convene.

"Don't you want to wait for Greta?"

Hugh had hoped for a few minutes with his older daughter before the meeting started. He'd called her that morning so she would know Vera had contacted him, but as she had so often in the past, she didn't take his call and didn't call him back.

"She knew what time we planned to begin," Vera said, taking over one of the wing chairs, thereby establishing herself as the focal point of the evening's activities.

Everyone but Hugh followed her lead and took a seat. He stood off to the side.

As he leaned against the wall and folded his arms across his chest, he smiled to himself and thought, old habits did die hard. Whenever Vera was front and center, he automatically stood to the side. Then again, he reminded himself, this was her arena. In his, he took front and center.

"First and foremost," Vera said, clearly directing her words to Martie, "let me say how delighted we all are that Lili is feeling

311

better. Also, let me thank you for allowing us to invade your home this evening. This was above and beyond and I know I speak for the others when I say we're truly grateful for your hospitality."

Martie nodded her appreciation for the kind words.

In an instant, Vera's smile was gone.

"Since this meeting was called to organize an effort to save HLI, let me give you an update. To put it bluntly: We're in trouble. Sales are way off. Our TV ratings are down. And at the close of trading today our stock hit an all-time low.

"Our legal problems are also mounting. Three former employees plan on pleading guilty to improper accounting practices. I can only assume they're hoping to trade dirt on me for leniency." Her eyes clouded and her mouth looked pinched. "If I'm guilty of anything, it's of delegating too much authority to others. I expected my staff to do the right thing. They assured me they were. It appears as if they lied, which makes me appear both stupid and culpable. I want to assure everyone in this room I'm neither of those things."

She took a breath, shrugged, and widened her eyes as if it were all a mystery to her.

"The federal prosecutor is moving forward with his investigation at breakneck speed, holding press conferences twice a day to announce new charges and to throw another barrel of chum to the sharks in the media. It's as if everyone's simply salivating at the thought of me being dressed by the state instead of Armani."

She proffered a feeble smile and quickly moved on.

"Craig Hemminger is the government's primary witness, but his testimony will be quickly followed by a number of other HLI employees, particularly those who worked in the area of finance."

"Don't worry about that," Bryan said. "I have to be present at all the depositions and they're obligated to turn over to us whatever evidence they produce. If there's nothing but hot air coming out of the prosecutor's office, we'll know it soon enough. If there's a problem, we'll know that too and deal with it in due course."

His voice resonated with confidence, but Vera wasn't reassured.

"How do we deal with the matter of Valentine Red?" She ran her fingers through her hair and shook her head. "I don't know if that's related to the attacks on HLI, but if these horrid happenings are part of a plot to weaken my company so it can be poached, I'm afraid it's succeeding."

Her chest heaved. She looked tired and vulnerable.

"Bryan," she said, visibly trying to gather strength. "Have you spoken to your friend at the NYPD?"

Bryan said that he had. "Tony Borzone confirmed that the poison in the lipstick from Lili's gift bag matched that taken from the Central Park victim. The chemical formulations were exact, which means they were mixed at the same time in the same container. The only remaining question is the delivery system. Since no lipstick was found at the scene, we have to assume by the width of the lines drawn on the victim's body that the tube was a regular size. The strokes were too broad to come from the minis."

That seemed to confirm Martie's fear that the contamination might be more widespread than they'd originally suspected. When she said as much, Vera asked her to recount her findings from her morning in Carteret.

"At first I rejected the idea that the kettles were the source of the poison because they appeared too large to be compromised without detection. I thought that was a positive development because it would have indicated that the lethal batch was limited. Then my guide told me about the giveaways at the Foundation gala."

"We made up four hundred and fifty gold tubes," Vera said. "Since we don't waste product, whatever mixture was left over would have been used for the minis."

"Which is too large a quantity to be poured by hand." Martie still couldn't figure out how that much poison could have been brought into the plant without being discovered.

"Could someone have removed a portion of the mix from the kettles and set it aside?" Bryan asked Vera, cuing in to Martie's thinking.

"I suppose. We do extract a small sampling to study before the batch is fully processed."

Vincent picked up the thread dangled by Bryan.

"Then we might not be talking about hundreds of mercury-laced lipsticks," he said. "Our guy could've taken a beaker full of hot lipstick from a kettle, swiped a couple of the fancy gold tubes, and whipped up his own giveaways."

Having seen the size of the kettles, that scenario made more sense to Martie.

"How many of these did you order?" she asked, holding up the Valentine tube she'd found in her Foundation goody bag. It was a gold tube with a small red enamel heart on the top. The mini Lili had been given was exactly the same, scaled down.

"It's our signature tube, so they're stock items. We use them for special events. Valentine's Day. Things like that."

"Which means they're around and available," Martie said, thinking aloud. "Since there had to be a count on how many lipsticks were made and shipped, either the compromised tubes were slipped into the gala order to be randomly distributed, or they were done separately for this nut job's personal use."

"Anyone with access to the plant would be able to get his hands on them," Hugh said. He turned to Wiggers. "I know this morning was preliminary, Vincent, but did you find any security loopholes?"

"Yeah," Wiggers said. "Me."

That got everyone's attention.

"While security in every other area is extremely tight, Ms. Hart, you employ an outside cleaning company. I gave them a dummied-up résumé and within an hour or two I was approved. Frankly, I don't think anyone checked my references."

"They must have," she said somewhat defensively. "They're bonded. I've never had so much as a powder puff stolen."

"Whoever's doing this isn't interested in stealing powder puffs. He's out to ruin your company and doesn't care if he kills a bunch of people in the process."

"You've suspected all along that this is part of a long-term plan," Martie said to Vera. "Whoever did this could have gotten the job and been working it until an opportunity presented itself."

"Or," Wiggers said, "he doesn't even work for CleanCo. When I got back to their main office I had to hand in my uniform. The supervisor told me they send them out to be laundered. There are a lot of spots along that chain where someone could have ripped one off."

"We still require a photo ID. And only the crew chief knows the password."

"That's true." Wiggers affirmed the fact that he couldn't have gotten into the plant without his crew chief.

Martie recalled Stella had to submit a thumbprint along with the photo ID. Later, she would ask Bryan to run the prints of everyone at CleanCo through the FBI database.

"Who's to say the crew chief or someone

on staff isn't in on this?" Bryan offered.

Hugh wasn't buying that. "What do they have to gain?"

"Money comes to mind," Bryan said. "Or vengeance."

Martie looked at Vera. The Hart Line meant the world to her. More to the point, it was her world.

Hugh also looked at Vera. He was still waiting for that list of enemies.

Bryan remained focused. "The poisoning of the lipsticks is only one of our problems. The most urgent, for sure, but it's not the only thing we have to worry about. There's a government investigation going on that could destroy HLI and send some people to jail."

Vera winced. The weight of all this was beginning to take its toll. She looked exhausted.

"There are also the personal threats against Vera." He turned to her. "Show them the latest."

Vera obediently went to her bag, slipped on latex gloves as Bryan had instructed her, and extracted the paper target. Just as she started to unfold it, the doorman buzzed. Martie quietly slipped out of the room and went to answer his call, then waited for the elevator to discharge its passenger.

"I got tied up," Greta said as she brushed by Martie.

She strode into the living room like an empress entering her court, her chin high, her lips pursed, her black silk blouse and loose trousers rippling as she walked.

She froze when she saw Hugh. She hadn't expected him to be there. Too late, she remembered his phone call.

Unnerved, she looked at Vera, who was holding up what appeared to be a bizarre cartoon.

"What is that?" she said with dramatic hauteur, grateful to have something other than her father on which to focus.

"Well, it's not a love note," Vera snapped sarcastically. She appeared embarrassed by Greta's entrance.

Greta, on the other hand, continued her intrusion by making a production of introducing herself to Wiggers, the one stranger in the room. She made just as much of a point of avoiding Hugh and Bryan.

Martie found that interesting. As far as she knew, Greta and her father hadn't seen each other in years. Greta and Bryan were supposed to be lovers, but he made no attempt to greet her.

Hugh walked over to welcome his daughter. He moved slowly, giving her

319

time to consider her response. His smile was warm. Still, Greta stiffened. Hugh hesitated, wanting to embrace her, yet uncertain as to whether or not he should.

"It's great to see you, Greta," Hugh said finally.

"Yes. Uh-huh." Greta was squirming like an insecure five-year-old. "Nice to see you too."

Eager to escape, Greta turned and quickly found a seat next to Wiggers. With a flick of her hair, she dismissed Hugh and directed her attention to Vera.

"When did you get that?" she asked.

"Last night. Bryan's going to take it and have it dusted for fingerprints."

Greta turned to Bryan, her expression sour. "Do you really think whoever's doing this is stupid enough to leave prints?"

"No, but we're going to dust it anyway. Now," he said to the rest of the gathering, "can we get back to what we were talking about before?"

The unspoken phrase "we were so rudely interrupted" just hung in the air.

Martie was positively rapt at the drama being played out in her living room.

Hugh was not. "You need to go back in," he said to Wiggers. "Check out the different crews. Who's new? Who left on bad

320

terms? Who was a part-timer? That kind of thing."

"Yes, sir," Wiggers said. "I know the drill."

Martie smiled. She bet he did.

That afternoon, Hugh told her he had sought Wiggers out after he heard he'd retired. He claimed he signed him up because if he could train Martie to follow orders, he could train anyone to do anything. That was Hugh's way of chiding her for being stubborn and headstrong; on a good day, he called it being tenacious and directed.

"Did that second lipstick victim die?" Greta asked. "Is that why we're sending the troops into Carteret?"

The silence in the room was stunning.

"That second lipstick victim is alive and well and sleeping in the bedroom down the hall, thank you." Martie was hot and didn't care who knew it. "My daughter was the second victim."

Greta was confused and rattled by the hostility being aimed at her from all corners.

"Forgive me," she said, glaring at Bryan. "Seriously. I had no way of knowing."

He'd made her look foolish. She wouldn't forget that.

"How did she get her hands on a tube of Valentine? It's not your color," she said to Martie.

Though it came out sounding like a criticism, even in her state of pique Martie understood it was a professional observation. Valentine Red was too blue for her.

Before she could respond, Vera offered a mea culpa.

"I brought Lili a gift of what I believed were Hart Line goodies. It turned out that wasn't the case. Fortunately, her nanny, Soledad, was quick-thinking and got Lili to the hospital in time. I can't even begin to imagine what might have happened if she hadn't."

Her devastation was sincere.

Martie was moved by the choke in Vera's voice.

"Did Detective Borzone's forensic lab test the other products in that bag?" she asked Bryan.

"They prioritized and tested the lipstick first. I assume we'll hear about the rest of it tomorrow or the next day."

"Is this same detective on the hunt for whoever's menacing Vera?" Greta's tone was snide.

"Yes."

"Well, that makes me feel all warm and

safe inside. He's doing a hell of a job." Greta opened her purse and pulled out a plastic baggie containing an envelope. Instead of handing it to Bryan, she passed it over to Hugh. "I received this in the mail."

Hugh took Vera's latex gloves and examined the envelope. There was a white powder inside and a note: *This is how we get rid of rats.*

"Is this the first threat you've received?" he asked, carefully putting what he assumed was rat poison back into the envelope, then back into the baggie.

"I had a couple of hang-ups, but this is the first tangible threat," she said.

An almost imperceptible arch of an eyebrow caught Hugh's attention.

"And you?" he said to Martie.

"The other night I was awakened by someone who found it amusing to breathe into the phone and not identify himself. I thought it might be a crank. Guess not."

Vera, visibly disturbed at the notion that her sins had been visited on her daughters, turned to Hugh. "You're in the security business. Assign someone to guard them."

"I already have," Hugh said. "And I've assigned someone to you."

Greta swallowed wrong and began coughing. Wiggers handed her a glass of water. When her throat cleared, she looked at her father as if he were insane.

"Call off your dogs! This is an image business. If Vera and I, the heads of that business, are under guard, what does that say? It says we're in trouble, and frankly, I don't think that's the message we should be putting out there."

Vera pursed her lips as she weighed Greta's words against Hugh's recommendation.

Bryan was also torn. As much as he wanted to protect the three women, he had to be able to mount a decent defense for his client. If all this harassment was just a cruel sidebar to the attacks against HLI, with no intention of going beyond the threats, and they overreacted, they could kill their case before it ever got to court. If it was in fact the work of a crazy man intent on doing the Hart women harm and they underreacted, they could be aiding and abetting a potential homicide.

"Greta isn't wrong about the perils of creating the wrong image," he said. "The mere fact that HLI is under investigation casts a negative pall over Vera. Plus, the public doesn't care enough to make the distinction between a bodyguard and a policeman. Pictures of Vera with some hulk watching her back could taint the jury pool."

"Not to mention the impact it would have on our already shaky stockholders," Greta warned.

Vera had heard enough. "Recall the guards, Hugh. Instead of worrying about who or what might be lurking out there, let's concentrate on solving the problems we know about. They're serious enough."

"Someone is threatening you," Hugh said, his jaw tight. "To me, that's far more serious than the price of your damned stock."

Vera shrugged. An odd calm had descended on her. It was as if she'd been asked to make a Solomonic decision. She made it and was comfortable with it.

"If they're trying to scare me," she said, "they have. But if they're doing this to defeat me, they're going to have to try a lot harder. I am not going to throw up my hands, hide in a closet, and hand over this company to some greedy bastard who just wants what he wants. Whoever it is, he's going to have to fight me for it."

Martie was cleaning up when the doorman buzzed to say one of her guests had forgotten something and was coming back up. Before she could ask who it was, her doorbell rang. She opened the door and found Greta on her threshold.

"The doorman said you forgot something?" Martie's voice was edged with annoyance.

"I forgot to apologize," Greta said with great humility. "For that comment about the second poisoning victim."

Martie was speechless.

"I had no idea it was your daughter. I needed to tell you how truly sorry I am."

Martie couldn't seem to come up with anything to say, so she said nothing.

"May I come in?" Without waiting for a response, Greta maneuvered her way into the apartment.

"I sounded completely heartless, I know, but honestly, I was caught off guard." She shrugged. An embarrassed, companionable smile flitted across her lips. "And you know how pissy I get when I'm left out of the loop."

Martie didn't know how to handle this new and improved, up-front and apologetic Greta. This certainly wasn't the person she'd been dealing with since her hire. Then again, she had been sprung on Greta, something that couldn't have been easy to swallow considering their past. And what Greta had said was true: She did get testy when she was the last to know anything.

"Fortunately," Martie said, opting to give her sister the benefit of the doubt, "Lili's over the worst of it. She's going to be okay."

Greta expelled a huge sigh of relief. "Thank goodness." She paused, nervously, it appeared. "Look, this whole thing with Lili got me thinking about us. It's been years since we've seen each other and I've been positively horrid, I know, but we're sisters. And we're grown-ups now. Isn't it time we put all this childish hostility behind us?"

It was Martie's turn to be caught off guard.

"We're working for the same company, which means we're going to be seeing each other every day. And with all the bad stuff that's going on at HLI, the threats to Vera — and to us — doesn't it seem foolish to waste so much energy on old rivalries?"

Greta's graciousness made Martie feel small and petty.

"It's certainly worth a try." Martie hoped her voice didn't sound forced.

"Mommy." Lili shuffled into the living room carrying the stuffed airplane Bryan had given her. Like a blankie, it hadn't left her side.

"Hi, sweetie," Martie said, scooping the sleepy child up into her arms. "Are you all right?"

"Uh-huh." She nodded and blinked her eyes, trying to adjust to the light. "I thought your meeting was over."

"It is."

Lili scrutinized Greta. "Were you at the meeting?"

"I was."

"Do you work with my mommy?"

"I do. I'm Greta Hart."

Lili heard the name and grinned. "Do you know the Queen of Hearts?"

"Vera," Martie said, translating.

"I'm her daughter," Greta said.

"Wow! It must be so neat being her daughter," Lili enthused.

Greta exchanged a knowing smile with Martie. "Sometimes it's very neat."

"She's my friend," Lili bragged.

"That's nice. Do you think I could be your friend too?"

Greta put out her hand. Lili accepted it and gave Greta a hearty shake. As she did, her airplane tumbled out of her other hand and onto the floor. Greta picked it up.

"What a colorful, fun airplane," she said, giving it back to Lili.

"My other new friend, Bryan Chalmers, gave it to me," Lili explained. "He promised to take me flying, but I got sick, so he gave me this to play with until I'm well enough to go in a real airplane."

Martie watched for a negative response, but there was none.

"You're very brave, Lili," Greta said. "I'd be too scared to fly a plane."

"My mommy used to fly planes."

"Your mommy's a lot braver than I am. Always has been."

Lili looked surprised. "Are you a friend of my mommy's?"

Before Greta could answer, Martie put Lili down on the floor and gently shooed her toward her room. "That's enough, Miss Busybody. Back to bed."

Lili looked disappointed. "Okay," she said, making it clear that she would have preferred to extend her visit with the Queen of Hearts' daughter.

"It was lovely meeting you," Greta said.

"I have to get lots of sleep so I can get better," Lili explained, following Martie out of the room. "When I do, will you come back so we can visit some more?"

"I'd love to."

Martie looked from her daughter to her sister, certain that at some point she'd fallen through the Looking Glass.

When she returned to the living room after tucking Lili in, she escorted Greta to the door.

"She's very special," Greta said to Martie.

"She liked you too."

"I'm glad." She walked to the elevator, pressed the button, and turned back to Martie. "And to answer Lili's question, if you'll let me, I'd like very much to be her mommy's friend."

Chapter 13

The morning newspapers were full of speculation about the fate of Hart Line International. The stock had dipped even lower, as had confidence in HLI's CEO, Vera Hart. Fueling the negative publicity were pictures of three former HLI executives being handcuffed and led out of their homes into police cars the day before and the anticipation about what might be revealed when the federal prosecutor deposed Craig Hemminger that afternoon. Even more titillating was the specter of Hemminger handing over incriminating tapes to back up his testimony. The media was positively salivating.

Vera Hart was unavailable for comment.

Bryan looked at his watch — again. Hemminger should have been at Darren Montgomery's office an hour ago. He couldn't imagine what could be keeping him. Blowing off a federal prosecutor wasn't the smartest thing to do, and Hemminger was a very smart man.

Vera must have called him ten times already. Hemminger's assertion that he had recorded dozens of incriminating conversations had put both Vera and Greta on edge. While Vera continued to assure Bryan she had never given Hemminger anything that could be construed as damaging, she remained concerned that the tapes had been doctored to implicate her. Vera knew Craig Hemminger hated her and had told Bryan so.

If that meeting at Valhalla was any indication of how Hemminger felt about Greta, he wasn't crazy about her either.

It was going on an hour and a half and Bryan was growing impatient. Hanging around Montgomery's reception area was a complete waste of time, but it made no sense to return to his office. He'd leave, Hemminger would show up, and he'd have to race downtown again.

With little else to occupy his mind, Bryan returned to last night's gathering. When he set aside his emotional reaction to being in Martie's apartment and seeing how full her life had been without him, the most worrisome discovery was that in addition to Vera, both Greta and Martie had been menaced. Whoever this at-large lunatic was and whatever his endgame was, right now he was intent on ratcheting up everyone's sense of peril. Judging by the looks on the faces of everyone in the room, he had succeeded.

The good news, if there was any, was that as much as Bryan disliked Hugh Phelps, he knew that despite Hugh's verbal acquiescence, the general would never pull his guards off. They would simply retreat a little farther into the shadows.

The envelope Greta had received and the phone threats bothered Bryan, but they were understandable; Greta was the COO of HLI. If Vera was a target, it made sense that Greta would be one as well. Martie's anonymous phone call was alarming because it made no sense. Why had she become a target? Was it because she'd been snooping around at the Carteret plant? Was it because whoever hated Vera had discovered Martie's consanguine connection? Or were his suspicions about listening devices in Vera's office being borne out and whoever was at the other end overheard how involved Martie was in HLI and decided to lump her together with the other two?

It didn't matter. Whatever the cause, the effect was the same. Someone was waging war against the Hart women, and despite

Vera's valiant attempt to file this battle under "business," this was coming across as a very, very personal vendetta.

Vera was holed up in her apartment. She didn't have the stomach to face the carnivores stalking her building. They had been gathering since before dawn. Inside, she wandered nervously from room to room, coffee cup in one hand, cell phone in the other. She let the answering machine pick up whatever calls came in on the landline.

Hugh had called to offer encouragement. So had Greta and Martie. Vera, who hadn't enjoyed the benefits of a family for years, found their solicitousness comforting. The thought of their concern prompted a brief smile.

Perhaps when Hugh had asked what she was up to, why she was *suddenly* so interested in Lili and Martie, she should have told him this was why. Because it felt good to have people worried about *her* well-being for a change and not just the well-being of her company. Instead, she'd told him it was because life *suddenly* seemed finite. But she supposed both feelings were born of the same startling notion: There was no such thing as "forever."

Vera was turning sixty. While it was a

milestone that deserved to be marked; it made her aware of the unsettling thought that a cap had been placed on her existence. Whether she lived another twenty years or thirty, an end was in sight.

She had always been a forward-thinking woman, which was why she'd never really contemplated her own mortality. Then, several months before, she had a health scare. A lump had been discovered in her breast. She'd had a mammogram as well as an MRI, but her doctors wanted to do a biopsy. She scheduled it for six o'clock in the morning at a private clinic. No one other than Vera and the medical team knew anything about it.

The day before the procedure, Greta insisted on having that excruciating conversation about succession. It wasn't unreasonable for Greta to want to know what Vera had in mind as the future of HLI. Nor was it unkind for her to raise the subject of Vera's eventual retirement. It was simply bad timing.

As she paced, she recalled the vitriol that had passed between them on that day. It was regrettable, but she couldn't take back what she'd said, nor would she forget what Greta had said.

Vera sneaked a peek outside. The swarm

was increasing. Now there were cameras positioned across the street, their lenses aimed up at her window. She backed away quickly, worried that someone had caught a picture of her peering out of her apartment like a caged animal.

Just then, that's how she felt, as if she had been hunted and held captive by outside forces that insisted upon making changes in her life she didn't ask for and didn't want.

There was only one other time that she'd felt this victimized and, oddly enough, it was when she had been facing another milestone birthday — thirty. Hollywood abandoned her, and shortly after that Hugh ended their marriage.

She wallowed in depression for months, but eventually anger and heartbreak became a powerful motivating force. Hugh may have thought she was flawed. Hollywood may have thought she was done. But the public didn't agree. She was an icon and they loved her. They didn't care that she no longer made movies, they still wanted to know what lipstick she was wearing and how she kept her skin soft and what shade of blush she used. So eventually it dawned on Vera that she should do what she'd been doing since she was nine years old: play to her fans. If they wanted to live like her and look like her and dress like her, she would sell them her.

Now she wondered how her fans would feel after the government finished presenting its case. Would they continue to gift her with their loyalty? Or would they believe Hemminger and abandon her?

She checked her watch.

That bastard! The thought of him testifying against her and using doctored tapes to bolster his lies enraged her to the point where she simply couldn't stay sequestered a moment longer. Bryan had advised her to stay out of sight and let him take care of things.

But Vera Hart wasn't a woman who let others take care of her. Or things.

Once again, Martie was headed for New Jersey. Before she left home, Martie faxed Vincent Wiggers a list of employees who had been dismissed from HLI over the past three years. Since both Vera and Greta seemed reluctant to go through their files, Martie bypassed them and befriended Sarah Searls, the head of human resources at HLI. When Martie explained that she was trying to find the whistle-blower who had put Vera on the hot seat and everyone's job in jeopardy, Sarah was eager to help in any way she could.

Martie forwarded the list to Wiggers, who would run the names through databases that might highlight anyone who presented a reasonable cause for further investigation. Since Bryan was tied up at court, Martie suggested that Wiggers coordinate his efforts with Tony Borzone; Borzone might have access to intel that Wiggers wouldn't.

When she arrived in Carteret, Mark Fortas, the plant administrator, greeted her. She had called the day before to set up this appointment under the pretext of needing to conduct a review of lab procedures. Fortas was extremely cooperative; it wouldn't serve his interests to be a hindrance, but to be fair, he had nothing to hide. Carteret was a model production facility.

Martie reassured him that she expected no wholesale changes, but left open the possibility of making whatever changes would increase cost efficiency. Fortas wholeheartedly agreed with the concept and then eagerly escorted Martie to the production area in the north quadrant so he could turn her over to Ian Bardwill, the head chemist.

As they passed through security, Martie paid strict attention to the time it took for their ID tags to register, how long before a fingerprint was requested, and the interval between that, acceptance, and entry. She wanted to know whether the system was programmed to work as quickly as possible or as thoroughly. Her conclusion was that speed was the primary concern.

Bardwill was far more pleasant than he was on their first encounter, greeting her this time with respectful familiarity. Her guess was he'd Googled her and after reading her history was willing to view her as a valued colleague rather than a celebrity hire.

A man of medium height and build, Bardwill was probably in his early forties. Plain-looking, he had solemn gray eyes that held such a steady gaze it was as if he were constantly peering through a microscope. When he extended his hand, Martie noticed how elegant his fingers were.

"Welcome," he said in soft voice that was scented with station. "It's a pleasure to see you again."

Martie followed suit and the three of them engaged in banalities for a few seconds. Fortas excused himself and Bardwill walked Martie through most of his procedures, showing her how the chemists worked up a formula and which tests they conducted to validate their conclusions. His methods weren't very different from the ones she'd used at Rockefeller. When she told him that he seemed pleased.

Bardwill's assistant, Wally Crocker, was also quite helpful, but his incessant offers of support felt forced. Martie couldn't decide whether he was trying to score points with his boss or her. Either way, she found him annoying.

When they were finished in the lab and had observed the production line for a time, Martie and Bardwill returned to his office, where he offered her some coffee. In return, Martie offered a few suggestions, the main one being a reorganization plan that would increase profitability and keep staffing at its present level by defining theaters of responsibility.

Bardwill responded with a broad smile of relief. He'd already worked up such a plan. He extracted a sheaf of papers and laid them out in front of Martie. They were personnel charts with time schematics coordinated with names, positions, production schedules, and financial projections.

"I presented this to the board several times, but the only response I got was they would take it under advisement."

Martie found that rather shortsighted.

"I had the impression Vera Hart was a visionary who never met an idea she wouldn't investigate. I didn't think this company operated that way."

Barwill studied Martie for a moment, as if deciding whether or not he could trust her with his opinions about their mutual employer.

"When I first came here," he said, opting to confide, "the corporate mantra was, 'Grow bigger and better.' If you conceived a new product or contrived a new way of doing things, it was tested and, if approved, properly financed. To me, that's why this company is such a whopping success. No matter how many new divisions she added, Vera Hart constantly reinvested in Hart Line stalwarts.

"Over the past few years, however, corporate policy changed to, 'Stay the course.' At first, I thought the shift in emphasis was because profits were being used to shore up the newer, less successful divisions like sportswear and home accessories. But when I reviewed the year-end statements, our bottom line showed the biggest losses, which made no sense. Judging by the constant demand for production and our low number of returns, there was no way we couldn't have made our numbers. And then some!

"When I heard the accusations of accounting fraud, I refused to believe it. In my experience Vera Hart was always tough as nails but on the up and up. More than once I heard her say that since it was her name on every package, there'd better not be anything inside that was less than perfect. She demanded quality and rejected anything that wasn't up to her standards. She also fired anyone who didn't perform at the highest level."

"Do you think she's guilty?"

"Who knows? Instead of borrowing from one division to strengthen another as I thought they were doing, she and her cronies might have been playing some kind of high-stakes shell game so they could inflate the value of the stock and stuff their pockets while the stuffing was good.

"It probably never crossed their minds, but most of their employees also hold stock in HLI. Many of us were banking on that for our retirement or for our children's college tuition or for emergencies. Now, not only is that stock in the toilet, but we're all tainted with the stink of their greed."

His anger was palpable. Martie knew he

was wondering where he'd find a job if Vera was indicted and Hart Line Cosmetics went bust.

"I'm new, so I don't know all the players," she said, fishing. "Do you think Hemminger could have orchestrated all this on his own?"

She'd seen the newspaper on his desk with the picture of Craig Hemminger on the front page, so she knew he was aware of Hemminger's impending court appearance.

"I'm not sure," Ian said, his thin lips pinched. "He was the CFO. Whether this shuffling of resources was his idea, Greta's orders, or Vera Hart's it doesn't matter. Hemminger had a staff of flunkies who carried out any assignments he found distasteful, so his fingerprints aren't going to be on anything criminal. You can go to the bank on that," he said with undisguised animosity. "You can be sure *he* did!"

When their prime witness hadn't showed by five o'clock that afternoon, Darren Montgomery asked the NYPD in the Nineteenth Precinct to check out Hemminger's apartment. Montgomery was convinced he'd skipped. Bryan feared he might have been forcibly encouraged not to testify. Neither was surprised when the officers reported he wasn't at home. There weren't any signs of a struggle; if anything, his apartment was compulsively neat. Two large suitcases were still on the floor of a storage area off the kitchen and nothing significant appeared to be missing from his closet. His car was still in the garage and a call to his bank reported no unusual activity on his accounts that day or in the days previous.

Judging by the evidence — or lack thereof — at his apartment, he hadn't run away and hadn't been kidnapped. Other than the fact that he hadn't shown up for a subpoenaed court appearance, there was nothing to say he was actually missing. One officer suggested Hemminger was in a bar somewhere tying on a big one.

It was as feasible an explanation as anything else, Bryan supposed. And if that turned out to be the case, Hemminger would have more to worry about than a hangover. Darren Montgomery didn't like to be stood up.

Martie spent a good deal of the day with Ian Bardwill. By the time she left, she had his commitment to cooperate with her restructuring. She also had a couple of theories about how Valentine Red might have been contaminated and a bad feeling about the inner workings of HLI's financial department. If Bardwill's observations were correct — and his powers seemed keen — something in the Big Apple offices of Vera Hart's conglomerate was rotten.

It did intrigue her that Bardwill was so forthcoming in his criticism. He didn't know her. She had come at the behest of the corporate leaders. Why was he so willing and so quick to disparage his bosses? It wasn't out of the realm of possibility that Ian Bardwill was the whistle-blower.

As she left the plant to head back to New York, she decided she needed to speak to someone about this. She couldn't discuss something this incriminating with Vera or, despite their recently negotiated truce, with Greta. This wasn't exactly Hugh's area of expertise, nor, in all fairness, was the dirty laundry of Vera's business any of his business. That left Bryan. She came to a red light, quickly found his cell phone number in her Palm Pilot, and jotted it down so she could call him the minute she hit the city.

She had just passed the exit for Rahway when her rental car lurched violently to the left. Two cars swerved to avoid her. With her heart drumming against her chest, she gripped the steering wheel with both hands and tried to control the car, but it seemed to have a mind of its own, reeling wildly from one lane to another. Quickly, she activated the hazard lights to alert other drivers that she was in trouble. Unsure as to what the problem was, which made finding a solution nearly impossible, she relied on instinct.

She pumped the brakes cautiously, hoping to slow the car down without making the skid worse. It was rush hour and traffic was heavy. In her rearview mirror she saw that some cars had pulled over to the side; she was whirling like a dervish and no one, including her, knew where she would land.

Frightened, she remembered that Bryan had given her lessons on defensive driving during one of their weekends together in the desert. It was one of his you-never-know-when-this-will-come-in-handy courses.

Pitching from one side of the Jersey Turnpike, Martie desperately tried to recall what Bryan had told her. She slowed the car, kept the wheel as straight as she could, pulled on the emergency brake, and braced herself. The tires screeched. The car yanked left and streaked across two lanes like a missile homing in on its target.

Martie hit the divider, head on.

Sometime after midnight a jogger spotted something near the shoreline on the West Side Highway opposite Riverside Park. It was the body of a well-dressed middle-aged man. His pockets had been picked clean, but there were no gunshot wounds, knife slices, ligature marks, or bruises that would have resulted from a beating or a fall. According to the state of the rigor, the ME estimated the victim had been dead at least twelve hours. Postmortem lividity indicated the man had not died in this place. The blades of grass and bits of dirt on his clothing as well as the positioning of the body led the police to conclude he had been dumped from a car and had rolled down to the river. The case was presenting as a homicide, but they couldn't be certain until an autopsy was performed. Which meant they had to find out who the man was so they could notify the next of kin and get permission to proceed.

A quick fingerprint check at the morgue identified him as Craig Hemminger.

Chapter 14

She didn't know how long she had been in the truck. She only knew how nauseous she was and how much she hurt. Her wrists and ankles were bound and she was lying flat on the floor looking up into the faces of her captors. While they all had to absorb the shocks of the bumpy ride, for her it was a nightmare. Each time the truck hit a mound or a rut, her broken limbs slapped against the metal floor, the pain so intense and localized it was like being stabbed with acid-tipped knives. She winced and her eyes teared, but she refused to cry out.

The two younger soldiers looked away; witnessing her discomfort made them uncomfortable. The other two hooted and laughed as if they were at a soccer game.

When the truck stopped, her heart began to race. She didn't know whether they had arrived at a hospital, the nearest prison, or simply a place where

Tariq planned to execute her.

The doors opened. She raised herself up on her left arm and peered out onto a flat wasteland in the middle of which stood a single-story building. Inwardly, she breathed a sigh of relief. Hospital or prison, she felt as if she'd just been granted a stay of execution.

Quickly, before either of the more sadistic Guards could push her out, she crabbed her way to the end of the truck and attempted to slide out without landing on her broken foot. The drop was too steep. She couldn't control her fall. When both feet hit the ground, a sharp, searing pain coursed up from the sole of her right foot, spiking to her brain like the mercury in a thermometer that had been dipped in hot water.

She wanted to scream, to let her voice carry the pain out of her body and disperse it into the air, but then they would think she was weak. Instead, she fell back against the truck, took a deep breath, and gritted her teeth until the agonizing spasm subsided.

While the others scurried about unloading whatever bounty they had procured during their sortie, Martie used her one good eye to scan the surrounding area; her mind hadn't completely dismissed the idea of escape, despite the physical reality that that was impossible. There was nothing to see except desert and sky, both of which were heavily cloaked in black. The building was also lightless, probably so the Americans weren't alerted to their position. The Iraqis didn't want to invite a bombing. At that moment, she wholeheartedly agreed with their thinking.

Tariq, who was growing impatient with the snail's pace of his associates, started barking orders at his prize pit bulls, the same two who'd laughed at her during the journey here. As he shouted at them Martie was able to make out their names: Amin and Khalid.

Eager to prove themselves, they jumped into the truck and hauled out three boxes of medical supplies, which Martie had packed personally, a couple of machine guns, several ammunition belts, and a large gun mount that couldn't have come from her chopper. Her Hawk was outfitted for medical evacuation; there was no room for heavy armament, which was why Apaches flew escort on search and rescue missions. As she watched them dance around with the mount on their shoulders, she shuddered. Not from the sight of them with a gun mount, but because that piece of equipment had to have come from another downed American plane.

Her first thought was that it might have been from the crash that initiated her mission. One of the pilots of that flight, Captain Ryan Lockhart, had survived, but was seriously injured. Her crew was on its way to rescue him when they had been shot down.

She tried calculating the coordinates she had been given on that plane relative to hers, but it was difficult. During flight she'd been preparing for Lockhart's initial treatment. When he'd radioed in he'd given her a list of his injuries, the most serious of which was a compound fracture of the femur. She was so engrossed with what she was doing that when her copter was hit, she had no sense of where they were.

She decided they couldn't have been too close. Tariq would have stopped to scavenge that plane and to bag another American trophy.

Then again, when a plane was shot out of the sky it wasn't unusual to find equipment scattered for miles. As for the captain, it was possible that another Republican Guard unit had already picked him up.

What had they done with him?

Her mind raced as she tried to be logical in the midst of insanity. Since they weren't near a city or even a large village, she concluded either he was dead or he was inside whatever that building was. If it was a prison and not a hospital, she would ask to tend to his injuries. The medical kits were there, prepped and ready. And she was supposed to be allowed to care for her own troops.

Martie's sense of purposeful relief faded quickly when a third possibility surfaced. If the gun mount wasn't from Lockhart's plane, it could have come from one of her Apache escorts. The thought of having lost even more of her unit was devastating.

Concerns about her safety and Lockhart's fate were instantly shelved, replaced by a sad reverie in which she forced herself to remember the faces and names of every soldier on those two planes.

Her silent mourning was interrupted by the other two members of Tariq's happy band of brothers, Yasin and Zarif. They ripped Martie away from the truck and shoved her toward the door of the prison. As she struggled to maneuver without inflicting further damage to her already ravaged body, she glanced at the faces of her young jailers and was struck by an odd gush of pity for them. She was a soldier too and on some strange level she understood their need to curry favor with a superior officer; the rougher they were with her, the more they impressed Tariq. The shame of it was that the Republican Guard wasn't the United States Army. They prized brutality over honorable behavior. The Geneva Convention held no favor here.

As she hobbled toward the squat, undistinguished structure, she couldn't decide which was worse: staying out in the desert where she risked being attacked by anyone and everyone, or going through that door, where she felt certain she'd be attacked.

Once inside, Yasin, the larger of the two, dragged her down a narrow, spare hallway of cement cinderblocks. The air was much colder than it had been outside and even under her flight suit she could feel her skin prickle. The atmosphere was dank and smelled like dirty socks. She began to shiver and the nausea returned. When they arrived at her cell, Yasin propped her against a wall while he unlocked a thick metal door. He shoved her in and locked the door behind him.

It felt good to be alone.

The space was meager, maybe eight feet by six feet. A wooden bench sized to accommodate a tall man ran the length of the long wall opposite the door. There was a window. It was small, barred, and beyond her reach, but Martie studied it anyway, quickly recognizing that even if she could find a way to get to it, it was too skimpy for her to get through. There was nothing on the floor to shield her from the cold. Nor were there any toilet facilities: no sink, no commode, no bucket.

There was a small square cutout in the door that was protected by a mesh grill. She tried to look out, but the grill was covered by some kind of curtain. It allowed them to watch her; she couldn't see them.

She made her way to the bench and practically collapsed. She was exhausted and hungry. She also had to pee.

"Guard!" she yelled.

Minutes passed with no response.

"Guard!" she yelled again.

Again there was no response, but she knew they were standing outside the door, peeking in. She could feel their eyes on her.

She yelled again, and this time the door opened. It was Khalid.

"I need to use the bathroom," she said. He looked befuddled. "Toilet. W.C."

His English was probably limited, but she was sure he understood basic words.

Obviously he did, because he tossed in a bucket and exited.

She knew they were watching, so she turned her back to the door. It wasn't an act of modesty; living in the desert had eliminated that perk of civilization. This was an act of defiance: If they were hoping for a strip show, she was going to do her best to deny them.

The first thing she did was lean over so she could bring the bucket closer to the bench. Then she unzipped her flight suit and extricated her left arm. Gingerly, she worked the top down over her broken right arm. She almost cried with relief when the upper part of her suit fell to her waist.

She stopped and thought for a minute about how to complete her disrobing *without revealing herself to them, but in the end she surrendered to the inevitable. She sat on the bench, pulled the zipper down to the crotch, and removed her left leg. She grabbed a hunk of the jumpsuit and, using it as a sling, raised her right leg onto the bench. Slowly, she rolled the pant leg down and over her mangled foot. The entire leg pulsed with pain.*

Also, she was freezing. Without the cover of her uniform and still suffering from the residual effects of the crash, her body temperature must have been a degree above igloo. She had to get this over with as quickly as possible.

When her body was calm, she slid her panties off. Then she bent down to pull the bucket close to the bench. Carefully, she positioned herself so that she could support herself with her left arm and leg and squat over the bucket. She closed her eyes to create a sense of privacy and relieved herself.

She hoisted herself back up onto the bench and prepared to go through the wrenching process of dressing herself when the door to her cell opened.

Amin and Khalid entered and slammed the door behind them.

When Martie opened her eyes, the scene was completely unfamiliar. She blinked, searching for the small square window that punctuated the short wall or the cement block nearest her head where she had kept track of the days of her captivity by scratching lines in the grout with Bryan's dime. When she didn't find her signposts, she worried that she had been transferred to another cell or another prison.

Her eyes were blurry and her body felt spongy. They must have given her drugs.

Why would they do that? she wondered, her brain struggling to sweep away the narcotic cobwebs and focus.

Perhaps they had videotaped her, drugging her so they could get her to say what they wanted her to say. They'd tried to coerce her into "confessing" on tape several times. All she would give them was the standard: name, rank, serial number, and date of birth. They demanded more, and threatened her with horrific cruelty if she didn't deliver. In her mind, short of killing her they'd already done the worst they were prepared to do.

Delilah.

If they'd transferred her, what had they done with the other prisoners? What had they done with Delilah?

Delilah Green was a specialist with the 233rd Transportation Company. She and another specialist, Eddy Handelman, were operating an HET — heavy equipment transfer vehicle — near the Kuwaiti/Saudi Arabian border. They were delivering a repaired tank to troops in the field when they made a wrong turn and came face to face with Iraqi troops in armored patrol vehicles. The Americans came under intense fire. The other HET managed to escape, but Delilah and Eddy had the heavier load and got stuck in the sand. They were taken prisoner and ultimately wound up in the same prison as Martie.

From the first, the Iraqis used Delilah as a threat. They'd tell Martie what they wanted from her: information about troop movements, descriptions of equipment, strategic planning, and, of course, a confession in which she denounced the USA and its warmongering government. After each negative response, aside from her own punishment, they made certain she heard the repercussions of her refusal to cooperate.

Martie turned her head to her left, toward the tiny hole in the wall that former prisoners had burrowed as a communications link between cells.

"Delilah," she whispered, needing to know whether there had been further reprisals. The ensuing silence terrified her.

For most POWs the only thing staving off insanity was contact with other prisoners, knowing that you weren't alone.

"Delilah," she whispered again, unable to conceal the panic she felt at her friend's nonresponsiveness.

"She's fine," a male voice said. "And you're fine."

Martie rubbed her eyes and shook her head to clear away the fog so she could see the face that belonged to the vaguely familiar baritone. When she recognized Bryan, she burst into tears. She had been rescued. She was safe.

He bent down to caress her head. She threw her arms around him and clung to him as if he were her lifeline.

"I thought I'd die in there," she said, her voice trembling with emotion. "I thought they'd kill me. Thank you. Thank you. Thank you."

Bryan realized she was reliving her captivity. Gently, he brought her back to the present.

"You weren't in Iraq, Martie," he said, pressing her close to him. He could feel her heart pounding against his chest. "You were in New Jersey." He used the slang pronunciation, "Joisey," in the hopes of eliciting a smile. He couldn't see it, but he could feel her cheek move against his. He could also feel the tears that had dampened her face. "You were playing bumper cars on the Jersey Turnpike."

She pulled away from him as images of that traumatic ride flooded back.

"I hit the divider," she said.

"Head-on. But the emergency brake was engaged and the car had slowed. The front end was totaled, but your seat belt was on, which was why you didn't go flying through the windshield. You did have a concussion and some bruising, so the doctors kept you for observation."

Martie processed the information, segregating various lines of thought.

"Was anyone else hurt?"

"No. Fortunately, motorists sensed that your swaying all over the road wasn't just because there was a woman at the wheel. They avoided you like the plague."

"There's no question I was a loose cannon."

"Someone headed south actually called the police, which is why they were there almost immediately after you crashed. The ambulance followed by a couple of minutes."

"I was zigzagging all over the road," she said, going back over what had happened, trying to sort it out. "It was sudden. Like a blowout, but I didn't hear anything. And the car didn't bounce along on the rim the way it would with a blowout. This was no accident, Bryan. Someone messed with that car. I'm sure of it."

"I agree with you and so do the police. They're on it."

"Good." Her next thought was her daughter. "Where's Lili?"

"Home."

"Who's with her? Soledad can't work at night." Her voice was scalloped with anxiety. "Did you call my father?"

"I called Delilah," he said, rejecting the impulse to tell her Hugh Phelps was the last person he would call for anything. "She and Lili are having a sleepover."

Martie relaxed, but only slightly. "Does she know what happened?"

Bryan shook his head. "I made an executive decision. I asked Delilah to tell her you had to go out of town on business, which, considering where you were, wasn't a total lie."

Martie smiled. He looked so proud of himself. As well he should be. For a man without children, his responses were spot on.

"Not that I'm not thrilled to see you, but why did they call you and not my father or Vera?"

"You had my number written on a piece of paper. They found it on the front seat." He grinned at her. "Couldn't get through another day without me, eh?"

He expected an amused scowl or a dismissive chuckle. What he got were more tears.

"I wouldn't have survived this accident if not for you," she said, her voice ringing with emotion. "Those stupid driving lessons you gave me probably saved my life."

Tiny rivulets were parading down her cheeks, but her lips managed to curl in a smile as she remembered them careening about the desert.

Bryan, recollecting the same scenes, took her hand, leaned over, and kissed her. "I'm glad I could help." His voice was husky.

"When can I get out of here?" Martie asked, flushed with feelings she couldn't deal with just then. "And by the way, where is *here?*"

"*Here* is Newark and you can't leave until one of your medical *compadres* says so."

Martie found the nurse's button and pushed it. She sat up slowly and checked herself out. She had no broken bones. She was only slightly groggy, but other than that she felt fine.

A man whose name tag identified him as Dr. Cooper approached. He was tall and solidly built with kind eyes and an easy smile poking out from beneath a neatly trimmed salt and pepper beard.

"Nice to see you awake," he said, automatically pressing his fingers to her wrist.

"I want out," she said.

"Me too."

He dropped her wrist and chuckled at his own joke. Then he pressed his stethoscope against her chest and listened. He looked into her eyes, palpated her skull, picked up her chart, studied the latest notations of her vitals, and, after warning her about headaches and other possible recurring symptoms, pronounced her free to go.

For Martie, the next issue was where she wanted to go. Bryan, who read the confusion on her face, offered a solution.

"Rather than upset Lili, why not come home with me? I promise to behave like an officer and a gentleman." He smirked and twitched his eyebrows in a poor imitation of Groucho Marx. "And if you're a really good girl, I promise bagels, cream cheese, and lox for breakfast."

"Pumpernickel bagels?"

"And mocha java coffee."

"You win," she said, waving the corner of her sheet in surrender. "I'm yours."

He laughed. In his heart, he wished that were so.

By the time they got back to Bryan's loft it was late. Martie had a king-sized headache and her body felt battered and black and blue, but she had too many disparate thoughts spinning around in her head to sleep. Bryan gave her some sweats and invited her to make herself comfortable while he fixed some tea.

After changing clothes and washing up, Martie felt wonderfully refreshed. She padded back into the living room and cozied into the corner of one of the couches so she could admire the apartment. It was very Bryan, ordered yet serene. The furniture was contemporary, cleanly cut with a few sharp edges, but the colors and fabrics were soft and inviting.

A perfect description of the man who lived here, she thought.

What surprised her was the sophistication. The Bryan she had known seemed more frat boy than city squire, but he didn't have his own place back then. He lived in government housing, which could never be coupled with urbane décor. It was much too oxymoronic.

She remembered that when they had talked about their future, both of them had declared themselves in favor of a house. His Teaneck childhood had instilled in him the desire for a fireplace and a kitchen big enough for family dinners, a community with Little League games, and a park where every July Fourth there were fireworks and an oom-pah band.

While she hadn't revealed the entirety of her past, she agreed that a yard was a must-have. The house on Roxbury Drive had a small backyard, which Vera had overwhelmed with a pool. Luckily, there was a wonderful park across the street where she and Hugh had played catch and he taught her how to bat. Most of the homes she lived in with Hugh and Connie after that were far more modest; army bases didn't lend themselves to grassy spreads and private swimming pools.

When they talked about furniture, again the Roxbury house was Martie's reference. She spoke of artifacts gathered from world travels, of beautifully arranged surroundings in which each element seemed to enhance every other element, of lush fabrications and subtle lighting.

Now it struck her as somewhat surprising that Bryan never caught on to the dichotomy in her recollections; he knew military homes and he knew Connie. He should have realized that she never would have been the chatelaine of such a manor as Martie described. But back then he wasn't analyzing her story for flaws; he thought he was listening to her dreams.

"I had some soup in the freezer." Bryan placed a large bowl of rich vegetable soup on the table in front of her. "Whenever I go to Teaneck, my mother loads me up with food from the Round Table. She's convinced that if not for her, I'd never eat anything healthy or hearty. She seems to think that bachelors exist on packaged mac and cheese and cheap wine."

Martie looked around his apartment and laughed. "Has she ever been here?"

Bryan chuckled. "Many times, but until there's a wife in residence, this is a way station, not a home."

She could tell by the slight flush to his cheeks, he didn't totally disagree with his mother.

Rather than trespass on what could become shaky ground for both of them, Martie concentrated on her soup. Bryan had brought out a bowl for himself and he too retreated into the comfort of warm food.

"I wish I knew exactly what happened," Martie said after her stomach was full. "To the car, I mean."

Bryan had called the New Jersey State Troopers from the hospital while Martie was being released.

"The preliminary police report says it was a tire, but you were right. It wasn't a standard blowout. Something damaged the sidewall."

That made sense. The car had driven beautifully on the way to Carteret. There'd been none of the wobbling that might have indicated a problem with the wheels.

"So someone did deliberately sabotage the car."

Bryan nodded. "Looks that way."

"Do the police have any ideas?"

"No, but I do." Bryan put down his soup, folded his arms onto his knees, and leaned toward Martie. "My guess is that the Carteret plant is where the contamination took place. Whoever's behind this didn't want you snooping around. This was a message to lay off."

Martie lowered her head and studied her hands as she considered what Bryan had said. Her right hand was striped with the thin lines of three surgeries needed to put her bones back in order. A sock covered her right foot, but underneath there were scars from the four surgeries required to get her up and walking again. She thought about Lili doubled over from poison and vomiting until she cried. She allowed the sight of that concrete divider to surface.

"I'm not going to do that," she said, looking up at Bryan, her lips set in a determined line. "You know that, don't you? I'm going to find this creep and I'm going to make him pay. For the woman in the park. For Lili. And for me."

Bryan heard the resolve in her voice and saw it in her eyes, but as much as he admired her courage, he needed to put the brakes on her quest for revenge. She didn't know about Craig Hemminger.

"I'm happy to sign on as your loyal deputy, Lieutenant Phelps, but pull back the reins for a minute. We don't know whether this is one person or a group. Whether this is specifically directed against you or it's part of a multipronged plan of intimidation aimed at anyone connected with Vera."

"Do the police know what caused the collapse of the tire's sidewall?"

He was grateful that she was so intent on her own accident that she hadn't asked about Hemminger's court appearance.

"It looks as if someone rammed a nail or spike into it. They sent it off to the lab for analysis." She eyed him quizzically. "They might be able to tell whether he used a shoe or a hammer and what kind of shoe and hammer we should be looking for."

"Do they have camera surveillance of the parking lot?" she asked. "Inside, they have cameras all over the place."

"I'll check it out first thing in the morning."

"I just realized something," Martie said, her eyes aglow with insight. "Since there are cameras watching who comes in and goes out of almost every door in the place, the person who contaminated the lipstick had to be familiar to the security crew."

"That would eliminate Wiggers's theory of a last-minute add-on to the cleaning detail. Any thoughts on the staff?"

"There's a guy named Wally Crocker who gives me the creeps." She laughed at her own words. "I know the courts wouldn't issue a warrant based on that kind of evidence, but he kept hanging around when I was meeting with his boss, Ian Bardwill. I couldn't shake the feeling that he wasn't really looking to help. Maybe he was looking to find out what I was doing there."

"I'll check him out as well." He stood, reached for her hand, and helped her to her feet. "Right now I'm checking you into the Chalmers hotel. It's late and you've had a full day."

Martie hesitated. Shakespeare's words "to sleep, perchance to dream" began to repeat like a thumping bass in her head. The last thing she wanted was to have another nightmare about her ten-night, nine-day sojourn in Iraq.

Bryan thought she lingered on the couch because she suddenly felt shy about staying in his apartment.

"I'm going to camp out on the couch in there," he said, pointing to a room behind the kitchen. "It's a second bedroom that I turned into a small office."

A subtle veil of relief wafted over Martie's face. She didn't think she was strong enough to deal with her attraction to him.

"I hate putting you out," she said.

"You're not." He helped her up, slid his arm around her waist, and nudged her forward. "I've slept in a lot less comfortable places, you know."

She flushed when she realized he was referring to their nights in the Saudi desert, and probably the Wings Motel outside of Fort Rucker. They spent more than a few nights in that fleabag. She swallowed a smile. Bryan always said the desert was nicer.

"I know nothing can compare to the sumptuous splendor of the Riyadh Ramada," he said, intuiting her thoughts as he opened the door to his bedroom. "But here, we have real beds with real sheets and no camels to worry about."

"That's a comfort."

He pulled back the blanket and invited her to climb in. She did, but instead of snuggling under the covers, she invited him to sit near her. Aside from not wanting to be alone, there was something she had to ask him.

Bryan was going to reject the suggestion — he also had a loose grip on his desires — but her expression was serious, not sensual. He did as she requested.

"What's wrong?"

"Tell me why this Valentine case means so much to you."

He shook his head. "You need —"

"I need to know."

He braced himself. "It's because of you."

Martie looked at him quizzically.

Bryan took his time, framing his words in his head. This was a conversation he'd envisioned many times over the years, but now that it was finally here, he found it difficult to begin.

"It started out being a totally subconscious thing," he said, clearly struggling with the best way to explain. "But from the day I left the army and entered the field of law enforcement, which was about eight years ago, I've been on a silent rampage to ensure the conviction of every sex offender I could. Whether it was while I was at the Bureau or during my time in the DA's office, if I caught the case, or if I could assist on the case, I made certain that anyone who committed a rape was sent away. Because you were raped and this is the only way I could avenge that crime."

Martie's breath caught in her throat. She had never told him the details of what happened in that prison.

"How did you find out?"

"When I returned stateside from Korea, I was stationed in California. One night I went to an off-base bar and ran into Eddy Handelman."

He was the soldier captured with Delilah.

"We hoisted a few and began to talk

about Desert Storm. After a couple of hours and more than a couple of drinks, he started to spill the details of his imprisonment."

Bryan stared at her, hard. She lowered her eyes.

"He was sick about what they did to you and Delilah."

Slowly, Martie raised her eyes. They were moist.

"He assumed I knew."

"How did you react?" Her voice stumbled.

His voice boomed. "How do you think I reacted? I was filled with rage." When she bit her lip, he realized she'd misunderstood. "Not at you," he said, far more softly. "Never at you. At them.

"I wanted to call you immediately, but I knew this wasn't something we could talk about on the phone. When I got back to Washington, I tried to call, but you had unlisted your number." His jaw tightened. "I contacted your father, but true to form he refused to tell me where you were."

Bryan had told Hugh he knew what had happened to Martie and was desperate to see her. Hugh told him he was too late, that Martie had moved on.

"He was only trying to protect me," she said weakly.

"From me? Why would he feel the need to do that? I loved you."

"So does he."

Bryan shook his head. There was no room in his heart for forgiveness when it came to General Hugh Phelps. Or himself.

"I shouldn't have listened to him. I should have tracked you down no matter where you went. But I didn't. I listened to him. And I lost you."

He got up off the bed and started to pace, circling about like an animal who'd been wounded and wanted to strike back at the first thing that crossed its path.

"I felt I didn't do right by you," he said. "When Handelman told me what happened, I felt I should have known. Or at the very least, I should have found a way to make you trust me with the truth. But I didn't.

"After I spoke to the general, I couldn't help but wonder if the reason you didn't confide in me was because I hadn't loved you enough. Or you hadn't loved me at all."

"I did love you, Bryan," Martie said, stunned that he ever could have doubted that. "But I didn't tell anyone, including my father, about the rape for months. Only my doctors knew."

Again, she lowered her eyes.

"What happened to me was very personal, very intimate, and very brutal. It didn't have anything to do with you or my father or anyone else. It was my experience and my task to get past it. I didn't want to hear your view of it, or Hugh's, or even the army's. I didn't want any suggestions or any advice or even any sympathy. All that mattered was how *I* felt about what happened to me and how *I* chose to heal." She looked at him. "Can you understand that?"

He did understand, but there was too much emotion in his throat to risk trying to speak.

"I've learned not to dwell on might-have-beens, Bryan," she said softly. "They're painful and unproductive. I focus on where I am now and where I want to be next."

He had stopped his perambulating and stood staring at her. He looked spent.

"The women whose cases you took on are lucky. Rape isn't an easy crime to prosecute honorably."

He knew she meant without allowing the defense to attack the victim on the stand, spinning everything from the way she wore her hair to how many dates she'd had since high school to make it appear that she "asked for it."

"I know you're not in the DA's office anymore, but it's important that you help find whoever killed that woman in Central Park and bring him to justice. It's the only way her family will have any peace."

His brown eyes grew dark as they fixed on hers. "Do you feel peace? Does Delilah?"

"That was war," she said quietly.

She didn't want to revisit that place or time, the dreams she'd had this evening had been more than enough reminiscence, but Bryan believed she and the woman in the park had suffered a similar indignity. She needed to separate the incidents, for his sake and hers.

"Delilah and I were prisoners of war, Bryan. They tortured us by violating us, but it wasn't anything worse than what they did to our men. Their goal was to humiliate us while making themselves feel powerful." She swallowed the emotion she felt lumping in her throat. "In the end I beat them, because I wasn't humiliated. I was a soldier who behaved in accordance to the standards set out by the army in which I served. I denied them their power because I didn't give them any information. I didn't give them their confession. And I didn't give them my soul."

Bryan flinched and looked away, as if he couldn't bear to see the scars of Martie's experience in her eyes.

She turned his face back to hers. Her gaze was firm, as was her voice.

"Most important," she said, "I survived."

Next to her, Bryan stirred. For a minute, she couldn't figure out what he was doing there. She had fallen asleep alone. They were both still in their sweats. Then it came back to her. Nightmares: hideous distortions of a hideous reality, twisted snapshots of a faceless woman in Central Park, Delilah, her, Amin and Khalid, merging together in a terrifying documentary.

She must have cried out. Knowing Bryan, he came running to comfort her.

Instinctively, she nestled closer to him. In response, Bryan's lips grazed her neck. He was awake, very much so, it seemed.

Martie didn't hesitate. She turned around and met his lips, her insides exploding the minute his tongue slipped into her mouth. The electricity she felt must have been contagious, because he pressed against her as if he would die if they were separated. His hands raked through her hair as his lips feasted on her lips and her neck.

She responded by sliding her arms around him. She felt his skin tighten at her touch.

Without disconnecting his mouth from hers, Bryan's hands quickly glided under her sweatshirt, trembling as they touched her breasts. She gasped as he reawakened a passion in her she thought she'd left behind in that other life. His hands journeyed across her body and her skin felt alive again, keenly sensitive to the touch of a man who loved her. He kissed her flesh and she felt as if she would burst with pleasure, but beyond the physical, automatic response to a sensual exchange, there was the liberating joy of feeling safe in this man's arms.

Eager, Martie moved away from him and stripped off the bulky fleece, freeing herself from its confines, and, by extension, freeing herself from the past.

Bryan looked at her with a question in his eyes.

"Yes," she whispered, smiling as she liberated him from his shirt.

"Okay, then," he said with a smile.

He devoured her and she him, each feasting on delights that tasted familiar, yet new. They made love as if it were the first time, full of passion and the joy of exploration. Yet it wasn't the first time, so each knew the other's pleasure spots, those secret places that acted as the catalyst for energizing every other part. Deftly, they aroused each other with the precision that comes from knowledge, but as it had been when they were lovers before, there always seemed to be something new to learn, another exciting door to open, another level of pitch to reach.

Bryan had never been with a woman as beautiful as Martie, nor one whose body meshed with his the way hers did. Outside of this bed, when he was better able to think, he would say it was because he'd never loved anyone the way he loved her, but just then, it was all about the fit and the feel. The way her breasts felt against his chest and fit his hands. The way their lips seemed to become one whenever they touched. The way their hands seemed to know instinctively where to go and what to do to extract the greatest pleasure possible. The way her skin felt so smooth and silky against his. The way it felt when her long, long legs were stretched alongside his, and then when they sinuously wrapped around him. But nothing compared to the way his body felt when it joined with hers, molded together in a heated union that rose above time and place. With other women he experienced sexual climaxes. With Martie, it was the culmination of an act of love.

For Martie, being with Bryan was like a homecoming, a return to a place she had loved being, a place she had sorely missed. Here, lying next to him, she felt secure and warm and thoroughly loved. So loved. Bryan knew how to hold her and caress her and kiss her and bring her to a peak of excitation that made her want to scream with the lusciousness of it all. He knew how to make her feel womanly and sensuous. He also knew how to make her feel cherished.

When they were spent, Bryan caressed Martie's hair and looked deep into her eyes. There was so much he wanted to say.

He started to speak, but she put a finger on his lips.

"Shhh." She kissed him good night and turned over to go to sleep.

It took him a while to absorb the miracle that had just occurred, but eventually he too drifted off.

Martie awakened slowly. She felt warm and safe, blanketed by a soft comforter and a strong arm.

An incongruous memory surfaced, probably prompted by the physical association of being held like that. It was the day the prison was liberated. After they had routed the Iraqis, Americans from the Fourth Armored Division came in to collect the POWs. There were five: three men, one of whom was Captain Lockhart, and Delilah and Martie. The soldiers unlocked each of the cells and approached the prisoners like precious objects. Carefully, they tended them and prepared them for their departure. They were dirty and battered and frail, but their rescuers made certain they left that hellhole of a prison with the dignity of heroes.

Tears came to Martie's eyes as she remembered trying to stand at attention when the brigade major entered her cell, the pain that shot through her when she forced her right arm up and her right hand into a salute. He returned her salute, then caught her before she fell.

She remembered him stepping aside to admit a female medic who was going to help her out of her yellow POW uniform and back into an army jumpsuit, then fit her with a better sling for her arm and a stabilizing boot for her shattered foot.

The picture that made the papers showed her walking toward the evacuation helicopter. In truth, she wasn't walking at all. Her left arm was draped around the major's shoulder. His arm was cinched firmly around her waist. Her feet were two inches above the ground.

As she lay in Bryan's arms and watched daylight insinuate itself on the world, she remembered how difficult it had been when she first returned stateside dealing with his anguish over his inability to prevent what had happened to her; and he only knew about her imprisonment. He felt as if the only way he could make up for his absence was to be ever-present. He pressed her to marry him, to let him take care of her.

Instead of his love feeling supportive, it was draining, even a bit overwhelming. At that time she had no strength, either emotional or physical, to comfort or reassure him. She needed all of her energy to be directed toward healing her wounds.

Years later, when she thought about his silence after the transfer to Korea, she realized that whatever the cause, it was probably for the best. She needed a blank slate, someone who would deal with her as she was, not someone who might be tempted to compare her to the woman she was before the war.

She had worked with her therapists to

put her experiences in perspective, to view them within the proper context, but at the end of the day, she was a woman who had been tortured and defiled. She survived, but she hadn't returned the same way she left. No POW does.

It hadn't been an easy road, or a straight one, but she had found her way back to life. She'd met Jack and fallen in love; not with the passion she'd had for Bryan, but comfort and security made up for a lot. She'd had a child; Lili was and would always be her reason for being. She'd returned to work; she could no longer operate with the same efficiency in the ER, but medical research had given her a haven and a purpose. And, she thought with amazed bemusement, she'd reunited with her mother — more or less.

That's not to say she didn't suffer setbacks. The recent recurrence of occasional daydreams and nightmares was one. And every now and then, when something triggered a memory, her heart rate spiked, she felt shaky and got the chills. But when she saw Delilah or Wiggers or Bryan, she didn't experience the strong physical pain or mental depression she would have in the years immediately following her return. Nor was she having problems concentrating or falling asleep.

She was able to talk about what happened and to see people who were reminders of the event without panicking or retreating; she, Lockhart, Delilah, and the other two Desert Storm veterans known as the Fallujah Five got together once a year, when possible. She could enjoy activities like going to Yankee games with Hugh and Lili, or the movies, or out to dinner with friends again. She had even begun to believe that her future might include marriage and old age.

"Are you awake?"

His voice made her acutely aware of the nearness of his body. It also aroused a heated desire to repeat last night's activity, to reclaim the intense, all-consuming love that had been theirs before the war and its aftereffects intervened. His arm was around her now, but she was still reliving last night and a hundred nights before that. She could feel his hands on her. She could remember how he tasted, how he smelled, how he looked when he loved her. She could remember how delicious it felt to have his lips navigate their way from her mouth, to her neck, to her breasts; how it felt to lie skin to skin and slowly, sensuously merge their bodies until they were one person, an entity that was only complete when each was bound to the other.

Martie luxuriated in her erotic imaginings; her body was alert and eager. They were cupped like spoons, a position that brought back memories of other mornings waking up similarly entwined.

"Martie?" he whispered, his breath brushing her ear. "Are you awake?"

"Yes" was on her lips when the ring of the telephone interrupted.

Bryan grabbed the phone and moved away from her.

"Greta?" he said.

The unwelcome, unsettling specter of her sister burst from the shadows, throwing cold water on Martie's hopes for a delicious morning with Bryan.

He slid out of bed and took the phone into the bathroom so he didn't disturb her.

It wasn't Bryan, however, who was disturbing Martie. It was Greta. Martie saw the hurt on her face at Vera's lakeside cottage when she realized Martie and Bryan had once been lovers. It was Greta offering a sincere apology and being sweet and auntlike with Lili. It was Greta asking Martie to put aside childhood hurts and try to be friends.

Martie was engulfed in a maelstrom of

guilt and defiance. On the one hand she didn't see why she should stand down and cede Bryan to someone else. Martie loved him too. The day she saw him at Valhalla, she knew that she'd never stopped loving him; last night proved that to be true. On the other hand, until a few weeks ago Bryan had been romantically involved with Greta. She hadn't stopped loving him either.

The bathroom opened. Bryan returned the phone to its crib and crossed to her side of the bed. She could feel him over her.

Martie closed her eyes and pretended to be asleep.

Chapter 15

Delilah was starstruck. Standing right there in front of her was the one and only Vera Hart.

"Oh. Wow! It's you. I can't believe it. Vera Hart," she stammered, as she opened the door to Bryan's loft. "What an honor. I'm such a major fan of yours. I try to use all your products, I mean when I can afford them and all, but I love —"

"Is Mr. Chalmers here?" Vera interrupted icily, double-checking the piece of paper her secretary had given her with Bryan's address.

Delilah blushed. She must have committed one of those faux pas things.

"Oh, sure," she said, nervously stepping aside. "They're inside."

Vera couldn't imagine who this scruffy blond creature was, nor did she care. Without so much as a "pardon me," she swept by Delilah on her way into the heart of the loft.

Martie and Bryan were seated next to

each other at a large rectangular table laden with coffee cups, half-filled plates and cups, as well as an enormous platter of bagels, cream cheese, lemons, sliced tomatoes, and assorted smoked fish. They were casually dressed. Bryan hadn't shaved. Martie's face was free of makeup.

"Well, isn't this lovely," Vera said as she eyed the cozy tableau, a sly smile gliding across her lips. "Am I intruding?" Her tone made it clear she hoped she was.

Delilah, unable to camouflage her devotion, parked herself a few feet away from Vera and openly adored her.

The object of this undiluted veneration was less than appreciative. Nettled, Vera narrowed her eyes as if trying to figure out who and what this stranger was, why she was there, and why she wouldn't go away.

"Would you care to join us?" Bryan said, swallowing a smile.

"That would be lovely," Vera replied.

Delilah rushed to pull out the chair at the head of the table.

Vera ignored her. She preferred the chair directly across from Bryan and Martie; the view was clear and unobstructed. When she was settled, she said to Delilah, "I'd like a cup of coffee, please. And a setting."

She turned back to Martie and Bryan,

expecting Delilah to do as she was instructed.

Martie was annoyed at Vera's discourtesy, but she held her tongue. To someone who didn't know their history, Delilah was an incongruity. Plus, Martie and Vera had never discussed her internment; she didn't know how much Vera knew. But during her brief employment at the Hart Line, she'd learned that Vera was nothing if not thorough. She'd probably read everything she could find on Desert Storm's POWs.

"Vera," she said in a tone that politely demanded attention, "this is my *friend,* Delilah Green. We served together in Iraq."

The minute Martie mentioned the girl's name and connected her to Iraq, Vera knew who she was. Her presence was just so out of context Vera hadn't placed her as the other female POW.

"Of course," she said, rising to shake Delilah's hand and turning on the charm. "Forgive me, dear. I'm so thrilled to finally get a chance to meet you."

She took Delilah's hand and warmly cupped it between both of hers.

"I apologize for my terrible manners. I didn't mean to sound as if I were issuing orders, I was simply —"

"No bother, ma'am. I didn't take no offense. Really. I'm deeply honored to make your acquaintance."

"And I yours," Vera said, wrapping Delilah in a maternal hug.

Martie silently congratulated Vera on her recovery. If Delilah had felt even the smallest slight, Vera's warmth had melted it away. Martie also congratulated herself on guessing correctly about Vera's penchant for research. Vera knew exactly who Delilah was.

"You really are gorgeous," Delilah gushed. "I gotta tell ya, bein' in a room with you and Martie makes me feel like a real ugly duckling."

"That only means that the swan in you has yet to come out," Vera said.

Delilah's eyes widened. "I never thought about it that way."

"It's my business to think about women that way." Vera narrowed her eyes and studied Delilah. "In fact, would you do something for me, Delilah?"

"Anything."

"I'd like you to be my guest at the Hart Line Spa." She leaned forward in a conspiratorial, woman-to-woman way. "Let my people help the swan in you emerge."

"Sure. I guess. Wow." Delilah wasn't

used to people like Vera Hart even looking at her twice, let alone taking an interest in her.

"Good, I'm glad that's settled."

Satisfied with the outcome, Vera eyed the table, turned, and started for the kitchen, presumably to get herself coffee.

"Oh, please, Ms. Hart," Delilah said. "It's my pleasure."

Martie waited for a satisfied smile to appear on the former actress's lips. Surprisingly, there was none.

When Delilah was out of earshot, Martie thanked Vera. "That was very generous. Thank you."

"You're welcome. It's my way of apologizing. I truly am sorry. I had no idea." She splayed her hands in a gesture of confession. "It's wrong, I know, but I do judge people by their appearance. Occupational hazard, I suppose."

"Delilah doesn't make the best impression," Martie said in reluctant agreement. "She hasn't led an easy life and it shows. What you need to understand is that despite superficial differences, she's my best friend. We take care of each other."

Vera wanted to say, "I understand," but they would have been empty words. There was no way to appreciate the depth of a friendship forged in captivity unless one had survived a similar experience.

Martie, seeking to bolster Vera's opinion of Delilah, bragged about how well Delilah was doing in her new job.

Vera was only half listening. She was much more interested in the bruise on Martie's cheek.

"What happened?" she said, pointing to the injury.

Before Martie could answer, Bryan provided a synopsis of recent events.

"Yesterday while Martie was at the plant in Carteret, someone sabotaged her car. On the way home she had an accident. My number was on the seat, so they called me. Rather than upset Lili, we decided she would come here. Delilah stayed with Lili and came by this morning with a change of clothes for Martie."

Vera's mouth tightened. "Are you all right?"

"I'm fine." It felt so strange to have her mother acting like a mother.

"Do you know who did this?" Vera didn't care which of them answered, as long as one of them did.

It was Bryan. "I spoke to the head of security this morning. He's sending me the tape from the cameras that overlook the parking lot."

Vera nodded, but she appeared deep in thought. Martie guessed she was visualizing the scene as well as riffling through a series of names, searching for possible culprits.

While she continued to ruminate, Delilah set down a plate, a napkin, and utensils so that Vera could have something to eat. Then she brought her a cup and poured some coffee. She was so obsequious, Martie was certain if Vera asked her to shine her shoes, Delilah would have gladly obliged.

Vera thanked Delilah and sipped her coffee, but her eyes didn't leave Martie's face. Suddenly she rose from her chair and leaned across the table, softly touching Martie's cheek.

"Are you sure you're all right?"

"Yes."

Vera turned to Bryan. "Is she?"

Like Martie, Bryan was taken aback by this unexpected maternal impulse. Too, he found it fascinating that Vera would assume he would be privy to matters Martie might consider private. As far as she knew, Bryan and Martie's only relationship had been a collegial one that had begun and ended at Fort Rucker. All he had said this morning was that his phone number had been in Martie's car. Why would Vera make such a leap?

Probably because she had known all along that they had been lovers, he realized. Suddenly the timing of their hiring at HLI seemed obvious. So did her little tea party at the lake house in Westchester. The question now was, why would she be going to such lengths to reunite them? And at Greta's expense.

"As far as I know, Vera, your daughter is okay."

"Good," she said, pleased that that had been settled. "Now let's discuss my other daughter. Where the hell is she?"

Martie was confused. Was that why Vera came down here? She was hoping to find Greta?

"I can't answer either of those questions," Bryan said. "Since you called this morning and asked me where she was, I've been trying to reach her. So far, I haven't had any luck."

Since you called this morning and asked where she was.

So it wasn't Greta who called, Martie thought, relief flooding her body.

"She's up to something," Vera insisted,

anxiously tapping her fingers on the table. "And whatever it is, I know I'm not going to like it."

"I don't know what she's up to," Delilah shouted from the kitchen where she'd gone to fix more coffee. "But I know where she is. She's on TV."

The barrage of flashbulbs practically blinded Greta, but she'd had enough practice at news conferences to be able to keep from blinking like a signal device on a battleship. As she approached the podium she sighted the reporters she could depend on for softballs, as well as those who traditionally came at her with a cleaver.

"Ladies and gentlemen, good morning."

She was dressed in head-to-toe Armani black, which she believed was appropriate considering her announcement.

"It is with deep regret and immeasurable personal sadness that I announce the death of the Hart Line's former CFO, Craig Hemminger."

Again the flashbulbs created a wall of light before her. The clamorous clicking of the cameras sounded like a swarm of crickets.

"Mr. Hemminger's body was found late yesterday. At the request of the police, I'm not permitted to release any further details other than that his death is a presumed homicide."

She paused and lowered her head. She waited for the room to follow her lead and offer a respectful moment of silence before looking up. When she did, her eyes were moist, but her voice vibrated with anger.

"Because of our great affection for Mr. Hemminger and our respect for his years of service, Hart Line International is offering a generous reward to anyone who comes forward with information that would lead to the capture and conviction of the person or persons responsible for this heinous act."

"Do you think he was murdered because he knew too much?" one of the piranhas in the front row asked.

Greta ignored him.

"How *generous* is the reward?" someone from the rear of the room shouted.

Greta ignored him too.

"I'm also here today to make you aware of another matter that isn't being formally investigated, but suddenly seems dangerously tied to Mr. Hemminger's death. For the past several months, Vera Hart has been the victim of a menacing stalker."

"Details, please?" The plea came from an ally, so Greta responded.

"There too, I'm not permitted to elaborate, but suffice it to say, there have been several credible death threats."

"Do you have any idea who might be targeting Ms. Hart?"

"Other than the government?" Greta replied with a cynical sneer. "Unfortunately, in times like these it's hard to know where a threat originates. The cosmetics industry is small and notoriously ruthless and the Hart Line does have rivals who conduct business as a blood sport, but I have no basis on which to point a finger at any of them, nor any inclination to do so.

"Whether we like it or not, this is a violent age in which the unstable can easily find the means to act out their deadly fantasies."

She shrugged, signaling her inability to comprehend the current state of world affairs. In the audience, heads nodded.

"Vera Hart was an internationally known movie star. This can't be the first lunatic fan she's ever encountered," said a skeptic off to the left.

"Hardly. Over the years Vera Hart has had her share of deranged admirers. They sent her pictures, letters, gifts, some even sent her their underwear, but none of them ever threatened her life."

"Do the police have any leads?"

"We're handling this privately."

"Why aren't the police on it?"

"Because before yesterday Vera Hart was simply another powerful public figure being taunted by an unhappy, or unhinged, private citizen. It wasn't a police matter because no one had died. Now someone has."

"What makes you so sure this is business-related?" another piranha said. "Why couldn't it be another celebrity obsessed wack job like Mark David Chapman or John Hinckley?" He was referring to the man who shot John Lennon and the man who stalked Jodie Foster and shot President Reagan.

"Because this particular wack job is also threatening to kill me."

The collective gasp was precisely the re-action Greta wanted.

"The CFO of the Hart Line is dead. The CEO receives death threats and menacing packages almost every day. And the COO recently received an envelope with a deadly powder."

The word *anthrax* flew around the room like a wasp. People automatically recoiled.

"Okay," Greta's reliable ally said, "I'll ask you again. Do you have any idea who might be behind this reign of terror?"

Greta paused, as if she were hesitant to reply for fear of lethal reprisal. "No, but if I were the police I'd start with the person who blew the whistle on Hart Line International. Anyone who does something that extreme has an agenda."

"Maybe the agenda was to shine a light on HLI's fraudulent accounting practices," a scandalmonger from an afternoon tabloid suggested.

"*Alleged*," Greta corrected. "Our books are scrupulously audited, with the results published quarterly in our stockholders' report."

"Hemminger claimed he had tapes that proved you exaggerated profit statements to please your stockholders."

"That's what he claimed."

"He must have had something on someone, because he was tossed out quicker than you can say *scapegoat*."

Greta bit her lip and nodded sadly.

"Ms. Hart's response to the government's inquiry was spontaneous and perhaps a bit precipitous. While I might have waited until we conducted our own in-house inquiry, she chose to clean house immediately." Her sigh expressed her regret at Vera's action. "I think Mr. Hemminger said he had tapes in a snit of revenge."

"So you don't think there were any tapes."

"No, sir, I do not."

"If Vera Hart is so innocent, why is the government pursuing her like a dog on the scent?" the correspondent of the *Atlanta Constitution* said.

"Because the American public doesn't know who Ken Lay or Dennis Kozlowski or Bernard Ebbers are. They do know Vera Hart. My guess is the government needed to create a buzz about their so-called crackdown on corporate corruption, so they made my mother their poster girl."

"Oh, please," a cable television reporter scoffed. "You mean to tell us you think the Justice Department tagged Vera Hart as a PR stunt?"

"The public's paying attention. I rest my case."

Greta was rewarded with a couple of chuckles and more than a few nods of agreement, mostly from women.

"Could this harassment be part of a hostile takeover?" one of the business reporters asked.

Greta considered the question before issuing a response.

"If these baseless accusations were lodged simply to create a furor that would devalue HLI stock and make it easier for someone to take over the company, I'd be angry, but I'd fight back. Death threats go way beyond corporate espionage, don't you think?"

"If this is as serious as you say, how come Vera Hart isn't the one breaking this news?" the tabloid pencil asked.

Greta's sigh said, how come indeed?

Tim Polatchek couldn't stop laughing. That so-called press conference was the funniest thing he'd seen in months. He reached out to his friend Johnny Walker and poured himself a fresh one. It was early, but what the hell!

He had to hand it to Greta. Her performance was brilliant. And fall-down hilarious. Seinfeld couldn't have done it better

Man, she hung Vera Hart out to dry. How good was that? She rubbed that dried-up old has-been's face in shit and came up smelling like a rose!

He especially liked that two-hankie moment of silence for the recently departed Craig Hemminger.

Like she gave a crap that he was dead. Whew! That was rich!

Baseless accusations!

How that woman could lie with such a straight face was beyond him! Those *accusations* were the dead-on truth. HLI had been inflating profits to bring a smile to the face of their fat-toad stockholders for years. And he should know. He was the cog in the machine that did it!

What would his father say if he knew that? Tim wondered. Too unimportant for them to bother with, eh? Not! He was simply flying under the radar.

But Dolph didn't know about such things. He was a friggin' Boy Scout. Always doing the honorable thing. Always obeying the rules. Never stealing so much as a penny from anyone!

So what did he get for his trouble? Canned, that's what. The minute the heat got turned on. Those corporate sons of bitches didn't even bother to clean their shoes before they booted Dolph Polatchek, Mr. Cellophane, out the door. They didn't give him severance or a bonus or a fucking Mickey Mouse watch! They gave him squat!

Dolph didn't deserve to be treated that way. He was one of the good guys. And the good guys were always supposed to win. Wasn't that the American way?

Well, soon shit was going to happen. And Old Dolph and his little boy Tim were going to get everything they ever wanted. And then some.

Vera watched the press conference in stony silence. Not so much as an eyelash fluttered. And when it was over, she simply turned to Bryan and said, "I need to speak to you. Privately."

Bryan was on his feet before she finished her sentence. He too wanted to discuss Greta's one-woman show, but not here.

"Stop!" Martie said, halting the two of them in their tracks. "Was she telling the truth? Was Craig Hemminger murdered?" Her body was tense as she looked from one to the other. "Why didn't anyone tell me?"

"I never even thought about it," Vera said honestly. "As far as I knew, you'd never even met the man."

Bryan reminded Martie she'd been in a hospital with a concussion.

"Do you think the two are related?" Martie said, wondering if there was a connection between Hemminger's death and her accident.

"I don't know," he said. "Anything's possible."

"Can we talk about it?"

"Absolutely."

Vera, who had been idling in the hall, practically stomped her foot in frustration. "Not now," she snapped. "Bryan and I have things to do."

"Okay, then. How about if I take you home?" he said.

"Wonderful idea," Vera said, visibly relieved.

She cautioned Martie about doing more than she should, thanked Delilah for her kindness, and hastened toward the door.

"Will you be here when I get back?" Bryan asked Martie.

She shook her head. "Delilah and I will clean up and then I'm going home to Lili."

"Of course. The princess is going to want her mommy."

Martie noticed that even the mention of Lili and he smiled.

"If you'd like, come on by when you and Vera have finished."

He nodded, waved to Delilah, and followed Vera to the elevator.

"I want one of them," Delilah declared.

"One of what?"

"One of him." For emphasis, Delilah

issued a loud, soldier's, "Hoo-ah!"

"Really."

"I said it before, and I'm sayin' it again: Bryan is a keeper."

Martie laughed. Delilah had always been an unabashed fan. "I hear ya."

"If only." Delilah harrumphed as she finished clearing the table.

Martie brought in the platter of appetizers so she could wrap up the leftovers and put them away.

"Either you grab that man up or some other woman's gonna," Delilah blurted, as if she couldn't hold that bit of advice in a moment longer. "He's a prize. And he's madly in love with you."

"I hope so," Martie confessed, "because I'm nuts about him."

"Bet the farm, honey. You want him, he's yours."

Greta's nagging likeness reappeared, taunting Martie. "What if he's still tied to someone else?"

"And who do you think he's tied to?"

"Greta Hart."

Delilah laughed so loud and so hard Martie feared she might burst a blood vessel. "That tight-ass? Not likely." She stared at Martie. "And by the way, what's up with Bryan referring to you as Ms.

Hart's daughter? What happened to Connie?"

Martie had forgotten whether she'd ever explained her complicated filial relationships to Delilah. She gave her the shortened version, which was stunning enough. Delilah had trouble comprehending the parsed story of Vera and Hugh, their marriage, their divorce, and the severing of ties. When Martie was done, she couldn't decide which part of the story Delilah found more unbelievable: that Vera was Martie's mother, or that the tight-ass was her sister.

"Well, that's a kick." She looked dazed and took a few moments to absorb the alteration in Martie's biography. "So how do you feel about her now? You seemed kinda cozy."

"Let's just say we're working on it."

"You do look exactly like her," Delilah said, staring at Martie as if viewing her and Vera on a split screen.

"So I've been told."

"Does Lili know?"

"No. She thinks Vera is the Queen of Hearts. And for now that's all she needs to know, Delilah."

Delilah raised her hands as if to take an oath. "I'm cool with that."

"Good. Now let's finish up here and get back uptown."

"First let's finish up our conversation about Prince Chalmers."

Martie put down the dish towel, put her hands on her hips, and confronted her friend. "How come we always talk about me and men? What about you? Why aren't you out looking for your prince?"

Delilah's expression morphed from the confidence of a prosecutor to the insecurity of a defendant. She didn't like to talk about herself, especially in regard to men.

"Why look for something that doesn't want to be found by you?"

"What does that mean?"

"I'm not like you, Martie. You're beautiful and smart and classy. You're the one men take home and marry. I'm the one they get down and dirty with on the side."

Delilah had said similar things in the past, but each time she heard the self-deprecation it cut Martie as deep as if it were the first time.

Delilah had never possessed a sense of worth. Her father had made his living digging in the bowels of the earth and died from his efforts. Her mother had cleaned other people's dirty clothes. They had scraped by without ever having enough money or time to do anything but work hard and sleep fast. Delilah never even heard the word *self-esteem* until an army recruiter told her it came with the uniform.

For her, the army opened the door to a supermarket of life choices. There were educational opportunities, vocational training, travel, and an introduction to people who hailed from places other than the mountains of West Virginia. She loved every aspect of it; she even enjoyed the rigors of Basic. It made her feel strong and fit, too healthy to die young like her dad.

Then came the Gulf War. When Delilah's battalion shipped out to Kuwait, she harbored the same fears as everyone else, but her apprehension was balanced by the pride she felt in serving her country. Also, she viewed going off to fight a war as not just the logical end of her training, but the final chapter in her reinvention.

She had worked hard to leave Piney Hollow behind and in many ways had succeeded, but Desert Storm was the ultimate test. She didn't minimize the impact of war; she knew she would come home from the desert transformed.

She did, but not in the way she planned.

Martie, like Delilah and other rape survivors, suffered psychological injury from her detention. She felt altered, but not damaged. She'd been a prisoner of war. Whatever indignities or persecution she'd endured were part of her duty to the uniform. She bore no shame because she knew she bore no responsibility for what was done to her.

Delilah felt damaged. She believed she hadn't resisted her assailants strenuously enough, that she had been victimized because she was weak, and that by allowing herself to be violated she had let her country down. During her treatment at the army hospital, psychiatrists tried to convince her that if submission meant her survival, it was an act of courage, not of cowardice. They reminded her of her survival training, how she was expected to do whatever she could to live to the next day. She hadn't given the Iraqis names or positions or anything that they really wanted. All she offered was a target for their violence.

Delilah had been in the cell next to Martie. She knew they were tormenting her as well, but she never heard Martie scream. She never heard Martie cry. She never heard Martie beg for her life. In an odd way, that became another form of torture, the torture of comparison. Alone in her cell with her fears, her guilt, her store of insecurities, and the irrational thought that comes with such stringent solitude, Delilah became convinced that she had received the harsher treatment because her character deficiencies invited it.

With no one to refute her imaginings, Delilah internalized that feeling of worthlessness and carried it with her into the civilian world.

Martie could never figure out whether it was because she had a stronger self-image going in, or because she'd grown up in the military and viewed her captivity from a different perspective, or because she'd simply been lucky to have Bryan when she came home and, later, Jack Abrams. Whatever the reason, she never felt she deserved what the Iraqis did to her. It devastated her that Delilah believed she did.

"You know what, Delilah," Martie said, suddenly filled with a sense of mission, "it's not that I'm classy and you're not, it's that you deliberately pick men who are going to treat you like crap and I don't."

Delilah recoiled at the sharpness in Martie's tone and the truth in her words.

"I'm not prettier than you. I take better care of myself. Am I better educated? Yes, but that doesn't mean I'm smarter. It just means I went to school longer. And as for Prince Charming, the last time I looked I was single, just like you. The difference is that if the opportunity to have a happily-ever-after presents itself, I'm willing to take the chance. Are you?"

Delilah lowered her head and stared at her shoes. Martie crossed the room and wrapped her friend in a loving embrace.

There were differences between them, Delilah wasn't wrong about that, but Martie believed they were material and cultural rather than intrinsic.

"You were an awfully brave soldier," Martie said, hugging Delilah close. "I was there in Fallujah and I was there when they pinned those medals on you, so don't try and tell me different."

Delilah pulled back and looked at Martie, tears of gratitude filling her eyes

"Wear those medals proudly, Delilah. They were given to you for the courage you displayed in a time of war."

"That was a long time ago," she whispered.

"Heroism doesn't have an expiration date," Martie said.

She wiped Delilah's eyes, then looked into them.

"I know how difficult it's been for you,

but that's because when you took off your uniform you forgot what Specialist Delilah Green was all about. Instead of marching headlong into a new life, you slid right back down the mountain to Piney Hollow."

Delilah grimaced, but rewarded Martie's perspicacity with a chuckle.

"Bring back the woman who earned that Bronze Star," Martie said. "Be the hero who survived Fallujah. Don't be a cowardly civilian."

"I don't want to be," Delilah confessed. "But I've been stuck in this rut for so long, I don't know how to be anything else."

It took a minute before a solution came to her, but when it did a huge grin illuminated Martie's face.

"Okay, transportation specialist, what do you do when a truck is mired in the mud and all it can do is spin its wheels?"

"You attach it to something stronger and you pull it out," Delilah said, eyeing Martie curiously.

"Exactly! You and I are now officially tied at the waist. I am going to pull you out of your rut if it's the last thing I do."

"And you're going to do this how?"

"By giving you a promotion."

Delilah folded her arms across her chest

and eyed Martie suspiciously. "To what?"

"Executive assistant."

"Come again?"

"How would you like to work for me at the Hart Line?"

"You're kidding."

"No, I'm not. You've got the skills. You proved that over at the shelter. I need an assistant and there's no one I'd rather have watching my back than you."

Delilah still wasn't convinced this was a good idea. Martie sensed she thought it was simply another form of charity.

"If I don't hire someone, Delilah, the human resources department will simply assign someone." She sensed a slight lowering of resistance. "Honestly, I'm not making up a job for you. It's there and it's going to be filled one way or another."

Delilah was bobbing her head up and down as if each fact were being entered and processed.

"I may be able to answer a phone and make appointments and work a computer, but I don't belong in some fancy office."

"Only because you don't think you do."

Delilah suddenly became obsessed with filling the dishwasher.

"Do you remember that recruiting slogan, 'Be all that you can be'?"

413

There was no response.

"Do you?" Martie persisted.

Delilah shut the door on the dishwasher and turned around to face Martie. "I've tried to better myself," she said, looking weary from that particular battle, "but I'm still that hick from Piney Hollow."

Martie refused to accept that. "Because it's comfortable, Delilah. It feels familiar, so instead of moving beyond, you continually seek the kind of people you left behind. If you really want to leave Piney Hollow, you have to venture out and travel in different circles so you can meet new people."

Delilah was struggling.

"I know it's scary, but it's not anything you can't handle. It's the same job you're doing at the shelter, just in a different place."

"What if I embarrass you?"

Martie had been waiting for that.

She looked Delilah squarely in the eye and said, "That is simply not possible, Specialist Green."

"I want you to draw up a rider to my will," Vera told Bryan once they were sequestered in her apartment, "that bequeaths my stock position in HLI to Martie. Since I own the controlling interest, she would take over the reins.

"As for Lili, I'll want to work out specific provisions for her education and her future that would withstand any court challenge that might be raised, but essentially the purpose of this rider is to confirm Martie as my corporate heir apparent and she and Lili as my main beneficiaries."

Bryan was thunderstruck. Vera had just cut Greta out of her life.

"I'm not an estate lawyer, Vera. You know that."

"Of course I know that! I have a dozen estate lawyers. If I had wanted one of them I would have called them. I want you because I don't want word of this to get out."

"To the press? Or to Greta?"

"Either."

"Why are you doing this?" Bryan asked, completely befuddled.

"Because what I'd really like to do is kill Greta," Vera said, with sober eyes and a forthrightness that eliminated any doubt about her sincerity, "but right now I don't think I'd get away with it."

Chapter 16

Tony Borzone's eyes hurt. He'd spent half the day on his computer searching databases. Bryan had checked ViCAP for deaths caused by mercuric chloride and come up empty. Tony was looking for rape/homicides in which there were lipstick drawings on the bodies.

He found one case in Florida, outside of Palm Beach, from 1999, and another in Georgia, near Atlanta, that occurred in August 2000. In both cases, the women were brutally assaulted at night in public parks; there were lipstick markings on the bodies. He jotted down the names of the detectives so he could call and question them to see if there were other similarities.

Borzone's partner, Frank O'Malley, was a meat-and-potatoes guy. He didn't like fancy food or elaborate theories. He wanted to work the case from the clues at the scene. Tony didn't like fancy food or elaborate theories either, but he was a big-picture guy. He believed in context, that often the clues at the scene are pieces from a larger puzzle. From the minute they caught this case he maintained that the killer wasn't a first-timer; the MO was too specific. Whoever did this had done it before. He also believed that the use of lipstick and the way the women were bound were the perp's signature and would eventually hang him. Which was why he was still at his desk, long after his shift was over and O'Malley had gone home.

He was about to shut down his computer when a small box in the corner of the screen flashed an announcement that there was a breaking news story: Greta Hart was holding a press conference. He double clicked to bring the page up full and listened in. When it was over, he leaned back in his chair and tried to digest the red meat that had just been tossed from the podium.

Murder. Stalkers. Death threats. Hints of anthrax. That was a lot to cram into a five-minute performance timed to air on the evening news.

On the face of it this case and the one he was working on weren't related. Yet just as he didn't believe the precise duplication of these rape/murders was accidental, neither did he think it was wise to ignore the murder of Craig Hemminger, the CFO of

417

the company that manufactured the lethal lipstick. He'd been on the job too long to ignore things that at first glance appeared to be way out in left field. Some dots were simply harder to connect than others.

Judging by the questions from the press and the bob and weave of Greta Hart, the consensus was that Hemminger was offed because he possessed incriminating tapes.

Borzone didn't buy it.

Yes, owning proof of someone's guilt was a powerful motive for murder — experience had proven that in case after case after case — but Hemminger's daily drumbeat about bringing down the house of Hart with his tapes made it sound like he was hoping for what Borzone called an Abracadabra: In high profile, white-collar crimes involving large sums of money, if the threat was serious enough there was a quid pro quo. If the offer was high enough, Abracadabra! The evidence disappeared.

If there really were tapes and they contained what Hemminger said they did, the Harts would pay, and pay big. Abracadabra!

But Hemminger was dead and no tapes were discovered.

The way Borzone saw it, there were three possibilities: Vera Hart made an offer but Hemminger was one of the rare ducks who was willing to turn down a fortune so he could have the greater satisfaction of seeing his bête noire put away; Hemminger had no tapes and was simply using the media to torment his former employer; or he had something explosive on someone else and that someone wanted him silenced.

Borzone scratched his head and stared at his computer screen.

So unless she knew exactly what happened, which it appeared she didn't, what the hell was Greta Hart's press conference all about?

First of all, he was certain the officers on the case had asked her not to make it public. She openly defied them. Why?

Second, since she was one of those suspected of being caught on those tapes, why would she put herself out there like that? Was she hiding in plain sight? Implying innocence by coming forward and taking the press on instead of doing the Fifth Amendment tap dance? Or was she racing to get to the microphones before Mommy Dearest could rat *her* out?

She sure took dead aim at her mother with that little smirk-and-sigh routine at the end. By not explaining where Vera was, she implied Vera had a reason not to be there. Again, why?

Why even bother to gun for Vera? The government already had her in their crosshairs. If Greta wanted revenge for some childhood trauma, all she had to do was sit back and let the justice system do its thing. Borzone wasn't following it closely, but from the little he'd read, things didn't look good for the former movie star. She could get time.

Speaking of time, he was wasting it thinking about rich folks' money problems. He had a murderer to find.

"You made it sound urgent," Bryan said, racing into Greta's office. After hearing about Craig Hemminger, everything felt like an emergency. "What's up?"

She was standing in the middle of the room looking uncharacteristically haggard. Her suit jacket was carelessly flung over the back of a chair, her lipstick had faded, her hair was mussed, and her eyes were red.

"I'm scared," she said without preamble. "I didn't know who else to call."

Tears dotted her cheeks. Her slender body trembled like a twig in a storm.

"It's okay," Bryan soothed. "I'm a bit rattled myself."

"Craig was murdered, thrown from a car like a piece of garbage," she said, hugging herself as if trying to dam a deluge of emotion.

On impulse, Bryan held her close. She felt thin and frail in his arms.

"I could be next."

"Don't go there," Bryan said.

She trembled. "Why not? A woman was murdered. I've been threatened. My mother's been threatened. Even Martie's received some unnerving phone calls. There's a maniac out there with a grudge against this company. Craig wasn't the first and he won't be the last."

Bryan wanted to tell her she was wrong, but he couldn't. He'd seen too many instances where vendettas took a number of lives before the criminals were caught.

"I'll call your father," he said. "He'll arrange protection."

"No," she said, looking at him with watery aqua eyes. "I told you. There's too much at stake. I don't want our stockholders to get the wrong message. And I don't want this bastard to think he's won."

"The win will be a lot bigger if you and Vera are hurt, don't you think? Let's not try to be a hero, okay?"

Greta stiffened. "Why not? Is it only

421

people in uniform who are allowed to be heroes?"

Her words came at him like a sniper's bullet. They were startling and well aimed.

"You know better than that, Greta."

"Do I?" She glared at him, unable to hold her tongue. "Aren't you impressed by stars and medals and citations for bravery?"

"I absolutely am," he said, taking her arm and firmly steering her toward the couch. "But I'd rather not have them conferred graveside, so don't be a fool. Let Hugh put a security detail on you and your mother."

She grumbled as she plunked herself down on the couch.

"At least until we know what happened to Hemminger, okay?"

She offered no response. Bryan thought she looked deflated. Her shoulders were hunched and she was sighing deeply. He brought her a glass of water and sat next to her.

"Drink," he commanded.

She obeyed, but not happily.

"I do think Lili needs a guard," she said suddenly.

"Lili?"

"I met her the other night, after the

meeting." Her mouth curled in a soft smile. "She's quite delightful."

"That she is, but when exactly did you meet her?" Bryan didn't remember Greta going anywhere near Lili's room while they were there.

"After everyone left, I went back upstairs to apologize to Martie for my insensitive comment about the second poisoning victim. I explained that no one, meaning you, had told me who the victim was." Her words were pointed and sharp.

Bryan accepted the criticism. "I am sorry about that," he said. "I didn't think it was my news to tell."

"Be that as it may, you might want to consider assigning a guard to her. Maybe even to Martie as well."

Bryan narrowed his eyes and stared at her.

"In case you're wondering, I also apologized to my sister. We've actually negotiated a truce." She smiled at his arched-eyebrow response. But then the smile faded. "Seriously, Bryan. Martie's new to HLI, so there shouldn't have been any threats made against her. The fact that there were means someone knows she's Vera's daughter, and in his sick mind that makes her a viable target."

"If I put a guard on her, why not you?"

"Because I'm a principal of the company. What I do could affect HLI's stock position. And whatever this crazy perceives as HLI's wrongdoings, Vera and I are responsible, not Martie."

Bryan leaned back into the corner of the couch and studied her. It wasn't often that Greta Hart looked vulnerable, but just then she did, and he felt for her. Someone was intent on doing harm to those associated with HLI. Hemminger was dead. Martie's car had been sabotaged, although Greta didn't know that. All three Hart women had received death threats. Still, there was an obvious question begging to be asked.

"If you're so worried about this guy winning, why go on national TV and give him the publicity he craves?"

Greta raised her arms and shrugged her shoulders in despair. "I panicked. I thought if I told the world about Craig's murder and the threats, the press would get off our backs and I could start to clean up this mess."

"Mess? What mess?" Bryan's stomach dropped to his feet.

"There is no mess," she said, rubbing her fingers together like a cricket. "I didn't mean to say that."

"Greta," Bryan said quietly, "do you know more than what you've said?"

She turned her head and clasped her hands, her posture one of deliberation.

"Are you protecting someone?"

She sighed and faced him. "If I tell you, will you believe me?"

"Is there a reason I shouldn't?"

She hesitated. "It's not out of the realm of possibility that you'll choose to believe my mother over me." She harrumphed. "She is the professional actress in the family."

"Your mother? What are you talking about?"

"I think Vera might be responsible for what's happening to HLI."

"What?"

"It's complicated," she said.

"I have nothing to do and nowhere to go."

She took another deep breath. "Last year she had a health scare that I think deeply affected her."

"Did she have a heart attack?" Bryan asked.

Greta shook her head. "No. She thought she had breast cancer. She had a biopsy and it came back negative."

"She must have been relieved."

"That's the thing. I don't know. She tried to hide it from me, but I found out anyway. I respected her privacy and never confronted her about it, but after that she began to change."

"In what way?"

"Her attitude toward me, for one."

She pursed her lips and elevated her chin in a pose of defensiveness. Bryan thought she seemed embarrassed by what she was about to say. And hurt.

"She used to trust me. She used to respect my opinions and my judgment. She rarely made a significant decision without consulting me. Suddenly, nothing I said or did pleased her.

"It was the same with Craig and her division directors. Where once she relied on us and encouraged us to work together as a team, suddenly it was as if she were a team of one and we were her rivals."

She shook her head and rubbed her eyes, as if it were all beyond her comprehension. "She was especially hard on Craig. They were lovers once, you know."

He didn't know that, but he didn't think it really mattered.

"I don't get it," Bryan said. "Why would

a *negative* biopsy prompt such a personality change?"

"Vera's an icon. Icons aren't supposed to die. They're supposed to live forever in the hearts and minds of their adoring fans."

"Your mother may be an icon, Greta, but she's also a very savvy businesswoman. I can't imagine her doing something to discredit that reputation."

"True, but when the key to your marketing success is your own youthful vigor and visage, aging can be a slap in the face."

"Okay," Bryan said, conceding. "I'll buy that."

"America has a love-hate relationship with its celebrities. Someone comes along who excites us: Movie star. Singer. Sports figure. Politician. We build them up, sprinkle them with the blinding glitter of assumed perfection, and inhale every detail of their lives as if they're truly godlike. Then one day we wake up and decide they're human after all. We so resent the disillusionment, we tear them apart like jackals. And then, we move on to the next."

Bryan had to admit he was as guilty as the next guy for participating in — and thereby perpetuating — that build up/tear down cycle of personality worship. He'd never thought about it from the vantage point of the worshipee, but it had to be devastating to have been revered to the point of mania and then to suddenly become a target of ridicule.

Vera, he realized, had experienced that idol insanity twice, as a child and again as an adult. To her credit, she emerged stronger and more focused than most. But now it was happening for a third time.

"There's no question in my mind that that cancer scare pushed her off her pins," Greta continued. "Immediately after, she became even more obsessive about HLI than she was before, if that's possible. And more possessive. She couldn't even entertain the concept of her precious company being led by anyone but her."

Her lips flattened into a tight line and her spine straightened.

"I had the extreme misfortune of asking her to name me as her heir apparent at about the same time that this was going on. She refused. When I asked why, she had no answer other than the Hart Line was hers and would always be hers. Aside from feeling hurt and unappreciated, I found that attitude completely irrational, especially coming from a woman who had taken such pride in bringing her company public."

Bryan couldn't argue the point, especially since Vera's intense passion for the Hart Line was constantly in evidence.

"Even after I found out about the biopsy, I still found it foolish not to set out a plan of succession. It wouldn't have done anything except pave the way for a smooth transition in case of her retirement or her death. No one was pushing her toward either, but I suppose she felt threatened because she refused to listen to anyone about anything. Sink or swim, she was going to captain her ship alone."

"Everyone has a mad moment," he said, trying to come up with a possible explanation. "Especially if death had come a little too close for comfort."

"I agree, but her mad moment was compounded by a recession, one which impacted quite heavily on our bigger-ticket items. Even though our products are moderately priced, no one *needs* a new couch or a new coat or a greenhouse filled with orchids. In hard times people make do."

"And women buy lipsticks," he said, recalling his mother's and his sister's theories about makeup being the cheapest lift around.

"Absolutely, but our rating is based on corporate totals, not individual divisions."

"Why wouldn't she just ride it out? HLI has been around long enough to have weathered other market dips. Why manipulate the numbers?"

"The Hart Line is my mother's life, Bryan. She wouldn't be able to get out of bed in the morning if she didn't have this office to come to and this company to run. She has nothing else."

The desolate undertone that accompanied that last comment cut. Greta was talking about herself as well. He wanted to address that, to recite her virtues et al., but it would have been condescending.

"With Craig gone I can't corroborate my suspicions, but don't believe Vera's claim that she never followed the day-to-day P&Ls. That's part of her public schtick, that she doesn't dirty her hands with business matters. She just makes the world a more beautiful place."

Greta sneered. "Believe me, she knew everything about HLI, from the shifting interest rates on business loans to which paper-supply company gave us the best prices on toilet tissue."

He'd only known Vera Hart for a short time, but Bryan was willing to bet that was true. She was too anal and egotistical to be a hands-off manager.

"When business began to slow, she grew concerned about our stock position, with good reason. If it were to diminish, we would have a hard time getting financing for acquisitions or R&D projects. And if we couldn't get financing, we'd have to use our own money. If we did that, our profits would be less and our stock price would fall. Similar circumstances have ruined more than one major company. Vera couldn't and wouldn't let that happen to the Hart Line."

Bryan sifted through everything Greta had said, mixing her thoughts with his own. It all made sense, but there were some loopholes in her theory.

"As COO, didn't you sign off on the financials?"

"I did, but that was a formality. My job is to make certain all our divisions are operating at peak efficiency. During the years in question, I knew some were doing exceptionally well while others were having difficulty meeting their projections, but I never put all the pieces together. That was Craig's responsibility. And, ultimately, Vera's."

Bryan would have pegged Greta as being highly compulsive about HLI's P&L, but in behemoth corporations it wasn't un-

usual for the COO to cede certain responsibilities to others.

"If asked, would Hemminger have gone
along with Vera's request to cook the
books?"

"He loved her." Greta's aquamarine eyes
locked on Bryan's as if to underline her
point. "He would have done anything for
her."

Bryan arose from the couch and began
to pace. He needed movement to think, as
well as distance between him and Greta.
Her constant double entendres were
making him claustrophobic.

"What about Hemminger's staff? Wouldn't
someone there have noticed what was
going on?"

"The way it's set up, each division has its
own accounting superintendent. Craig was
the clearinghouse. That's probably why
Vera involved him and not one of his un-
derlings."

"But then someone blew the whistle."
Bryan wondered if what Greta had just
said eliminated a member of Hemminger's
staff as the one who tipped off the government about the possibility of fraud.

"And the government pounced. I don't
think she planned on that. Nor did
Craig."

"But why would Vera fire him? That dares him to betray her."

"True, but one, I don't think she ever thought he would sell her out. My mother believes that once you fall in love with her, it's a forever thing." Again Greta looked at Bryan. "She can't comprehend that someone could be madly in love with you one day and be over it the next."

"And two?" Bryan said, refusing to revisit their relationship.

She paused, her body language signaling an intense struggle between fealty to her mother and loyalty to the company for which she served as COO.

"And two, she didn't know he was taping their conversations."

Bryan ceased his pacing. "Are you suggesting Vera killed Hemminger?"

"I know it seems too incredible to even contemplate," she said, fresh tears forming, "but someone was on those tapes and I know it wasn't me."

Bryan stared at her. It did seem incredible, but if his years in the Bureau and the DA's office had taught him anything, it was that murderers weren't a homogenized lot. They came from every social strata, every ethnic group, all ages, and both genders. If the motive was strong enough, the means were available, and the opportunity presented itself, those who might be disposed to kill, would.

"It's a huge leap from playing with numbers to committing murder, Greta."

She nodded, clearly upset at herself for even having such a horrible thought, let alone putting it out there like an accusation.

"Her freedom is at stake, Bryan. You said it yourself. If she's found guilty, she could get ten years in prison. If you were facing that possibility, wouldn't you be desperate enough to do something irrational?"

The more Greta said, the worse Bryan felt. Attorneys never asked their clients about their guilt; the assumption was that they were innocent. Also, that avoided the possibility of an attorney being accused of suborning perjury when questioning his client on the witness stand.

"What about the threats?" he said. "Are you implying that she's the one who sent those packages and notes to you and placed those phone calls to Martie?"

Greta's silence was loud.

"And that she's been inventing the death threats that were sent to her as well?"

"She's a clever woman. If this is part of

some long-range strategy, Bryan, believe me, she has every detail worked out to the nth degree."

"What about the poisoning of the lipstick?"

Greta shook her head. "No. She wouldn't do that."

Bryan found her vehement defense impressive, but confusing.

"If you believe she deliberately committed fraud and that she might have arranged for someone's death, why are you so certain she isn't capable of this?"

"I'm not certain of anything, but I know how much that particular brand means to her. It was her first success. I don't think she'd tarnish its image."

They were interrupted by a knock on the door. Greta gave permission for whomever it was to enter. It was the man from the mailroom.

"This just came for you, Ms. Hart."

He handed her a FedEx package. She thanked him, closed the door behind him, and ripped the paper zipper that would open the envelope. Inside, she found another envelope. When she took it out and looked at it, she sprang back and dropped it on the floor.

"It looks just like the envelope that held

the rat poison," she said, breathlessly.

Bryan took out his handkerchief and reached for the envelope. To him, it appeared to be a standard office white, but so had the other envelope. She had a right to be scared. Carefully, he lifted up the envelope and opened the flap. Inside was a note written in lipstick: *I'm going to paint the town Valentine Red.*

Delilah had gone. Lili was asleep. And Martie had exhausted herself trying to find a connection between her car accident and Craig Hemminger's murder. There simply didn't seem to be a solid line linking the two events. There was the fuzzy line that said everything that happened to anyone associated with HLI was related, but that would require a grand conspiracy to be at work.

Vera believed there was a conspiracy. She felt the bottom line to all this was a concerted effort to wrest control of her empire away from her, which would mean the conspiracy might well be grand; HLI was grand. That certainly would explain the troubles with the FDA, the whistle-blowing to the government to challenge Vera's competency and ensure high-profile press coverage to damage her reputation. Even the death threats might have been issued to rattle Vera so that she appeared vulnerable and weak, not in full control of her faculties.

Combined, all those actions were supposed to bring down the price of the stock so that a takeover was possible, and to inspire the stockholders to demand a change in ownership because they believed it was necessary. Martie got that.

The piece that didn't fit was the contamination of Valentine Red, which led to the murder of the woman in Central Park. No savvy businessman would want to risk his fortune or reputation on rehabilitating a company burdened with that kind of negative publicity.

So, Martie thought, deciding to follow her own advice and examine each issue separately, start with the money.

From what she could tell, there had been no wholesale inflation of profits to cater to stockholders, as had been alleged. There was, however, enough shifting of profits and losses to make HLI's books look like a shell game. Martie suspected that was to cover an inordinate amount of skimming. And since embezzlement on that scale usually involved more than one person, she needed to determine the identity of the person behind it.

It could have been Hemminger. If the stories about his affair with Vera and the scathing personal and financial consequences of that liaison were true, he certainly had motive. As the chief financial officer he had unfettered access to the books, which provided him with both means and opportunity.

But even if he was the general in this secret war against HLI, Martie doubted he could have pulled off such a huge manipulation of money by himself. So how many soldiers did he have working under him, and did each of them have knowledge of the whole operation or only of their individual tasks?

What if one of these soldiers suddenly realized Hemminger had involved him in something highly illegal and decided to mutiny?

Why kill the guy who's going to take the fall for everyone else?

Because he's going to spill his guts, Martie thought. He's going to name names and send all those loyal soldiers to the brig.

Okay, so who ordered her car sabotaged? Was it the general of this greedy band of brothers? Or was it the same lone disenchanted soldier who had doctored the books, and then, when he became over-come with guilt, killed his leader?

But Martie had nothing to do with the accounting scandal. Whoever decreed that she should be eliminated feared being implicated in something far more treacherous than cooked books. He feared being charged with murder.

So was the soldier who fudged the numbers the same one who doctored Valentine Red? And was the contamination of Valentine Red part of the overall plan?

One action didn't support the other, Martie thought, going back to her notion that destroying the signature brand of a company was contradictory with normal takeover goals.

What if there were two enemy camps, both with the same ultimate goal, but each with its own stratagem? What if they were working at cross-purposes? That would certainly explain the incompatibility of methodology. Put another way: The right hand had no idea what the left hand was doing.

What she had to figure out was who was controlling each of those hands and what it was they were trying to grab.

Martie's brain suddenly felt fried. She was tired and should have gone to bed, but she was still waiting for Bryan.

As she curled up in the corner of her sofa, she couldn't stop thinking about how delicious it had been being with him. Like a teenage girl after her first kiss, Martie's head exploded with fantasies about love and marriage and happily-ever-after. If she'd had a pad and pencil she probably would have scribbled *Mrs. Bryan Chalmers* all over it, with hearts and arrows and all that gooey stuff. Of course, her fantasies included Lili, but how perfect was it that Lili was already crazy about Bryan? Having him join their lives would be easy.

She closed her eyes and luxuriated in her fancy, but not for long. Though she tried to close her ears to it, her inner voice intruded, cautioning that her imagination was running away with her.

There was the lingering question of Greta. When Martie returned home, Lili was atwitter with a gift that had been sent to her by "our new friend, Greta." It was a stuffed bear in an aviator's outfit called Amelia Bearhart. It was such an adorable gift and so thoughtful, Martie had been flooded with a tidal wave of guilt about poaching her sister's lover.

She struggled with it all day long, but ultimately she decided that, bottom line, she loved Bryan and wanted him in her life. Last night she had made that clear. If Greta loved him, Martie was certain she too had made her feelings obvious. That left it up to Bryan to choose.

Martie shifted position on the couch, turning over, trying to find a place where she felt comfortable.

Earlier, when she had confessed to being in love with Bryan again, Delilah had asked if this was a rekindling of a fire that had never gone out, or if Martie was stirring these ashes because her bed was empty and her nights were cold.

It was a good question.

After Jack died, Martie had called a moratorium on dating. If she went out, it was sporadic at best and usually because someone fixed her up and she felt it was rude to waste that effort by not accepting the date. She blamed her reluctance to fling herself back into the singles pool on her schedule, Lili, her therapy, her newly defined standards for a potential husband, and the fact that being single was exhausting. They were all valid reasons for sitting on the sidelines of life. They were also excuses.

Looking at it through an analyst's eye, she supposed she allowed herself to get into the habit of staying home, of using her child or a good friend or family as substitutes for a lover. After all, if there was someone readily available to supply her with emotional succor, why bother with something as inherently depressing as the bar scene? Or with risking rejection? Or with winding up with the wrong man and feeling like a fool?

Delilah, in her homespun way, had been warning Martie to make certain that her renewed infatuation with Bryan was real and not just nostalgia for the safety she'd felt before her life went awry.

That was good advice.

Martie was convinced that most people who suffered from PTSD longed for an Elysium. Who wouldn't pray for a chance to excise a hideous chapter in one's life? Who wouldn't leap at an opportunity to purge themselves of a traumatic event by hiding behind someone from the past?

She wondered whether Bryan represented that chance. If that were so, taking him from Greta seemed doubly wrong.

No, she told herself. Her feelings for Bryan weren't about turning back the clock.

Speaking of clocks, Martie looked at hers. It was nearly ten. Concerned, she

442

called Bryan's apartment. Vera probably had made him jump through a hundred lawyerly hoops and he had gone home whipped.

There was no answer.

She called his office.

No answer there either.

She thought about calling Vera, but their rapprochement wasn't far enough along for her to feel comfortable making Vera her confidante.

Curious, she dialed the number of the security desk and asked if Mr. Chalmers had checked in.

"Yes, Dr. Phelps. He signed in at about five this afternoon."

"Is he still there?"

"No, ma'am. He and Ms. Hart left around seven."

"Vera or Greta?" she asked, holding her breath.

"Greta. Is there anything I can help you with?"

"No. Thanks. It's nothing important."

As she put down the phone, she felt a lump gather in her throat. It appeared as if Bryan had already made his choice.

Chapter 17

Lieutenant Eric Roberts of the Twenty-fourth Precinct wasn't known for his sense of humor. He was a perpetually preoccupied man who took life very seriously. He was also obsessively organized and placed a high premium on punctuality. To him, lateness was a sign of arrogance, a declaration that your time was more important than the time of whomever you were supposed to meet. He was not a man who tolerated that kind of conceit, which was why he was tapping his foot impatiently when Bryan and Greta finally arrived at the stationhouse on West 100th Street.

Tony Borzone, Lieutenant Gary Douglas from the Nineteenth, and Pete Doyle from the NYPD Crime Scene Unit had been waiting for thirty-seven minutes.

Bryan had called Borzone and told him about the envelope. It was his suggestion that the three detectives convene to see if their cases overlapped. Doyle was there to take custody of the envelope that had been sent to Greta and take it back to the lab for analysis.

After Doyle had gone, Bryan introduced Greta to the other officers. When Borzone extended his hand, Greta pulled hers back and stared at him with the same inquisitive repulsion she might have for a Komodo dragon.

"So you're the one working the Central Park case?"

"That I am." Borzone found her tone surprisingly rude for a denizen of the social set. He always thought members of her circle would rather die than be discourteous. It was supposed to have something to do with breeding.

"You're not doing a very good job."

"I'm sorry to disappoint you, Ms. Hart. I'll work harder. I promise."

"Please do," Greta said in her most imperious voice.

"Can we stop this bullshit and get down to business?" Roberts had had enough. He led them down the hall to the larger of his interrogation rooms.

"Where would you like us to sit?" Greta asked, looking around the dingy place and wishing for a Windex bottle.

"This isn't a dinner party, Miss Hart. Sit wherever you want."

While Greta settled herself and huffed about Borzone and the untidiness of her surroundings, the detectives took Bryan aside and discussed how to proceed.

Zones of responsibility were easily established by respecting NYPD precinct boundaries. Hemminger was found near the Hudson River close to Eighty-eighth Street, which was within Roberts's purview; since his was the active case, the meeting was held at his house. The lipstick murder had been committed in Borzone's Central Park. Both Greta and Vera Hart lived on the Upper East Side, which was Gary Douglas's Nineteenth.

Lieutenant Roberts believed his investigation into the murder of Craig Hemminger took precedence. While Bryan didn't downplay the importance of solving that homicide as quickly as possible, he argued that Hemminger was already dead. Greta Hart was alive, but it was becoming increasingly clear that her life, as well as her mother's, might be in danger. To him, the priority was to prevent them from suffering the same fate as their colleague.

Douglas, whose presence had been requested because the threats had been levied against two high-profile women living in his precinct, and Borzone, whose connection to the Hemminger case was tenuous, were content to let Roberts take the lead. They would sit back, listen, and observe.

"As I'm sure you realize," Roberts began, "having three homicide detectives from three different precincts conduct an interview is highly unusual, Ms. Hart, but we're faced with an usual situation, so if you don't mind, I'll ask for your indulgence." Roberts tried to smile, but it was an unfamiliar exercise.

"I'm happy to cooperate, Lieutenant. Aside from my obvious desire to find the person who killed Mr. Hemminger, I'm rather worried about my own survival."

She shot a look at Borzone, as if he were personally to blame for her predicament.

"Speaking of Mr. Hemminger, when did you last speak to him?"

"A couple of days ago."

"Did you call him or did he call you?"

"I called to see how he was doing."

"Why?"

Greta tilted her head to the side, her expression quizzical. This interview was supposed to be about the Valentine threat.

Bryan grimaced. He should have known that a hard-nosed cop like Roberts wouldn't agree to a parley about poison pen letters unless he intended to get something out of it.

"We had worked together for years," Greta said. "I felt bad that he was dismissed and wanted to find out how he was."

Roberts walked over to a folder at the head of the table, opened it, and glanced at the top sheet. "Your phone call was very short. Less than two minutes. Either he told you he was fine or told you to bug off. Which was it?"

Greta glanced over at Bryan. She was surprised the police had pulled the phone logs. He wasn't.

"The latter," she said.

Her normally pale skin had turned a preternatural shade of white, but her voice remained firm.

"How'd you feel about that?"

"Sad."

"According to several people who were present at the board meeting when he was canned, he had a bit of a temper tantrum. True?"

"He was upset, yes."

"I was told that he reserved some of his harshest criticism for you."

Roberts patrolled the narrow room, forcing Greta to move her head in order to follow him.

"He did, but it's quite normal for someone who has just been humiliated in front of his peers to lash out," she said with complete sangfroid. "I didn't take it personally."

"Really?"

"Really." Her tone was slightly mocking.

"You're tough," Roberts said, making it clear he didn't find that quality particularly admirable in a woman.

"Yes, I am." Her tone let him know she thought toughness was one of her best traits. "Considering the circumstances, I wasn't surprised by his outburst, which is why I didn't take umbrage at it. It was character-logical."

"Character-logical." Roberts ran his fingers through his already scruffy hair and pursed his lips as he considered the phrase. "That's shrink talk. You go to a shrink?"

"Not presently."

Roberts arched an eyebrow. "What does that mean, 'character-logical'?"

"It means that the person's actions are consistent with his personality," she said, sounding like a Psych 101 professor.

Bryan cringed. Not only was she antagonizing Roberts, but she was underestimating him. He might not have her scholastic degrees, but he was canny, and if she had anything that would help him find his killer, he was going to get it out of her.

"Craig Hemminger was tightly wound," Greta said, expanding her explanation. "He was a man who lived a narrow existence of limited pleasures, which resulted in a rather constipated personality. He had been through an ugly divorce, was estranged from his children, was deeply in debt, had few friends and no hobbies. For him, work was paramount. When that was taken away, he freaked. He reacted the same way anyone, including you, Lieutenant, might react if the center of your universe had suddenly been marked off limits. He lashed out at those he believed were responsible for his desolation, in this case my mother and me. Character-logical."

Roberts didn't comment. He simply continued his pantherlike perambulation around the metal table.

Bryan watched him carefully. He wasn't there in the capacity of Greta's attorney, but if her rights were violated, he would step in. Roberts was coming close.

"He said he had tapes that could incriminate you."

"And Vera Hart," Greta added.

"Correct. So?"

Greta shrugged. "I've never seen those

tapes, let alone heard what's on them. Have you?"

"Not yet, but my boys are going over his apartment as we speak."

Greta crossed her legs, flung an arm over the back of her chair, and leaned back in an unflinching, self-possessed pose.

Bryan understood that Greta's years as COO of a major corporation led her to believe that a show of confidence denied weakness. But this wasn't a boardroom and the people in attendance weren't stockholders. They were seasoned detectives.

"Were you ever up to Mr. Hemminger's apartment?" Roberts asked. "I mean, just in case we find your fingerprints. We wouldn't want to jump to any wrong conclusions."

Greta's lips pinched with annoyance. "Of course I've been to Craig's apartment." There was a decided edge to her voice. "Many times. We were colleagues."

"Don't you have offices for collegial discussions?"

Her jaw clenched. "Offices have interruptions," she said, as if she were speaking to a four-year-old.

Roberts was unfazed. "Did he ever visit your apartment? To discuss business, of course."

Greta slapped her hand on the table and glared at him. "That's it!" she said. "For the last time: Craig Hemminger and I were business associates. We often went over corporate matters after hours. We were never involved in anything other than a business relationship. I'm distraught that someone took his life and I will do whatever is necessary to assist you in your search for his killer, but I came here because there is a lunatic out there who has threatened my life, my mother's life, my sister's life, and now the lives of innocent women throughout the city. That scares the hell out me. Why doesn't that concern any of you?"

She looked from one to the other, but instead of her gaze lingering on Borzone, or her current combatant, Roberts, she focused now on Gary Douglas.

"I'm certain that you and Detective Borzone have spoken about the woman who was raped and murdered in Central Park."

Douglas affirmed her assumption with a nod.

"And I know that you're aware of the involvement of a poisoned product from my company." She balled her fists and leaned toward Douglas, her body tightly coiled. "That's hideous to me, Lieutenant. That someone would take something that's supposed to make women feel beautiful and use it as an instrument of murder."

Her outrage filled the small room with a scorching energy that was hard to ignore.

"Has there been any progress on tracking down the contamination site?" Douglas asked, including Bryan in his scope.

"We're fairly certain that the corruption took place at the Carteret, New Jersey, plant," Bryan said.

Greta turned to him, curious as to what he knew and why she hadn't been filled in.

"Dr. Marta Phelps was returning from a second visit to that plant when she was in a car accident on the New Jersey Turnpike. State troopers took possession of the car and have confirmed that a sharp object was found in the sidewall of the right rear tire. The object is now at their forensic lab undergoing further tests."

"Are you certain the car was sabotaged?" Greta's hand flew to her throat. She appeared genuinely thunderstruck.

"Yes." Despite their truce and Greta's apparent shock, Bryan noted that her first question was about the car, not how Martie had fared.

"Is she all right?"

"Yes."

While the other lieutenant ignored the exchange, Borzone was fascinated. During the early days of their friendship he and Bryan had spent a number of gut-spilling nights at bars. Borzone always thought those kinds of nights were the male equivalent of a teenage girl's slumber party. Whether it was lack of sleep or too much liquor, the effect was the same: Your defenses were lowered enough to tell all and you did. On several of those nights, Bryan talked about the love he lost. Borzone was almost certain her name was Martie Phelps.

"Was Dr. Phelps hurt?" he asked.

"She was taken to the hospital with a concussion and some minor injuries and, after a period of observation, released."

Oh, yeah, Borzone thought, looking at Bryan's face. That was the one.

"My assumption, which is shared by Vera Hart, is that whoever poisoned the lipsticks was indeed working out of that plant and that this attempt on Dr. Phelps's life was to prevent her from getting any closer to discovering his identity. Also, I believe it was meant to warn anyone who might want to follow her lead."

Gary Douglas, a man with a quiet nature that seemed at odds with his broad shoulders and muscular body, stroked his chin thoughtfully. "According to Ms. Hart's latest missive, the killer is threatening to go wide. Is that possible?" he said. "Is the contaminated product contained?"

"We don't know."

"That's not very reassuring."

"We're doing everything we can," Greta said, inserting herself into the conversation. "We manufacture lipsticks in large numbers. What we haven't yet established is whether an entire kettle was poisoned, which would mean hundreds of lethal lipsticks in the market, or whether a smaller quantity was tainted."

"We're leaning toward the latter," Bryan said quickly, noting the look of panic on the faces of the three men responsible for the safety of New York's citizenry. "After Dr. Phelps's first visit to Carteret she concluded that security procedures in the main production area were sufficient. She believes that the perp used one of the samples that are periodically taken from the kettles for color correction. The assumption is that he took lipstick tubes from stock and filled them with the poisoned liquid. What we don't know is how he distributed them."

Borzone's thick eyebrows knitted together. "How do you ship your lipsticks?" he asked Greta.

"In cardboard boxes."

"How many lipsticks in a box?"

"Twelve."

"How many boxes would a sample pitcher fill?"

"One. Two if it were a skimpy pour."

Bryan could tell Tony was counting how many weapons were loose in the general public. He was also trying to figure out where his suspect would've gotten his hands on a fancy lipstick tube.

"Are they shipped alone or with other products?"

"Usually a store's entire order is put together and then boxed in larger shipping cartons. By the way, Lieutenant, I have asked the head of distribution for Hart Line Cosmetics to give me the dates when the most recent batches of Valentine Red were shipped, along with the names and addresses of the accounts to whom they were delivered."

"Thank you, Ms. Hart. That would be most helpful."

"I hate to be a Cassandra, but for all we know this horrible deed was done some time ago. We have smaller accounts like large drugstores and beauty salons that we supply with product, mostly as an accommodation to a market without access to a department store. They don't sell out as quickly, which means these lipsticks could have been on their shelves for a while. It also means their names might not come up in the list I requested."

"Then I'll need a list of those smaller outlets as well."

"Absolutely."

Bryan watched with interest as Greta and Tony Borzone practiced the ancient art of cooperation. Greta's attitude toward Tony changed dramatically once he turned his detective skills on to a problem she wanted solved.

Tony turned to Douglas. "I'll keep you up on all of this, Gary."

"Good. I'll want to see the stores, both large and small, within the metropolitan area."

"I gather Hemminger was completely out of this particular loop. Is that right, Ms. Hart?" Roberts, who'd been respectfully silent during the exchange about the lipsticks, reasserted himself.

Greta resented his intrusion. "Obviously. He was the chief financial officer. He had nothing to do with formulation of product, production, or distribution, other than to be certain it was all done with the greatest cost efficiency."

"I guess, since he was scheduled to be deposed for fraud on the day he was murdered, he wasn't doing such a good job."

"Alleged fraud, Lieutenant."

"I stand corrected."

Roberts offered Greta a gallant bow of his head. She wasn't charmed.

"Did you think he was doing a good job?"

"Yes. I assumed he was."

"Assumed. I find that curious, Ms. Hart. If you and he discussed business as often as you indicated, how come you didn't know what was going on?"

Greta shifted position in her seat, unable to keep from showing her discomfort. "We discussed either the broader picture or specific problems within the divisions, Lieutenant. Not everyday numbers."

"Okay, so who would he have talked to about the fact that the everyday numbers didn't add up?"

"The head of HLI."

"Vera Hart."

"Yes. She is the head of the company."

"Speaking of Vera Hart, what was her relationship to the deceased?"

"Ask her."

"I'm asking you."

458

Bryan bounded to his feet. Vera's affair with Hemminger was bound to come out sooner or later, but since it could implicate Vera when it did, he would prefer that it come from her.

"You know what, it's been a long day, Lieutenant," Bryan said. "I'd like to take Ms. Hart home, if that's all right with you."

"I'm not sure we're finished," Roberts said, his voice tight with girdled annoyance.

"Since your line of questioning shifted to Vera Hart rather than Greta, I assumed you were."

Bryan turned to Borzone. "Do you have any more questions, Tony?"

"Not right now, no." Borzone stifled a smile, but not his curiosity. Bryan was acting very lawyerly all of a sudden.

"Gary?"

"No questions," Lieutenant Douglas said. "But I would appreciate it if you'd bring over the other letters and copies of the e-mails."

"First thing in the morning," Bryan said. "Okay, Greta, it's time to leave."

She stood, collected her belongings, and smiled at Roberts. "Good night, Lieutenant," she said as Bryan held the door for her. "I hate to leave so soon, but as Mr. Chalmers said, it's been a long day."

"Yes, it has," Roberts replied, bristling at her smugness. "But don't worry. I'm sure we'll see each other again real soon."

"When will that lab person get back to us on my note?" Greta asked in the limousine on the way back to her apartment.

"It shouldn't take long. Doyle works fast."

"What's he going to do?"

"He'll dust for fingerprints. If he finds any, he'll run them through the system. I expect he'll also test the lipstick for mercuric chloride."

He was crisp and to the point.

"I'm sorry if I was rude to your friends," she said. "Death threats have a way of rendering me thoughtless."

She was being flirtatious. Bryan wasn't in the mood. Something about that whole interview felt off, but he couldn't put his finger on it.

"Tony's a good man and a good cop. He's doing the best he can. So is Roberts."

"I thought I was very helpful to both. Didn't you?"

"Eventually."

Greta responded to the chill emanating from him by wrapping her pashmina around her shoulders. Earlier, she felt they had closed some of the gap between them. He'd come the minute she called. He'd been concerned about her well-being, caring and kind. He'd been responsive to her fears, calling this meeting on her behalf, accompanying her uptown, acting as her shield. Now he was sitting on the other side of the limo, the distance between them widening again.

"It's late. You must be hungry," she said, as if presenting him with a reason for his crankiness. "How about if I have Luther stop and pick something up for dinner?"

"No. Thanks. I've asked Luther to drop me off at home first, if that's all right with you."

It wasn't all right with her at all.

"Of course. Whatever you wish."

They rode in silence, he trying to identify the root of his discomfort, she trying to gauge how far she could push him.

"May I ask you a question?"

"Certainly."

"Did you end that meeting to protect me or Vera?"

She reached for his hand, offering him another chance to be the knight she longed for him to be. He refused the gesture.

"Does it matter?"

To her it mattered a great deal. So did his rejection of her advances.

"Yes," she said, her temper breaking loose of its restraints, "because if you were protecting Vera, you're a sucker."

"Good to know."

"I told you not to take the job at HLI, Bryan," she said, his sarcasm stoking her anger. "I warned you she was up to something, but you didn't listen."

"And what exactly is she up to?"

"Let's see. She has an entire law firm at her disposal and yet she hires you, a man with no corporate experience, to be her attorney. Then, a couple of days later, she hires your former lover to head up a completely unnecessary new division of Hart Line Cosmetics. Do you really think that was a coincidence?"

Actually, he didn't. Especially after Vera's visit to his loft that morning.

"She hired Martie so that when the shit hit the fan you'd be so blinded by the fact that she's your girlfriend's mother that you wouldn't look too closely at what she was doing. She's playing you, Bryan, and when she's finished your career will be in ruins."

Even if Greta was one hundred percent correct, Bryan didn't like having his intelligence and his integrity challenged.

"You haven't answered the question," he said with practiced calm. "What is she up to?"

"Honestly, I don't really know. I'm not even sure she really knows."

Bryan shook his head, his expression one of impatience and growing disgust. "I think you're the one playing games, Greta."

She appeared stung by the insult. "You want to think the worst of me, don't you?" she said, breasting her shawl defensively.

"Give me a reason to think otherwise."

"Okay, the truth is I'm convinced Vera's having a breakdown."

"And you're convinced of this why?"

"Aside from her bizarre behavior at work, there's her sudden fascination with all things familial. She's placing undue trust in my father, a man she's loathed for most of her life, and getting all warm and fuzzy with a daughter she hasn't given a hoot about in years."

"This may shock you, but it sounds to me as if she's trying to reunite her family."

"Why would she do that?" Greta scoffed. "Despite the crap her press releases would have you believe, Vera Hart isn't Betty Crocker."

Bryan agreed it was difficult to imagine

Vera Hart in a kitchen with children and a dog without a camera recording it for an upcoming edition of her television show, but after what he had witnessed this morning between Vera and Martie, it was impossible for him to completely discount a desire for reunification.

"Maybe what you heard about the results of that biopsy was wrong," he suggested

"Not possible," Greta said with annoying finality. "I got my information from a highly reliable source."

"When I was at the Bureau we called highly reliable sources snitches," he said. "And since we're sharing intelligence, let me give you the benefit of my experience in the field: If you can pay to get information, Greta, your mother can pay to make sure that what she doesn't want to get out, doesn't."

They pulled up in front of his building. Bryan opened the door and quickly stepped into the street.

"I don't know what's going on, Greta, but if Vera isn't having a breakdown and isn't dying of cancer and hasn't done any of the heinous things you're accusing her of doing, she's going to come right back at you. And it won't be pretty."

Greta simply stared at his back as he turned and headed for his building, an eddy of hot tears pooling in her eyes.

The phone rang. Martie's arm snaked out from beneath the covers. She grabbed the receiver and pressed it against her ear.

"Hullo," she mumbled, her brain caught in the middle distance between sleep and wakefulness.

The silence on the other end encouraged her to go back to sleep, but that was difficult. Her slumber had been restless, interrupted by a montage of unsettling images: Bryan and Greta, a dead Hemminger, her own body lying on an asphalt surface, as well as the usual denizens of her nightmares.

She was about to return the phone to its cradle when she heard breathing on the other end.

Her eyes opened and her senses went on alert, another hangover from her military background.

"Hello," she said again, straining to hear anything that might help identify her caller — background noises, sounds that might indicate physical conditions like wheezing or sniffling.

All that greeted her was an unnerving

stillness fraught with evil intent.

It reminded Martie of the explosive hush she'd heard described by her patients at the base hospital. They said it occurred just before an attack. It was an unusual quiescence: one that shuddered with the dreadful anticipation of that shrill whistle that announced a rocket had been launched and was heading to its target. Some of her patients had been inside tanks camouflaged by sand berms when they heard it. Others were in trenches. None would ever forget it.

One soldier told her that the silence was so weighted it felt as if the universe were holding its breath.

Martie had heard that bone-chilling hush only once: lying alone in the desert beneath the fuselage of her Hawk.

This quiet wasn't as heavy, but this wasn't Iraq. And now she had a choice. She could either indulge her caller by playing his game, or she could start her own game.

Carefully, she depressed the button on the phone, hoping it sounded like a wiretap being initiated. Then she waited.

When he didn't speak or hang up, she began to ramble as if she had been in-structed to keep him on the line for three minutes until a trace had been completed. As expected, the call was ended almost immediately after she began her nonsensical rant.

She stared at the phone, as if the intensity of her gaze would produce a picture of her tormenter, or at least a clue as to his or her identity. And, as she had earlier this evening, she tried to fit this into the growing puzzle of activity. Was the caller that soldier gone around the bend? Was he the one who thought she should die on the New Jersey Turnpike? Was he the one who put her daughter in the hospital? And Craig Hemminger in the morgue?

A small shadow appeared in the doorway to her bedroom. Martie smiled. This little ghost padded across the room with her fuzzy airplane and her blankie and climbed up onto Martie's bed.

"Hi, sweetie," she said, stroking Lili's back.

"Hi, Mommy." Lili snuggled next to Martie, who held up the blanket for her daughter to burrow under. "Who was on the phone?" she asked.

"It was a wrong number."

Lili nodded. "I thought maybe it was Bryan again."

"Bryan?"

"Uh-huh. He called yesterday while you were away and we made a play date." She looked up at Martie with stars in her eyes. "He's going to take me flying, just like he promised. I thought that was him getting your permission."

He must have called Lili earlier in the day, before the police notified him of Martie's accident.

"No, sweetie, that wasn't Bryan."

"I can go, can't I, Mommy?"

"We'll see."

A couple of hours ago Martie would have said absolutely yes, but she didn't feel the same way now that she knew he was still involved with Greta. It was bad enough she was hurt. She didn't want her daughter to be hurt also.

"You said I could," Lili reminded her. "I've been looking forward to it. Pleeeeeease, Mommy?"

Before Martie could answer, the phone rang again. Lili went to answer it. Martie grabbed the receiver from her. She didn't want Lili to hear that hideous breathing.

"Hello."

"I'm sorry I'm calling so late," Bryan said. "I wanted to tell you why I couldn't stop by. I got tied up and —"

Martie put the phone down.

"Who was it?" Lili asked.

"Another wrong number," Martie said.

Tripp staggered to the door, half awake and still half drunk. He couldn't imagine who would be ringing his bell at four in the morning, but if it was the chippy he'd been humping before he went unconscious, he could rouse himself to go at it again.

He opened the door, but instead of some hot little redhead there were two large men shoving badges in his face. One of them, a large cocoa-colored man with a shaved head and hands big enough to palm a beach ball, leaned on the doorjamb. The other one, a doughy Irishman who looked like he could polish off a keg in a single sitting, filled the rest of the doorway.

"Let's go, Runyon," the Irishman said. "We're going to take a little ride."

"Where?" Tripp was struggling to make sense of what was happening to him.

"Not far. We're practically around the corner."

"I'm not going anywhere with you," he said, now fully awake.

"I don't remember my partner asking you," the darker man said. "Now be a good boy and get yourself dressed."

"Why?"

"Because we said so?"

Tripp folded his arms across his chest and struck a noble pose. He forgot he was wearing underwear and not princely velvet robes.

"I'm sorry, but that's not a reason for rousting me out of my home in the middle of the night. Either provide me with cause or say good night."

"Okay, I'll try it again." He leaned in so that his face was only inches away from Tripp's. "Because you're under arrest on suspicion of murder, asshole. That good enough for ya?"

Chapter 18

Martie called Vera and Hugh at the crack of dawn and asked them to come to her apartment after Soledad took Lili to school. When Hugh arrived, Martie told him about her visit to Carteret.

Needless to say, Hugh was not pleased to hear that Martie had been in a non-accidental car crash, nor that the person who brought her home from the hospital was Bryan Chalmers. He refrained from questioning her about why Bryan had been called and not him, concentrating instead on the issue of the sabotage. Martie told him all she knew, which wasn't very much.

When Vera arrived, Martie asked how difficult it would be to organize a meeting of HLI personnel. She preempted questions about Greta and Bryan by simply saying Hugh and Vera were the two she felt were needed to put her plan into action. Everyone else was extraneous.

Hugh found that comment telling.

Vera found it disturbing; the last time

she'd seen Martie and Bryan together, they were basking in the afterglow.

Martie didn't allow either of them to linger on the point. "We need to have this meeting today," she stressed.

"It might be a bit complicated," Vera said, "but it can be done. Why?"

"I've been sifting through all the disparate information we have to see if I can find a connection between any two things. The only real link we have is that the sabotage of my car seems to verify that Carteret was the contamination site."

Vera and Hugh nodded in agreement.

"The night we had that pow-wow here, Wiggers made a big point about the security system and the level of familiarity it would take to pass through without detection. I thought about that when I was out at Carteret this time. Since I'm new to the company, I was asked to identify myself several times. Also I noticed how many checkpoints there were. It struck me that since the people manning those security cameras didn't pick up anybody who didn't belong, the person who poisoned the lipsticks has to be an HLI employee."

"The Hart Line employs thousands of people." Vera sounded discouraged.

"That only means we have to narrow the

prospect pool." Martie sounded focused and upbeat. "Correct me if I'm wrong," she said to Vera, "but mid- or lower-level employees from the New York office, or any of the other plants or offices, would not be familiar to the cameras in Carteret."

"True," Vera said.

"Okay, if we eliminate them, that leaves those on the management level. I'd like to get them in one room and have them watched by some trained observers." She looked at Hugh. "There's one guy in particular I'd like watched, Wally Crocker. He's the one I think played with the tire on my car."

Hugh's lips and eyes narrowed until they became two parallel lines, straight and hard.

"Don't snap on that pit bull collar yet, Dad. Crocker isn't the brains behind the lipstick contamination. He's a gofer. There'll be plenty of time to deal with him after we find out whom he's working with or for."

Hugh mumbled something that sounded like agreement, but since it came boxed with a low growl it was virtually unintelligible.

Vera, anxious to put the wheels into motion, excused herself to call her secretary.

"Why didn't you want Greta here?" Hugh asked once Vera left the room.

"She's too negative," Martie replied, opting not to mention their après-meeting chat or the gift Greta sent to Lili. "She elevates even the smallest thing into a major confrontation, and frankly I don't have the energy to deal with her this morning."

Hugh listened to the words, but he listened even more carefully to the tone in which they were delivered. Martie's criticism of Greta's contrary behavior was perfectly justified; Greta did challenge every word out of Martie's mouth. So why sound defensive?

"And Bryan?" he asked, pegging him as the root.

"I didn't see any reason for him to be here."

Hugh had mixed feelings about Martie's apparent change of heart. While he hadn't been thrilled that she and Bryan had been working on a reunion of sorts, he was less thrilled at the thought that Bryan might have hurt Martie.

"Everything's arranged," Vera said. "Tess has sent out a general notice. Everyone in New York will be there. As for Carteret and Suffern, we have vans that will bring everyone into the city. It's set for noon. Is that all right?"

Martie marveled at Vera's efficiency. "It's perfect."

"Not yet," Vera cautioned. "First we have to hammer out the details. That's where the devil is, you know."

The reception area for Hart Line International executives was on the sixty-fourth floor of the HLI building on Madison Avenue. In keeping with Vera's penchant for constant redecoration, this elegant suite was redone every other year. As with her various homes, Vera believed in practicing what she preached, or, to be more precise, living with what she sold.

This decorative cycle was more contemporary than the last, with four large couches and several bergère chairs forming a gracious seating area that seemed to float in the generous space. As always, Vera upgraded her rooms with antiques and artwork that few of her customers could afford, bought and paid for by HLI, of course. This year's *mise-en-scène* was accessorized with several Chinese Ming Dynasty tables and mirrors, an Adolph Gottlieb, and a Richard Diebenkorn.

The *objets* on the antique tables, however, were all from the Faux Fabulous line of the Vera Hart Home Collection.

The view from the suite, which reversed the downtown cityscapes seen from the gym, was spectacular. It afforded visitors and those staff members lucky enough to be allowed admittance the unique experience of looking out on the exquisite living landscape of Central Park.

This day was unusually clear and the park was a cheerful montage of primary colors: the bright yellow of the sun, the green of the trees and great lawns, the blue of the sky, and the brilliant dots of red from caps or T-shirts or shorts sported by New Yorkers taking advantage of the day and their midtown playground.

Inside, however, the mood was gray and muddied.

Over a hundred people were expected at this compulsory meeting. Everyone with a title had been summoned and no one dared to decline an invitation from Vera Hart. Tess had been given the task of greeting the horde, checking off names on an attendance list, as well as keeping her ears opened for any seditious conversation.

As loyal and well meaning as Tess was, she would not be the sole intelligence gatherer. Hugh had sprinkled several of his agents throughout the room. Key among them was Vincent Wiggers; his assignment was Wally Crocker.

Martie had described Crocker and Ian Bardwill to Wiggers. After listening carefully and asking a few pointed questions, he concurred that it was unlikely a grunt like Crocker had acted on his own.

"The worm's being paid," Vincent said. "And from what you just told me, not by Bardwill. He doesn't have enough cash for payoffs."

"He's also far more principled," Martie said, holding on to her suspicion that he might have been the whistle-blower.

Martie was mingling with some of the incoming staffers when Bryan excused her from the group and ushered her off to the side.

"Why did you hang up on me last night?"

"It was late."

"You were awake. I heard it in your voice."

"Lili was with me."

"So what?"

"I have things to do, Bryan."

She started to leave, but he grabbed her arm.

"Uh-uh," he insisted. "You are not walking away from me again. I let that

477

happen once and lived to regret it. I'm not letting it happen a second time."

"It's not totally up to you," she said, her heart tearing in half.

Bryan moved so close to her she could barely breathe. "I don't know what this arctic freeze is about, Martie, but I know you love me. I felt it."

"I was still groggy from the drugs," she said, looking away. "It was just sex. Nothing more."

"You can lie to yourself and you can try to lie to me, but I know what I felt."

"Please, Bryan. Let me go."

He lifted her chin so that she could see the honesty in his eyes.

"I love you, Martie Phelps," he said. "And because we're in a public place I'll let you leave, but I am not letting you go. This time I intend to fight for you until I win you. And no one is going to get in my way. Not your father or your mother or your sister or you."

Her mouth twitched, which meant that someone in that litany of family members spooked her. Bryan's natural assumption was that the general was doing a repeat performance of his Chalmers condemnation.

Martie pulled free from his grasp.

"You can put up as much resistance as you want," he said to her back as she walked away, "but I can't lose. I've got Lili on my side."

In spite of herself, Martie smiled.

Vera was down the hall in her private office when Greta walked in waving the memo about the meeting in her hand.

"Why wasn't I briefed on this?" she demanded to know.

"Because it's my meeting, not yours." Vera didn't look up. She continued studying the papers arrayed in front of her.

"What the hell does that mean?"

"I believe it's self-explanatory. Now, if you'll excuse me."

"I will not!" Greta peered over the desk, trying to see what Vera was poring over so intently. "What are you doing?"

Vera looked up, rested her arms on top of her papers, folded her hands in front of her, and looked at Greta with the dispassion of a bank clerk. Her eyes were cold. Her mouth was tight, but her tone was calm, a well-modulated contrast to Greta's shrillness.

"I'm going over personnel lists," she said.

"Why?"

"I'm checking to see who's been naughty and who's been nice."

"Look, if you're angry about that press conference, let me explain." Greta's voice was an amalgam of forced apology mixed with nervousness that no apology would suffice. "I couldn't get in touch with you and I felt that something needed to be done. Craig's death was horrible, but the timing of it put us in a terrible light. I couldn't let the media run rampant with speculation and unsubstantiated accusations. I held a press conference so the world would know the horror we've been living with, the horror of your cyber-stalking and our repeated death threats."

Vera's upper lip twitched with amusement at Greta's attempt at bonding.

"I know you didn't want that kind of publicity, but that was before a Hart Line employee was murdered."

Vera continued to stare silently at Greta.

"I did try to reach you," she reiterated. "Where were you, by the way?" she said with a tinge of insinuation.

"At home. And if your next question is, 'Can anyone verify that?' the answer is yes."

Greta was playing amateur detective. Vera didn't deal with amateurs.

"Really, Mother, I'm not accusing you of anything. I simply wanted to —"

"Get out, Greta."

"What?"

"You heard me. I'm busy."

Greta's skin flushed almost as red as her hair.

"I almost forgot," Vera said, handing Greta an envelope. "I got you something."

Greta eyed the envelope suspiciously. "What is it?"

"Take it. It's not rat poison. Although . . ." Vera tilted her head and waved her hand as if to say, "If the shoe fits."

Greta's lips flattened against her teeth, making her look positively wolverine.

"It's a gift certificate."

"For what?"

"A much-needed vacation."

"I don't need a vacation," Greta hissed.

"Oh, darling, I disagree. Watching you yesterday was highly disturbing. There seemed to be no question that the stress of all *our death threats* had gotten the better of you. Why else would you have behaved so traitorously?"

There was a deep rumbling undertone to Vera's calm exterior, like a volcano building to a heated eruption.

"Why else would you have aired our private matters to the public after I repeatedly asked you not to? Why else would you have implicated me with your silence?" She leaned forward, her posture menacing. "It's a month's stay at the Golden Door. Go. Get a facial and a massage. Take early morning hikes. Use the steam room. Learn yoga. Do whatever the hell you want, but go."

Greta took the envelope, but she didn't open it. Instead, she ripped it into a dozen pieces, dropped them on Vera's desk, and stormed out.

Vera brushed the scraps away.

"Well," she said, calmly returning to her lists, "that went well."

In the rush of getting this meeting organized, Martie had almost forgotten that Delilah was starting work at the Hart Line, but when Martie arrived at the office, there she was, seated behind a noticeably organized desk. She was wearing a simple navy blue pantsuit, her blond hair was pulled back in a neat ponytail, her fingernails were cleanly manicured, and her makeup was subdued. Martie couldn't remember ever seeing Delilah look this pretty. Without the garish artifice that had been her costume, she was lovely.

"Well, good-bye, Piney Hollow, and hello, New York," Martie said, her eyes wide with approval. "You look incredible!"

Delilah blushed. "Thanks."

Martie had a lump in her throat looking at her friend's transformation. It was only surface, but still . . .

"Do you like the results?"

"A lot. It doesn't look like me or feel like me, but if I'm going to do like you say and move in different circles, I gotta dress the part." She tilted her head down the hall at the other HLI staffers. "I don't look out of place, do I?"

It made Martie's heart sing to see how pleased she was with her sameness; desert camis or tailored navy blue pantsuits, a uniform provided a certain amount of comfort.

"Absolutely not," Martie said. "You're a bona fide Hart-Liner."

Delilah sighed happily. She'd obviously worked very hard for that compliment.

"Now," Martie said, "did anyone show you around?"

"The human resources person. She was real nice. Introduced me to everyone, showed me the lay of the land, all that stuff. She also told me there's a big meeting happening here at noon, so let's stop wasting time on me. What can I do to help you?"

"You can get my office in shape, for starters. Since I've been here, things have been so hectic I still haven't unpacked all my files from Rockefeller, let alone set up my address book."

Delilah bounded to her feet and practically saluted. "Piece of cake!"

"I want to thank you all for coming," Vera said, standing behind a modest podium and speaking into a microphone. "I promise I'll be brief."

She smiled and the large assembly tittered. Vera was always brief. She said whatever it was she had to say and that was that. No fluff. No fuss.

"Yesterday, we received the horrible news that Craig Hemminger was murdered."

She looked out and acknowledged some of the sad nods and mumbled regrets.

"Despite his recent departure, Craig served us long and well. Let us all remember him kindly."

As her staff indulged in a moment of mourning, Vera reconnoitered. Hugh was in the back. Sprinkled in and among the crowd were several of his agents, listening and watching for any questionable behavior. Greta stood off to the side, sulking. Her eyes were fixed on Martie, who was several rows in front of her.

Bryan was up front, slightly behind Vera. His eyes were also on Martie.

"Today, some detectives might want to question you. You're not suspects. They're simply looking for information. Please be as helpful as you can.

"For those of you who were concerned about what you heard at Greta's press conference yesterday, I'd like to give you the facts and clear up some points Ms. Hart left rather foggy."

Out of the corner of her eye, she saw Greta stiffen.

"Though my attorney, Mr. Chalmers, has cautioned me not to comment on any matters concerning the ongoing investigation, I feel compelled to ask you to trust me. Remember who I am and what this company means to me. Think about how hard we've worked to make the Hart Line the success that it is. And then decide whether I would do anything to put it, you, or me in this kind of jeopardy.

"Now on to the death threats."

A frisson of nervousness swept through the room. Instinctively, some people appeared to shrink into themselves, as if trying to hide from whatever demons might be skulking about. Others surreptitiously stole a glance at their neighbors, wondering.

"It's true that Greta and I have received some very unpleasant mail." She smiled, but the pall over the room was too heavy to allow any lightness to filter through. "I wish I knew who was doing this, but I don't. I wish I knew why they were doing this, but I don't. Which is why all of it has been turned over to the police."

Again, she smiled, but this time with a resignation so unlike her that a few eyes popped.

"All of a sudden," she said, with a tinge of tremor in her voice, "I don't seem to be able to get through a day without a lawyer or a detective. It's my worst nightmare.

"As for the possibility that all of this hideousness is part of a takeover plot?" She shrugged. "If you know who's behind it, please let me know."

A nervous titter greeted her inquiry.

She turned so that she was facing Greta. Her mouth tightened and her eyes became pieces of aqua ice.

"Actually, that was not a throwaway comment. Yesterday, Greta offered a reward for anyone who provided tips that might lead to the arrest of Craig's murderer. While that was exceedingly generous, since HLI is a public company it wouldn't be proper to commit those kinds of funds to something so personal. Which must mean that Greta intended to pay that reward from her own pocket."

Greta glared back at Vera with the heated venom of a rattlesnake.

"And since, as she so eloquently put it, we had such great affection and respect for Mr. Hemminger, my guess is that the amount of her reward couldn't have been less than two hundred and fifty thousand dollars."

Greta dug her nails into her palms so hard she practically drew blood.

"Not only am I willing to double that, but I'll offer the same amount to anyone who can provide information that will lead us to the person responsible for this assault on the Hart Line. Someone killed Craig Hemminger. And someone is trying to kill my company. I want them both brought to justice."

The outburst of applause and the bleacher-worthy cheers made Vera's executive suite sound like a stadium.

She motioned for her fans to quiet

down. When they did, she thanked everyone for their support.

"And now," she said with an exaggerated sigh, "for the good news."

An appreciative chuckle told her that her staff could use some good news.

"Dr. Phelps," she said, smiling at Martie and inviting her up to the podium, "would you join me, please?"

Confused, Martie crossed the room and stood by her mother.

"A couple of weeks ago my office issued a press release announcing the hire of Dr. Marta Phelps to head up our exciting new skin care research project. I'm sure you all remember that she was the winner of a Hart Foundation Woman of the Year Award."

The applause was warm and respectful and wary. They were waiting for the other shoe to drop.

"I'm especially thrilled to have someone of Dr. Phelps's caliber join the Hart Line family, because this exceedingly brilliant woman is also a member of my family."

She turned to Martie, who was as surprised at this announcement as everyone else.

"Ladies and gentlemen, meet my younger daughter, Martie Phelps."

Relief fired the crowd with enthusiasm. There were squeals of surprise and lots of grandmotherly clucking about how beautiful Martie was and how much she looked like their peerless leader. There were also the inevitable head swivels that went from Martie to Greta and back again, comparing and contrasting the two female offspring of the legendary Vera Hart.

Greta felt as if Vera had fired a twelve-gauge shotgun directly into her chest. Struck and hurting, she tilted her head down and away from the curious stares, automatically bringing her hand up to her right eye to hide the imperfection she was certain everyone saw and was talking about.

Vera, milking the moment, walked out from behind the podium, took Martie by the hand, and began to introduce her to the staff. Even those who'd already met Martie rushed to greet her again. Few wanted to miss a chance to get up close and personal.

Not everyone in the room was moved by this Hallmark moment, however.

Greta disappeared as quickly as she could.

Tim Polatchek wasn't far behind.

Vera's day at the office ended the way it began: having her decisions challenged by her daughter.

"What was that all about?" Martie said, still befuddled by her surprise coming-out party.

"You didn't like my speech?" Vera's brow furrowed with concern. "I thought I struck just the right tone."

"Your speech was fine," Martie admitted. "It was quite good, in fact."

Vera smiled beatifically. "Thank you, dear."

"It was the ending I wasn't sure I liked."

"No? Why not?"

"Because I feel as if you used me, as if that whole intro-to-the-folks routine was a manipulation."

"To what end?" Vera's eyes were wide with innocence.

"To get Greta's goat, for one."

Vera peered at Martie. "I would have thought you'd like that."

Martie flushed with an inadvertent confession that, indeed, that would be a guilty pleasure.

Slyly, Vera said, "For whatever it's worth, it did get her goat. But I didn't do that on your behalf. I owed her one and I don't like to leave debts unfulfilled."

Martie studied the weave of the carpet as her blush faded and her embarrassment ebbed. It was difficult to admit that at her age she might still be playing "gotcha" with her older sister.

"I also owed you one."

Martie looked up at Vera, curious.

"For the *Mainstreet* article."

Vera watched Martie's face register surprise. And suspicion. She didn't blame her for feeling either.

"The world should have seen me with my younger daughter then. I thought perhaps I could make up for that horrible omission by introducing you to my smaller world today."

Martie was dumbstruck.

"I don't think I ever apologized to you for that terrible day, did I?"

Martie just shook her head. She was so full of feeling she was afraid to speak.

"Well, I am sorrier than you'll ever know."

"It was a long time ago," Martie said crisply, wanting to put an end to this discussion.

"Yes, it was," Vera said, noting Martie's discomfort. "At the time, I was so caught up in trying to resurrect my career I let a

491

number of very important things slide. I didn't pay attention to my marriage. Or my daughters." Her voice grew soft. "I should have known that you wouldn't have done anything to make that day difficult for me. In my heart I probably did know it. But in my head, I was focused solely on my needs. Unfortunately, I paid dearly for that self-absorption."

"Look, Vera," Martie said, "I accept your apology, but if you don't mind, I'd like to move on. I don't see any point in re-visiting the past. It can't do anything except open old wounds, and frankly I can't see why anyone would want to do that. They hurt enough the first time around."

Vera eyed Martie carefully. Something had happened with Bryan, something very disappointing. Vera longed to ask, but knew she couldn't. They hadn't walked far enough across the bridge yet for that.

"If you wish," Vera said, conceding. "Hugh, why don't you join us?"

Martie looked from one to the other as her father entered from Vera's anteroom.

"I have a small screen on my desk," Vera explained, pointing to the square silver frame Martie had assumed held a photograph. "It allows me to see who's waiting for an appointment."

Martie, who was not a cynic by nature, couldn't help but wonder whether Vera's apology was for her benefit or Hugh's.

Vera did not miss her expression of distrust.

"What did Mr. Wiggers have to report on that Crocker person?" Vera asked Hugh, shifting Martie's attention on to something else.

"He said Crocker never showed."

Vera opened a folder on her desk and slid her finger down the list of attendees.

"That's correct. According to Tess's records, he was the only one who didn't."

"I ran his address," Hugh said. "Wiggers and a partner are on their way to see if Mr. Crocker is under the weather or hiding under his bed."

Vera pursed her lips. "Did the others pick up anything of merit?"

"No. We watched Bardwill just in case Martie read him wrong, but," Hugh said, smiling at his daughter, "as usual, her instincts were spot on."

"I wouldn't discount anyone based on my instincts," she said. "My radar's a little off these days."

Vera could tell that Hugh had no idea what Martie was talking about, probably because he was still rooting against Bryan.

"I thought I recognized someone in the crowd," Martie continued, "but I couldn't place his face."

"Is he someone you met during your visits to Carteret?" Vera asked. "Or someone you met at the offices here?"

Martie's brow wrinkled as she sorted out her impressions. "That's the thing. When I noticed him I knew I'd met him way before I came to work for HLI. The problem is, I don't know where I met him or when."

"Could you have worked with him in Washington?" Hugh offered. "Or when you were in the army?"

Martie shook her head. "I don't know. Maybe."

"Our personnel files contain pictures," Vera said. "If you'd like you can go through them."

"That's probably a good idea, but we have so much else to do."

"Martie," Hugh said. "If you think this guy might give us a lead on anything, finding out who he is has to top your list of priorities."

"Let's sweat Crocker first," Martie said. "If he turns out to be a dud, I'll be happy to take a trip down memory lane."

Chapter 19

The dark-skinned detective, Otis Franklin, stood next to Tripp and stared down at him. While his ebony eyes held no particular menace, his presence was intimidating. Tripp was tall. Otis was big enough to be a condominium.

"State your name."

"Trevor Hollingsworth Runyon III," he said, hoping he sounded more self-assured than he felt.

"Address."

"Seven eighty-three Park Avenue."

Franklin harrumphed.

Tripp cringed. He'd thought his station would impress the detective; it did everyone else.

"Occupation."

"I'm with the Seafarer Bank."

"What do you do for the Seafarer Bank?" Franklin's partner, Donnelly, asked. He was at the far end of the table, scribbling on a large yellow pad.

"I examine properties for potential mortgages."

"Sounds exciting," Otis said. "And really important."

"The Seafarer Bank is my family's business. And yes, being able to properly assess the value of a property is extremely important."

Donnelly and Franklin looked at each other. Their expressions were mocking.

"Have you always worked for Daddy?" Donnelly said.

Tripp wanted to punch the Irishman in the mouth, but wisely restrained himself. Aside from the stupidity of smashing a policeman in his own stationhouse, there was the possibility of reprisal from Otis.

"No. Previously I was employed by Hart Line International."

"Oh, I see," Donnelly said, as if the lightbulb over his head had just been switched on. "Before you worked for Daddy, you worked for the missus."

"It sounds quite terrible when you put it like that, but yes."

The two detectives heard the embarrassment in Tripp's voice and shifted to a kinder, gentler approach.

"A man's got to do what a man's got to do," Donnelly said. "I don't envy you, though, buddy. Working with women all day long? Gotta be tough."

"You have no idea," Tripp said, feeling as if finally they'd found common ground.

"You didn't have to sell makeup or make cookies or shit like that, did you?" Otis asked, cringing at the thought.

Tripp laughed. "No. I was in charge of distribution. I made sure the shit was shipped." He laughed, amused by his own joke.

Otis smiled too. "Sounds like it wasn't a bad gig."

"Actually, it was a pretty good gig."

"So why'd you leave Hart Line?" Donnelly asked.

Tripp sat back in his chair, folded his arms across his chest, and huffed. "My wife divorced me, so her mother fired me."

"Whoa! That must have pissed you off something fierce," Otis said, sympathetically.

"In a word, yes."

"Undeserved, huh?"

"Absolutely."

"You were there a long time, weren't you?" Donnelly asked, he too sounding like he understood Tripp's outrage.

"Years."

"Bet you worked your ass off for them too."

"You bet I did!"

"Sucks, man." Otis folded his incredibly

large body onto the modest metal chair across from Tripp. "Must've been a bitch keeping up with all that paperwork with your ass stuck in the saddle of your polo pony, huh?"

Tripp's color drained. He had been so busy with his male bonding that he forgot the males in question were NYPD detectives and not his bar buddies.

"Whether I was in New York or Palm Beach, I did my job," he said, with an air of hauteur. "You don't have to be stuck behind a desk all day long to be efficient, you know." He sniffed. "I resent your implication that I was a laggard."

Otis stretched across the table, bringing his face close to Tripp's. "I resent assholes who send death threats."

Tripp recoiled. "What death threats? I never did any such thing." Beads of sweat traced the line of his forehead. "Who told you that? Must have been Vera Hart, that fucking bitch! She's out of control, I tell you. Out of control!"

His eyes were wide and he was puffing like a runner after a marathon.

What if Vera showed them those pictures of him and that boy?

"Let's review the facts." Otis was unfazed by Tripp's vehement denial. "Your wife divorced you. Your mother-in-law canned you. You had to go running back to your father for a job. And you're mightily pissed off. That right?"

Tripp was afraid to speak.

"That right?"

With Otis looming over him, he was afraid not to speak.

"Right," he muttered.

"Well, guess what Trevor Hollingsworth Runyon III, the two women you're pissed at have been receiving some really serious death threats."

"I didn't send them!" Tripp was so nervous he could barely think straight.

"No? That's funny, because guess whose fingerprints were on the most recent envelope?"

Tripp shook his head. "Not possible."

Fear had intensified the blue of his eyes and dried his mouth. He began to lick his lips like a man who'd been marooned in the desert.

"It's a mistake. I'm telling you. I didn't send any threats to anyone."

If she had someone who could doctor those pictures, she could've found someone to duplicate his fingerprints.

"Are you and Greta Hart on good terms?"

"I told you we're divorced. How friendly do you think we are?"

He wasn't thinking too clearly, but he knew enough not to mention that he made sexual house calls to his ex.

"How unfriendly are you?"

"Not terribly." It didn't seem smart to tell them that basically he detested Greta either.

"I don't get that," Donnelly said, honestly.

"Greta and I move in circles where after a divorce it's considered déclassé to be spiteful." He spit out a laugh that was wracked with cynicism. "It makes all the others at the cocktail party uncomfortable."

"How about your ex-mother-in-law?" Otis asked. "Sounds to me like you got a real hard-on for her."

"I can't stand her, but I didn't threaten her life."

"Why, because the folks at your cocktail party might not think that was classy?"

Tripp smirked. "*Au contraire!* Gossiping about Vera Hart is a national pastime, gentlemen, especially these days. Didn't you know that?"

"Not a fan favorite, eh?" Otis said.

Tripp shook his head, quite emphatically, Otis thought.

"Men hate her because she's as successful as the best of them and more successful than most."

"Then women must love her."

Tripp scoffed. "Hardly! She comes off as too damn perfect. She makes them look like they don't measure up, so they hate her too."

Donnelly ripped a page off his pad and tossed it across the room to a wastebasket.

"Your family has money, right?"

"Old money," Tripp said, making certain the other men knew the difference between the Runyons and the Harts.

"So why'd you want money from the Harts?"

How'd they know about that? Tripp wondered. They must have spoken to Vera. Or the lawyers he had contacted about suing Greta.

"I thought I deserved compensation," he said. "Beyond my severance package, that is."

"Who'd you go to? Hemminger?"

"Yes, but then they fired him too."

"How'd you feel about what happened to him?"

Tripp shrugged. "It's a terrible thing, being accused of fraud. He could go to jail for a long time." He shivered. "I wasn't crazy about the guy, but I wouldn't wish that on anyone."

"Well, your wish came true, Runyon. Hemminger's not going to have to worry about going to jail," Donnelly said. "He's asleep on a slab."

Tripp began to hyperventilate. "Do you mean he's dead?"

"Duh! Unless the guy has some strange nighttime habits and relatives in Transylvania, yeah, that's what I mean."

Tripp clutched at his chest and gulped for air.

Otis wasn't moved by the dramatic response.

"I take it you didn't know," he said to Tripp.

"No. How would I know?"

"Newspapers. Television. Radio. Telephone. Are you living in this world?"

"I was . . . partying." He sighed, trying to catch his breath. "Look. When you picked me up, I was half in the bag and you know it."

"Because you got the money you were demanding and were out celebrating? Or because you didn't and you'd done something stupid?"

As he waited for Tripp's response, Donnelly's pencil was still. So was the air in the cramped, windowless room.

Tripp's head swung from one detective to another.

"What are you talking about?"

"Hemminger's doorman says you came to visit him the day before he was murdered." Donnelly's voice was low.

"Murdered? Holy shit!" Tripp's face was ashen. His hands were cold and he was so nervous he was afraid he might wet himself.

"What did you want with Hemminger?"

It took a minute for him to search his brain for a memory.

"He called and said there were some personal items from my desk he wanted me to pick up." Tripp's voice was hollow. "I told him there was nothing there that meant anything to me, but he insisted."

He furrowed his brow as if thinking were an effort.

"Actually, he demanded that I come get the stuff, which frankly I thought was a little strange, but the guy was being hounded by the feds." Sheepishly, he looked at his two interrogators. "That could make you do strange things."

"So what happened when you were with him?"

"Nothing. We talked about HLI for a

couple of minutes, he handed me this carton, and we said good-bye. I wished him luck with the deposition and left."

"What was in the carton?"

"I don't know. I never opened it."

"We're going to want to see it."

Tripp looked at Otis and nodded obediently. He felt sick.

"You know," Donnelly said, "there are some people who think that whoever's sending these death threats to Greta and Vera Hart is the same guy who offed Hemminger. What do you think?"

"I think I need a lawyer," Tripp said glumly.

Enid Polatchek was so distressed about what was happening to Vera Hart, she'd taken to her bed. From the minute her eyes opened in the morning until the instant they closed at night, they were glued to Vera-vision: the cooking shows, the garden shows, the craft specials, the decorating makeovers, the cosmetics infomercials, and, of course, the news. If for one inexplicable moment the airways were Hartless, Enid filled the void with one of her treasury of tapes.

For Enid, this compulsive TV viewing had taken on the proportion of a religious vigil; if she continued to have faith and demonstrated that faith by watching every second of programming about her idol, Vera would be saved. And Enid would be rewarded in heaven.

Dolph couldn't stand being around her fanaticism, listening to her constant rant about the hypocrisy of society and the Armageddon it was inviting with its false accusations and insidious lies about the Holy Hart. Though it wasn't as far away as he would have liked, he moved into Tim's old room.

He hadn't gone in there for years. He'd forgotten how strange his son had been as a child. Tim's hobbies weren't the usual intrigue with fire engines and frogs. He'd always had more of an interest in chemistry and war. Instead of his shelves holding baseball or football trophies, they used to be arrayed with miniature soldiers representing all of the world's great wars.

Dolph always thought Tim became enamored with the military because it represented power. Tim was an outcast in school, frequently bullied by boys who took advantage of those who were smaller or weaker. Alone in his room, however, he could pit one group against another and know that his side would wind up victorious.

Vicarious vengeance, Dolph supposed.

It was Tim's interest in chemistry, oddly enough, that bound him to his mother. When Tim was a child, Enid entertained him with the chemistry of the kitchen, teaching him to make things like yeast dough and Jell-O and cupcakes. Dolph remembered how fascinated Tim had been to pour hot water over a colored powder, put it into the refrigerator, and after a while take it out and have this solid mass that jiggled on his plate.

Of course, once he started playing with chemistry sets, he graduated from Jell-O to minor explosives, but that seemed like a natural, healthy progression for a young lad. Truth be told, Dolph had been worried that his son spent so much time in an apron, so when he took an interest in chemistry, Dolph built Tim a small laboratory in the basement, right next to his own workshop.

Many a Saturday the Polatchek men spent in that basement, Dolph building small pieces of furniture, none of which Enid would allow upstairs, and Tim conducting various experiments. Those were happy times, Dolph recalled. He loved being with his son, and if they couldn't share Little League games or varsity basketball or wrestling meets, they always had the basement.

Spurred by nostalgia, Dolph went downstairs, tiptoeing so he didn't have to explain himself to his wife. He locked the door behind him as he'd always done when he and Tim retreated to their "clubhouse"; this was private property: *men only.* He flicked on the light and looked around. A melancholic rush came over him, filling his eyes with tears of reminiscence.

All his handcrafted furniture was there: the Papa Bear and Timmy Bear chairs he'd made when Tim was three years old; the vitrines he'd made to showcase Tim's soldier collection, which had been moved downstairs; the lab bench and storage cabinets he'd constructed; the card table they used to play gin whenever they wanted to escape Enid; the closets he built to store Tim's uniforms and old clothes.

Dolph revisited each and every piece, allowing himself to bathe in the memories of time spent in this concrete sanctuary. When he came to Tim's lab, his shoulders straightened with pride. Tim still used this area as a retreat. He had an apartment in New York, but he didn't have room for a lab there, so whenever he felt the need to tinker, he drove out to the house. About six months before, he was down here three weekends in a row, tinkering away. Dolph had wanted to return to his workbench and work alongside his son the way they had in the old days, but Tim seemed preoccupied, so Dolph respected his privacy and stayed upstairs.

Besides, right about then he'd had his own problems to sort out. Which reminded him, he wondered if the police had made any progress in capturing the man who killed Tim's boss.

Vera accompanied Hugh to the police station on Sixty-seventh Street so they could show the police a picture of Wally Crocker. Even though much of the evidence to date was circumstantial, Hugh wanted the police to issue an all-points bulletin for Crocker, whom Hugh suspected of trying to murder Martie. Plus, it appeared as if Crocker had played some role in the contamination of the Valentine Red lipstick which was used in the commission of a murder.

Wiggers, who was going to meet them there, had called to say it looked like the guy had left town in a hurry, hence the APB. His apartment was a mess: drawers and closet doors flung open, discarded clothes strewn about, empty liquor bottles littering the floor, dirty dishes in the sink.

Hugh and Vera were on their way to speak with Lieutenant Gary Douglas when Trevor Runyon, his son, Tripp, and a man who had the distinct air of a high-priced attorney descended the stairs. Trevor was holding Tripp's elbow, steering him as if the man were a five-year-old boy; the lawyer was trailing behind like a geisha. Trevor's face looked as if it had been permanently frozen into a scowl, his jaw and the lines around his mouth were that hard and fixed.

Hugh found it interesting that when Trevor spotted Vera, his brow knitted even tighter.

"Trevor." Vera eyed the two Runyons carefully. "Tripp. Fancy meeting you here," she said with a hint of a smirk.

"You stinking bitch!" Tripp lunged at Vera, his eyes narrowed to arrowlike slits, his hands reaching for her throat. If Trevor hadn't had a firm grip on him, Tripp might easily have strangled her.

"Get your pet monkey off me," Vera snarled, moving closer to Hugh.

Trevor yanked on Tripp's arm. The lawyer reminded them both where they were. But Trevor wasn't finished. He turned to Vera and hissed, "It's a pity we're in a police station. Anywhere else and I would let him have at you."

Vera dismissed his threat with an imperious wave of her hand. "As if this poor excuse for a man could possibly hurt me."

Tripp wanted to rip her heart out of her chest, but off to the side he noticed Otis and Donnelly watching him. With such a vague threat — "paint the town" — and a single fingerprint on a ubiquitous envelope, they'd been forced to release Tripp, but he'd been warned not to leave town.

Trevor didn't care who was in the audience. "You are a bitch," he said, too low for most of the police who were watching the verbal wrestling match to hear. "And believe me, I will get you where it'll hurt you the most."

"As always, Trevor," Vera mocked, "big talk, little stick, no action."

Runyon's face turned so red it looked as if it might explode.

Otis, who'd seen enough, ended the contretemps.

"Okay, boys and girls, break it up." He pointed to the Runyons. "If you two don't leave now, I'll make sure you spend the night at Rikers. As for you," he said, looking at Vera and Hugh, "whatever your business is in this house, either take care of it or say buh-bye."

"We're here to see Lieutenant Douglas," Hugh explained.

"Right this way," Otis said, leading them upstairs.

As the Runyons were going out, Vincent Wiggers was coming in. When they passed each other in the doorway, Wiggers heard the older man say, "How stupid can you be, sending those women death threats?"

The younger man was insistent in his denial. "I didn't do it! I don't care how they got my fingerprints on that fucking envelope, I didn't do it!"

Wiggers slowed his pace.

"I've waited years to get even," the older man said. "If you ruined this for me, I'll kill you myself."

Chapter 20

It wasn't even eight o'clock in the morning and already Bryan was having a very bad day. Actually, he was having a very bad couple of days. First there was Martie's inexplicable freeze. When she hung up on him the other night he tried to excuse it as fatigue, but her attitude toward him at the meeting the day before made it clear that the only thing she was tired of was him.

He had wanted to talk to her again, but his desk was piled high with things marked "urgent." Greta's news conference announcing the murder of Craig Hemminger and her revelation about death threats being sent to America's favorite diva had the press in a tizzy. Bryan was beginning to long for the relative calm of the district attorney's office.

Then he had a setback on Vera's e-mails. He'd called Bob Blanton, a buddy of his at the Bureau, and asked him to trace their origin. So far, none of Blanton's attempts had panned out.

And now, over breakfast, Borzone gave him an unsettling update on the Central Park case. They had an ID on the victim and were tracing her steps on the days preceding her murder. She was thirty-five years old, an executive at an advertising agency, divorced, dating, but no one in particular according to her friends. She was involved in a major presentation that week, so her hours were longer than usual. The only time she left her office was to go home or to a nearby gym for a quick workout. She did manage to squeeze in a haircut, however.

"Work is one thing," a comely coworker told Borzone. "A good haircut is everything."

What piqued Borzone's interest was that her haircut was at the Hart Line Spa.

According to the manager, the vic was a regular. She came in that day for a haircut and a manicure; she was in and out in an hour and a half. There were no receipts for any purchases.

"When I asked if she might have bought a tube of Valentine Red some other time," Borzone told Bryan, "the woman's upper lip curled as if I passed Limburger cheese under her nose. Evidently this lady would never have worn red. She was the Parfait Pink type."

Bryan's brow pleated with frustration. "I can't believe there's no connection between her being at that spa and the murder weapon being a Hart Line lipstick. It's got coincidence written all over it, and —"

"You don't believe in coincidences," Borzone said, finishing Bryan's thought.

"Do you?"

"Normally, I don't."

"But?"

Borzone filled Bryan in on the other two cases he'd found.

"I spoke to the detectives in charge of both cases and the MO is identical. The DOA in Palm Beach was snatched after leaving a spa."

"A Hart Line Spa, I take it."

Borzone nodded grimly. "She was raped and beaten, bound with her T-shirt, written all over with lipstick, and left in a nearby park. She was dead at the scene.

"The vic in Atlanta worked in the PR department for Hart Line Atlanta. She was also found in a park. Same set of circumstances, but she survived."

"Were the lipsticks Valentine Red?"

"Yes, but neither one was poisoned."

"Is that good news or bad news?"

Borzone shrugged. "The three cases are definitely the work of the same man, because the MO is exactly the same. All three victims had a vague connection to Hart Line, but not in a way that appears significant. It's probably a coincidence born of convenience and not something that links these murders to your investigation or provides a clear-cut motive."

"What about the fact that the lipstick in all of the cases is specifically Hart Line Cosmetics' Valentine Red."

"A criminal profiler would say two things: The killer defaces his victims to humiliate them. He's one of those mopes who commit crimes against women to compensate for feelings of inadequacy or to extract vengeance for repeated female rejection. Guys like this hate their mommies and blame women for everything bad in their lives. My guess is that this guy's mommy's favorite lipstick was Valentine Red."

Bryan sighed with frustration. Borzone was right, but that analysis fit more men than Bryan could count. They needed something more specific.

"What about the add-on of the mercuric chloride?"

"Either our guy is ramping up his murderous delights because simply raping and beating the shit out of these women isn't getting him off like it used to, or he got hold of the laced lipstick by accident."

"That's a couple of accidents and coincidences," Bryan noted.

"Combined with three identically committed murders. We're looking at a serial killer who's going to kill again, and soon, if we don't catch him."

"It doesn't sound as if you have a lot to go on."

"It would certainly make things easier if we could pinpoint the source for the tainted Valentine Reds, but you heard Greta Hart. It's everywhere."

Bryan nodded and pushed his home fries around on the plate.

"How's that doctor doing?" Borzone asked, changing the subject. "The one who was in the car accident."

"Fine."

"She the one?"

"What one?"

"The one who stole your heart and refuses to give it back."

Bryan stopped playing with his food. He looked up and in place of NYPD Detective Anthony Borzone he saw a friend. And just then, that's exactly what he needed.

"Oh, that one," Bryan said with a wry smile. "Yup. She's it."

He told Borzone about how they'd run

516

into each other at the gala, how one thing had led to another, and how he thought they had been given a second chance.

"So what happened? You two hit a bump in the road?"

"More like a crater." Bryan shrugged. "She's acting as if I did something seriously wrong. Maybe I did, but for the life of me, I can't figure out what it is."

"What's your relationship with the Hart woman?" Tony asked.

"There is no relationship. There was, but not anymore." Bryan laughed. "And by the way, the Hart woman is Dr. Phelps's sister."

Tony leaned back and stared at Bryan, who filled him in on the familial ties between Greta and Martie.

"That's what you did wrong, my friend," Borzone said when Bryan was finished. "You broke one of the Ten Commandments of Dating: Thou shalt not do sisters."

"I didn't know they were sisters," Bryan explained.

"Doesn't matter," Borzone said as his cell phone rang. "You were with both of them. And now both of them hate you. A lot."

Bryan sank down in the booth, feeling

completely dejected. "Could this day get any worse?" he muttered.

"Yes," Borzone said, hanging up from his call. "Your friend Delilah Green was just rushed to the hospital. She was found in the park, badly beaten and covered in lipstick."

Bryan was pacing in the lobby when Martie and Lili arrived. He'd called Martie on his way over to New York Hospital to tell her about Delilah.

"What happened? She was supposed to come by my apartment last night after work and never showed."

Bryan glanced at Lili. He didn't want to describe Delilah's condition in front of her.

"Soledad had an early doctor's appointment," Martie said, explaining why she brought Lili to the hospital.

Still, Bryan hesitated.

"Mommy, I'm going to stand over there so Bryan can tell you what happened to Delilah." She looked up at him. "It's not nice, is it?"

"No, Lili, it's not."

"Then I shouldn't hear it."

"No, you shouldn't." Bryan couldn't help smiling at Lili. "You're very smart and very wise for a girl your age."

"Yes," Lili said with complete self-assurance. "I am."

She walked over to the information desk and struck up a conversation with one of the grandmotherly volunteers.

Bryan filled Martie in.

Her hand flew to her mouth and her eyes filled with tears.

"Who would do that to her?" she moaned, her expression pained. Suddenly her color evaporated. Her voice was scratchy. "Was she raped?"

"No." Bryan wanted to kick himself. He should have told her that immediately.

Martie almost collapsed with relief. "Thank God."

"Are you okay, Mommy?" Lili had seen Martie's reaction and ran right over.

Martie bent down and kissed the top of Lili's head. "Yes, sweetie. I'm upset that Delilah's hurt, that's all."

Lili's mouth turned down and wobbled. "Me too." She looked like she was about to cry.

"Why don't you go up and see Delilah?" Bryan said to Martie. "I'm conducting a city-wide taste test for hospital coffee shops and I need an assistant. How about you?" he said to Lili. "You interested in helping me out?"

A big smile illuminated the little girl's face.

Martie was torn. She didn't want Lili getting too close to Bryan, but she needed to see Delilah, so she agreed.

"I won't be long," she said.

"Take your time," Lili said, eagerly reaching for Bryan's hand. "And give Delilah a kiss for me."

"I will."

Martie ran for the elevator, but her eyes were drawn back to the sight of Bryan and her daughter, hand in hand and fully engaged with each other. As the elevator doors closed, Martie sighed. She wasn't a woman who dwelled on life's might-have-beens. At a very young age she learned that they only made you sad and weighed you down. But this one had a particular sting to it. This wasn't only her lost opportunity. It was Lili's as well.

Bryan and Lili were in the midst of a very serious debate: whether Bryan's butter pecan ice cream was better than Lili's vanilla fudge. Bryan made the case that butter pecan had the added bonus of a crunch. Lili countered that her fudge swirl offered a different kind of plus, but a plus nonetheless. They argued about which flavor lent itself better to toppings like butterscotch, hot fudge, wet nuts, sprinkles, or whipped cream. In the end, it was a standoff.

"So are we going flying next Saturday?" Lili asked when the serious business of the ice cream was completed.

"I hope so," Bryan said. "We still have to get your mom's okay."

Lili nodded. "I know. That's why I thought it was you who called the other night."

He was about to say he did, when Lili added, "but Mommy said they were wrong numbers."

They? Numbers?

"There were two calls not from me?" He looked crushed, as if he were jealous of Martie's many admirers. The last thing he wanted to do was alarm her.

Lili nodded. "Uh-huh. The first one woke me up. I climbed into Mommy's bed and then the wrong number called again. I thought it was you. Mommy said no."

The second call probably was from him. The first was the same lunatic who'd called Martie before. Borzone had told him the police found Tripp Runyon's fingerprints on the envelope containing that threat about "painting the town Valentine Red" and had brought him in for questioning. Bryan didn't believe he would have placed a breather, as Borzone labeled those types of phone calls, the same day he was interrogated by the police. No one could be that stupid or that brazen. Which told Bryan the midnight breather was someone other than Tripp Runyon.

And possibly, someone completely unrelated to the death threats levied against Greta and Vera.

Bryan found that interesting. And scary. That meant whoever was placing those calls wasn't tormenting Martie because she was related to Vera Hart or worked for HLI. This caller hated Martie Phelps.

Two things other than the obvious concerned Bryan. Martie hadn't mentioned this latest call to Borzone. And he hadn't mentioned to anyone that there had been someone at the meeting who kept staring at Martie, and not in an admiring way.

Worse, he looked vaguely familiar and Bryan couldn't place him.

"She has several broken ribs, a cracked cheekbone, contusions on the face and chest, and some internal injuries that required surgery," Dr. Darika Bhansali told Martie.

Martie was sick at the thought of the pain Delilah must have endured.

"We had to remove her spleen and her left lung had been punctured by one of her broken ribs, but she'll be fine."

"Was she poisoned by the lipstick?"

Dr. Bhansali shook her head. "The detective told me about the other case, so we ran a check for mercuric chloride. There was none."

Martie was relieved.

"Where is Delilah now?"

"In her room resting."

"May I see her?"

Dr. Bhansali, a small Indian woman with a soothing voice and reassuring manner, told Martie she could visit, but only for a short while.

"She needs her rest."

"I understand."

The room was dark, with only the light above her bed illuminated. The air was still and warm. Delilah's eyes were black and blue. Her left cheek was heavily bandaged. Her other cheek and her neck were marred by angry scratches. She was hooked up to heart and blood pressure monitors, as well as an IV which conveyed both fluids and painkillers. Her eyes were closed and her breathing was shallow.

Martie ran her fingers across Delilah's forehead, smoothing a lock of blond hair off her battered face. Her throat lumped with tears she didn't want to shed.

Twenty-four hours ago, Delilah had embarked on a new life. She had looked so pretty, sounded so confident, and felt so accepted by the world she'd always wanted to be part of. Yet at the end of that glorious new day she wound up beaten and tossed naked in the park like a pile of garbage. A deep, ferocious anger stirred inside Martie.

What kind of sick bastard did this?

Simmering right alongside that anger was her own guilt at not having called the police when Delilah still hadn't shown up three hours after she'd been expected. If she had reported it, the police might have found her sooner, or caught her attacker, or something. But Martie didn't call, because she didn't have as much faith in Delilah as she should have. She was afraid of where the police might find Delilah and what she might have been doing.

"What happened?" Delilah's voice was weak and garbled thanks to her broken cheekbone and the sedatives.

"You decided that the easiest way to meet an eligible doctor was to have your spleen removed," Martie said, swallowing her tears while trying to sound upbeat. "I don't think I would've thought of that. Boy, are you clever."

Delilah nodded. "My middle name."

Her tongue skipped across her lips; both were dry. Martie found a glass of water and held the straw to Delilah's mouth. She sipped haltingly. It was obviously difficult for her to swallow and to speak.

"Bryan's downstairs." Martie knew Delilah would be pleased about that.

"Saw him."

Her head lolled to the side, directing Martie's gaze to a table where a cuddly white teddy bear holding a get well sign held court. Martie smiled.

"He's with Lili," she said.

Delilah's eyes opened wide. She tried to speak, but Martie spared her the effort.

"I won't let her see you. I'll just tell her you're sleeping. She'll understand. She's been in the hospital."

Delilah's eyes teared as they fixed on Martie's.

"I fought back," she said with quiet pride. "I wouldn't let them rape me."

Them? "There was more than one?" Bryan never said anything about there being more than one assailant on the Central Park case.

"Not sure. Blindfolded."

Again, she licked her lips. Martie gave her more water. She coughed half of it up and groaned from the pain. Her eyes closed and her body stiffened as she waited for the throbbing to subside.

"Thought there were two," she whispered, barely able to get the words out. "Could be wrong."

Martie didn't press her. She could have been recalling Fallujah and mixing that experience up with this one. Or this was a copycat crime. The lipstick was Valentine Red, but it wasn't poisoned and the assailant hadn't twisted her T-shirt around her head the way the Central Park rapist had done.

"He hurt me," Delilah said as she pressed the button that released another dose of painkiller.

He. Now it was only one.

"I know, but you're safe, the doctors say you're going to be fine, and the police are going to get the freak that did this to you! I promise."

Delilah nodded, then closed her eyes and drifted back into the haze of a medicated sleep.

As Martie left her room, she thought about how many other people had made promises to Delilah and broken them. She vowed she would not be one of them.

Tony Borzone had just left his partner outside the Nineteenth. Since this new case and their Central Park homicide were related, he and Frank had come to confer with Douglas and his squad. They shared details, sources, and ideas about where to look next. Off Borzone's info about the Central Park case and the other two lipstick murders he'd uncovered, Douglas's men were over at the Hart Line Spa canvassing the employees.

After bidding Frank good-bye, Borzone walked over to New York Hospital to meet Bryan and fill him in. When he entered the lobby he spotted Bryan on a couch with a little girl. They were laughing and talking quietly. A tall, strikingly beautiful woman approached. Tony knew immediately who she was. He stood off to the side so he could observe the group dynamic without being noticed.

The little girl was the spitting image of her mother. And both of them were clones of the famous Vera Hart.

Pretty good gene pool, Borzone thought.

The woman, Dr. Phelps, appeared agitated and uneasy. She refused to look Bryan in the eye. In Borzone's opinion, that spoke volumes. She had strong feelings for Bryan, but something had put her in full retreat.

Her daughter, who was holding fast to Bryan's hand, appeared reluctant to leave him. Bryan wasn't helping. He maintained his grip on the girl's hand while talking to her mother, refusing to let go of either.

They looked like a family in crisis, but, Borzone reminded himself, they weren't a family.

Over Dr. Phelps's shoulder, Bryan noticed him and waved him over. Inside, Borzone chuckled. Nothing like being used as a stalling tactic.

Bryan introduced them all, paying special attention to Lili. Often, men used children to garner points with women they wanted to bed or wed, depending on their intentions, but from what Borzone could tell, Bryan had genuine affection for this child. And she for him.

"You're the gentleman who's working on the other case," Martie said, glancing down at Lili to explain why she couldn't be more specific.

"I am. This one too," he said, letting her know he was keeping an eye on her friend.

"I appreciate that. She means a lot to me."

Lili tugged at Martie's slacks. "Are you talking about Delilah?"

"Yes, sweetie, I am."

Lili looked up at Tony, her expression quite serious. "There are some very bad people out there, Lieutenant Borzone," she said, pronouncing the *e* like an *i* so that his name rhymed with *macaroni*. "One hurt my friend Delilah so she had to have surgery. Another bad man put stuff in my special lipstick to make it taste yucky and I had to go to the hospital too. That's not nice."

"No," Borzone said, "it's not, but my partner Frank and I are going to find whoever did these things."

"Are you going to put them in jail?"

"You bet we are."

"Good." She smiled at him. "I feel much better now."

No wonder Bryan was crazy about this kid, Borzone thought.

"We have to go," Martie said, taking Lili's hand.

" 'Bye, Bryan," Lili said, pulling on his arm until he lowered his head for a kiss on the cheek. "I had fun with our taste test."

"Me too," Bryan said.

" 'Bye, Lieutenant Borzoni," she said. "Nice to meet you."

"Nice to meet you too, Lili."

Martie smiled at Borzone, clasped her daughter's hand, and without a word to Bryan took her leave.

"Whatever you did, get down on your knees and beg for forgiveness," Borzone said.

"I told you. I don't know what I did."

"Apologize anyway!"

"I would if I could. Did the Nineteenth have anything?"

"They're over at the spa now."

"What's your take on all this? Is it a copycat or are we looking at the same guy, minus the poison?"

"I'm not sure, which is why I'm going upstairs to talk to Ms. Green. Why don't you tag along? Number one, she trusts you. And number two, I see this as my good deed for the year."

"How so?"

Borzone gave Bryan a sly smile. "I figure if you help catch the punk that whaled on her friend, you might score some points with the doc."

"I just need you to tell me whatever you remember," Borzone said to Delilah.

"I left work late. It was my first day. I was going to Martie's to celebrate."

She stopped to take a breath and gather her strength.

"I left the building and turned down the side street when someone jumped me."

Bryan was standing by her side, holding her hand for support. His jaw was tight.

"Did you see your attacker?"

Delilah shook her head. "He pressed something to my nose and I blacked out."

"How did it smell?"

"Sort of sweet."

"Chloroform," Borzone said.

"When I woke up I was by the water. Under a highway, I think."

"What did you see?"

"I was blindfolded, but I could hear water sloshing alongside me and cars above me." She squinted, as if trying to recall every detail she could. "The sound was only coming from three directions, so I must have been up against a wall."

Borzone was impressed by how keen Delilah's recollections were.

"Were you bound?"

She shook her head. A tight smile flickered on her lips. She obviously considered that a mistake.

"When I woke up and realized what had happened, I stayed real still so whoever it was would think I was out cold. I just lay on the ground and waited and planned what to do when they came at me." Her expression was intense. "No way was anybody going to rape me. Not while I had a breath left in me."

"Could you tell how many there were?"

Delilah sighed. "I'm not too clear on that. At first I was sure there was only one. He watched me for a while. I could feel his eyes on me. He was making my skin crawl, but I kept still.

"Then he walked toward me." A memory surfaced. "He must have had rubber-soled boots on because they didn't click on the stones. When he started to rip off my clothes, I held my breath and waited until his head was near my arm. Then I grabbed the collar of his shirt and twisted it until I heard him choke. Then I kneed him. Hard. He let go of me and groaned, so I must have slammed him dead in the groin."

There was no pity in her eyes for any pain she might have inflicted on her attacker.

"It was after that that he lit into me."

She had passed out after the beating, but woke up for a brief moment, during which she thought she recalled hearing a one-sided conversation.

"He was talking to someone, but whoever it was either didn't answer or spoke so softly I didn't hear."

"Could he have been on the phone?"

"No. I don't think so. First of all he wasn't yelling the way most folks do with a cell phone. And I could feel the other person's presence. You know what I mean?"

"Yes, I do," Borzone said. "Did that second person hurt you?"

Delilah shook her head.

"He stayed back, almost as if he didn't want to come near me for some reason."

"Do you think it's because you know him?" Bryan asked.

"Maybe."

"Was there anything you remember about the one who attacked you that might help us? Height? Weight? Hair?"

Delilah struggled. Again she closed her eyes, as if she needed to feel blindfolded to remember the incident as it happened.

"He was strong, that's for sure. Probably works out. His hair was short and he had some facial hair, one of those five o'clock stubbles. I felt it rub against my skin. And he had on way too much cologne." She scrunched up her nose as if she could smell it even now.

"Do you remember what kind of scent it was?" Bryan asked.

"Sharp. The kind fancy men with slicked-back hair usually wear."

Bryan guessed Delilah had culled that fact from one of her waitressing gigs.

Slowly, she opened her eyes. "I haven't been much help, have I?"

"That's not so, Ms. Green," Borzone assured her. "Your sense of recall under stress is remarkable."

Delilah laughed. "I've had some major league training in that area."

Borzone smiled. "So I've heard."

"You're a mighty brave woman, Delilah."

"Thanks, Bryan, but truth be known, I'm real tired of being brave. For once in my life, I'd like to feel safe."

Chapter 21

"Why don't you come up?" Vera said to Hugh as the taxi pulled up in front of her building. They had been at his office reviewing security procedures. "Bonita can fix us something for dinner or, if you prefer, we can order in."

Hugh had several matters he wanted to discuss with Vera, so he agreed.

Her apartment was a large sprawl on the top floor of a building on Park Avenue, which to Hugh seemed apt: Vera was a bona fide star; why not live close to the sky? It was glamorous befitting its chatelaine, with museum-quality art and antiques, yet Hugh found it delightfully inviting. The prices of the furniture had gone up exponentially, but she hadn't changed the essence of her style since Roxbury.

In the main salon the walls were the color of *crème anglaise* spiced with sprinkles of nutmeg and cinnamon. Dollops of black added drama, but it was the colorful Dubuffet over the fireplace, the sinuous

Arp sculpture in the corner, and the Picasso above the sofa that took his breath away.

Vera suggested that they enjoy a cocktail in the sitting room, another visual feast. The couch was caramel leather, softened with plump suede cushions and a paisley cashmere throw. There were two modern takes on the old club chair in the same warm color of the couch, but they were upholstered in butter-soft wool. In the corner were a round ebony table and four chairs, plus another stunning painting, but that was not the artistic focus of this room. The draw here was a recessed box painted burnt orange that showcased a remarkable collection of small teapots.

Hugh smiled because he recognized them immediately as coming from the Yixing region of China, an area known for its unique purple clay. His smile broadened when he noticed three minuscule teapots arranged on a tri-step platform in descending size. He'd brought them back from the Orient shortly after Martie was born; one for each of his girls, he'd said.

"I hope you approve," Vera said, pointing to her collection with obvious pride. "I provided a few friends for the girls."

He laughed. "The girls," as Vera had dubbed them when he gave them to her, had been made by a contemporary artist who made them as tiny as he did to honor, and to wink at, the ancient custom of teapots holding only enough for a single serving; the Chinese used to carry Yixing teapots with them and drink from the spout instead of a cup.

Vera's teapots were larger, but not by much, and hers were definitely not modern-day.

"They look as if they're in very fine company," Hugh said, guessing they were from the Ming Dynasty of the late 1600s. One or two looked like they might have been made even earlier.

Vera smiled. "They seem happy."

She offered him a seat and a cocktail. Bonita was going to prepare them a light supper and then leave.

"Talk to me about Trevor Runyon," Hugh said, getting right to the point.

"What about him?"

"He hates you."

"I ruined his life."

She said it so calmly she might have been talking about the weather.

"Would he have been one of those on that enemies list you refused to give me?"

"Yes. Craig Hemminger would have been another."

"Hemminger?" Hugh didn't like the sound of this.

Vera leaned back into the corner of the couch and sipped her wine.

Hugh guessed that she was deliberating how much to tell him.

"The enemies list I resisted giving you would have included the names of a small but select group of powerful men. I took them as lovers. After they had left their wives and their children for me, I dumped them."

Again, her calm was stunning.

"This sounds like the polar opposite of a fan club, Vera."

"That's a good way to put it," she said, musing on the notion. "None of them adores me. I made certain of that."

"You make it sound as if it was all pre-meditated. Was it?"

Vera studied her manicure. "At the time I didn't think so."

When she looked up there was a defensive tilt to her chin.

"A few years ago, I went into therapy." She laughed. "What a rude awakening that was! In case you haven't dabbled in the fine art of psychiatry, a little *aperçu:* The path of self-discovery and realization is a painful one."

Hugh knew her well enough to understand that for Vera to relive the pressures of a childhood spent in the limelight, trying to please her parents first and the rest of the world second, and then the degrading darkness of the "has-been" must have been torturous. Revisiting their marriage and its dissolution probably wasn't easy either.

"When my therapist and I finally got around to these men and their ruination, I discovered that not only had I planned their devastation, but when it was accomplished, I celebrated."

"That sounds rather cold." And disturbing, Hugh thought.

She stared into her wine glass. "Perhaps, but it's honest."

"Why would you consciously ruin men's lives?"

"To get back at you."

Hugh put down his scotch. "I don't understand."

"When you left me I was at the low point in my life," she said. "My career was in ruins. I was hurt and confused and frightened and I was doing everything I could to regain a foothold in an industry that had used me and tossed me aside like a dirty tissue.

"Instead of supporting me and loving me no matter what, you walked out on me. And when you did, Hugh Phelps, you broke my heart."

Her voice remained steady, but tears gathered in her eyes.

"You humiliated me in front of my children and the world. You left me emotionally devastated and on the brink of financial ruin. And in case that wasn't enough, you took my baby with you.

"It sounds demented, I know, but somewhere in my subconscious the only way I could regain my self-esteem and even the score was to break as many hearts as I could. And to leave men the way you left me: devastated, broke, and alone."

Hugh felt as if she had fired a cannonball at his chest.

"I never realized." His voice was scratchy and small.

"Never realized what? That I adored you? That you and the girls were everything to me?"

"I thought your career was everything to you."

She shook her head, amazed at his complete lack of insight.

"My career was everything to *you*. You fell in love with a movie star, Hugh. That's *what* you married. And that's *what* you wanted.

"When my career tanked and I was no longer your celebrity wife, you grew angry because I had let you down. I wasn't the idealized woman you paraded around on your arm like a trophy. I was an ordinary woman, and that was *not* what you wanted."

"Is that what you think?" he asked, rattled because some of what she had said rang true.

"It's what I know."

He rubbed his eyes with his fist, as if trying to erase the reality she was forcing him to confront.

"We weren't a flesh-and-blood couple, Hugh. We were cardboard stereotypes. You were the soldier, the über-male. I was the Hollywood star, the über-female. Together we were the darlings of the media because we embodied perfection.

"But then my star faded and my ideal partner left me, declaring to one and all that I was no longer fit to worship."

All the color had drained from Hugh's face. He appeared stricken.

"In a way, you did me a favor. When you

challenged my idea about the Hart Line, dismissing it and me as frivolous, I became determined to make you eat your words."

"Which I have," Hugh admitted. "Many times over."

"Nice to know," Vera said. She smiled, but with only a whisper of the victory to which they both knew she was entitled.

"Maybe I should try this therapy stuff," he said.

"Be prepared."

"To find out that I'm not perfect? I already know that."

Vera laughed. "You think you do, but you don't. You're too much of a control freak, which means you're still not comfortable with the notion of imperfection, especially your own."

"And what exactly am I controlling? Certainly not you."

"Martie."

He grumbled defensively and gulped his scotch. "How so?"

"By doing everything you can to make sure she and Bryan Chalmers don't wind up together."

He started to speak, but she stopped him.

"Really, Hugh! They love each other. Why can't you see that?"

"He made things difficult for her when she returned from Iraq."

"What happened to her made things difficult, not Bryan."

"He was pushing her, which wasn't helping her recovery."

"So you shipped him off to Korea as fast as you could."

"She needed time to heal."

"And now?"

He squirmed in his chair. "It won't work."

She fixed her aquamarine eyes on him, drawing his gaze like a magnet. "Why not? Don't you believe in second chances?"

The double entendre hung in the air like a rain cloud about to burst.

"If it didn't work the first time, why not accept it and move on?"

"Because sometimes life interferes with destiny," she said, wondering if that was his explanation for marrying Connie.

"And you think we can reclaim our destiny?"

"I think that if an opportunity presents itself, we have to help the universe along."

She rose from the couch and walked over to him, rested her hands on the arms of the chair, and lowered her face until it was inches from his.

"They're soul mates, Hugh."

The closeness of her was intoxicating.

"Two people who are meant to be together. Stop resisting the pull of the universe." Her voice was hypnotic. "Let it happen."

He took her face in his hands and brought her lips to meet his. When he kissed her, the familiarity of her mouth against his sent a surge of feeling through him that was so intense it caught him off guard.

In his pocket, his cell phone rang.

Vera eased away from him.

He stared at her, his insides eddying like a whirlpool.

"Your phone," she said, snapping him out of his reverie.

His lips curled into a wry smile as he flipped open the phone and put it to his ear.

"Now?" he said, scowling. He closed the phone and looked at Vera. "That was Bryan. He needs to talk to me about Martie."

Vera laughed at the irony.

"Yeah, yeah," Hugh said as he rose from the chair. "I know. Second chances. Help the universe along. Yada, yada, yada."

He took her in his arms and kissed her again, deeper this time.

"What about my universe?" he said.

"I have a company in peril, two daughters in harm's way, and death threats to worry about," she said. "When my world is where I want it to be, we'll talk about your universe. Right now it's first things first."

Martie picked up her mail and she and Lili went upstairs. When they walked into their apartment, Martie sent Lili off to her room to get ready for dinner while she emptied the groceries and looked through the mail. There was the usual assortment of bills and flyers, plus a large envelope with no stamp and no return address.

Nervous, she patted down the envelope to see if it contained a letter bomb. When she felt relatively certain that it didn't, she opened it and emptied its contents onto the table.

They were photographs of Lili: close-ups of her at school, walking with Soledad, playing catch in the park with Hugh, food-shopping with Martie, sitting with Bryan in the hospital this afternoon.

Martie's heart pounded in her chest. She looked inside the envelope for a note, but there was none. None was needed. The implication that Lili could be targeted for harm anytime, anywhere was clear.

Her eyes welled with angry tears. Delilah was in the hospital. Lili's life was being threatened, again. There had been an attempt on her life. Craig Hemminger had been murdered. A woman in Central Park had been raped and murdered. Her mother and sister were both victims of a hate campaign. And she had a late-night caller whose only goal was to terrify her.

She looked at the pictures again and wiped her eyes, refusing to surrender to the fear this person wanted her to feel.

I will not be tortured twice in my life, she thought, her backbone stiffening.

Quickly, so Lili didn't wander in and see them, she put the pictures back in the envelope and stuffed the envelope in her purse.

Martie wasn't certain why this was happening or who was behind it, but this drip-drip-drip siege of persecution had to end. To stop it, she had to divorce herself from the emotion those pictures evoked and work the issue through, coolly and logically.

What she wanted to do was call Bryan, tell him about the photographs, and ask him what he thought, but she couldn't do that. When she was around him she was too emotional; she couldn't allow her feelings to cloud her judgment and cause her to make mistakes. There was too much at stake.

She dialed Hugh's office. He wasn't there. She dialed his cell phone. It was busy.

She called Vincent Wiggers. He too was unavailable.

It's okay, she told herself. She didn't have to borrow courage. It wasn't the first time she'd been on her own.

Primola was a cozy neighborhood restaurant on Sixty-fourth Street and Second Avenue. The patrons were mostly regulars who had their favorite tables up front, which meant they didn't pay much attention to those who weren't regulars and were seated in the back. Hugh and Bryan were in restaurant Siberia, which was exactly where they wanted to be.

"What's this all about?" Hugh asked, after they had ordered and the waiter had brought their drinks.

Bryan had asked to meet Hugh for a beer somewhere, but the general was hungry.

It was awkward, just the two of them, which was why Bryan jumped right in.

"Did you know that Martie's still getting those breather phone calls?"

"No." Hugh's lips pursed with annoyance: (A) that he didn't know, and (B) that Bryan Chalmers was the one to fill him in.

"I didn't think so, but I thought it was important that you were aware they were still going on."

"How do you know this? Were you there when the call came in?"

Ever the father, Bryan thought. Hugh was checking to see if Bryan was spending nights at Martie's.

"No, sir. I found out quite by accident."

Hugh looked at him quizzically.

"I spent some time with Lili this afternoon and she told me. Evidently Martie claimed it was a wrong number."

He deliberately neglected to mention that he had called Martie that same night.

Hugh tapped his fingers on the table, running this information around in his head.

"I'm more than a little surprised that you weren't aware of this, General," Bryan said respectfully. "I was under the impression that Martie confided in you. Why do you think she's keeping this to herself?"

"Because she prides herself on being self-sufficient. And she's stubborn."

"I can't imagine where she gets that

from," Bryan muttered, not too subtly under his breath.

Hugh, thinking about Vera, shocked Bryan by laughing. "Six of one, half a dozen of the other."

Bryan tipped his glass at Hugh. That was the first congenial moment the two men had shared since Martie was rescued ten years before.

"I've asked my friend, Lieutenant Tony Borzone, to see if he can get the LUDs from the other night. If he can, at least we'll know where that call originated."

"Good," Hugh said. "It'll be interesting to see if it turns out to be Tripp Runyon."

Bryan nodded, but without conviction. Despite the fingerprints, he didn't think Tripp was the one calling Martie and said so.

"Why not?" Hugh asked.

"I'm not sure he even knows who she is. And frightening her isn't going to get him what he wants, which is the kind of big-time money he can only get from Vera or Greta."

"True. By the way, thank you for responding so quickly to that latest letter to Greta. We aren't close, as you know, but she is my daughter and I don't want any harm to come to her."

"I understand, General. I'm glad I was there when she received it."

"Was Lieutenant Borzone the one you called?"

"Yes. He's working the homicide involving Valentine Red."

Hugh sipped his scotch, studying Bryan over the rim of his glass. "You seem to have a close relationship with him. Was he at the Bureau when you were there?"

"No. I met him when I was in the DA's office."

"Special case?"

"Every rape case is special to me."

Hugh put down his glass. "Because of Martie."

"Yes, sir."

Hugh saw how raw Bryan's feelings still were and for the first time realized that he and Bryan had something primal in common: His feelings about those who raped and tortured his daughter would never abate; he shouldn't expect more of Bryan than he believed was possible for himself.

"There's another thing I think you need to know," Bryan was saying. "Delilah Green is in the hospital."

Hugh confessed he didn't know about that either.

Bryan explained what had happened, the similarities to the Central Park case and the differences. He also confided in him about the other two cases Borzone had turned up.

"Does he think there's a link between these crimes and the government investigation of HLI?"

"No." He explained Tony's theory about the coincidence of convenience. "But I think this attack on Delilah was specifically meant to frighten Martie."

"Why do you say that?"

"Because Greta doesn't know Delilah and Vera only met her once. She's Martie's best friend and Martie is the one hot on the trail of whoever poisoned Valentine Red."

"Who the hell is doing this?" Hugh was having trouble disguising his frustration. "And for what reason?"

Actually, he realized with a start, Vera had given him a motive earlier. And possibly a name: Trevor Runyon.

"Vera thinks someone is trying to steal HLI out from under her," Bryan said.

Trevor Runyon was sounding more and more like a suspect, Hugh thought.

"The only thing that doesn't make sense is why a corporate raider would go these murderous lengths and taint the products that make HLI the financial powerhouse that it is. Especially the signature lipstick."

"To extract a very personal vengeance against Vera." Hugh threw that out there to see if Bryan was aware of Vera's former relationship to the senior Runyon.

"Do you have someone specific in mind, General?"

Hugh debated how much to tell Bryan. Vera had revealed the details of her past affairs in confidence. Then again, Vera had hired Bryan to defend her against her accusers.

"What do you know about Trevor Runyon?"

"He's the head of the Seafarer Bank, which funds many of HLI's acquisitions."

"He and Vera were once involved."

Bryan could tell by Hugh's expression that this was a dicey subject.

"I take it the relationship ended badly."

"Yes."

"And you think it's possible that Runyon is spearheading the takeover effort?"

"He has both the motivation and the resources."

"If he succeeded, it would devastate Vera, that's for sure." Bryan was somewhat reluctant to pin everything that was happening on the Runyons. "But is he the kind to torment women with death threats? And is he capable of murder?"

"I don't know about Trevor, but what about Tripp? Yesterday at the police station Vera referred to him as Trevor's pet monkey. It could be that in order to remain on the family payroll, he does whatever he's told to do."

He was wearing the kind of fancy cologne men with slicked-back hair wear.

"They would still need someone on the inside."

"Hemminger?"

"That could very well be," Bryan agreed. "He was involved with Vera at one time also."

Hugh appeared almost embarrassed at the mention of yet another of Vera's former lovers. It was beginning to sound as if there was a rather large men's club consisting solely of Vera Hart's rejected suitors.

"Maybe they got rid of him because he was the only one who could point a solid finger at them," Bryan said, filling in the silence.

"What about that Wally Crocker, the one from Carteret whom you think sabotaged Martie's car?"

"He could've been paid to contaminate the products and protect that information," Bryan said. "He is a chemist and he has disappeared, which certainly makes him look guilty, but there's someone else I'm concerned about. At the meeting this afternoon, there was a man who kept staring at Martie, and not in a flattering way. He wasn't standing with Ian Bardwill or anyone from Carteret, nor did he appear to be chummy with the Suffern staff."

"So you think he's based in New York."

Bryan nodded. "He looked vaguely familiar to me, General, but I can't place him."

"Funny, Martie said the same thing. She noticed someone whom I'm assuming is this same guy, but she couldn't place him either." Hugh popped an olive in his mouth. "If both of you recognized him, could he have been at Rucker?"

Bryan shrugged. "I doubt it. I would've remembered the guys who were there when Martie was. Most of them were my students."

"How about Saudi Arabia?"

"That's certainly possible," Bryan said. "But that was a staging area. There were thousands of troops stationed there."

"How do you suggest we track this guy down?"

Bryan almost fell off his chair. Lieutenant General Hugh Phelps was actually asking his opinion. It was staggering.

"By going through the personnel files. I'm hoping a name will pop out."

The waiter brought their food and for the next several minutes they concentrated on that.

"So what are your intentions toward my daughters?" Hugh said suddenly with a sly smile. "You've been involved with both of them."

Bryan blushed like a schoolboy, but decided the time had come to take the general on.

"It's true that Greta and I dated for a time, but I'm in love with only one of your daughters, sir, the same one I loved ten years ago and will probably still love ten years from now: Martie. As for my intentions, they've always been honorable. I wish you could see that."

"What makes you think I don't?"

"Your attitude towards me, for one. To say that you're hostile would be putting it mildly. Which leads me to believe that the minute you knew Martie and I had reconciled, you poured ice water on the relationship just as you did before. The only difference is that this time you can't order me out of town."

"You're saying you and Martie had reconciled."

"Yes, sir."

"And suddenly she doesn't want anything to do with you."

"It appears that way, yes."

"And you think it's my fault."

"Yes, sir, I do."

"Well, I'm sorry to tell you this, son, but I am not to blame for the failure of your relationship with Martie. If it's over, you screwed it up all by yourself."

Chapter 22

Martie barely slept. She'd spent most of the night analyzing what she knew and what to do about all she didn't know.

Proceeding with a researcher's sense of organization, she created two columns representing the camps she believed were engaged in this war of emotional terrorism. Then she listed each act of intimidation in the column she felt seemed most appropriate. When her analysis was complete, she studied the empirical data with the same detached, analytical eye she used when conducting chemical experiments or assessing a patient.

In the end, she concluded that the camp that had targeted her was trying to bring down HLI by eliminating consumer confidence, thereby killing the bottom line and ultimately devastating the value of HLI stock. When she interfered with that goal, she painted a bull's-eye on her chest, and, by extension, Lili's.

The other camp, the one that was menacing Vera and Greta, was more interested in a corporate takeover. Their goal was to diminish Vera's stature with her stockholders by accusing her of accounting fraud and by subjecting her to a government investigation, as well as a public flogging.

It was interesting to note that, while both Vera and Greta were being harassed, neither of them had actually been attacked. That suggested that perhaps the death threats were bogus. They were not precursors to an action, but were part of a negative public relations assault designed to make Vera especially appear incapable of warding off the intended takeover. For all intents and purposes, this camp's intention was to effect a bloodless coup.

So while the goal of both camps appeared to be the same — the ouster of Vera Hart as head of Hart Line International — none of the facts indicated that they were working in concert. It was definitely one hand versus the other.

What Martie didn't know was who was running the two camps and who was working with them. The only soldier's name she knew was Wally Crocker, and for the time being he was AWOL.

The identity of the man at the meeting

was also of interest because she was certain he too was a soldier in this war. She didn't know with which camp he was aligned, but he was staring at her with such animus there was no question that he considered her an enemy. She had no idea why.

The only way to answer that question was to find out who he was, and she intended to do that by taking Vera's suggestion and going through the personnel files as soon as Soledad arrived.

For her peace of mind, she had decided that Lili and Soledad would stay home today. If Lili didn't leave the apartment, she was safe.

As she waited for Soledad, Martie wandered around her living room, mentally reviewing everything one more time, seeking nuances she might have dismissed too readily or reevaluating things she might have elevated beyond their true importance.

As she perambulated, she fluffed cushions and straightened the pictures on her special photo table.

Her eyes grew moist as she looked at all the pictures of Lili. How could anyone want to hurt her?

She picked up the picture of Jack holding his infant daughter and wondered how he would feel about all this. Her mouth curled into a wobbly smile. No need to think too hard about that. He'd be furious. Lili was his baby girl. He would protect her with his life.

An odd, unbidden thought intruded: Bryan would protect Lili too. He adored her.

Of course, he claimed to love Martie, but then went off with Greta.

Martie shook her head, chasing Bryan Chalmers away.

As she put the picture of Jack and Lili back in its place, her eye was drawn to another picture. And another man. The one from the meeting. He was there in the picture of her Desert Storm unit.

But he couldn't have been in New York yesterday. He was dead.

Bryan was in the Central Park police station watching Frank O'Malley and Tony Borzone finish up their interrogation of Lester Krumholtz, a janitor at the Hart Line Spa that NYPD uniforms picked up at a relative's apartment in Queens where he'd been hiding out.

When Douglas's detectives had gone to the Hart Line Spa, they were told that Krumholtz hadn't shown up for work since the woman was found in the park. A quick check with Palm Beach had him working there at the time of that attack. A warrant for his arrest went out and every lipstick at the spa was confiscated and forwarded to the lab for analysis.

Krumholtz, a beefy man of six feet, two hundred pounds, had pasty white skin, bulging eyes, and a thinning pate. He started out being defiant, completely outraged that he had even been brought in for questioning. After two hours of intense grilling, he broke under the strain of trying to deny his guilt.

Neither detective bought his story because he had no story to tell. He had no alibi for the night in question. Employees at the spa said he had worked late that evening and confirmed that he would have been around at the same time the victim had come in for her haircut. According to preliminary reports, Krumholtz's DNA matched the semen taken from the New York DOA, as well as from the women in the other lipstick cases. And, Borzone and O'Malley told him, his photograph had been faxed to Atlanta. The woman there had positively identified him as her attacker.

While Krumholtz wrote out his statement, Tony came out.

"You did a great job," Bryan said.

Borzone accepted the compliment, but not without reservations.

"That only solves one problem. This guy didn't poison that lipstick and he didn't beat up Delilah Green, Bryan. Whatever's going on, it's not over yet."

Eric Roberts loved the fizz he got when he came close to solving a murder. It started as a growl low in his belly when he heard about a homicide. He hated the notion that one human being thought he had the right to take the life of another human being. The growl became lighter and rose up through his throat as each clue piled up on top of the one before it, becoming a giant evidentiary finger singling out the person who had committed the crime. And when that person was apprehended and Roberts knew he had a solid case to hand over to the DA's office, the growl became a fizz.

The Hemminger case had been slow to produce so much as a single bubble. The ME's office conducted an autopsy that showed Craig Hemminger died of a massive overdose of digoxin. Since digoxin was a drug in common usage at most hospitals, tracing it would be tedious.

Then Pete Doyle came back with an ID for the fingerprint on the "paint the town" threat and Douglas's detectives brought Tripp Runyon in for questioning.

Runyon was a big name and one that seemed tightly bound to the Harts. That also popped a bubble for Roberts, especially since he and Douglas both agreed with Doyle it was strange that there was only one print. When people put a note inside an envelope, they held the envelope in one hand while inserting the note with the other. If someone had been wearing gloves there would have been no prints; if he wasn't wearing gloves there should have been a set of prints. Also, it was difficult to wipe prints off paper.

Doyle's guess was that someone had transferred the fingerprint from another surface, wood or glass or some other solid that would produce a clear image. That indicated that someone might have been setting Runyon up to take the fall for the lipstick murder.

Then Douglas told Roberts about the carton Hemminger gave Runyon. Both lieutenants believed the tapes Hemminger claimed would incriminate Greta and Vera Hart were in that carton.

That produced an even bigger bubble.

And then a witness came forward, a young man who'd been out jogging and noticed a car parked alongside the West Side Highway near where Hemminger's body had been found. It was a Lincoln Town Car with three passengers idling in one of the lay-by's. There was a man in the driver's seat, a second man and a woman in the back. The witness confessed to being nosy, but also said he continued to run, so his descriptions were vague. The driver could have been anyone: average height, sandy brown hair, average build. The description of the man in the back fit Hemminger, but the woman was more difficult to describe. She had on a hat and sunglasses and was sitting deep in the corner of the car. The good news was that the jogger picked up the license plate: HLI 1.

According to the MVB, that car belonged to Vera Hart.

Bryan returned to his office. He and Vera were supposed to be meeting about her defense. Darren Montgomery had no intention of postponing his moment in the spotlight just because his prime witness was murdered. He was moving forward on his investigation into accounting fraud at HLI and had notified Bryan he intended to depose Vera at the end of the week.

Bryan was also waiting for the personnel files. He intended to look through them until he found the man who'd been visually obsessed with Martie.

Until they arrived, he pulled up the HLI personnel calendar on his computer. Vera was obsessive about accounting for people's time, so there was a general calendar that listed tapings, public appearances, product launches, research trials, store openings, major interdivisional meetings, anything related to the business of Hart Line International was listed. Bryan wanted to see who was where on the dates Vera received those threatening e-mails. He wanted to have something to cross-reference when Bob Blanton got back to him.

If he found anything interesting, he might bounce it off Hugh Phelps when he arrived. Bryan had surprised himself by inviting Hugh to join him this afternoon. At dinner the previous evening, the general had been adamant that he'd had nothing to do with Martie's cold shoulder. Even more interesting was that instead of sounding pleased at the broken state of their relationship, he encouraged Bryan to give Martie time.

"Being thrown into this pressure cooker

along with a mother and sister she's had nothing to do with in years has been difficult," he confided. "Add to that a revival of a romance that was also linked to another time and place, and it just might have been too much in too short a period of time. Give her the space to sort it out. If it's meant to be, it'll happen."

Bryan had been stunned. "Forgive me, sir, if I ask why the sudden change of heart? You've never exactly been one of my cheerleaders."

Hugh smothered a smile. "Recently, someone whose opinion I value counseled me on the miracle of second chances."

Bryan guessed he was referring to Vera.

"We don't always get them, but when we do, according to my friend, we should take advantage of them."

"I wholeheartedly agree, sir. Believe me, I tried."

Hugh looked at him through his hawkish gray eyes. He could tell Chalmers had no idea why Martie had backed away from him. Hugh didn't know either.

"My advice, young man, would be to try again. And this time, try harder."

Bryan had been mulling over the general's words when Hugh walked into Bryan's office. At the same time, someone from human resources delivered the personnel picture book. And his phone rang.

It was Borzone. Bryan, hoping it was good news about finding the freak who was poisoning Hart Line products, put him on speakerphone so Hugh could listen in.

"Wally Crocker was arrested early this morning in some fleabag motel off the Jersey Turnpike. Fortunately he's a bit of a wimp-ass. The boys had barely finished asking him his name and he started squealing like a pig."

"Who'd he give up?"

"A guy named Tim Polatchek. Ever heard of him?"

Hugh's face went white.

"The name sounds familiar."

Bryan paused as he tried to recall where he might have heard it.

"He's a dead man," Bryan said, more to himself than to Tony as he quickly riffled through the files until he got to the *P*'s.

"Uh-uh. Polatchek's very much alive. Our buddies over in Jersey got a warrant to go into his parents' home, and guess what they found."

"Mercuric chloride."

"And a couple of other lethal chemicals. How'd you know?"

Bryan stared at the face of the man he'd seen at the meeting.

"He was a pharmacy specialist in the army. Served in Desert Storm. He was supposed to have died in a helicopter crash."

"Maybe there are two Tim Polatcheks," Borzone said, "because his parents insist their baby boy is alive and well, but missing."

"Find him," Bryan urged Borzone. "My gut says he knows we're on to him and he's about to launch his last hurrah."

Borzone's response frightened both Hugh and Bryan. "My gut says the same thing."

Bryan put down the phone and stared at Hugh. "I thought Polatchek died in that crash," he said quietly.

"He didn't."

"You said he did, General." Bryan's words came through gritted teeth. Hugh Phelps was not the only military man in the room. To Bryan, certain things were sacrosanct, as they should have been to a highly decorated officer. Like honesty and the awarding of medals.

Hugh braced and looked at the younger man, knowing that what he was about to say would take the polish off his stars.

"I lied."

Chapter 23

"Thanks for the box." Otis Franklin grinned at Tripp, his white teeth in sharp contrast to his dark skin.

Tripp Runyon had the opposite color scheme going: his skin was hoary white, but the bags under his eyes were charcoal gray.

"No problem," he said.

Tripp thought he'd drop the carton off and be free to leave. When Franklin and Donnelly brought him back upstairs, he began to panic.

"We've got a few more questions. You don't mind, do ya, buddy?"

"No. Sure. Okay." It wasn't okay at all, but he didn't see that he had a choice.

Donnelly smiled and offered him a seat, his mien one of complete reassurance. "We're trying to help you out here, Runyon," he said. "Frankly, we think someone's setting you up and we want you to help us find out who that son of a bitch is."

Tripp looked from one detective to the other, but said nothing. His attorney had warned him about the good-cop/bad-cop routine and how sometimes detectives softened you up by being nice and then sprang the trap.

Also, he knew that while Otis and Donnelly were interviewing him, other detectives were digging around in that stupid carton Hemminger had given him. Tripp had no idea what was in there, but it couldn't be good, and that frightened him.

"There was one fingerprint on that envelope and it was yours. But," Donnelly said, "we think someone transferred that fingerprint onto the envelope to frame you."

Tripp looked confused.

"Did you have drinks with anyone you think might be out to screw you over?"

Tripp immediately thought of the drink he had at Greta's, but he hadn't mentioned that the last time, so it probably wasn't a good idea to bring it up now. Besides, the threat had been sent to her.

"Vera Hart," he said, recalling that breakfast with her at the diner. "I told you she hates me."

"You also said you hate her," Otis reminded him. "You wouldn't be throwing her name out just to get back at her, would you?"

Tripp shook his head. "She wants to hurt me and she's got people who can help her do it."

"What kind of people?" Otis asked, slightly incredulous, yet curious.

"The kind that can make it look as if you did something you didn't."

Hemminger's tapes were fascinating, but for Lieutenants Roberts and Douglas some questions remained.

Did Hemminger dupe Runyon into holding on to the tapes for safekeeping or did Tripp take them to use as leverage against his former wife and her mother in his quest for a major payoff?

The other question was whether the tapes were copies or the originals. Either way, they were damning.

As was Runyon's tale about Vera and the doctored photographs.

There was also the matter of Delilah Green. Before they would let Tripp leave, Douglas's detectives asked where he and his father had gone after leaving the station house. His "No place special" was unsatisfactory.

Tripp was put into a holding cell. One

team of detectives was sent out to find Trevor Runyon and question him as to his whereabouts on the night Delilah was abducted. And Otis and Franklin were commanded to bring in the formidable Vera Hart.

They had questions for her as well.

Delilah was sleeping. Martie stood by her bed and gently touched her fingers. Her eyes fluttered. Martie smiled.

"How now?" she said.

Delilah's lips lifted for a brief smile, but her eyes remained closed.

"How now?" was what they used to ask each other through the hole in the wall in Fallujah.

Delilah's response, "Not now," was good. It meant she was okay. "Ow now," would have told Martie she was hurting.

Martie ran her hand down Delilah's arm in a makeshift caress.

"Have the police found him?" Her voice was still little more than a raspy whisper.

"Not yet, but they're working on it."

"Good." Slowly, Delilah scanned Martie's face. "How now, you?"

"Someone I thought was dead has resurfaced. Someone from Iraq."

Delilah wheezed and her eyes widened. "Who?"

"You didn't know him."

"What's he doing?"

"Nothing I can point a definite finger at, but somehow I think he's involved in a plot to ruin the Hart Line."

Her breathing sounded labored. Martie thought about calling for the nurse. Instead, she gave Delilah some water and dabbed her brow with a damp cloth.

"Did he poison the lipstick?" Delilah wanted to know. "The one that hurt Lili?"

Martie shrugged. "Maybe. I'm having trouble putting it all together."

Delilah inhaled. It seemed to take every ounce of energy she possessed.

"Ask Bryan."

"Bryan?"

Her eyes blinked. "He called. Said he needed to find you."

"Bryan and I are having a time-out," Martie said, deciding that was the most innocuous explanation she could offer. "And I have things to do, so much as I'd love to listen to you sing the praises of Bryan Chalmers —"

Suddenly there was a lot of loud beeping. The monitors were blinking furiously. Delilah's eyes were closed and her mouth was slack. Her chest was still. When Martie put her hand under Delilah's nose, she could barely feel any air.

She ran into the hall yelling for help, but they were already on the way with a crash cart. One of the doctors told her to step aside and leave the doorway clear.

She thought about telling them she was a doctor, but the last thing she wanted to do was interfere with their routine and break the natural rhythm of a team. Instead, she moved down toward the end of the corridor, her eyes and ears trained on Delilah's room.

She could tell by the instructions the doctors were giving and by the equipment that had been wheeled in that Delilah was in distress. Her guess was that Delilah's heart had stopped and they were trying to jolt her back to life.

The thought of losing Delilah crushed her. She wrapped her arms around herself and squeezed tightly, as if trying to contain the tidal wave of emotion that was enveloping her. Tears streamed down her cheeks, but her eyes remained fixed on that room. Mentally, she went through the procedures she imagined were being performed on Delilah and counted each precious minute that went by without anyone coming out to tell her the crisis had passed. She was so absorbed in what was happening up the hall, she never realized someone had come up behind her until she felt a gun in her back.

"If you open your mouth I'll kill you right here," he said.

"Soledad, it's Vera Hart."

"Hi, Ms. Hart. How are you?"

"I'm fine, dear, but the car is downstairs waiting for you and Lili."

"Me and Lili? Where are we going?"

"Didn't Dr. Phelps tell you about our special party?"

Soledad had gotten to Martie's apartment late. Martie had left in a hurry. She must have forgotten.

"No, ma'am."

"We're filming a children's party for my television show and Lili is going to be our star."

"Oh, she'll love that." Soledad would love that too. She'd never seen a television show being filmed.

"Yes, but we're running late, so could you bring her downstairs now?"

Soledad hung up the phone and ran into Lili's room to tell her they were going to a party with the Queen of Hearts.

They were out the door two minutes later.

On the way down in the elevator, Soledad tried to call Martie to tell her where they were going, but Martie didn't answer, so she left a message.

Otis Franklin didn't like doormen at snooty apartment buildings. Just because a guy wore a uniform and had a whistle didn't make him important.

Sven Lingstrom, the doorman at Vera Hart's building, clearly believed the gold braid, the whistle, the white gloves, and the scrambled eggs on his hat declared him part of New York City's elite. He forgot that when he went home at night, *he* didn't have a doorman.

Donnelly said they were there to see Vera Hart and asked to be buzzed up. Lingstrom demanded to see their badges. They complied. He dialed her apartment.

After several minutes, it became apparent that Ms. Hart was not at home.

"Did you see her go out?" Donnelly said.

"No, but I might have been assisting someone else."

Otis asked whether Vera Hart garaged her car in the building. The man recoiled.

"This building does not have garage facilities," he sniffed. "Those residents who don't have their own cars and drivers either keep their cars at a nearby garage or have regular car services that they use to transport them around the city."

Okay. Otis asked where Vera Hart garaged her car. Lingstrom told them it was around the corner, down a block.

"Do you know most of your residents' drivers by sight?"

"Of course."

Donnelly asked him if he recalled whether or not Vera Hart used her car on the previous Wednesday, the day Hemminger was murdered.

"Did she go out that day, do you remember?"

"To be honest, Officer, that whole week was a blur. There were so many reporters camped out on the sidewalk, you could barely get in and out of the building."

"Look, Mr. Lingstrom," Donnelly said, "we respect your desire to protect the tenants, but we're investigating a homicide. This is important. Did anyone come to see Ms. Hart? Did she go out? Did she call for her car?"

Lingstrom looked uncomfortable.

"Mr. Lingstrom?"

"I wouldn't know whether she went out or not," he confessed, humiliated to have to say he wasn't fully aware of the tenants' coming and goings. "With all that was going on, Ms. Hart had taken to wearing disguises and using the service entrance on the side of the building. Our more famous residents often do that," he confided.

"Did she take cabs or use a car service?"

"Sometimes, I think. But she also used her own car. Of course, then, if her driver was coming to pick her up, he'd wait around the corner."

"Does Ms. Hart have a housekeeper?" Otis asked.

"Yes, Bonita Rivas."

"Does she live in?"

"No. She comes in five days a week. Sometimes, if Ms. Hart is having a dinner party, she'll come in on a weekend, but not usually."

"Did she come in that day?"

Lingstrom had to think. "I'm not exactly sure if it was that particular day, but one day last week she didn't come in until around noon."

"Noon?" Otis said, noting that Hemminger was killed between seven and ten in the morning. "Are you sure?"

"Yes. I remember because I remarked that it was well past Bonita's usual time. She said Ms. Hart had told her she needed to be alone. She had some things to clear up."

Yeah, Otis thought. Like getting rid of a government witness whose testimony was going to send your butt to jail.

Chapter 24

She couldn't be certain, but she thought seven days had passed. She could see sunrises and sunsets through her tiny window, but now and then the Iraqis covered the window in order to disorient her sense of time. On those days they would often withhold food and dramatically alter the temperature.

In a strange way she didn't mind those days because her captors left her alone. Of course, her gratefulness for that oasis of solitude was tempered by the fact that if they were ignoring her they were torturing someone else.

She didn't mind when they skipped a meal. Aside from the tastelessness of the food, relieving herself was so difficult, the less she ate the easier it was. She didn't even mind the loss of light. She was weak and sleep was restorative.

As for the hot/cold environment, she was freezing even when they had the temperature on broil because she had ripped off a sleeve and a pant leg to create makeshift casts for her broken bones. She knew they weren't healing correctly, but at least if she could keep them somewhat immobile and lie still the pain was not excruciating.

To pass the time and to keep her focused on the positive, she would close her eyes and visualize the surgeries she would need when she reached the States. Not only did this reassure her that her limbs could be restored, but it blocked the nightmarish reruns of the crash and the loss of her unit. Each time she did this, she tried a different surgical technique to clear away the scar tissue, reknit her shattered bones with screws and metal plates, repair blood vessels and nerves, and reconnect tendons in a way that would restore flexibility and strength.

After a week of virtual operations she amused herself with the notion that after this, she really could perform those surgeries in her sleep.

When she wasn't negotiating her way around the OR, she was thinking hard about two things: her survival training and her captors. She needed to remember one so she could deal with the other. Also, she had to know her enemy.

The two who seemed to delight in abusing her were Amin and Khalid. They had raped her that first day, and each day since they had come into her cell leering as if they intended to repeat their brutalities. They didn't, but that didn't mean they wouldn't.

Yasin and Zarif were different. They had actually performed tiny acts of kindness. Yasin had helped her tie the fabric cast on her leg. Zarif had seen her shivering during one of the cold spells through the peekaboo in the door and had come in to cover her with a blanket.

They both would beat a hasty retreat the instant they heard footsteps in the hall. Sometimes they yelled profanities at her and slammed the door behind them. She was certain they both told tall tales about what each had done to her or said to her when he was alone in her cell, but Martie believed that was so they could maintain their tough-guy images. Basically they were kids who had been dragged from their homes by the Baathists and ordered to become soldiers in Saddam's army.

Tariq had interrogated her only once; otherwise he'd been notably absent. During the hours she'd spent in his office, *his main objective had been to find out about the number of troops in Iraq, their movements, and which units were based where, but she could tell he was alternately fascinated and repulsed by the fact that she was an officer and therefore an equal.*

In between demands for pertinent military information, which she refused to provide, he asked a number of personal questions: Was she married or single, did she have children, why did she become a doctor and, most intriguing to him, a soldier? He had trouble understanding why a woman would want to do that. In his world women were supposed to be veiled and subservient. In Saudi Arabia they weren't allowed to drive, let alone fly. In other Arab countries girls couldn't go to school or be treated by a male physician. Those who became doctors couldn't treat men. Women were supposed to tend their children, keep the home, and obey their men. If they did those things, they would be honored. If they didn't, they would be reviled, or worse.

As she lay on her wooden bench and thought about Tariq and the culture that bred him, it dawned on her that while he might not object to his men roughing her up, raping her might be unacceptable.

Another deterrent to unmilitary behavior toward her was that the war was
going badly for the Iraqis. Tariq's desperation to know troop movements was
probably more self-protection than anything else. Any moment the Americans
could storm his position and vanquish his
brigade. If he was taken prisoner and it
was known he abused an American officer, and a female officer at that, he
might have to pay in kind.

It was night. She could tell because the
color filling the tiny square that masquer-
aded as a window was gray. When the
Iraqis covered it, it was black.

Her body clock also told her it was
night because she was hungry. She didn't
have much of an appetite, but her body
could go just so long without growling for
nourishment.

The big metal door opened. Khalid entered holding a food tray. There was no
steam coming from the plate, so whatever it was, it wasn't hot. It was probably
a stale roll and dates or tomatoes or left-
over couscous.

Martie wasn't surprised at the paucity
of the menu. They were deep in the heart
of Iraq in the middle of a war. Supply

lines were being bombed constantly and whatever food was available would be sent to the front lines. No one was going to care whether American POWs were well fed.

Khalid, who was wearing sandals and a white woolen robe worn by Arab men, dropped the tray onto the floor in front of her. This was a subtle form of torment. He knew how hard it was for her to move. If she wanted to eat, she was going to have to bend over and lift that tray onto the bench.

As she reached down with her good arm, he pushed the tray a few inches away with his foot.

She never looked up. She bent over a little more and stretched farther to capture the tray, knowing he would push it several more inches away. He did. She tried again, and again he pushed it with his foot, laughing at her predicament.

Martie had had enough. Gritting her teeth, she propelled herself off the bench, moving toward him and jamming her good shoulder into his groin. He yelped in pain. She swallowed hers.

Within seconds she was on her feet and ready for him. He came at her, his hand raised to strike. With the tray in her hand, she lunged at him, swiping the edge across the side of his head, cutting his forehead and drawing blood.

Like an injured bear he lumbered toward her, roaring with indignation and threatening her in Arabic.

She knew he meant to hurt her badly this time. Her strength was limited, as was her agility. The one resource she had was her lungs and so she screamed as loud as she could, "Rape!"

Khalid didn't know that word, although he should have, but he knew she was attracting unwanted attention. He balled his hand into a fist and punched her hard in the stomach, doubling her over.

She fell and the pain almost overwhelmed her, but she refused to surrender. She slid her hand under her body and secured a weapon.

Khalid didn't know whether or not she was conscious, but he intended to punish her. As he climbed onto her, her hand came up and she slashed him with a broken shard from her dinner plate.

At that same moment the metal door opened and Tariq came storming into the cell. He saw Khalid on top of Martie and ordered him to get off. When Khalid didn't budge, Tariq pulled on Khalid's robe until he was practically choking the large man.

"He raped me," Martie said, struggling to her feet and pointing an accusing finger at her attacker. It didn't matter when it occurred; it was the truth. "He raped me."

Her body was trembling, but her eyes were steady and fixed on Tariq.

"He can't do that," she said. "I'm a prisoner of war and an officer of the United States Army."

She was delivering a message: There were rules about these things and his men had broken those rules.

Khalid, sulking next to his commanding officer, was humiliated and angry. He couldn't believe that she had bested him. He tried to explain to Tariq, but he was ordered out.

"He won't be bothering you again," Tariq said to Martie.

As Khalid went to follow his leader, he turned and glared at Martie as if issuing a warning.

Without flinching, she said, "Allah would be ashamed."

She never saw Khalid again.

Enid Polatchek was outraged. How dare these troopers barge into her house and say those terrible things. Her son would never harm Vera Hart.

"She's like a god to us," Enid protested when New Jersey State Trooper Halligan told her Tim had poisoned several Hart Line products. "Tim loves her."

Dolph would have liked to have taken Enid aside and told her to shut up, that she sounded like a moron, but she wouldn't listen, so why bother? Besides, if he wanted to be charitable, this was a nightmare for her.

It hadn't been as shocking for Dolph. When the troopers came to the door and presented them with a warrant to search the premises, he knew they would head right for the basement and Tim's lab. In his head, he'd known that Tim was up to no good on his recent visits; in his heart he didn't want to know what it was his son was doing.

Enid, of course, had paid no attention. Tim's visits created occasions for her to cook something she'd seen Vera Hart prepare on one of her programs, evenings when she could dress up in a Hart Line Original and use the makeup Tim brought her and feel as if she were almost as flawless as her idol.

If Dolph thought Enid would throw herself around the ankles of the trooper who removed some of the materials from Tim's bench, he was afraid she would get one of her carving knives and cut the heart out of the police officer who asked to see whatever makeup Tim had given her.

"I will not!" She folded her arms across her chest, stomped her foot, and harrumphed. She was Everywoman, standing tall against the evil marauders who would seek to invade her domain and pillage her family's goods.

"I'm sorry, Mrs. Polatchek," the trooper said, "but I have a court order here that says you will."

"Why would you take my makeup?" she said, sniffling like a baby whose pacifier had been taken away. "It's Hart Line makeup."

As if that were a reason to obstruct justice.

"It may be poisoned," Sergeant Halligan cautioned.

Falling on deaf ears, Dolph wanted to say.

Then again, Enid had been feeling poorly lately. Her color was poor and she'd been having trouble sleeping. She was depressed and anxious and complained of headaches. Too, for a woman who loved food and had never had a problem, she was having stomach pains.

Dolph had thought she was going through Hart withdrawal, that she was so physically traumatized by what was happening with Vera Hart that it had literally made her sick.

Now he wondered.

"Call Martie," Bryan said to Hugh as he ripped Tim's picture out of the file. "If Polatchek's the one who told Crocker to punch that hole in Martie's tire, he intends to kill her."

Hugh dialed Martie's number. He let it ring until her answering machine picked up. He left a message and dialed her cell phone. She didn't pick that up either.

Bryan, watching this, was becoming more anxious by the minute. And more annoyed at Lieutenant General Hugh Phelps.

"Her cell is off," Hugh said. "And no one answered at the apartment."

They looked at each other, each mirroring the other's panic.

"Lili," Bryan said. "Where the hell is Lili?"

"Maybe Martie took her and went out of town until this whole thing is finished."

"Why would she do that?"

"With Delilah being hurt, she might have decided not to wait around for the next bomb to explode."

"Delilah," Bryan said, reaching for the phone. He dialed the number of the hospital and asked for the nurses' station. Once connected, he asked for a specific nurse, Lisa Friedman, the one assigned to Delilah Green. "Did a Dr. Phelps come to visit Delilah?"

"Yes," she said. "But she didn't stay long. Delilah had an emergency."

"What kind of emergency?"

"I can't discuss this over the phone, Mr. Chalmers."

Bryan had a bad feeling. "Did anyone other than Dr. Phelps visit Delilah today?"

"Her brother."

As far as Bryan knew, Delilah had no contact with her family. It seemed highly unlikely that one of her brothers would show up out of the blue.

"When did Dr. Phelps leave?" He was already on his feet.

"I'm not sure." The nurse was uncomfortable. She knew the police were keeping tabs on Delilah's visitors. "I'm sorry to tell you, Mr. Chalmers, but due to Ms. Green's emergency, I didn't see her leave."

"And Delilah's brother?"

"I think he had gone by the time Dr. Phelps arrived."

But she didn't see him either. Bryan's uneasiness was growing.

Adding to his discomfort was the fact that Vera was uncharacteristically late.

Bryan dialed an internal number. Like the others, that one went unanswered. Two other numbers and he was practically out the door.

"Let's go," he said to Hugh. "I can't reach Greta or Vera either."

Hugh's jaw went rigid. "Where are we going? I want Wiggers to meet us. My guess is we're dealing with a hostage situation and we're going to need all the experienced manpower we can get."

Bryan agreed.

"First we're going to the hospital so that I can find out what exactly happened to Delilah and confirm who it was that visited her. Then we're going to find the missing Hart women. And on our way, General, you're going to explain to me why you lied about Tim Polatchek."

Chapter 25

Vincent Wiggers was waiting outside the hospital in a black BMW SUV. Bryan had been expecting a Hummer, but they attracted too much attention. This was one of the most ubiquitous cars on the road.

As Phelps had promised, in the rear was everything a SOC — Special Operation Corps — unit might need: tactical vests, boots, woodland camouflage, a backpack fitted with entry tools like a sledgehammer and bolt cutters, smoke grenades, explosives, rope, rappelling harnesses and hooks, flashlights, handcuffs, batons, 9mm pistols with boxes of extra magazines, tactical assault gloves, two M-16 sniper rifles, and an M-60 machine gun. Needless to say, the side and rear windows were tinted to prevent anyone from seeing in.

"Where to?" Wiggers said.

Hugh, completely unaccustomed to someone else being in charge, turned to Bryan, his expression one of mild bemusement. "I don't rightly know. Any ideas?"

"I know exactly where they are," Bryan said, and gave Wiggers the directions.

Then he called Borzone. "Did they find anything?"

On the way to the hospital Bryan had called Borzone, told him his suspicions, and asked for some uniformed police to check out both Vera's and Greta's apartments.

"Vera Hart's apartment was neat as a pin," Tony said. "There was no sign of anything except an anal compulsive."

"And Greta's?"

"Not so lucky there. Her apartment was a mess. Furniture was turned over. Clothes were strewn about. But since there's only one apartment to a floor, there are no nosy neighbors to report unusual noises or strange people in the hall. And speaking of strange people, no one seems to know where Trevor Runyon is."

"What about Tripp?"

"They had to kick him. Nothing to hold him on."

"Were the tapes in that box?"

"Want to know whose voice is on them?"

Bryan tensed. He did and he didn't.

"You're not going to be happy, counselor."

Borzone told him.

"Have you gotten back the LUDs on Trevor Runyon's phones?"

"We're running them now."

Bryan had pinpointed Polatchek as his prime suspect, but he didn't want to be careless and eliminate any other possibilities. "Do you think we should be worried, Tony?"

"The Runyon men aren't too crazy about the Hart women, so yeah."

"Did anyone see Greta leave?"

"According to her doorman, she didn't come out the front door. She could have been playing dress-up so no one recognized her, or if she was abducted, they used the service entrance.

"Her car isn't in her garage either, but the man on duty didn't remember her taking it out. We've got a call in to the night attendant to see what he knows." Borzone paused. "Listen, the day Hemminger was supposed to be deposed, did you speak to your client?"

"Several times."

"That morning or that afternoon?"

"Morning."

"Cell or landline?"

"Landline. She was home. I called on her private line. What's this about?"

"Just clearing up some confusion. We

think someone borrowed Vera's car that day."

Bryan's stomach knotted. "Any sign of Polatchek?"

"Nope. His parents don't have a clue. By the way, the father, Dolph Polatchek, insisted that his wife be brought to a hospital. He thinks sonny-boy might have poisoned his mommy's makeup too."

"He used his mother as a guinea pig?" Bryan was appalled.

"Looks that way. We've got all her cosmetics at the lab."

"How about Crocker?"

"He lawyered up and has been imitating a clam since the suit arrived."

"Keep in touch."

"By the way, Chalmers, where the hell are you?"

"On the road."

"Going where?"

"To play soldier."

"Where is she?" Lili asked impatiently. "And where's the party?"

"I don't know, honey." Soledad wasn't impatient, she was nervous. They had been waiting for more than an hour. "I'm sure she's just getting everything ready."

"I hope so. I'm bored."

Soledad told Lili she agreed, but inside she knew something was wrong, terribly wrong.

When Vera Hart's driver picked them up, he explained that Ms. Hart had gone on ahead to set up the party and would meet them there. He hustled them in the car, closed the window between the front and back seats, and never said another word until they reached Valhalla.

Then he ushered them into the studio and left. Still without telling them anything.

Lili called him "creepy."

"To say the least," Soledad said, wishing she knew what was going on.

"Can we go out and play until the Queen of Hearts shows up?" Lili asked with a slight whine to her voice.

"Sure. Let's go."

Soledad thought going outside was a good idea. She knew they weren't close to the highway, but it was a manageable walk. If Vera Hart didn't arrive within the next fifteen minutes, she was going to take Lili and make a run for it.

The two of them went to the door. Soledad tried the doorknob. It was locked. There was another door, but that was locked as well. Quickly, she looked around for another exit. There was none. Nor was there any other means of escape. While there were several large windows in the kitchen part of the studio, they were fake. The scenery they looked out on was a painted canvas dropcloth.

The studio was a completely interior space. With the doors locked from the outside, she and Lili were trapped.

"Okay," Bryan said to Hugh, "we have about forty minutes. Tell me about Polatchek."

Hugh didn't have to explain who Tim Polatchek was and how he knew Martie. Polatchek had been one of the pharmacy specialists in Martie's battalion. When the search and rescue call came in that day, one of the Pathfinders who usually flew with her crew was sick.

Pathfinders for the 101st Airborne Division were skilled infantrymen deployed to provide site security for helicopter missions. Usually they parachuted into an area ahead of an extraction so they could mark off landing or drop zones for the pilots. In search and rescue efforts, they were there to monitor landings through radio contact with Pathfinders on the ground.

With an empty seat on the copter, the

officer in charge of operations for the battalion ordered Polatchek to board. They might have to fight the Iraqis for Captain Lockhart; he wanted as many trained hands as they could transport.

The Black Hawk crashed and everyone except Martie was presumed dead.

"Polatchek survived," Hugh said. "After the Iraqis took Martie away, he dug himself out of the sand and escaped. Ultimately, he radioed back to base and got himself extracted. He was brought to Kuwait."

"To you?" Bryan asked.

Hugh had been a deputy commander of the Allied Forces in Desert Storm based in Kuwait.

"As a matter of fact, yes."

"Was he awake when she was captured?" Bryan's voice was tight with barely contained rage. The thought that Polatchek allowed them to take Martie without a fight was more than he could fathom.

"I think so," Hugh said. "He denied it, but over the course of a lengthy interrogation he mentioned the Republican Guard. He wouldn't have known that unless he saw their red berets. When the inconsistency of his testimony was pointed out to him, he claimed he was lucky he knew his own name, that the trauma of hitting the ground at one hundred and forty miles an hour had wreaked havoc on his senses and his memory."

That was certainly possible, but Bryan refused to give Polatchek any quarter.

Hugh sensed that Bryan didn't understand why he had.

"Look, Bryan, I wanted to kill the fucker with my own hands, so I know how you feel, but I was the deputy commander. Polatchek was one of my soldiers. He had been shot down by the enemy and injured."

Bryan recognized Hugh's situation as one of those hideous moral dilemmas that test one's code of ethics, but he couldn't get past the fact that Polatchek left the woman Bryan loved undefended in the desert.

"Your daughter was a POW." His words sounded judgmental, but his tone acknowledged the conflict

Hugh's eyes closed and he nodded. Even after ten years, the incident was painful.

"At that moment all I cared about was Martie," he said. "If I thought that exacting my revenge on that yellow-bellied coward would have gotten her out of that hellhole in Fallujah, I would have. But just then, he didn't matter."

"You did nothing?" Bryan was incredulous.

Hugh sighed. Bryan suspected the general was about to make a confession.

"Not exactly. I had him flown into Ramstein and admitted to the psych ward at the army hospital in Stuttgart for evaluation. The papers accompanying his transfer didn't recommend anything specific, but the tone of my issuance was that he was a candidate for a Section Eight."

A Section Eight was an army discharge given to those deemed unfit for military service. Usually the cause was mental instability; Corporal Klinger in *M*A*S*H* was the archetypal model for this kind of dismissal.

"Ultimately that's what they did." A look of smug satisfaction crossed Hugh's face. "He aided and abetted his own discharge because he was a quivering wreck the whole time he was in the hospital and never told a straight story about what happened in the desert. The psychiatrists thought the crash created a permanent psychic trauma."

"And you? What do you think happened?"

"He played dead until those Iraqi bastards took my daughter away."

Bryan remembered Martie telling him

601

she had hallucinated while she was lying beneath the fuselage that she thought one of the sand berms had moved. Since no one appeared, she thought she had been mistaken.

"He deserved whatever he got," Hugh said in a voice of steel.

When a soldier was discharged as a Section Eight it wasn't easy getting employment if the employers checked army records. If they were seeking recommendations, being booted from the army because they thought you were a nutcase was not exactly a prime reference.

Of course, Polatchek might not have mentioned his military experience. Without a draft, employers didn't check military records as a matter of rote.

"Why did you let Martie believe he died in that crash? Why not tell her what you did?"

"For the same reasons I shipped you to Korea and practically banished Delilah from her life. I wanted to protect my daughter," he said, his voice breaking. "I wanted her to heal, not to be constantly reminded of those nine terrible days."

He crossed and uncrossed his legs, unable to get comfortable.

"You saw her when she came out of

Fallujah," Hugh said. "She was thread-thin. She was severely injured. She had been beaten and violated. Why would I tell her that if Polatchek had been an honorable soldier, she might not have been taken prisoner? He had a pistol. He could have taken them by surprise. If she thought he was dead, so did they."

His eyes had turned flinty, yet Bryan saw tears lurking in the corners.

He understood because thinking about Martie as a POW always brought tears to his eyes. No matter how evolved he was, no matter how courageous and capable he knew Martie was, there was this primal impulse that said as the male he was supposed to protect the female at all costs. He didn't and he carried with him the burden of that failure.

Hugh Phelps's burden had to be doubly heavy. Martie was not only his daughter, but also a soldier under his command. He had failed her twice.

"I never told her Polatchek died," Hugh said. "And I never told her he survived. I never mentioned his name at all."

Bryan wanted to fault Hugh for his dishonesty, but he couldn't. He might have done the same thing in Hugh's place.

"He didn't receive any medals, did he?"

Bryan asked. The thought galled him.

"No. I would've had to recommend him for them." A sly smile crept onto Hugh's lips. "I guess those papers got lost along with his transfer notification."

Bryan was astounded. Lieutenant General Hugh Phelps, Mr. Perfection, Mr. By-the-Book, hadn't filed transfer papers? He had deliberately let a soldier slip through the cracks.

With no transfer papers, Polatchek's commanding officers would have believed what Martie believed, that Polatchek had died when the Hawk went down. The hospital in Ramstein wouldn't have followed up because they would have assumed Hugh had sent Polatchek's transfer orders to the 101st base.

Polatchek didn't know it, but essentially he had been lost. Thanks to Hugh Phelps.

"Is that why you retired?" Bryan asked.

"Yes."

"Does anyone else know what Polatchek did?"

"It's in his records, but he was in a psych ward when he blabbed about hiding from the enemy, so no one acted on it."

"Does anyone know what you did?"

"Only me," Wiggers said.

Bryan was so absorbed in what Hugh was

saying, he'd forgotten all about Wiggers.

Bryan looked at Hugh, then at Wiggers.

"I flew to Ramstein to see Martie after she was rescued," Wiggers said. "Naturally, the general was there. We had never met, but sitting in the visitor's area he and I discovered we had something in common: We both cared deeply about Martie Phelps.

"The longer she was there, the antsier he seemed to get, especially when they insisted that she be examined by the head doctors. I chalked it up to Martie being so frail and all, but the more I was around him the more I realized it was something else."

"I was terrified that Martie and Polatchek would run into each other," Hugh explained.

Bryan wondered if his fear was that seeing Polatchek would upset Martie or that he might have to confess what he had done. Probably both.

"The general needed a friend just then," Wiggers said. "And I'm a good listener."

Martie loved Wiggers. Now Bryan knew why. Humility was a wonderful complement to courage. Vincent Wiggers not only had both of those qualities, but he also knew how to keep a secret.

"You realize that Polatchek may have

taken your two daughters and your ex-wife hostage," Bryan said to Hugh. "Are you going to be able to control yourself, sir?"

"Probably not," Hugh replied with admirable candor. "That's why I brought you and Wiggers along."

Chapter 26

Martie awoke and found herself on a wooden bench in a dimly lit space with a wide metal door. Groggy and disoriented, she searched for the window high up on the wall to see if it was day or night and for the peekaboo in the middle of the door to see if someone was watching her or she was alone.

She spotted neither of those markers, but as her eyes continued their exploration she found a somewhat disheveled Vera staring at her from the other end of the bench.

Martie blinked. It could be a hallucination. Or she might have been drugged. She did have the headache and cottony feeling that often accompanied sedatives.

"Are you okay?" Vera whispered.

Martie went to sit up and realized her hands were cuffed behind her back. She could tell by the feel they were Flex-Cuffs, the notched plastic kind that resembled the zipper-type ties packaged with some plastic bags. She raised herself upright and looked over at Vera. Her hands were also cuffed; her feet were bound with rope.

"I think so," Martie said, automatically reconnoitering her surroundings.

It was a room with high ceilings and concrete walls, not unlike her cell in Fallujah except it was much larger and much better equipped. Opposite the bench was a wall of shelves. Some were stocked with provisions like canned goods, paper supplies, and bottled water. Others held bedrolls, blankets, and kitchen items. There were a table and four chairs, a portable stove, a refrigerator, a sink, a radio, and a small television, all neatly and attractively arranged.

Tucked in between the ceiling and the top shelf was a clock and a monitor that transmitted security coverage of the estate. Since there was only one monitor and the pictures were constantly changing, Martie concluded there was a 360-degree camera mounted somewhere on the property.

On her right was a narrower door that might have opened onto a bathroom, and next to that a double set of doors that probably concealed a closet.

"Is this your Valhalla bunker?" she asked Vera.

"Yes."

"It's charming," Martie said admiringly. Only Vera Hart would decorate a security bunker.

"It's also impenetrable."

Vera looked scared. For Martie, that was a first. Even as a child she never remembered Vera being anything but in complete control. Then again, this was not exactly Vera's milieu.

"In today's world," she said, "nothing is impenetrable."

She didn't want to frighten her mother more than she already was, but they were hostages. A reality check was in order.

"Is this what it was like?" Vera asked. Her voice was small and tinged with awe.

"You mean Fallujah?"

Vera nodded. She looked haggard and worn.

"The accommodations weren't quite as luxurious, but the isolation was the same. So was the fear of what might be next."

"I've been sitting here watching you sleep and thinking. I never fully appreciated what you endured. I respected your fortitude and admired your courage, but I don't think I truly understood what you went through, until now." She sighed. Her breath was feathery. "I don't know if I can do this."

609

"Yes, you can," Martie declared with conviction.

Vera looked unsure. She had been confined to this underground dungeon for hours. She was faint with hunger and overwhelmed by the horrors created by her imagination.

"You're a survivor. This is just a different kind of test, but you can do it. I know you can."

Vera tried to regain her usual confidence, but this was a different kind of test, one for which she didn't believe she was prepared.

Martie, having bolstered Vera as best she could, recognized that she needed to take charge, and quickly. There was no telling when their captors would arrive and what the agenda would be when they did.

Her ankles also had been bound with rope, but not tightly. She slid close to Vera, lay face down on the bench, and put her feet near Vera's hands.

"Turn around and untie me," she said.

Vera's nervousness made her movements awkward and slower than Martie would have liked, but she got the job done.

Quickly, Martie rose from the bench and toured the cement square, assessing their options. There were few. All the knives and forks had been removed, as had the pots. There were no china plates, only paper. The glasses were thick plastic. The only cooking utensils were wooden spoons and rubber tongs, neither of which made an intimidating weapon.

She turned around so she could use her hands to open the door to the bathroom. It was compact, with no window, no towel hooks, and no mirror other than the one on the door of the medicine cabinet. She'd have to rip the door off and smash it to get a piece of glass, which was not a viable option. The noise would eliminate the element of surprise.

The closet wasn't fruitful either. It was a Joan Crawford special with no wire hangers, only big fat plastic ones. They were black and, as plastic hangers go, they were chic, but for her purposes they were useless.

"Well," she said to Vera, "congratulations. You created an incredible hideout to protect you against any and all circumstances when the enemy is without. Unfortunately, our enemies are going to attack from within."

The question was how well trained the enemies were. She knew about Polatchek, but having figured out what he'd done in the desert, she decided his core was soft. Realizing that he was the one who'd poisoned the lipsticks and tampered with Delilah's IV only confirmed that; he preferred killing and maiming at a distance rather than getting up close and personal with his victims. Nonetheless, Martie knew better than to underestimate PFC Timothy Polatchek. He'd managed to escape capture by the Iraqis and he'd kidnapped her from a hospital and transported her up to Westchester without anyone noticing.

Martie returned to the bench. She was still feeling a bit wobbly and wanted to conserve her energy for what was to come.

"Tell me about the bunker. Is there an emergency escape route?"

"No. That's the only way in or out."

Vera inclined her head to their left. The door was wide and high and thick and made of steel.

"Is that the only security camera?"

"Yes. With the lake bordering the property on the back end and woodlands along the sides, the camera covers the open area."

"Is there a fence around the perimeter?"

"Yes. It's high and topped with sharp metal spikes to discourage trespassers."

Martie's eyes narrowed as she considered their options.

"How much trouble are we in?" Vera said.

"We're at our captors' mercy, that's for sure. Plus, I don't think anyone's going to realize we're missing for quite a while."

"Then we're on our own." Vera's voice was low and scalloped with worry.

"Yes, but we're not alone," Martie said with the practiced calm of a surgeon. "We have each other. And I'm not exactly inexperienced. You just follow my lead and stay strong and we'll be fine."

Vera bit her lip and nodded as she summoned the courage that a few minutes before had deserted her.

"In a situation like this you have to rely on your strengths. One of your greatest strengths is that you're task-oriented," Martie said softly. "Right now your only task is to stay alive until you can be rescued."

Vera started to question the feasibility of anyone coming for them, but Martie stopped her.

"Focus," she said evenly. "Focus on the task at hand. Eliminate all extraneous thoughts. Just focus."

Vera was trying, Martie could see that, but she wasn't a soldier. She hadn't had Martie's training.

"We're going to get out of this," Martie promised. "Just hang in there."

"Okay," Vera said with a forced smile. "You lead. I'll follow."

Martie's legs felt tight. As she stretched them out, she noticed a few grayish fibers clinging to the outside of her pant leg. She raised her leg and bent her knee so she could examine them more closely. They were short, coarse hairs, the kind that made up the carpet in the trunk of a car.

"How and when did you get here?" she asked Vera, wondering if Vera had been in the same car as she was.

"I drove up at around seven this morning."

A clock on the wall over the stove said it was six-thirty in the evening. No wonder Vera looked wan and unkempt. Six-thirty. Soledad would be wondering where she was. She hoped Lili wasn't frightened. Maybe Soledad called Hugh. He'd be happy to babysit Lili.

And Delilah. What happened to Delilah? Martie didn't know whether she was dead or alive.

"Greta called at the crack of dawn," Vera went on. "She had figured out who the whistle-blower was. She said she called him and told him she had proof that he

614

was lying about what he'd told the feds and he should come to Valhalla for a sit-down between the three of us."

"Did she say who it was?"

"Trevor Runyon."

Martie's eyes widened.

"He finances most of your acquisitions. Why would he want to ruin your company?"

"To do unto me what I had done unto him."

Vera gave Martie the short version of her desperately dysfunctional relationship with Trevor.

Listening to Vera, Martie realized Greta's story was highly plausible. Runyon could have alerted the government to financial misdeeds because as a major investor in HLI he had access to the figures. He could have tipped off the feds, demanded a certain amount of anonymity for his testimony, and then sat back and watched Vera squirm. Once the stock bottomed out, he would tender offers to buy HLI in the name of dummy companies incorporated in the Caymans. He would have destroyed Vera's company, taken it over without exposing himself, and built it up again with him, not her, reaping the benefits of the Vera Hart name. It would be sweet revenge indeed.

From the little she knew about Trevor Runyon, he didn't strike her as the type to get his hands dirty with things like hand grenades and death threats. But he was the type to hire someone to do those things for him. And Delilah did say there were two attackers and one had remained suspiciously silent.

"What happened when you got here? How did you wind up down in this place?"

"I don't honestly know. Greta and I were in the Colonial waiting for him. We had a cup of coffee and talked about the investigation. The next thing I knew, I woke up here."

"Where is Greta?"

"I have no idea. I'm worried that whoever did this to us might have done something truly hideous to her."

Martie wasn't sure about that, but for now Vera seemed determined to hang on to the illusion that Greta was also a victim, so she kept her skepticism to herself.

"Do you know someone named Tim Polatchek?"

"He's the one who tried to rescue you after you had been shot down."

"What?"

"He told me all about it when he came

looking for a job. He said that he was on the Black Hawk with you."

"He was." *That weasel.*

Martie was furious that he would mangle the facts to get a job with an unsuspecting Vera.

Vera was confused by Martie's sudden hostility. "He said when it crashed he was knocked unconscious. By the time he came to, you were gone and the others were dead. He found the radio and contacted another helicopter so he could give them his location. He said he was sure you were thrown from the copter and by the time they arrived he would have found you."

"And so you gave him a job."

"Of course." She looked at Martie, hurt that she wouldn't immediately understand why. "I was grateful."

Martie's jaw tightened.

"Why do you ask?"

"Because he's the one who poisoned Valentine Red."

"And I did one hell of a job, if I do say so myself," Tim declared proudly as he entered the bunker. "You've always preached brand identification, Ms. Hart. Well, thanks to me, your brand is going to be in headlines all across the country. I think I deserve a promotion for that, don't you?"

He stood at the doorway with his arms akimbo, his hair closely shorn, his green eyes ablaze with anticipated glory. He was garbed in full desert camouflage, the pale beige in sharp contrast to the near-black of the walls. Hanging from his belt was a holstered 9mm and an assault knife. Martie was certain he had another knife hidden inside the top part of his boot, and possibly another gun.

"And you, Lieutenant. Did you enjoy your ride up here?" he asked, clearly quite proud of himself.

Martie didn't respond.

"I asked you a question."

She stared at him, but remained speechless.

Next to her, Vera tensed.

"Your daughter and her nanny enjoyed their ride," he taunted. "They might not have if they knew you were in the trunk, so I didn't say anything. I don't like being a spoiler."

Martie bounded off the bench.

"Where's Lili?" she shrieked, as she reared back and launched a karate kick dead into his chest.

He recoiled and yelped from the pain, but he recovered quickly. He pushed Martie with such force she hit the floor and slammed against the bench. The impact hammered the small of her back.

"I knew a cat like you wouldn't have lost her tongue," he said, panting and snarling and hovering over her as she scrambled up onto the bench.

"Where is she, you freak?" she shouted at him. "What did you do with her and Soledad?"

The only fear she had was that he had done to them what he did to Delilah.

Polatchek looked from Martie to Vera and back to Martie again. He was regrouping. She'd caught him off guard. He couldn't let that happen again.

"Where is my daughter?" Martie's voice was so highly pitched it could've shattered glass, had there been any.

"Shut the fuck up," he screamed. "They're fine."

"They'd better be."

"Or you'll do what? Kill me?"

"No," Martie said. "I'll hurt you really bad and then I'll leave you to die. Just like you did to me."

Bryan had needed time and silence to absorb all that Hugh had told him. Wiggers and the general gave him both.

They had just made the turn off the

Cross Westchester Parkway onto Route 684 when Bryan's cell phone rang. It was Bob Blanton.

"You're sure. . . . Okay, thanks."

His forehead creased as he processed the information he'd just received.

"Where are we going, by the way?" Hugh asked Bryan. He was curious about the call, but if it was relevant Bryan would tell them in due time.

"Vera has a compound in Bedford," Bryan said, still slightly distracted. "There's a Homeland Security–style bunker on the premises. My bet is that's where Polatchek took them."

"How the hell would a grunt like Polatchek know what Vera has on one of her estates?"

"He didn't," Bryan said, facing the general. "Greta did."

Hugh's eyes narrowed sharply. "You think she's behind all of this?"

"Yes, sir, I do."

"But her apartment was ransacked. She received death threats."

"There were a couple of pieces of furniture overturned and a few items of clothing on the floor. She staged it, General, just like she sent death threats to Vera and, for good measure, to herself."

"How do you know that?"

"That phone call was from a friend of mine at the Bureau who traced the origins of the e-mails sent to Vera. Each was sent from a city where there's an HLI plant. On a hunch, I had sent him a list of all HLI's assets as a jumping-off point.

"On another hunch, I checked Greta's schedule over the past several weeks while I was waiting for you. She was in each of those cities on the dates the e-mails were sent. Bob said they confirmed that the e-mails came from HLI factory computers. For corroboration, he called the plant manager in Little Rock, who confirmed that Greta had used his office and his computer during her visit. He's calling the others as we speak."

Hugh scratched his head. "I can't say that thought hasn't been rattling around the fringes of my brain for a while," he confessed quietly. "I guess I just didn't want to think that she could do something like that."

Wiggers weighed in with a loud harrumph. He didn't like Greta from the get-go.

"You're not alone, General," Bryan said, sick at the thought that he was once romantically involved with her. "I was taken in as well."

"Don't beat yourself up, gentlemen," Wiggers said. "You're forgetting: Greta Hart is the daughter of a famous actress."

It vexed Martie that it had taken her so long to see it, but now she was certain: Greta was not only the leader of one of the camps, but probably the driving force behind this entire operation. Her ambition to replace Vera was too naked and too raw for her not to be an obvious choice. What had thrown Martie and everyone else off were the death threats. They'd been a good touch. So was her apology and the gift to Lili.

Greta was brilliant; Martie had always known that. She was also Machiavellian: ruthless and efficient enough to strategize a coup of this magnitude. To pull it off with impunity, however, she needed someone in place to take the blame in case her plans hit a snag.

Hemminger and Trevor Runyon sprang to mind, but Hemminger was dead. That left Runyon.

Martie had to assume that Greta knew about Vera's relationship with her ex-father-in-law and the bitter feelings that had emanated from their breakup. She probably filed it away under "just in case."

When she created the strategy for the take-over of HLI Trevor Runyon became the perfect foil. He was HLI's primary source of funds and Greta had been married to his son, so he was perceived to have an insider's knowledge of the workings of the company. He was known to have an entrepreneurial bent. And he carried an Olympic-sized torch for her mother, so pointing the finger at him for seeking to ruin Vera was beyond logical.

As for Runyon, it must have been a snap to seduce him into joining forces to bring Vera down. Hatred made for strange bedfellows.

Martie pegged Tim Polatchek as leader of camp number two when she recognized him in the photograph in her living room. It took a while to jog her brain, but when she recalled that his specialty was pharmacology, she knew immediately he was the one who had played Mr. Wizard with the Hart Line cosmetics.

What she couldn't figure out was how Greta had enlisted him and whether he was an adjutant or a foot soldier.

Soon enough, she'd have her chance to ask.

The door opened and in walked Greta garbed in Ninja black: boots, pants, turtleneck, protective vest, and a tight black cap that covered all her hair, save a slick red ponytail. Like Polatchek she wore a BDU — Basic Duty Uniform — belt equipped with a holstered semiautomatic, a sheathed assault knife, and pockets to hold extra ammo magazines. She was armed for battle.

"Well, isn't this nice?" She dropped a big black duffel bag on the floor and smiled as she surveyed the scene she'd worked so hard to set. "I'd say it's a family reunion, but Daddy's not here."

She pursed her lips and tapped her index finger against them. The smile faded.

"Then again, Daddy was never *here*. He was always *there*. Isn't that so, Martie? Oops! I forgot. You left *here* to go *there* with him."

Martie offered no response. None was required. This was a monologue, not a conversation.

Greta clasped her hands behind her back and paced in front of the bench like Patton reviewing the troops. Behind her, Polatchek stood at ease.

Martie found the whole scene almost comical, but kept it to herself. Knowing that Lili and Soledad were somewhere on the estate had stifled her impulse to take

Greta on. Until she knew where they were and whether they were safe, she would play the role assigned to her as the good prisoner. Greta could have her moment.

"Why are her feet unbound?" Greta shouted at Tim, pointing at Martie.

That answers one question, Martie thought. Polatchek was a foot soldier.

"The knots must have come undone. Shitty rope."

"Rope? I told you to get the plastic restraints."

Greta glared at him. He glared back. However, he retied the bonds around her ankles.

Interesting, Martie thought. Foot soldiers were usually cowed by the disapproval of their superior officer. Perhaps there was a mutiny under way.

Over their heads, Martie stole a glance at the monitor. It was almost seven-thirty. She had hoped to see movement of some kind, but everything was still.

The last time Martie had been here it was a hive of activity, between the landscapers and the maids and the studio technicians. Of course, there had been a lunch and a board meeting and a taping of a TV show that day. Martie had no idea how much staff was normally on the property, but however many there were, Greta must have given them the day off. She didn't want any witnesses.

"What the hell is this all about?" Vera had been as patient as she was capable of being. It was late. She was tired and hungry and achy. Despite Martie's directive, she couldn't remain silent a moment longer.

"What is this about? This is about me, Mother dear," Greta declared. "I've decided I'm sick of waiting for you to do the right thing and name me as your successor. So I'm simply going to succeed."

Martie prayed that Vera wouldn't say, "over my dead body."

She didn't. Instead, she leaned back and said, "You think so?"

"I know so." Greta's face was so hard it looked like it had been carved from granite. Her eyes were aflame with years of perceived insult.

Vera laughed, further enraging Greta.

"I wouldn't laugh, if I were you," Martie said to Vera, eager to defuse the situation. "Greta's smart and she's determined. She devised a plan to snatch your company right out from under your nose, and guess what? It's working. You're under investigation. She's partnered up with Trevor

626

Runyon, and as soon as your stock bottoms out, she's going to take over HLI whether you agree to it or not. Am I right?"

Greta's lips pressed against her teeth in a feral smile.

"Clever, getting the head of Seafarer Bank to partner with you."

"He's not my partner. He's a convenience. As soon as I'm fully in charge, he's gone." She chuckled at her own cunning. "And he won't be able to complain. If the business community finds out he participated in this, he's ruined."

"I'm impressed," Martie said.

"A compliment from the family's highly decorated war hero." Greta offered Martie a sarcastic salute. "I'm honored. But why are you so surprised? I'm a general's daughter too, you know."

The tremor in her voice told Martie that was something Greta had waited a long time to say.

"A good general always has a plan. What's yours, Greta? Are you going to kill Vera to get control or are you just going to threaten to harm her granddaughter to force her hand?"

Polatchek folded his arms across his chest and snickered. "Did you do it?" he asked. As he did, he inadvertently glanced over at the duffel.

Martie feared it was filled with explosives.

Greta glowered at Polatchek. Then she bent her head to the side and studied Martie for a moment or two.

"It certainly would be a lot less messy if she agreed to my demands. I suggest you convince her."

Martie breathed a quick sigh of relief. Lili was fine, for now. But if Greta had set out dynamite bundles and she was here, either she was carrying a remote detonator or she had used proximity detonators; whoever went near the dynamite would be blown to bits.

"Why don't you just do it?" Martie said to Vera, desperately trying to buy time.

Maybe Hugh called the apartment and when he didn't get an answer realized something was wrong. Maybe Bryan had figured out who Greta really was and what she was up to. Maybe the police had found something to implicate her. But even if all that occurred, how would they know to come to Valhalla? And how would they find this damn bunker?

"The company's going to be worthless once news gets out about a woman dying from this Bruce Willis wannabe's handiwork," she said, sneering at Polatchek.

Pitting one against the other was always a good tactic; it rerouted their attention from the hostages to each other.

"Who's going to buy makeup or anything else from the Hart Line when they find out Valentine Red's been poisoned?"

Greta's expression turned black. While she didn't utter the words "Whatever possessed you?" her anger at his unauthorized action overwhelmed the room.

Tim didn't respond, but squared himself as if anticipating a bullet to the chest.

"You know what I can't figure out?" Martie hoped she sounded conciliatory. "Why he'd screw you over like that, especially after you paid him all that hush money."

Martie was shooting blind here, but both Greta's and Tim's faces said she'd hit her target.

"He was the guy who stole all those millions for you, set up the accounts in the Caymans, and doctored the books to cover it all up. You had to feel pretty confident about him refusing to testify against you because you made him rich." She shook her head. "So how does he repay your generosity? He destroys the Hart Line's signature brand."

Vera was outraged. "You mean to tell me

that this nothing of a man stole from me and then poisoned my products so that a woman died and my Lili got sick? You should rot in hell, Tim whatever-your-name-is!"

Polatchek quailed at her insult. He'd worked for her for years and she didn't know his name? Vera Hart was treating him the same way Enid did, belittling him, diminishing him, dismissing him. His hand flew to his holster.

"I don't think Tim meant to kill that woman," Martie said, again trying to bring it down a notch. "He simply screwed up. He's good at that."

Polatchek started to lunge at her, but Greta held up her arm. She wanted to hear what Martie had to say.

This time she directed her comments to Tim. "I'm not sure why, but I think you just wanted a couple of women to get sick enough to give Hart Line some bad press."

In spite of himself, Polatchek nodded in agreement. Vera gasped at his silent admission.

"You forgot to calculate the fact that the mercuric chloride might intensify within the lipstick compound." She clucked her tongue like a disapproving teacher. "You didn't do your homework, Timmy, and because of that you messed up Greta's big plan. Not smart."

Polatchek rushed to defend himself to Greta, blathering on about how he was only trying to accelerate the stock drop, but his words sounded hollow.

"And you killed my friend Delilah Green, you stinking worm! Why? To hurt me? Well, congratulations, you succeeded, but in the doing you've left behind a trail of dead bodies that you're going to have to explain. And," she hissed at Greta, "since he's your boy, so will you."

Greta glared at Tim with such heat Martie was surprised he didn't melt. Obviously Greta hadn't known about whatever Polatchek did to Delilah in the hospital either.

As she listened to Polatchek and Greta spar, a memory surfaced. Tim Polatchek was the only person she'd ever told that Vera Hart was her mother. They had been drinking one night and she'd had one too many. He'd gone on and on about what a pain in the ass his mother was, about how ridiculous she was and how her idol was Vera Hart. He told Martie how Enid would stand in the kitchen and imitate every move Vera Hart made, worshiping her image on the TV screen to the point of it being beyond religious. Nothing Vera Hart did was wrong. Nothing he did was ever right. Tim hated her. He couldn't imagine anyone having a mother more difficult to deal with than Enid Polatchek.

Martie asked him to imagine how horrific it must have been to be Vera Hart's daughter.

He conceded that might be worse than being Enid Polatchek's son. That's when Martie fessed up about her parentage.

Now she wondered whether this was some kind of circuitous vengeance, that destroying Vera was really his way of getting back at Enid.

As if on cue, Vera pulled a Vera: She made herself the center of attention by delivering a heated aria on what the two nincompoops playing soldier had done; by attempting to conduct a coup they had brought an international company to the brink of ruin. In her diatribe, she belittled Tim and berated her daughter to the point where both were stunned by her disdain.

Over their heads, Martie checked the monitor. A dark BMW had pulled up to the gates of the estate. The driver pressed a code into the security box and the gates opened. Martie held her breath. The driver was Vincent Wiggers. There were others in the car, but it was too dark for her to identify them. An educated guess said it was Hugh and Bryan.

Inside, she smiled. The cavalry had arrived.

But if Greta turned around now, Martie and Vera were as good as dead.

Chapter 27

They approached the gate slowly so they could scan the perimeter and take stock. It was dusk, that end of day when shadows got long and one's vision was compromised. They doused their lights so as not to attract attention and idled for a moment to be certain they hadn't been spotted. When it appeared all was clear, they moved toward the entrance of Valhalla.

Fortunately, when Vera had asked Hugh to take on the task of protecting her and her daughters, she had given him the security codes for all of her residences and her office. She had also given him a list of whatever other safeguards she'd had installed, which was how Hugh knew there was only one camera. It was perched above the guardhouse, which thankfully was empty.

Wiggers punched in the code. The gates opened. As they did, Bryan jumped out of the car, scaled the gates, and knocked the camera off its brace. Once that was disabled, he climbed back into the car. Wiggers made a sharp left.

The plan was to hug the tree line and circumnavigate the compound, staying out of sight of the various buildings in case Greta and whoever was helping her were posted at the windows. Their goal was simple: Disable any sentries — human or otherwise — locate the bunker, and find a way inside.

The only hint they had about where the bunker might be was Bryan's recollection of his tour of the grounds. Vera had passed the barn and was heading toward the lake cottage when he'd inquired about the bunker. She acknowledged that it was in the vicinity, but pointedly avoided showing him precisely where.

Not far from the entrance, they came upon the Colonial. Large and white and gracious, it stood on a rise like a proud symbol of an earlier, simpler time. It appeared to be dark and still and empty.

Wiggers wanted to get rid of the car. Bryan pointed to the rear of the house, which was banked by two centuries-old maples. Their thick foliage made the ground beneath them black as pitch. An ink-colored car would completely disappear. Also, as Hugh pointed out, after they retrieved their hostages they'd want to be nearer, not farther, from the exit.

"We'll proceed on foot," the general commanded.

They changed into their camos and loaded their backpacks, their eyes constantly scanning the horizon to prevent an ambush in case they had been spotted. Bryan provided each of them with a hastily sketched layout of the grounds if for some reason they got separated.

On the way up they had decided to bypass the lake cottage and the Tudor; they were unlikely bases. The lake cottage had only one reasonable means of egress, and that was through the front door. Out back the lake was large and, since it was private, surrounded by heavily forested land enclosed with a high fence. There were too many obstacles to overcome to achieve a quick and seamless escape.

The Tudor was way off to the right, on the other side of the greenhouses. Bryan felt it had too much open ground between it and where he believed the bunker was to make sense as a staging area.

Their focus narrowed to the barn and the bunker.

The sun had set. The air was clear and slightly cool, a typical spring evening.

There was only a quarter moon and it sat low in the sky, creating a dark, opaque background. The estate was large, spread out, and isolated, so sound was at a minimum: some birds chirping, the occasional rustling of leaves when a denizen of the forest scooted from one place to another, the lapping of the water against the lakeshore. The quietude worked to their benefit because they would be able to hear an enemy approaching. It worked to their detriment because the enemy could hear them.

With their night goggles in place and weapons drawn, they slipped behind the Colonial and headed deep into the compound toward the barn.

Bryan acted as the Pathfinder. Bent over and hunkered close to the ground, he strained to recall the way to the lumbering structure that housed Vera Hart's studio. His fellow soldiers followed several paces behind, they too running fast and low.

Finally, the outline of the barn loomed large against the sky. Cautious about cracking a branch or kicking a stone or creating any other noise that might alert a watchman, he kept his eyes on the ground ahead, checking for impediments.

It was small, but it didn't belong, so it

caught his attention. He stopped, raised his goggles, bent down low, and shone his flashlight on the object. It was a red reflector shaped like heart. He recognized it immediately.

When the others caught up to him, he held up the decoration from her little sneaker.

"They've got Lili," he said.

The screen on the monitor went blank. Mentally, Martie gave the guys a "Hooah!" for knocking out the camera. Knowing there were boots on the grounds gave her hope, but even if they found the bunker quickly, penetrating it would take time, something she and Vera had very little of.

Also, there were Lili and Soledad. Martie prayed that Bryan and Hugh would make certain to rescue them first. In the meantime she would do whatever she could to make sure she and Vera survived until the Special Ops unit arrived.

If she didn't die in Fallujah, she wasn't going to die in Valhalla.

"I have to use the bathroom," she announced.

Polatchek growled as if she had said, "Okay, I'd like to leave now."

"I have to use the bathroom," she repeated, daring Greta to deny her this most basic request. "You and Vera seem to have a lot to discuss, none of which involves me, and since I'm sure you have additional cuffs tucked away in one of your pouches, you can restrain me after I'm finished."

Reluctantly, Greta jerked her head at Polatchek to take care of it. While he untied Martie's ankles and removed the plastic cuffs, she went to the duffel and extracted a set of documents, which she waved in front of Vera.

"You're going to sign these," she commanded. "They turn the reins of HLI over to me. Because I'm a fair and reasonable person and recognize your years of service, I've given you a generous severance package. But you're out as of today."

Vera may not have had military experience, but she knew Greta intended to get her signature on those papers and then kill her. That a child she had borne could so cold-heartedly plan her murder was too chilling to contemplate. It froze all thought except one: Her other daughter had to figure a way out of this.

"Get me my glasses," Vera said. "I don't sign anything without reading it."

Martie silently congratulated the newbie recruit on that maneuver. It was a good stall.

Martie went into the bathroom and closed the door. Polatchek stood guard outside.

Once that monitor went dark, Martie realized she had to take some kind of action or she and Vera would be dead before help could get to them. The only place there might be something she could use as a weapon was in that bathroom. When she'd looked around before, she hadn't seen anything that could be of any help. Then she remembered the light fixture was covered by a ventilated screen. If the slats were made of metal, she might be able to break one off and hide it in her slacks.

The instant the door closed, Martie leaped up onto the toilet and then onto the edge of the sink. The gods must have been with her, because the screen was metal and it wasn't screwed into the ceiling. Praying she didn't fall, she extended her hand until it reached the screen. She lifted it, turned it on its side, and slid it out, thrilled to note that it was two slats longer on each side than the opening.

She jumped down off the sink so she could apply the pressure necessary to snap one of the slats out of its frame.

It broke off easily. She was so grateful she almost cried.

The good news was that the edges were now jagged and extremely sharp. The bad news was that the slat was too long for her to sit with it tucked into her belt. She'd have to break it in half.

"What the hell are you doing in there?" Polatchek groused. "Hurry up."

Martie climbed back up onto the sink and returned the screen to the ceiling, checking to be sure the missing slat wasn't visible. Then she jumped down and stepped on one end of the metal strip, bending it until it snapped. The instant it did, she flushed the toilet to cover the noise.

She tucked one shiv into her pants and slipped the other one into the water tank. She turned on the faucet to make Polatchek think she was washing her hands, but instead sat on the toilet seat to be sure she wouldn't stab herself when she returned to the bench.

Then she opened the door.

"Took you long enough."

Martie sneered at him as if he were a foul odor.

"She's next," Martie said, pointing to Vera. "She's been sitting here for hours without relief."

Greta was growing frustrated by the

pace, but in the big picture these picayune requests didn't matter. The end was in sight.

"Get her cuffed and then undo the other one," she said to Polatchek.

"Turn around."

Martie complied, but she extended her arms out so his hands wouldn't be anywhere near her back. Also, she put her fingers together but held her hands slightly apart so that when he snapped on the cuffs the plastic wouldn't be as tight around her wrists as it would be if her wrists were pressed together. She was banking on his anxiety to lessen his attention to detail.

After he'd finished, he gripped her elbow and dragged her back to the bench.

"You enjoy being a tough guy, don't you?" she said as he tied her ankles. "Funny how brave you can be when the enemy is two women on a bench and not five Iraqis in a desert. Then, you were a coward."

"Shut up!" He jumped to his feet and slapped her across the face. He was trembling with rage and humiliation.

Martie never even flinched. When it came to abuse, he was an amateur.

"You're wasting time," Greta snapped. "Undo Vera's restraints."

He untied her ankles and cut her cuffs.

Vera stretched her arms, groaning from the pain of having been kept in one position for so long. She longed to say or do something to Greta, but Martie had insisted she go to the bathroom. Something was in there she was supposed to get.

Polatchek pushed her inside and closed the door.

"Don't take too long," he said with bloated authority.

Vera studied every inch of the bathroom floor, including behind the toilet. She saw nothing. She did have to relieve herself, so she did, using the respite as a chance to survey the rest of the room. The sink was empty. The medicine cabinet was too obvious. The coil that held the toilet paper roll in its place was still intact. She looked up. The fan was whirring gently.

Then she saw it. The screen that covered the fluorescent lightbulbs was slightly askew, not so anybody else would have noticed, but she would never have allowed it to be so much as a thirty-second of an inch off. Someone had moved it. As she stood to flush the toilet, she realized there was only one place to hide anything in here. Carefully, she lifted the top of the tank. Inside was a broken piece of metal; she recognized it immediately as one of the slats from that screen.

She took it out, dried it with toilet tissue, and stuck it in the back of her pants. She replaced the top, flushed the toilet, rinsed her hands, and opened the door with a flourish.

She was armed and ready.

"Do you have any idea how sweet this is?" Greta said when Vera was out of the room.

"What is, playing soldier? If you want a real rush you should try the real thing, right, Polatchek?"

"Can it."

Martie laughed as if a command from him were the equivalent to an order from the Cookie Monster. As she did, she extracted the shiv.

Polatchek's eyes narrowed to slits. He pulled his lips together so tightly there was nothing but a straight line where his mouth should have been. Occasionally, his head jerked as if he had a tic. His control was ebbing.

Martie intended to push him to the brink. While it was true that the crazier he got the more dangerous it was for her and

Vera, by the same token if he became a loose cannon Greta was equally vulnerable.

"I'm going to get Bryan back," Greta proclaimed with a defiant lift of her chin. "He loved me once. He's going to love me again."

As ridiculous as it was considering the circumstances, Martie exulted. Bryan hadn't gone back to Greta.

"How can you be so sure?" Martie asked, needing to be sure.

"He came with me to the police station when he thought I had been threatened. He defended me. He protected me. He comforted me. That's how I know he still loves me."

She sounded like a nursery-schooler listing the reasons she should be allowed to stay up late. She'd be pathetic if she weren't so pathological.

The door to the bathroom opened. Vera walked out like the diva that she was.

"Feel better?" Martie said.

"Greatly relieved," Vera replied.

Martie smiled.

Greta barked at Polatchek, who reattached Vera's cuffs and her ankle ties.

He finished and resumed his "at ease" stance at Greta's side.

"Do you know why he poisoned those products?" Martie said to Greta. "His mommy is a big fan of our mommy. She watches Vera's shows religiously and thinks she's the most perfect human being God ever created."

Polatchek's hand twitched against his holster.

"You promised him money, but destroying his mother's idol was much more appealing."

"Shut up, bitch!" He pulled his weapon and pointed it at Martie.

Vera gasped. Greta's head snapped in his direction.

Whatever she had promised him must have been far more appealing than killing Martie, because he reholstered his gun.

"Once again," Martie continued, "Timmy screwed up. Not only did he destroy his mommy's favorite personality, but he destroyed the Hart Line as well."

The plastic band was proving tough to cut. She leaned back up against the wall, pressed the shiv against her back, and drew her wrists against it. Nothing. Then it dawned on her: Use the ragged edge of the slat to widen the teeth of the zipper that locked the cuff around the wrists.

She turned to Vera, hoping her two captors would look that way as well so she could continue her work.

"Sign the stupid papers and give her the company already. She's convinced she's a better CEO than you. If she thinks she can pull HLI out of the toilet, let her try."

On cue, Vera pulled her broken slat from her waistband, glanced over at Martie to see what she was doing, and imitated the action.

"That would be interesting," she said. "I never remember a time when Greta didn't want to be me or to bask in the reflection of my fame."

"What the hell are you talking about?"

"Whenever you met anybody new you immediately announced that you were Vera Hart's daughter, didn't you? You loved seeing the look of recognition in people's eyes, especially if they seemed to envy you. There was nothing you liked better than reaping the benefits that came with being my offspring."

Greta appeared momentarily flustered. She wanted to get those papers signed so she could end this charade, but Vera had touched a nerve.

"I'm sure Martie did the same thing."

"I doubt it. For most of her life, I don't

think she even thought of me as her mother."

Martie was focused on bisecting her cuffs, but even so, she caught the pain in that statement.

"She hated you," Polatchek said, eager to contribute.

"And you know this how?"

"She told me so. We were drunk one night and she railed on and on about how tough it was to be Vera Hart's little girl."

He laughed, but it was the sad sound of an empty soul.

"We were comparing childhoods. We couldn't decide whose was worse."

This conversation was giving Martie the time she needed, but for Vera it couldn't have been easy.

"Actually," Tim continued, undeterred by Greta's angry scowl, "you and Enid both lose. The worst parent on the planet has to be that fucking General Phelps. What a hard-ass he is."

"He was a hard-ass with you because you were a terrible soldier," Martie said, guessing that Polatchek had had a run-in with her father after she was captured. "You dishonored the uniform, Tim. No true military person would forgive you for that."

He started for her again, but Vera interrupted.

"Did she tell you that she was General
Phelps's daughter?"

She knew it was irrelevant whether or
not Martie bragged about her father, but
she couldn't help herself.

"She didn't have to. Everyone knew."

Martie was almost free.

Vera pursed her lips and appeared
thoughtful. "How interesting, to have a
contest judging the quality of one's parents. Over the years I often wondered who
was better: Hugh or I. Of course, one way
to decide was to determine which of our
daughters was the more accomplished,
more well-adjusted adult." She leaned forward as if confiding a great truth. "It's that
old nature versus nurture conundrum.
Quite fascinating, really. After all, you
didn't grow up in the same household. I
raised you. Hugh raised Martie. You're
both grown women now, so I suppose the
contest is over." Her aquamarine eyes
blazed. "What do you think, Greta? Do I
win or does Hugh?"

"I win," Greta said, stomping across the
room and standing directly in front of
Vera. "I win!"

"Not quite," Vera said with complete

aplomb. "If you kill me, you get nothing."

Martie stopped what she was doing.

"What do you mean?" Greta's face was tight and red.

"I changed my will. You don't get my business, my stock, or any of my assets. You don't get so much as a bauble or a bead from my estate. And in case you think that after I'm dead you can change it back, you can't. It's airtight."

"Who'd you leave it all to, her?" Greta's finger shook as she pointed at Martie.

"No. I left it in a trust."

"A trust?" Greta was visibly shaken. With all her planning and all her strategizing, she hadn't considered Vera's will. Dead or alive, Vera still ruled.

"We did all this for nothing?" Polatchek went ballistic. "I can't fucking believe it! All these years laboring over those books, and now it's for shit!"

He started pacing, his breath coming in short puffs.

"I worked like a slave for my payoff. You kept saying you had it all under control. You told me you'd make me CFO when you took over. You told me you'd give me a piece of the company."

He laughed, but the sound was manic.

"I helped you kill Hemminger so he

wouldn't give those tapes to the prosecutor. I did what you said and beat up her friend to throw the police off the track. And now there's no payoff?"

"Shut up, Tim."

"No. I want them to know you blackmailed me. You made me do your bidding by using my army records. Well, I'm not taking the heat for your fuckup."

He spun around and glowered at Martie. His eyes were wide and wild.

"You think I did this for the money, but believe me, that was just a bonus. The real reason I teamed up with Greta was that we had something major in common: We both hated you, your father, *and* her. The three of you ruined our lives."

He got up into Greta's face, shoving her back away from Vera.

"You talked about revenge, about getting even, about finally having it all. You thought you were so smart. You told me you had this major plan that couldn't fail. Well, news flash — the old bitch outfoxed you. She beat you, and there's nothing you can do about it."

Martie cringed. There was something Greta could do. And she did.

She pulled her gun and shot him.

Bryan and Wiggers did a quick check on the barn door for explosives. When they didn't find any, Hugh broke the lock and rushed in. Bryan and Wiggers went on ahead to search for the bunker. Hugh wasn't going anywhere until he found his granddaughter. Using his flashlight and the instructions Bryan had given him on the interior layout, he made his way to the back where the studio was. His fingers shook as he opened the door.

"GG," Lili yelled when she saw him. She ran into his waiting arms and hugged him.

He held her close, unable to imagine the world without her in it.

"Come," he said to Soledad, clutching Lili. "We have to get out of here."

Wiggers had warned Hugh that despite the lack of proximity bundles, he was certain explosives had been laid out. Bryan agreed. Greta hadn't kidnapped Lili for show. She had a detonator on her that she was fully prepared to use. Hugh was to get Lili and Soledad out of the barn as quickly as possible. Bryan and Wiggers would try to get to the bunker before the blow button was pressed.

Hugh held Lili and led Soledad out of the barn. The three of them headed for the lake cottage. Bryan had remembered seeing a motorboat moored at the dock. If necessary, Hugh could take the boat to the far end of the lake. In his backpack were wire cutters he could use to cut the fence. Wiggers and Bryan would pick them up, or they'd run for it. Either way, they'd have a head start.

It was difficult locating the bunker in the dark. Bryan recalled seeing a patch of grass that was a slightly different shade of green than the rest of the lawn when he and Vera drove by, but now everything was gray. He did remember the land was high; digging a bunker required depth. Also, it wasn't far from a stand of birch trees.

He and Wiggers sleuthed along the tree line using their flashlights to see if they could spot a vent or a drain or something that would indicate the bunker was near.

Wiggers ran headlong into an antenna. If he hadn't had goggles on, it would have taken an eye out.

"Pssst." He summoned Bryan and showed him what he'd found. "It's close."

They walked from the trees out, shining their flashlights on the ground. Wiggers noticed a split in the grass, as if a piece of sod had been dislodged. The two of them got on their knees and felt around. The grass wasn't as cold or as damp as the surrounding greenery. Quickly, they pulled out shovels and began to dig. They didn't have to go down very far. The sod was on top of something that looked like a large wooden planter.

When they lifted it off, they saw a metal hatch similar to those on submarines.

Wiggers turned the wheel and raised the cover. There were stairs leading down into the earth. Before descending, he placed a small flare on the side of the hatch so if for some reason Hugh came looking for them, he'd know where they were.

They were scoping out the hallway and the metal door when they heard a muffled sound coming from within the chamber. There was no mistaking it. It was a gunshot.

Bryan's heart sank.

Tim Polatchek lay in a pool of his own blood. He was alive, but barely.

Vera was horrified. Suddenly, overcome by fatigue and hunger and fear, she began to cry.

"Congratulations," Martie said, unfazed by her sister's brutality, but worried about

Vera's fading stamina. "Now you're an army of one."

She could feel the plastic giving way. It couldn't happen soon enough. Greta had gone over the edge.

"That's not very good planning, Greta. A real soldier would know better than to leave herself without backup."

"I don't need backup. I have this." She unsnapped from a loop on her belt something that looked like a key to an expensive European car. "If I press this little button, there'll be a big bang at Vera's precious barn and your daughter and her nanny will be blown apart."

Vera's head fell and she groaned with psychic pain. "I can't believe this is happening. I simply can't believe this," she muttered, caught in an eddy of self-recrimination and helplessness.

"Believe it!" Greta shouted at her. "Not only are you going to sign those papers, but you're going to add something that overrides your will. If you don't, I'll kill you and her and them," she said, taunting them with the detonator.

Martie looked into Greta's eyes. They were the eyes of a predator, focused but empty. She couldn't begin to fathom what turned a person into something so evil.

"Why would you do that? Lili's a child. She never did anything to you."

"Why would I do that? Because I hate you! And I hate her!" she said, pointing to Vera. "And I hate that self-centered swash-buckler who has the nerve to call himself a father."

Greta was livid. A lifetime of slights and insecurities and unfulfilled needs had knitted together and pricked at her like a hair shirt.

She began to pace again. Every now and then she looked down at Tim, whose breathing was so shallow his chest hardly moved.

"Why don't you let me help him?" Martie nodded toward Polatchek. The irony of her being forced sit on the side-lines and let him die didn't escape her. "You don't need another murder on your hands."

"I didn't kill Hemminger," Greta insisted. "He did. I didn't do anything. He did it all."

"Let me stem the bleeding, at least."

Greta spun around and aimed her pistol at Martie's head.

"Why, so you can be a hero again? No way! I'm sick to death of your heroics. I'm sick to death of you!"

Her body was quaking with the accelerated rage that often preceded a breakdown. Martie wouldn't care except that Greta literally held Lili's life in her hand.

"Look," Martie said, changing tactics. "You want control of HLI. Fine. Vera will sign the papers, won't you?"

"Undo my hands," Vera said, hiding the slat beneath her. "And give me a pen. You want the Hart Line? It's yours."

Greta had waited so long to hear those words, she never considered the consequences of releasing one of her prisoners. Keeping an eye and her pistol trained on Martie, Greta reached behind Vera and unlocked her restraints.

"You make one false move and I'll blow her head off."

"Give me the papers," Vera said.

Greta complied, handing over the documents and a pen.

"And you?" she said to Martie, confident that things were once again going her way. "What are you going to do for me?"

"I'll leave the Hart Line. I'll leave New York, if that will make you happy. Just end this."

"Make me happy! What a joke. I haven't been happy since the day you were born. How could I be, when you steal every chance I have at it? I had a father until you stole him. I had a lover and you stole him too. And now, it appears, you've even stolen the affection of my mother."

She laughed, but the sound was one of cosmic pathos.

"To think I volunteered to live with her. I had a choice and I chose her. How foolish was that? You left and wound up with a father and a mother and a life. I wound up with a string of governesses."

She was pacing more furiously now, talking more to herself than either Martie or Vera.

"I stayed because I thought she needed me. I thought she needed someone to love her and take care of her and encourage her. But Vera Hart doesn't need anyone. She's an island unto herself."

She snorted with frustration.

"She was never home. She was always at work." Greta's voice was low and hoarse, strained with emotion. "So I went to work with her, again thinking she'd be pleased, that she would love me, that she would one day look at me and realize that I was the only continuous presence in her stinking ego-centered life. But did she? No. She was too busy staring at herself in the mirror or patting herself on the back for her singular success or pining away for the general who dumped her or thinking about you, the child who left her."

Her entire body quaked with the sting of her rejection.

"Why shouldn't I want you all dead? With you out of the way, Bryan will come back to me. And without her or you or your brat, my father will have no one else to love but me."

Amazingly, for the first time in nearly an hour Greta's eye suddenly caught the monitor.

"Shit!" She stared at the black and white snow on the screen, knowing that someone had breached the gate. "Who's here?" she shouted, spinning around to face Martie and Vera. "Who did you bring here?"

The plastic band finally split. With the speed of a missile, Martie bent over, cut the rope binding her feet, and lunged headlong at Greta. As she flung her to the ground, she tried to dislodge the detonator from Greta's hand, but she was too late.

The hatch was open so they heard it, the hideous sound of dynamite exploding and a building bursting apart. The ground shook. An angry orange haze veiled the sky.

Wiggers and Bryan stared at each other and at Hugh Phelps, who was racing down the steps.

"The barn just blew," he announced.

"What are you doing here?" Bryan said. "Where are Lili and Soledad?"

"I brought them to the car and told them to get off the estate. Soledad's headed into town so she can tell the police what's going on and arrange for reinforcements."

"Good thinking, General," Bryan said.

"The farther away they are, the safer they are," Hugh said, thinking as a grandfather, not as a general. "And I needed to be here. Vera and my daughters are in there."

Before Hugh joined them, Bryan and Wiggers had determined the only way to get inside the bunker was to blow the door down. They dotted the doorframe with a series of blasting caps and RDX, an explosive compound which, when detonated, would slice right through the steel. There was a risk that when the door exploded they would be hurt by flying debris, but it was risk they had to take. Greta and Polatchek had already killed Hemminger, brutally assaulted Delilah, and kidnapped four people. Someone had fired a weapon and had blown up the barn believing two innocents were in there. Neither of them had anything more to lose.

"If my daughter is dead, I'll kill you with my bare hands," Martie said to Greta, whom she had pinned to the floor.

Greta issued a hysterical laugh. "*If* she's dead? Of course she's dead. I put enough dynamite around that studio to blow up Westchester County."

Martie unbuckled Greta's belt, searching for cuffs. There were none. Greta hadn't planned on them being here long enough to require replacements.

Vera hopped close to Martie so she could take Greta's knife and cut the ropes around her ankles. When she was free, she grabbed Polatchek's gun and aimed it at her older daughter.

"Do you know how to fire a weapon?" Martie asked, taking Greta's, emptying it of its magazine, and tossing it across the room.

"No. That makes me dangerous, doesn't it?"

"Keep it on her," Martie said. "I need to work on him."

It had been a long time since Martie had

dealt with patients, especially under battle-field conditions. She worried that her fingers wouldn't work and that she wouldn't remember what to do. She had no choice but to try.

She took Polatchek's knife, ran to the stove, and sterilized it. Then she took a bedsheet from the neatly piled stack on one of the shelves, crafted a tourniquet and several bandage strips.

The bullet had punctured his stomach. With no exit wound, Martie could assume it was lodged there. Internal bleeding was flooding his body cavity. If he didn't have surgery soon, he would die. The best Martie could do was try to remove the bullet and stanch the bleeding until the rescue team could extract him and get him to a hospital.

Greta sat up slowly. Vera's eyes remained fixed and focused.

"You don't want to hurt me," Greta said. With Martie fully absorbed saving Polatchek, she hoped to rattle Vera, grab the gun, and shoot them both.

"Don't I?"

Vera aimed and fired.

After measuring the length of the hallway, Wiggers had placed the explosives so the door would fall out toward them. He wasn't quite finished, but when they heard the shot they knew they'd run out of time.

The three of them positioned themselves on the steps, put plugs in their ears, braced themselves against the wall, and turned their heads away from the blast.

Wiggers pressed the detonator. The sound was deafening. The door thundered to the ground. Without waiting for the debris to stop falling, Bryan leaped off the stairs onto the door and bounded into the bunker chamber. Wiggers and Hugh were on his heels. All three had their guns drawn.

Martie was lying on top of Polatchek. Both bodies were still.

Greta was on her knees; Vera was also on the floor. Greta had a grip on Vera's arm and a gun pressed against her back. There was a bloody gash on the side of Vera's head. Debris from the shattered doorframe and material shaken loose from the shelves lay strewn all about.

"Don't come any farther or I'll kill her." Greta's eyes bored into Bryan.

A second later Wiggers and Hugh entered.

Greta realized she was outnumbered.

She stared at her father, her body shaking from shock and rage and desperation.

"Did you come to save me, Daddy?" she said. "Well, you're too late. You're years too late."

Bryan started for Martie, who was extricating herself from Polatchek.

"I'm warning you," Greta repeated, shoving the barrel of the gun into Vera's back. "I'm warning all of you. I'll kill her."

Bryan's arm remained outstretched, his pistol pointed at Greta's head.

"You wouldn't shoot me," she said in a voice that practically pleaded for him not to contradict her.

"No, but I would." Wiggers took aim. "Put the gun down."

She'd forgotten about Wiggers. He had no stake in her survival, no emotional connection to her. Still, she stood her ground, holding on to Vera, glaring at her enemies. Her eyes were full of pent-up rage and tears as she looked from Wiggers to Bryan to her father.

"Put it down," Wiggers said again.

"Please, Greta," Hugh said. "Do as he says."

When Greta didn't move, he fired. The bullet grazed her arm. She dropped the gun. Wiggers cuffed her.

Vera jumped up and moved away from Greta, but she was light-headed, swooned and started to fall. Hugh caught her and carried her back to the bench.

Bryan ran to Martie, who was slowly rising to her feet.

"Careful," she said. "He's barely hanging on."

Bryan looked down at Polatchek. A bloody knife and bullet lay by his side. His midsection was tightly wrapped in bands of floral sheets from the Hart Home Line Collection.

Outside the chamber the police and EMTs had arrived and were lowering stretchers and medical equipment. Wiggers appointed himself traffic coordinator. The first to go was Polatchek. After the EMTs had secured him to the stretcher, the head of the unit congratulated Martie on her work.

"Nice piece of emergency surgery," he said with obvious admiration. "This guy owes you."

"You have no idea," Bryan said as he watched the stretcher leave.

Wiggers held on to Greta until Polatchek had been hoisted up and out. When the passageway was clear, he happily handed her over to the police.

As she was led away, she looked back at her parents, who were huddled together, and at the sister she'd hated her entire life, who was being protected by the man Greta had thought would love her for the rest of her life.

"I can't believe you saved him," she said, her tone acrid and bitter. "I guess that's the difference between you and me. I would've let that loser die."

No one said a word.

The minute she'd gone, Martie asked about Lili and Soledad. "Is my baby okay?"

"Yes," Hugh said, reassuring her with a hug. "They're both fine. The local police had someone drive them home. I didn't want Lili to see any of this."

"Thank you," Martie said, choking over the lump in her throat. "How'd you find her?"

"Bryan found her." Hugh's voice was filled with respect and, Martie thought, a touch of honest affection. "He was the general of this operation, not me. He found all of you. I'm beyond grateful, son."

He saluted a modest and surprised Bryan.

The salute triggered a memory Martie had locked away in a corner of her heart so she could remain focused throughout this hideous siege. Delilah. Her color deathly pale. Her body still.

"Polatchek killed Delilah," she said, letting the tears fall. It was the first time she allowed herself to mourn. "He beat her, tried to rape her, and when that wasn't enough to satisfy him, he killed her." She doubled over with fatigue and grief. "I can't believe she's gone."

"She's not." Bryan gripped Martie's arms, forcing her to look at him. "She's going to be all right."

"She is?" Martie's voice was disbelieving. She had been in the hall when the defibrillator was wheeled in.

"Polatchek injected epinephrine into her IV. It accelerated her heartbeat and spiked her metabolic rate to near-catastrophic levels, but the team got to her in time."

"Thank God." Martie was overcome with relief.

Bryan wiped a few tears off her cheeks. "She'll be out of the hospital in a few days."

"What happened here?" Wiggers said when he returned from making certain that Greta was gone.

Martie collected herself and provided a brief synopsis.

"Man! I taught you well." Wiggers grinned with self-congratulation.

"Yes, you did," Martie said, embracing her former drill sergeant. "Make a plan and then be prepared to change the plan."

"Right on, Lieutenant." Wiggers expressed his approval with a loud whoop. "I tell you, if this wasn't a make-believe bunker you could've earned yourself a few more ribbons."

"I'll tell you who deserves a few ribbons. She does." Martie pointed to Vera and smiled broadly. "She's the best recruit this woman's army has ever seen."

Bryan looked from Martie to Vera. "Who fired that second shot?"

"I did," Vera said proudly. "Martie was working on that Polatchek person. I was guarding Greta." She turned to Martie, an anguished expression on her face. "You didn't think I was aiming at her, did you?"

"Never." Martie remembered how even when she was cuffed and bound, Vera hadn't wanted to embrace the idea that Greta was her enemy. "I knew you wouldn't do that."

Vera shook her head. She couldn't even begin to fathom how it had come to this, how she would have had a pistol in her hand pointed at her firstborn.

"Actually I was aiming at the bedding, but I missed and hit the clock instead." She shrugged and tried to make light of it, but her lips were wobbly. "Nobody's perfect, I guess."

Martie walked over to Vera and warmly embraced her. "I'm proud of you, Mom," she said.

Vera's eyes filled with grateful, happy tears. Her hand gently brushed Martie's face.

"And I am so unbelievably proud of you."

As Hugh watched his ex-wife and his daughter reunite, his face glowed with pleasure and then grew dark.

Vera knew why.

"Martie got the best of us," she said gently. "Greta got the worst."

She kissed Martie on the cheek, broke free of her embrace, and went to Hugh's side.

"But she's still ours. Now let's act like parents and go to the police station to see what we can do to help her."

"I'll drive," Wiggers said, wanting to leave Martie and Bryan alone.

"How did you know where to find us?" Martie asked after they'd gone. "And how did you ever find Lili?"

Bryan reached into his pocket. When he opened his hand, Lili's reflector heart and his good luck dime lay in the palm.

"One provided the luck for me to find the other," he said, his voice choking on might-have-beens. "Once I knew Hugh would take care of Lili, Wiggers and I came after you and Vera."

Martie, who'd been so strong and so stoic, saw the heart and the dime, heard the caring in his voice about her daughter and her mother, and wept.

Bryan held her in his arms.

"I love you," he said, his lips against her hair. "In case I didn't make that clear ten years ago or last week or the other night or just now: I love you."

Martie raised her head off his shoulder, reached inside her sweater, and brought out the chain that held her dime.

"You've always been clear," she said. "It was me who couldn't see through the fog."

"And now?"

"I love you, Bryan Chalmers. Even more than I did ten years ago and last week and the other night." She kissed him softly. "And by the way, thanks for rescuing me."

"My pleasure, my lady," he said with a gallant bow.

"And my daughter."

"Also my pleasure." Bryan looked deep into her eyes, getting lost in the pool of aqua. "In case you couldn't guess, I've fallen madly in love with your daughter."

A warm, safe, wonderful feeling washed over her. It felt as if she'd been driving through a snowstorm and finally came to a house where the lights were on and the fire was burning. Someone was waiting for her to come home.

"Lili doesn't like it when I speak for her, but I don't think she'd mind me saying she has a thing for you too."

"Good, because I intend to ask her permission to marry you."

"And when exactly do you plan on doing that?"

"Tomorrow, when I take her flying."

Martie started to protest, but he stopped her.

"I promised her and I like to keep my promises. Besides, if we're going to be a family, I need Lili in my corner."

Martie laughed. "To protect you against what? Or whom?"

"How about your parents?"

"How about them?"

"In the spirit of full disclosure, I confess that I don't love your mother, but she's growing on me. She's smart and she's tough, but underneath that immaculate, not-a-hair-out-of-place exterior is a top-notch lady who's earned my respect as well as my affection."

"And my father?" Martie asked.

That slow, sly smile she loved so much crept over his mouth.

"Let's just say I'm working on it." He took her in his arms again and held her close. "I'm not perfect, you know."

"Good," she said, nestling against him. "I don't like perfect. Nobody does."

JAN 2 2 2019

Sudlersville Memorial Library
Post Office Box 112
Sudlersville, MD 21668